ON SECRET SERVICE

Detective-Mystery Stories Based on Real Cases Solved By Government Agents

BY
WILLIAM NELSON TAFT

ON SECRET SERVICE

I
A FLASH IN THE NIGHT

We were sitting in the lobby of the Willard, Bill Quinn and I, watching the constant stream of politicians, pretty women, and petty office seekers who drift constantly through the heart of Washington.

Suddenly, under his breath, I heard Quinn mutter, "Hello!" and, following his eyes, I saw a trim, dapper, almost effeminate-looking chap of about twenty-five strolling through Peacock Alley as if he didn't have a care in the world.

"What's the matter?" I inquired. "Somebody who oughtn't to be here?"

"Not at all. He's got a perfect right to be anywhere he pleases, but I didn't know he was home. Last time I heard of him he was in Seattle, mixed up with those riots that Ole Hanson handled so well."

"Bolshevist?"

"Hardly," and Quinn smiled. "Don't you know Jimmy Callahan? Well, it's scarcely the province of a Secret Service man to impress his face upon everyone ... the secret wouldn't last long. No, Jimmy was working on the other end of the Seattle affair. Trying to locate the men behind the move—and I understand he did it[2] fairly well, too. But what else would you expect from the man who solved that submarine tangle in Norfolk?"

Quinn must have read the look of interest in my face, for he continued, almost without a pause: "Did you ever hear the inside of that case? One of the most remarkable in the whole history of the Secret Service, and that's saying a good deal. I don't suppose it would do any harm to spill it, so let's move over there in a corner and I'll relate a few details of a case where the second hand of a watch played a leading role."

The whole thing started back in the spring of 1918 [said Quinn, who held down a soft berth in the Treasury Department as a reward for a game leg obtained during a counterfeiting raid on Long Island].

Along about then, if you remember, the Germans let loose a lot of boasting statements as to what they were going to do to American ships and American shipping. Transports were going to be sunk, commerce crippled and all that sort of thing. While not a word of it got into the papers, there were a bunch of people right here in Washington who took these threats seriously—for the Hun's most powerful weapon appeared to be in his submarines, and if a fleet of them once got going off the coast we'd lose a lot of valuable men and time landing them.

Then came the sinking of the *Carolina* and those other ships off the Jersey coast. Altogether it looked like a warm summer.

One afternoon the Chief sent for Callahan, who'd just come back from taking care of some job down on the border, and told him his troubles.

"Jimmy," said the Chief, "somebody on this side is giving those damn Huns a whole lot of information that they haven't any business getting. You know about[3] those boats they've sunk already, of course. They're only small fry. What they're laying for is a transport, another *Tuscania* that they can stab in the dark and make their getaway. The point that's worrying us is that the U-boats must be getting their information from some one over here. The sinking of the *Carolina* proves that. No submarine, operating on general cruising orders, could possibly have known when that ship was due or what course she was going to take. Every precaution was taken at San Juan to keep her sailing a secret, but of course you can't hide every detail of that kind. She got out. Some one saw her, wired the information up the coast here and the man we've got to nab tipped the U-boat off.

"Of course we could go at it from Porto Rico, but that would mean wasting a whole lot more time than we can afford. It's not so much a question of the other end of the cable as it is who transmitted the message to the submarine—and how!

"It's your job to find out before they score a real hit."

Callahan, knowing the way things are handled in the little suite on the west side of the Treasury Building, asked for the file containing the available information and found it very meager indeed.

Details of the sinking of the *Carolina* were included, among them the fact that the *U-37* had been waiting directly in the path of the steamer, though the latter was using a course entirely different from the one the New York and Porto Rico S. S. Company's boats generally took. The evidence of a number of passengers was that the submarine didn't appear a bit surprised at the size of her prey, but went about the whole affair in a businesslike manner. The meat of the report was contained in the final paragraph, stating that one of the German officers had boasted that they "would get a lot more ships[4] in the same way," adding, "Don't worry—we'll be notified when they are going to sail."

Of course, Callahan reasoned, this might be simply a piece of Teutonic bravado—but there was more than an even chance that it was the truth, particularly when taken in conjunction with the sinking of the *Texel* and the *Pinar del Rio* and the fact that the *Carolina's* course was so accurately known.

But how in the name of Heaven had they gotten their information?

Callahan knew that the four principal ports of embarkation for troops—Boston, New York, Norfolk, and Charleston—were shrouded in a mantle of secrecy which it was almost impossible to penetrate. Some months before, when he had been working on the case which grew out of the disappearance of the plans of the battleship *Pennsylvania*, he had had occasion to make a number of guarded inquiries in naval circles in New York, and he recalled that it had been necessary not only to show his badge, but to submit to the most searching scrutiny before he was allowed to see the men he wished to reach. He therefore felt certain that no outsider could have dug up the specific information in the short space of time at their disposal.

But, arguing that it had been obtained, the way in which it had been passed on to the U-boat also presented a puzzle.

Was there a secret submarine base on the coast?

Had some German, more daring than the rest, actually come ashore and penetrated into the very lines of the Service?

Had he laid a plan whereby he could repeat this operation as often as necessary?

Or did the answer lie in a concealed wireless, operating[5] upon information supplied through underground channels?

These were only a few of the questions which raced through Callahan's mind. The submarine base he dismissed as impracticable. He knew that the *Thor*, the *Unita*, the *Macedonia*, and nine other vessels had, at the beginning of the war, cleared from American ports under false papers with the intention of supplying German warships with oil, coal, and food. He also knew that, of the million and a half dollars' worth of supplies, less than one-sixth had ever been transshipped. Therefore, having failed so signally here, the Germans would hardly try the same scheme again.

The rumor that German officers had actually come into New York, where they were supposed to have been seen in a theater, was also rather far-fetched. So the wireless theory seemed to be the most tenable. But even a wireless cannot conceal its existence from the other stations indefinitely. Of course, it was possible that it might be located on some unfrequented part of the coast—but then how could the operator obtain the information which he transmitted to the U-boat?

Callahan gave it up in despair—for that night. He was tired and he felt that eight hours' sleep would do him more good than thrashing around with a problem for which there appeared to be no solution; a problem which, after all, he couldn't even be sure existed.

Maybe, he thought, drowsily, as he turned off the light—maybe the German on the U-boat was only boasting, after all—or, maybe....

The first thing Jimmy did the next morning was to call upon the head of the recently organized Intelligence Bureau of the War Department—not the Intelligence Division which has charge of censorship and the handling[6] of news, but the bureau which bears the same relation to the army that the Secret Service does to the Treasury Department.

"From what ports are transports sailing within the next couple of weeks?" he inquired of the officer in charge.

"From Boston, New York, Norfolk, and Charleston," was the reply—merely confirming Callahan's previous belief. He had hoped that the ground would be more limited, because he wanted to have the honor of solving this problem by himself, and it was hardly possible for him to cover the entire Atlantic Coast.

"Where's the biggest ship sailing from?" was his next question.

"There's one that clears Norfolk at daylight on Monday morning with twelve thousand men aboard...."

"Norfolk?" interrupted Callahan. "I thought most of the big ones left from New York or Boston."

"So they do, generally. But these men are from Virginia and North Carolina. Therefore it's easier to ship them right out of Norfolk—saves time and congestion of the railroads. As it happens, the ship they're going on is one of the largest that will clear for ten days or more. All of the other big ones are on the other side."

"Then," cut in Callahan, "if the Germans wanted to make a ten-strike they'd lay for that boat?"

"They sure would—and one torpedo well placed would make the *Tuscania* look like a Sunday-school picnic. But what's the idea? Got a tip that the Huns are going to try to grab her?"

"No, not a tip," Callahan called back over his shoulder, for he was already halfway out of the door; "just a hunch—and I'm going to play it for all it's worth!"

The next morning, safely ensconced at the Monticello under the name of "Robert P. Oliver, of Williamsport,[7] Pa." Callahan admitted to himself that he was indeed working on nothing more than a "hunch," and not a very well-defined one at that. The only point that appeared actually to back up his theory that the information was coming from Norfolk was the fact that the U-boat was known to be operating between New York and the Virginia capes. New York itself was well guarded and the surrounding country was continually patrolled by operatives of all kinds. It was the logical point to watch, and therefore it would be much more difficult to obtain and transmit information there than it would be in the vicinity of Norfolk, where military and naval operations were not conducted on as large a scale nor with as great an amount of secrecy.

Norfolk, Callahan found, was rather proud of her new-found glory. For years she had basked in the social prestige of the Chamberlin, the annual gathering of the Fleet at Hampton Roads and the military pomp and ceremony attendant upon the operations of Fortress Monroe. But the war had brought a new thrill. Norfolk was now one of the principal ports of embarkation for the men going abroad. Norfolk had finally taken her rank with New York and Boston—the rank to which her harbor entitled her.

Callahan reached Norfolk on Wednesday morning. The *America*, according to the information he had received from the War Department, would clear at daybreak Monday—but at noon on Saturday the Secret Service operative had very little more knowledge than when he arrived. He had found that there was a rumor to the effect that two U-boats were waiting off the Capes for the transport, which, of course, would have the benefit of the usual convoy.

"But," as one army officer phrased it, "what's the use[8] of a convoy if they know just where you are? Germany would willingly lose a sub. or two to get us, and, with the sea that's been running for the past ten days, there'd be no hope of saving more than half the boys."

Spurred by the rapidity with which time was passing and the fact that he sensed a thrill of danger—an intuition of impending peril—around the *America*, Callahan spent the better part of Friday night and all Saturday morning running down tips that proved to be groundless. A man with a German name was reported to be working in secret upon some invention in an isolated house on Willoughby Spit; a woman, concerning whom little was known, had been seen frequently in the company of two lieutenants slated to sail on the *America*; a house in Newport News emitted strange "clacking" sounds at night.

But the alleged German proved to be a photographer of unassailable loyalty, putting in extra hours trying to develop a new process of color printing. The woman came from one of the oldest families in Richmond and had known the two lieutenants for years. The house in Newport News proved to be the residence of a young man who hoped some day to sell a photoplay scenario, the irregular clacking noise being made by a typewriter operated none too steadily.

"That's what happens to most of the 'clues' that people hand you," Callahan mused as he sat before his open window on Saturday evening, with less than thirty-six hours left before the *America* was scheduled to leave. "Some fellows have luck with them, but I'll be hanged if I ever did. Here I'm working in the dark on a case that I'm not even positive exists. That infernal submarine may be laying off Boston at this minute, waiting for the ship that leaves there Tuesday. Maybe they don't get any word from shore at all.... Maybe they just...."[9]

But here he was brought up with a sudden jar that concentrated all his mental faculties along an entirely different road.

Gazing out over the lights of the city, scarcely aware that he saw them, his subconscious mind had been following for the past three minutes something apparently usual, but in reality entirely out of the ordinary.

"By George!" he muttered, "I wonder...."

Then, taking his watch from his pocket, his eyes alternated between a point several blocks distant—a point over the roofs of the houses—and the second hand of his timepiece. Less than a minute elapsed before he reached for a pencil and commenced to jot down dots and dashes on the back of an envelope. When, a quarter of an hour later, he found that the dashes had become monotonous—as he expected they would—he reached for the telephone and asked to be connected with the private wire of the Navy Department in Washington.

"Let me speak to Mr. Thurber at once," he directed. "Operative Callahan, S. S., speaking.... Hello! that you, Thurber?... This is Callahan. I'm in Norfolk and I want to know whether you can read this code. You can figure it out if anybody can. Ready?...

Dash, dash, dash, dot, dash, dash, dot—" and he continued until he had repeated the entire series of symbols that he had plucked out of the night.

"Sounds like a variation of the International Morse," came the comment from the other end of the wire—from Thurber, librarian of the Navy Department and one of the leading American authorities on code and ciphers. "May take a little time to figure it out, but it doesn't look difficult. Where can I reach you?"

"I'm at the Monticello—name of Robert P. Oliver. Put in a call for me as soon as you see the light on it. I've[10] got something important to do right now," and he hung up without another word.

A quick grab for his hat, a pat under his arm, to make sure that the holster holding the automatic was in place, and Callahan was on his way downstairs.

Once in the street, he quickened his pace and was soon gazing skyward at the corner of two deserted thoroughfares not many blocks from the Monticello. A few minutes' consultation with his watch confirmed his impression that everything was right again and he commenced his search for the night watchman.

"Who," he inquired of that individual, "has charge of the operation of that phonograph sign on the roof?"

"Doan know fuh certain, suh, but Ah think it's operated by a man down the street a piece. He's got charge of a bunch of them sort o' things. Mighty funny kinder way to earn a livin', Ah calls it—flashing on an' off all night long...."

"But where's he work from?" interrupted Callahan, fearful that the negro's garrulousness might delay him unduly.

"Straight down this street three blocks, suh. Then turn one block to yo' left and yo' cain't miss the place. Electrical Advertisin' Headquarters they calls it. Thank you, suh," and Callahan was gone almost before the watchman could grasp the fact that he held a five-dollar bill instead of a dollar, as he thought.

It didn't take the Secret Service man long to locate the place he sought, and on the top floor he found a dark, swarthy individual bending over the complicated apparatus which operated a number of the electric signs throughout the city. Before the other knew it, Callahan was in the room—his back to the door and his automatic ready for action.[11]

"Up with your hands!" snapped Callahan. "Higher! That's better. Now tell me where you got that information you flashed out to sea to-night by means of that phonograph sign up the street. Quick! I haven't any time to waste."

"*Si, si, señor*," stammered the man who faced him. "But I understand not the English very well."

"All right," countered Callahan. "Let's try it in Spanish," and he repeated his demands in that language.

Volubly the Spaniard—or Mexican, as he later turned out to be—maintained that he had received no information, nor had he transmitted any. He claimed his only duty was to watch the "drums" which operated the signs mechanically.

"No drum in the world could make that sign flash like it did to-night," Callahan cut in. "For more than fifteen minutes you sent a variation of the Morse code seaward. Come on—I'll give you just one minute to tell me, or I'll bend this gun over your head."

Before the minute had elapsed, the Mexican commenced his confession. He had been paid a hundred dollars a week, he claimed, to flash a certain series of signals every Saturday night, precisely at nine o'clock. The message itself—a series of dots and dashes which he produced from his pocket as evidence of his truthfulness—had reached him on Saturday morning for the two preceding weeks. He didn't know what it meant. All he did was to disconnect the drum which operated the sign and move the switch himself.

Payment for each week's work, he stated, was inclosed with the next week's message. Where it came from he didn't know, but the envelope was postmarked Washington.

With his revolver concealed in his coat pocket, but with its muzzle in the small of the Mexican's back, Callahan[12] marched his captive back to the hotel and up into his room. As he opened the door the telephone rang out, and, ordering the other to stand with his face to the wall in a corner—"and be damn sure not to make a move"—the government agent answered the call. As he expected, it was Thurber.

"The code's a cinch," came the voice over the wire from Washington. "But the message is infernally important. It's in German, and evidently you picked it up about two sentences from the start. The part you gave me states that the transport *America*, with twelve thousand men aboard, will leave Norfolk at daylight Monday. The route the ship will take is distinctly stated, as is the personnel of her convoy. Where'd you get the message?"

"Flashes in the night," answered Callahan. "I noticed that an electric sign wasn't behaving regularly—so I jotted down its signals and passed them on to you. The next important point is whether the message is complete enough for you to reconstruct the code. Have you got all the letters?"

"Yes, every one of them."

"Then take down this message, put it into that dot-and-dash code and send it to me by special messenger on one of the navy torpedo boats to-night. It's a matter of life and death to thousands of men!" and Callahan dictated three sentences over the wire. "Got that?" he inquired. "Good! Get busy and hurry it down. I've got to have it in the morning."

"Turn around," he directed the Mexican, as he replaced the receiver. "Were you to send these messages only on Saturday night?"

"*Si, señor.* Save that I was told that there might be occasions when I had to do the same thing on Sunday night, too."[13]

"At nine o'clock?"

"*Si, señor.*"

Callahan smiled. Things were breaking better than he had dared hope. It meant that the U-boat would be watching for the signal the following night. Then, with proper emphasis of the automatic, he gave the Mexican his orders. He was to return to his office with Callahan and go about his business as usual, with the certainty that if he tried any foolishness the revolver could act more quickly than he. Accompanied by the government agent, he was to come back to the Monticello and spend the night in Callahan's room, remaining there until the next evening when he would—promptly at nine o'clock and under the direction of an expert in telegraphy—send the message which Callahan would hand him.

That's practically all there is to the story.

"All?" I echoed, when Quinn paused. "What do you mean, 'all'? What was the message Callahan sent? What happened to the Mexican? Who sent the letter and the money from Washington?"

"Nothing much happened to the Mexican," replied my informant, with a smile. "They found that he was telling the truth, so they just sent him over the border with instructions not to show himself north of the Rio Grande. As for the letter—that took the Post Office, the Department of Justice, and the Secret Service the better part of three months to trace. But they finally located the sender, two weeks after she (yes, it was a woman, and a darned pretty one at that) had made her getaway. I understand they got her in England and sentenced her to penal servitude for some twenty years or more. In spite of the war, the Anglo-Saxon race hasn't completely overcome its prejudice against the death penalty for women."[14]

"But the message Callahan sent?" I persisted.

"That was short and to the point. As I recall it, it ran something like this: 'Urgent—Route of *America* changed. She clears at daylight, but takes a course exactly ten miles south of one previously stated. Be there.'

"The U-boat was there, all right. But so were four hydroplanes and half a dozen destroyers, all carrying the Stars and Stripes!"

[15]

II
THE MINT MYSTERY

"Mr Drummond! Wire for Mr. Drummond! Mr. Drummond, please!"

It was the monotonous, oft-repeated call of a Western Union boy—according to my friend Bill Quinn, formerly of the United States Secret Service—that really was responsible for solving the mystery which surrounded the disappearance of $130,000 in gold from the Philadelphia Mint.

"The boy himself didn't have a thing to do with the gold or the finding of it," admitted Quinn, "but his persistence was responsible for locating Drummond, of the Secret Service, just as he was about to start on a well-earned vacation in the Maine woods. Uncle Sam's sleuths don't get any too much time off, you know, and a month or so in a part of the world where they don't know anything about international intrigues and don't care about counterfeiting is a blessing not to be despised.

"That's the reason the boy had to be persistent when he was paging Drummond.

"The operative had a hunch that it was a summons to another case and he was dog tired. But the boy kept singing out the name through the train and finally landed his man, thus being indirectly responsible for the solution of a mystery that might have remained unsolved for weeks—and incidentally saved the government nearly[16] every cent of the one hundred and thirty thousand dollars."

When Drummond opened the telegram [continued Quinn] he found that it was a summons to Philadelphia, signed by Hamlin, Assistant Secretary of the Treasury.

"Preston needs you at once. Extremely important," read the wire—and, as Drummond was fully aware that Preston was Director of the United States Mint, it didn't take much deduction to figure that something had gone wrong in the big building on Spring Garden Street where a large part of the country's money is coined.

But even the lure of the chase—something you read a lot about in detective stories, but find too seldom in the real hard work of tracing criminals—did not offset Drummond's disappointment in having to defer his vacation. Grumbling, he gathered his bags and cut across New York to the Pennsylvania Station, where he was fortunate enough to be able to make a train on the point of leaving for Philadelphia. At the Mint he found Director Preston and Superintendent Bosbyshell awaiting him.

"Mr. Hamlin wired that he had instructed you to come up at once," said the director. "But we had hardly hoped that you could make it so soon."

"Wire reached me on board a train that would have pulled out of Grand Central Station in another three minutes," growled Drummond. "I was on my way to Maine to forget all about work for a month. But," and his face broke into a smile, "since they did find me, what's the trouble?"

"Trouble enough," replied the director. "Some hundred and thirty thousand dollars in gold is missing from the Mint!"

"What!" Even Drummond was shaken out of his professional[17] calm, not to mention his grouch. Robbery of the United States Treasury or one of the government Mints was a favorite dream with criminals, but—save for the memorable occasion when a gang was found trying to tunnel under Fifteenth Street in Washington—there had been no time when the scheme was more than visionary.

"Are you certain? Isn't there any chance for a mistake?"

The questions were perfunctory, rather than hopeful.

"Unfortunately, not the least," continued Preston. "Somebody has made away with a hundred and thirty thousand dollars worth of the government's money. Seven hundred pounds of gold is missing and there isn't a trace to show how or where it went. The vault doors haven't been tampered with. The combination of the grille inside the vault is intact. Everything, apparently, is as it should be—but fifty bars of gold are missing."

"And each bar," mused Drummond, "weighs—"

"Fourteen pounds," cut in the superintendent.

Drummond looked at him in surprise.

"I beg your pardon," said Preston. "This is Mr. Bosbyshell, superintendent of the Mint. This thing has gotten on my nerves so that I didn't have the common decency to introduce you. Mr. Bosbyshell was with me when we discovered that the gold was missing."

"When was that?"

"Yesterday afternoon," replied the director. "Every now and then—at irregular intervals—we weigh all the gold in the Mint, to make sure that everything is as it should be. Nothing wrong was discovered until we reached Vault Six, but there fifty bars were missing. There wasn't any chance of error. The records showed precisely how much should have been there and the scales showed how much there was, to the fraction of an ounce.[18]

"But even if we had only counted the bars, instead of weighing each one separately, the theft would have been instantly discovered, for the vault contained exactly fifty bars less than it should have. It was then that I wired Washington and asked for assistance from the Secret Service."

"Thus spoiling my vacation," muttered Drummond. "How many men know the combination to the vault door?"

"Only two," replied the superintendent. "Cochrane, who is the official weigher, and myself. Cochrane is above suspicion. He's been here for the past thirty years and there hasn't been a single complaint against him in all that time."

Drummond looked as if he would like to ask Preston if the same could be said for the superintendent, but he contented himself with listening as Bosbyshell continued:

"But even if Cochrane or I—yes, I'm just as much to be suspected as he—could have managed to open the vault door unseen, we could not have gotten inside the iron grille which guards the gold in the interior of the vault. That is always kept locked, with a combination known to two other men only. There's too much gold in each one of these vaults to take any chance with, which is the reason for this double protection. Two men—Cochrane and I—handle the combination to the vault door and open it whenever necessary. Two others—Jamison and Strubel—are the only ones that know how to open the grille door. One of them has to be present whenever the bars are put in or taken away, for the men who can get inside the vault cannot enter the grille, and the men who can manipulate the grille door can't get into the vault."

"It certainly sounds like a burglar-proof combination," commented Drummond. "Is there any possibility for[19] conspiracy between"—and he hesitated for the fraction of a second—"between Cochrane and either of the men who can open the grille door?"

"Apparently not the least in the world," replied Preston. "So far as we know they are all as honest as the day—"

"But the fact remains," Drummond interrupted, "that the gold is missing."

"Exactly—but the grille door was sealed with the official governmental stamp when we entered the vault yesterday. That stamp is applied only in the presence of both men who know the combination. So the conspiracy, if there be any, must have included Cochrane, Strubel, and Jamison—instead of being a two-man job."

"How much gold did you say was missing?" inquired the Treasury operative, taking another tack.

"Seven hundred pounds—fifty bars of fourteen pounds each," answered Bosbyshell. "That's another problem that defies explanation. How could one man carry away all that gold without being seen? He'd need a dray to cart it off, and we're very careful about what goes out of the Mint. There's a guard at the front door all the time, and no one is allowed to leave with a package of any kind until it has been examined and passed."

A grunt was Drummond's only comment—and those who knew the Secret Service man best would have interpreted the sound to mean studious digestion of facts, rather than admission of even temporary defeat.

It was one of the government detective's pet theories that every crime, no matter how puzzling, could be solved by application of common-sense principles and the rules of logic. "The criminal with brains," he was fond of saying, "will deliberately try to throw you off the scent. Then you've got to take your time and separate the wheat[20] from the chaff—the false leads from the true. But the man who commits a crime on the spur of the moment—or who flatters himself that he hasn't left a single clue behind—is the one who's easy to catch. The cleverest crook in the world can't enter a room without leaving his visiting card in some way or other. It's up to you to find that card and read the name on it. And common sense is the best reading glass."

Requesting that his mission be kept secret, Drummond said that he would like to examine Vault No. Six.

"Let Cochrane open the vault for me and then have Jamison and Strubel open the grille," he directed.

"Unless Mr. Bosbyshell opened the vault door," Preston reminded him, "there's no one but Cochrane who could do it. It won't be necessary, however, to have either of the others open the grille—the door was taken from its hinges this morning in order the better to examine the place and it hasn't yet been replaced."

"All right," agreed Drummond. "Let's have Cochrane work the outer combination, then. I'll have a look at the other two later."

Accompanied by the director and the superintendent, Drummond made his way to the basement where they were joined by the official weigher, a man well over fifty, who was introduced by Preston to "Mr. Drummond, a visitor who is desirous of seeing the vaults."

"I understand that you are the only man who can open them," said the detective. "Suppose we look into this one," as he stopped, as if by accident, before Vault No. 6.

Cochrane, without a word, bent forward and commenced to twirl the combination. A few spins to the right, a few to the left, back to the right, to the left once more—and he pulled at the heavy door expectantly. But it failed to budge.[21]

Again he bent over the combination, spinning it rapidly. Still the door refused to open.

"I'm afraid I'll have to ask you to help me with this, Superintendent," Cochrane said, finally. "It doesn't seem to work, somehow."

But, under Bosbyshell's manipulation, the door swung back almost instantly.

"Nothing wrong with the combination," commented Preston.

Drummond smiled. "Has the combination been changed recently?" he asked.

"Not for the past month," Bosbyshell replied. "We usually switch all of them six times a year, just as a general precaution—but this has been the same for the past few weeks. Ever since the fifteenth of last month, to be precise."

Inside the vault Drummond found that, as Preston had stated, the door to the grille had been taken from its hinges, to facilitate the work of the men who had weighed the gold, and had not been replaced.

"Where are the gold bars?" asked the detective. "The place looks like it had been well looted."

"They were all taken out this morning, to be carefully weighed," was Preston's reply.

"I'd like to see some of them stacked up there along the side of the grille, if it isn't too much trouble."

"Surely," said Bosbyshell. "I'll have the men bring them in at once."

As soon as the superintendent had left the room, Drummond requested that the door of the grille be placed in its usual position, and Cochrane set it up level with the floor, leaning against the supports at the side.

"Is that the way it always stays?" inquired the Secret Service man.[22]

"No, sir, but it's pretty heavy to handle, and I thought you just wanted to get a general idea of things."

"I'd like to see it in place, if you don't mind. Here, I'll help you with it—but we better slip our coats off, for it looks like a man's-sized job," and he removed his coat as he spoke.

After Cochrane had followed his example, the two of them hung the heavy door from its hinges and stepped back to get the effect. But Drummond's eyes were fixed, not upon the entrance to the grille, but on the middle of Cochrane's back, and, when the opportunity offered an instant later, he shifted his gaze to the waist of the elder man's trousers. Something that he saw there caused the shadow of a smile to flit across his face.

"Thanks," he said. "That will do nicely," and he made a quick gesture to Preston that he would like to have Cochrane leave the vault.

"Very much obliged, Mr. Cochrane," said the director. "We won't bother you any more. You might ask those men to hurry in with the bars, if you will."

And the weigher, pausing only to secure his coat, left the vault.

"Why all the stage setting?" inquired Preston. "You don't suspect...."

"I don't suspect a thing," Drummond smiled, searching for his own coat, "beyond the fact that the solution to the mystery is so simple as to be almost absurd. By the way, have you noticed those scratches on the bars of the grille, about four feet from the floor?"

"No, I hadn't," admitted the director. "But what of them? These vaults aren't new, you know, and I dare say you'd find similar marks on the grille bars in any of the others."

"I hope not," Drummond replied, grimly, "for that[23] would almost certainly mean a shortage of gold in other sections of the Mint. Incidentally, has all the rest of the gold been weighed?"

"Every ounce of it."

"Nothing missing?"

"Outside of the seven hundred pounds from this vault, not a particle."

"Good—then I'll be willing to lay a small wager that you can't find the duplicates of these scratches anywhere else in the Mint." And Drummond smiled at the director's perplexity.

When the men arrived with a truck loaded with gold bars, they stacked them—at the superintendent's direction—along the side of the grille nearest the vault entrance.

"Is that the way they are usually arranged?" inquired Drummond.

"Yes—the grille bars are of tempered steel and the openings between them are too small to permit anyone to put his hand through. Therefore, as we are somewhat pressed for space, we stack them up right along the outer wall of the grille and then work back. It saves time and labor in bringing them in."

"Is this the way the door of the grille ordinarily hangs?"

Bosbyshell inspected it a moment before he replied.

"Yes," he said. "It appears to be all right. It was purposely made to swing clear of the floor and the ceiling so that it might not become jammed. The combination and the use of the seal prevents its being opened by anyone who has no business in the grille."

"And the seal was intact when you came in yesterday afternoon?"

"It was."

"Thanks," said Drummond; "that was all I wanted to know," and he made his way upstairs with a smile which[24] seemed to say that his vacation in the Maine woods had not been indefinitely postponed.

Once back in the director's office, the government operative asked permission to use the telephone, and, calling the Philadelphia office of the Secret Service, requested that three agents be assigned to meet him down town as soon as possible.

"Have you a record of the home address of the people employed in the Mint?" Drummond inquired of the director, as he hung up the receiver.

"Surely," said Preston, producing a typewritten list from the drawer of his desk.

"I'll borrow this for a while, if I may. I'll probably be back with it before three o'clock—and bring some news with me, too," and the operative was out of the room before Preston could frame a single question.

As a matter of fact, the clock in the director's office pointed to two-thirty when Drummond returned, accompanied by the three men who had been assigned to assist him.

"Have you discovered anything?" Preston demanded.

"Let's have Cochrane up here first," Drummond smiled. "I can't be positive until I've talked to him. You might have the superintendent in, too. He'll be interested in developments, I think."

Bosbyshell was the first to arrive, and, at Drummond's request, took up a position on the far side of the room. As soon as he had entered, two of the other Secret Service men ranged themselves on the other side of the doorway and, the moment Cochrane came in, closed the door behind him.

"Cochrane," said Drummond, "what did you do with the seven hundred pounds of gold that you took from Vault No. Six during the past few weeks?"[25]

"What—what—" stammered the weigher.

"There's no use bluffing," continued the detective. "We've got the goods on you. The only thing missing is the gold itself, and the sooner you turn it over the more lenient the government will be with you. I know how you got the bars out of the grille—a piece of bent wire was sufficient to dislodge them from the top of the pile nearest the grille bars

11

and it was easy to slip them under the door. No wonder the seal was never tampered with. It wasn't necessary for you to go inside the grille at all.

"But, more than that, I know how you carried the bars, one at a time, out of the Mint. It took these three men less than an hour this afternoon to find the tailor who fixed the false pocket in the front of your trousers—the next time you try a job of this kind you better attend to all these details yourself—and it needed only one look at your suspenders this morning to see that they were a good deal wider and heavier than necessary. That long coat you are in the habit of wearing is just the thing to cover up any suspicious bulge in your garments and the guard at the door, knowing you, would never think of telling you to stop unless you carried a package or something else contrary to orders.

"The people in your neighborhood say that they've seen queer bluish lights in the basement of your house on Woodland Avenue. So I suspect you've been melting that gold up and hiding it somewhere, ready for a quick getaway.

"Yes, Cochrane, we've got the goods on you and if you want to save half of a twenty-year sentence—which at your age means life—come across with the information. Where is the gold?"

"In the old sewer pipe," faltered the weigher, who appeared to have aged ten years while Drummond was[26] speaking. "In the old sewer pipe that leads from my basement."

"Good!" exclaimed Drummond. "I think Mr. Preston will use his influence with the court to see that your sentence isn't any heavier than necessary. It's worth that much to guard the Mint against future losses of the same kind, isn't it, Mr. Director?"

"It surely is," replied Preston. "But how in the name of Heaven did you get the answer so quickly?"

Drummond delayed his answer until Cochrane, accompanied by the three Secret Service men, had left the room. Then—

"Nothing but common sense," he said. "You remember those scratches I called your attention to—the ones on the side of the grille bars? They were a clear indication of the way in which the gold had been taken from the grille—knocked down from the top of the pile with a piece of wire and pulled under the door of the grille. That eliminated Jamison and Strubel immediately. They needn't have gone to that trouble, even if it had been possible for them to get into the vault in the first place.

"But I had my suspicions of Cochrane when he was unable to open the vault door. That pointed to nervousness, and nervousness indicated a guilty conscience. I made the hanging of the grille door an excuse to get him to shed his coat—though I did want to see whether the door came all the way down to the floor—and I noted that his suspenders were very broad and his trousers abnormally wide around the waist. He didn't want to take any chances with that extra fourteen pounds of gold, you know. It would never do to drop it in the street.

"The rest is merely corroborative. I found that bluish lights had been observed in the basement of Cochrane's house, and one of my men located the tailor who had[27] enlarged his trousers. That's really all there was to it."

With that Drummond started to the door, only to be stopped by Director Preston's inquiry as to where he was going.

"On my vacation, which you interrupted this morning," replied the Secret Service man.

"It's a good thing I did," Preston called after him. "If Cochrane had really gotten away with that gold we might never have caught him."

"Which," as Bill Quinn said, when he finished his narrative, "is the reason I claim that the telegraph boy who persisted in paging Drummond is the one who was really responsible for the saving of some hundred and thirty thousand dollars that belonged to Uncle Sam."

"But, surely," I said, "that case was an exception. In rapidity of action, I mean. Don't governmental investigations usually take a long time?"

"Frequently," admitted Quinn, "they drag on and on for months—sometimes years. But it's seldom that Uncle Sam fails to land his man—even though the trail leads into the realms of royalty, as in the Ypiranga case. That happened before the World War opened, but it gave the State Department a mighty good line on what to expect from Germany."

[28]

III
THE YPIRANGA CASE

"Mexico," said Bill Quinn, who now holds a soft berth in the Treasury Department by virtue of an injury received in the line of duty—during a raid on counterfeiters a few years ago, to be precise—"is back on the first page of the papers again after being crowded off for some four years because of the World War. Funny coincidence, that, when you remember that it was this same Mexico that gave us our first indication of the way we might expect Germany to behave."

"Huh?" I said, a bit startled. "What do you mean? The first spark of the war was kindled in Serbia, not Mexico. Outside of the rumblings of the Algeciras case and one or two other minor affairs, there wasn't the slightest indication of the conflict to come."

"No?" and Quinn's eyebrows went up in interrogation. "How about the Ypiranga case?"

"The which?"

"The Ypiranga case—the one where Jack Stewart stumbled across a clue in a Mexico City café which led all the way to Berlin and back to Washington and threatened to precipitate a row before the Kaiser was quite ready for it?"

"No," I admitted, "that's a page of underground history that I haven't read—and I must confess that I don't know Stewart, either."

"Probably not," said the former Secret Service man.[29] "He wasn't connected with any of the branches of the government that get into print very often. As a matter of fact, the very existence of the organization to which he belonged isn't given any too much publicity. Everyone knows of the Secret Service and the men who make the investigations for the Department of Justice and the Post-office Department—but the Department of State, for obvious reasons, conducts its inquiries in a rather more diplomatic manner. Its agents have to pose as commercial investigators, or something else equally as prosaic. Their salaries are, as a general thing, paid out of the President's private allowance or out of the fund given to the department 'for use as it may see fit.' Less than half a dozen people know the actual status of the organization or the names of its members at any one time, and its exploits are recorded only in the archives of the State Department."

"But who," I persisted, as Quinn stopped, "was Jack Stewart and what was the nature of the affair upon which he stumbled in Mexico City?"

Stewart [replied Quinn] was just a quiet, ordinary sort of chap, the kind that you'd expect to find behind a desk in the State Department, sorting out consular reports and handling routine stuff. Nothing exceptional about him at all—which was probably one reason for his being selected for work as a secret agent of the Department. It doesn't do, you know, to pick men who are conspicuous, either in their dress or manner. Too easy to spot and remember them. The chap who's swallowed up in the crowd is the one who can get by with a whole lot of quiet work without being suspected.

When they sent Jack down to Mexico they didn't have the slightest idea he'd uncover anything as big as he did.[30] The country south of the Rio Grande, if you recall, had been none too quiet for some time prior to 1914. Taft had had his troubles with it ever since the end of the Diaz regime, and when Wilson came in the "Mexican question" was a legacy that caused the men in the State Department to spend a good many sleepless nights.

All sorts of rumors, most of them wild and bloody, floated up through official and unofficial channels. The one fact that seemed to be certain was that Mexico was none too friendly to the United States, and that some other nation was behind this feeling, keeping it constantly stirred up and overlooking no opportunity to add fuel to the flame. Three or four other members of the State Department's secret organization had been wandering around picking up leads for some months past and, upon the return of one of these to Washington, Stewart was sent to replace him.

His instructions were simple and delightfully indefinite. He was to proceed to Mexico City, posing as the investigator for a financial house in New York which was on the lookout for a soft concession from the Mexican government. This would give him an opportunity to seek the acquaintance of Mexican officials and lend an air of plausibility to practically any line that he found it necessary to follow. But, once at the capital with his alibis well established, he was to overlook nothing which might throw light upon the question that had been bothering Washington for some time past—just which one of the foreign powers was fanning the Mexican unrest and to what lengths it was prepared to go?

Of course, the State Department suspected—just as we now know—that Berlin was behind the movement, but at that time there was no indication of the reason. In the light of later events, however, the plan is plain. Germany,[31] feeling certain that the greatest war Europe had ever known was a matter of the immediate future, was laying her plans to keep other nations out of the conflict. She figured that Mexico was the best foil for the United States and that our pitifully small army would have its hands full with troubles at home. If not, she intended to let Japan enter into the equation—as shown by the Zimmerman note some two years later.

When Stewart got to Mexico City, it did not take him long to discover that there was an undercurrent of animosity to the United States which made itself felt in numberless ways. Some of the Mexican papers, apparently on a stronger financial basis than ever before, were outspoken in their criticism of American dollars and American dealings. The people as a whole, long dominated by Diaz, were being stirred to resentment of the "Gringoes," who "sought to purchase the soul of a nation as well as its mineral wealth." The improvements which American capital had made were entirely overlooked, and the spotlight of subsidized publicity was thrown upon the encroachments of the hated Yankees.

All this Stewart reported to Washington, and in reply was politely informed that, while interesting, it was hardly news. The State Department had known all this for months. The question was: Where was the money coming from and what was the immediate object of the game?

"Take your time and don't bother us unless you find something definite to report," was the substance of the instructions cabled to Stewart.

The secret agent, therefore, contented himself with lounging around the very inviting cafés of the Mexican capital and making friends with such officials as might be able to drop scraps of information.

It was November when he first hit Mexico City. It[32] was nearly the middle of April before he picked up anything at all worth while. Of course, in the meantime he had uncovered a number of leads—but every one of them was blind. For a day or two, or a week at most, they would hold out glowing promise of something big just around the corner. Then, when he got to the end of the rainbow, he would find an empty pail in place of the pot of gold he had hoped for.

It wasn't surprising, therefore, that Stewart was growing tired of the life of continual mystery, of developments that never developed, of secrets that were empty and surprises that faded away into nothing.

It was on the 13th of April, while seated at a little table in front of a sidewalk café on the Calles de Victoria, that the American agent obtained his first real clue to the impending disaster.

When two Mexicans whom he knew by sight, but not by name, sat down at a table near his he pricked up his ears purely by instinct, rather than through any real hope of obtaining information of value.

The arrival of the usual sugared drinks was followed by a few words of guarded conversation, and then one of the Mexicans remarked, in a tone a trifle louder than necessary, that "the United States is a nation of cowardly women, dollar worshipers who are afraid to fight, and braggarts who would not dare to back up their threats."

It was an effort for Stewart to remain immersed in the newspaper propped up in front of him. Often as he had heard these sentiments expressed, his Southern blood still rose involuntarily—until his logic reminded him that his mission was not to start a quarrel, but to end one. He knew that no good could ensue from his taking up the challenge, and the very fact that the speaker had raised his voice gave him the tip that the words were uttered[33] for his especial benefit, to find out whether he understood Spanish—for he made no attempt to disguise his nationality.

With a smile which did not show on his lips, Stewart summoned the waiter and in atrocious Spanish ordered another glass of lemonade. His complete knowledge of the language was the one thing which he had managed to keep entirely under cover ever since reaching Mexico, for he figured that the natives would speak more freely in his presence if they believed he could not gather what they were discussing.

The trick worked to perfection.

"Pig-headed Yankee," commented the Mexican who had first spoken. "Lemonade! Pah!—they haven't the nerve to take a man's drink!" and he drained his glass of *pulque* at a single gulp.

The other, who had not spoken above a whisper, raised his glass and regarded it in silence for a moment. Then—"Prosit," he said, and drank.

"*Nom di Dio*," warned his companion. "Be careful! The American hog does not speak Spanish well enough to understand those who use it fluently, but he may speak German."

Stewart smothered a smile behind his paper. Spanish had always been a hobby of his—but he only knew about three words in German!

"I understand," continued the Mexican, "that Victoriano is preparing for the coup, just as I always figured he would" (Stewart knew that "Victoriano" was the familiar form in which the populace referred to Victoriano Huerta, self-appointed President of Mexico and the man who had steadfastly defied the American government in every way possible, taking care not to allow matters to reach such a hot stage that he could handle them through[34] diplomatic promises to see that things "improved in the future").

"*El Presidente* has always been careful to protect himself"—the speaker went on—"but now that you have brought definite assurance from our friends that the money and the arms will be forthcoming within the fortnight there is nothing further to fear from the Yankee pigs. It will be easy to stir up sentiment against them here overnight, and before they can mass their handful of troops along the Rio Grande we will have retaken Texas and wiped out the insult of 'forty-eight. What is the latest news from the ship?"

"The ——?" inquired the man across the table, but his Teutonic intonation of what was evidently a Spanish name was so jumbled that all Stewart could catch was the first syllable—something that sounded like "*Eep.*"

"Is that the name?" asked the Mexican.

"Yes," replied the other. "She sailed from Hamburg on the seventh. Allowing two weeks for the passage—she isn't fast, you know—that would bring her into Vera Cruz about the twenty-first. Once there, the arms can be landed and...."

The events of the next few minutes moved so rapidly that, when Stewart had time to catch his breath, he found it difficult to reconstruct the affair with accuracy.

He recalled that he had been so interested in the conversation at the next table that he had failed to notice the approach of the only other man he knew in the State Department's secret organization—Dawson, who had been prowling around the West Coast on an errand similar to his. Before he knew it Dawson had clapped him on the back and exclaimed: "Hello, Jack! Didn't expect to see you here—thought you'd be looking over things in the vicinity of the Palace."[35]

The words themselves were innocent enough, but—they were spoken in fluent, rapid Spanish and Stewart had shown that he understood!

"*Sapristi!*" hissed the Mexican. "Did you see?" and he bent forward to whisper hurriedly to his companion.

Stewart recovered himself instantly, but the damage had been done.

"Hello, Dawson," he answered in English, trusting that the men at the next table had not noted his slip. "Sit down and have something? Rotten weather, isn't it? And not a lead in sight. These Mexicans seem to be afraid to enter into any contract that ties them up more than a year—and eighteen revolutions can happen in that time."

As Dawson seated himself, Stewart gave him a hasty sign to be careful. Watching the Mexican and his companion out of the corner of his eye, he steered the conversation into harmless channels, but a moment later the pair at the next table called the waiter, gave some whispered instructions, and left.

"What's the matter?" asked Dawson.

"Nothing—except that I involuntarily registered a knowledge of Spanish when you spoke to me just now, and I've spent several months building up a reputation for knowing less about the language than anyone in Mexico City. As luck would have it, there was a couple seated at the next table who were giving me what sounded like the first real dope I've had since I got here. I'll tell you about it later. The question now is to get back to the hotel before that precious pair get in their dirty work. A code message to Washington is all I ask—but, if I'm not mistaken, we are going to have our work cut out for us on the way back."

"Scott! Serious as that, is it?" muttered Dawson.[36] "Well, there are two of us and I'd like to see their whole dam' army try to stop us. Let's go!"

"Wait a minute," counseled Stewart. "There's no real hurry, for they wouldn't dare try to start anything in the open. In case we get separated or—if anything should happen—wire the Department in code that a vessel with a Spanish name—something that begins with 'Eep'—has cleared Hamburg, loaded with guns and ammunition. Expected at Vera Cruz about the twenty-first. Germany's behind the whole plot. Now I'll settle up and we'll move."

But as he reached for his pocketbook a Mexican swaggering along the sidewalk deliberately stumbled against his chair and sent him sprawling. Dawson was on his feet in an instant, his fists clenched and ready for action.

But Stewart had noted that the Mexican had three companions and that one of the men who had occupied the adjoining table was watching the affair from a vantage point half a block away.

With a leap that was catlike in its agility, Stewart seized the swaggering native by the legs in a football tackle, and upset him against his assistants.

"Quick, this way!" he called to Dawson, starting up the street away from the watcher at the far corner. As he ran, his hand slipped into his coat pocket where the small, but extremely efficient, automatic with which all government agents are supplied usually rested. But the gun wasn't there! Apparently it had slipped out in the scuffle a moment before.

Hardly had he realized that he was unarmed before he and Dawson were confronted by five other natives coming from the opposite direction. The meager lighting system of the Mexican capital, however, was rather a help than a detriment, for in the struggle which followed it was practically impossible to tell friend from foe. The two[37] Americans, standing shoulder to shoulder, had the added advantage of teamwork—something which the natives had never learned.

"Don't use your gun if you can help it," Stewart warned. "We don't want the police in on this!"

As he spoke his fist shot out and the leader of the attacking party sprawled in the street. No sound came from Dawson, beyond a grunt, as he landed on the man he had singled out of the bunch. The ten seconds that followed were jammed with action, punctuated with the shrill cries for reinforcements from the Mexicans, and brightened here and there by the dull light from down the street which glinted off the long knives— the favorite weapon of the Latin-American fighter.

Stewart and Dawson realized that they must not only fight, but fight fast. Every second brought closer the arrival of help from the rear, but Dawson waited until he could hear the reinforcements almost upon them before he gave the word to break through. Then—

"Come on, Jack!" he called. "Let's go!"

Heads down, fists moving with piston-like precision, the two Americans plowed their way through. Dawson swore later that he felt at least one rib give under the impact of the blows and he knew that he nursed a sore wrist for days, but Stewart claimed that his energies were concentrated solely on the scrap and that he didn't have time to receive any impression of what was going on. He knew that he had to fight his way out—that it was essential for one of them to reach the telegraph office or the embassy with the news they carried.

It was a case of fight like the devil and trust to luck and the darkness for aid.

Almost before they knew it, they had broken through the trio in front of them and had turned down the Calles[38] Ancha, running in a form that would have done credit to a college track team. Behind them they heard the muffled oaths of their pursuers as they fell over the party they had just left.

"They don't want to attract the police any more than we do," gasped Dawson. "They don't dare shoot!"

But as he spoke there came the z-z-i-pp of a bullet, accompanied by the sharp crack of a revolver somewhere behind them.

"Careful," warned Stewart. "We've got to skirt that street light ahead. Duck and—"

But with that he crumpled up, a bullet through his hip.

Without an instant's hesitation Dawson stooped, swung his companion over his shoulder, and staggered on, his right hand groping for his automatic. Once out of the glare of the arc light, he felt that he would be safe, at least for a moment.

Then, clattering toward them, he heard a sound that spelled safety—one of the open nighthawk cabs that prowl around the streets of the Mexican capital.

Shifting Stewart so that his feet rested on the ground, he wheeled and raked the street behind him with a fusillade from his automatic. There was only a dull mass of whitish clothing some fifty yards away at which to aim, but he knew that the counter-attack would probably gain a few precious seconds of time—time sufficient to stop the cab and to put his plan into operation.

The moment the cab came into the circle of light from the street lamp Dawson dragged his companion toward it, seized the horse's bridle with his free hand and ordered the driver to halt.

Before the cabby had recovered his wits the two Americans were in the vehicle and Dawson had his revolver pressed none too gently into the small of the driver's back.[39] The weapon was empty, but the Mexican didn't know that, and he responded instantly to Dawson's order to turn around and drive "as if seventy devils of Hades were after him!"

Outside of a few stray shots that followed as they disappeared up the street, the drive to the Embassy was uneventful, and, once under the shelter of the American flag, the rest was easy.

Stewart, it developed, had sustained only a flesh wound through the muscles of his hip—painful, but not dangerous. Within ten minutes after he had reached O'Shaughnessy's office he was dictating a code wire to Washington—a cable which stated that a vessel with a Spanish name, commencing with something that sounded like "Eep," had cleared Hamburg on the seventh, loaded with arms and ammunition destined to advance the interests of Mexican revolutionists and to hamper the efforts of the United States to preserve order south of the border.

The wire reached Washington at noon of the following day and was instantly transmitted to Berlin, with instructions to Ambassador Gerard to look into the matter and report immediately.

Vessel in question is probably the *Ypiranga* [stated a code the following morning]. Cleared Hamburg on date mentioned, presumably loaded with grain. Rumors here of large shipment of arms to some Latin American republic. Practically certain that Wilhelmstrasse is behind the move, but impossible to obtain confirmation. Motive unknown.

Ten minutes after this message had been decoded the newspaper correspondents at the White House noted that a special Cabinet meeting had been called, but no announcement was made of its purpose or of the business transacted, beyond the admission that "the insult to the flag at Tampico had been considered."[40]

Promptly at noon the great wireless station at Arlington flashed a message to Admiral Mayo, in command of the squadron off the Mexican coast. In effect, it read:

Proceed immediately to Vera Cruz. Await arrival of steamer *Ypiranga*, loaded with arms. Prevent landing at any cost. Blockade upon pretext of recent insult to flag. Atlantic Fleet ordered to your support.

"The rest of the story," concluded Quinn, "is a matter of history. How the fleet bottled up the harbor at Vera Cruz, how it was forced to send a landing party ashore under fire, and how seventeen American sailors lost their lives during the guerrilla attack which followed. All that was spread across the front pages of American papers in big black type—but the fact that a steamer named the *Ypiranga* had been held up by the American fleet and forced to anchor at a safe distance offshore, under the guns of the flagship, was given little space. Apparently it was a minor incident—but in reality it was the crux of the whole situation, an indication of Germany's rancor, which was to burst its bounds before four months had passed, another case in which the arm of Uncle Sam had been long enough to stretch halfway across a continent and nip impending disaster."

"But," I inquired, as he paused, "what became of Dawson and Stewart?"

"That I don't know," replied Quinn. "The last time I heard of Jack he had a captain's commission in France and was following up his feud with the Hun that started in Mexico City four months before the rest of the world dreamed of war. Dawson, I believe, is still in the Department, and rendered valuable assistance in combating German propaganda in Chile and Peru. He'll probably[41] be rewarded with a consular job in some out-of-the-way hole, for, now that the war is over, the organization to which he belongs will gradually dwindle to its previous small proportions.

"Strange, wasn't it, how that pair stumbled across one of the first tentacles of the World War in front of a café in Mexico City? That's one beauty of government detective work—you never know when the monotony is going to be blown wide open by the biggest thing you ever happened upon.

"There was little Mary McNilless, who turned up the clue which prevented an explosion, compared to which the Black Tom affair would have been a Sunday-school party. She never dreamed that she would prevent the loss of millions of dollars' worth of property and at least a score of lives, but she did—without moving from her desk."

"How?" I asked.

But Quinn yawned, looked at his watch, and said: "That's entirely too long a story to spin right now. It's past my bedtime, and Mrs. Quinn's likely to be fussy if I'm not home by twelve at least. She says that now I have an office job she can at least count on my being round to guard the house—something that she never could do before. So let's leave Mary for another time. Goodnight"—and he was off.

[42]

IV
THE CLUE ON SHELF 45

"Of course, it is possible that patriotism might have prompted Mary McNilless to locate the clue which prevented an explosion that would have seriously hampered the munitions industry of the United States—but the fact remains that she did it principally because she was in love with Dick Walters, and Dick happened to be in the Secret Service. It was one case where Cupid scored over Mars."

Bill Quinn eased the game leg which he won as the trophy of a counterfeiting raid some years before into a more comfortable position, reached for his pipe and tobacco pouch, and settled himself for another reminiscence of the Service with which he had formerly been actively connected.

"Mary was—and doubtless still is—one of those red-headed, blue-eyed Irish beauties whom nature has peppered with just enough freckles to make them alluring, evidences that the sun itself couldn't help kissing her. But, from all I've been able to gather, the sun was in a class by itself. Until Dick Walters came upon the scene, Miss McNilless held herself strictly aloof from masculine company and much preferred to spend an evening with her books than to take a trip to Coney or any of the other resorts where a girl's kisses pass as current coin in payment for three or four hours' outing.

"Dick was just the kind of chap that would have appealed to Mary, or to 'most any other girl, for that matter.[43] Maybe you remember him. He used to be at the White House during Taft's regime, but they shifted most of the force soon after Wilson came in and Dick was sent out to the Coast on an opium hunt that kept him busy for more than a year. In fact, he came east just in time to be assigned to the von Ewald case—and, incidentally, to fall foul of Mary and Cupid, a pair that you couldn't tie, much less beat."

The von Ewald case [Quinn continued, after pausing a moment to repack his pipe] was one of the many exploits of the Secret Service that never got in the papers. To be strictly truthful, it wasn't as much a triumph for the S. S. as it was for Mary McNilless—and, besides, we weren't at war with Germany at that time, so it had to be kept rather dark.

But Germany was at war with us. You remember the Black Tom explosion in August, nineteen sixteen? Well, if the plans of von Ewald and his associates hadn't been frustrated by a little red-headed girl with exceptional powers of observation, there would have been a detonation in Wilmington, Delaware, that would have made the Black Tom affair, with its damage of thirty millions of dollars, sound like the college yell of a deaf-and-dumb institute.

As far back as January, nineteen sixteen, the Secret Service knew that there were a number of Germans in New York who desired nothing so much as to hinder the munitions industry of the United States, despite the fact that we were a neutral nation.

From Harry Newton, the leader in the second plot to destroy the Welland Canal, and from Paul Seib, who was implicated in the attempt to destroy shipping at Hoboken, they forced the information that the conspirators received their orders and drew their pay from a man of many[44] aliases, known to his associates as "Number eight fifty-nine" and occasionally, to the world at large, as "von Ewald."

This much was known in Washington—but, when you came to analyze the information, it didn't amount to a whole lot. It's one thing to know that some one is plotting murder and arson on a wholesale scale, but discovering the identity of that individual is an entirely different proposition, one which called for all the finesse and obstinacy for which the governmental detective services are famous.

Another factor that complicated the situation was that speed was essential. The problem was entirely different from a counterfeiting or smuggling case, where you can be content to let the people on the other side of the table make as many moves as they wish, with the practical certainty that you'll land them sooner or later. "Give them plenty of rope and they'll land in Leavenworth" is a favorite axiom in the Service—but here you had to conserve your rope to the uttermost. Every day that passed meant that some new plot was that much nearer completion—that millions of dollars in property and the lives of no-one-knew-how-many people were still in danger.

So the order went forward from the headquarters of the Service, "Get the man known as von Ewald and get him quick!"

Secret Service men, Postal inspectors, and Department of Justice agents were called in from all parts of the country and rushed to New York, until the metropolis looked like the headquarters of a convention of governmental detectives. Grogan, the chap that landed Perry, the master-counterfeiter, was there, as were George MacMasters and Sid Shields, who prevented the revolution in Cuba three or four years ago. Jimmy Reynolds was borrowed from the Internal Revenue Bureau, and Althouse, who[45] spoke German like a native, was brought up from the border where he had been working on a propaganda case just across the line.

There must have been forty men turned loose on this assignment alone, and, in the course of the search for von Ewald, there were a number of other developments scarcely less important than the main issue. At least two of these—the Trenton taxicab tangle and the affair of the girl at the switchboard—are exploits worthy of separate mention.

But, in spite of the great array of detective talent, no one could get a line on von Ewald.

In April, when Dick Walters returned from the Coast, the other men in the Service were frankly skeptical as to whether there was a von Ewald at all. They had come to look upon him as a myth, a bugaboo. They couldn't deny that there must be some guiding spirit to the Teutonic plots, but they rather favored the theory that several men, rather than one, were to blame.

Walters' instructions were just like the rest—to go to New York and stick on the job until the German conspirator was apprehended.

"Maybe it's one man, maybe there're half a dozen," the chief admitted, "but we've got to nail 'em. The very fact that they haven't started anything of consequence since the early part of the year would appear to point to renewed activity very shortly. It's up to you and the other men already in New York to prevent the success of any of these plots."

Walters listened patiently to all the dope that had been gathered and then figured, as had every new man, that it was up to him to do a little sleuthing of his own.

The headquarters of the German agents was supposed to be somewhere in Greenwich Village, on one of those[46] half-grown alleys that always threatens to meet itself coming back. But more than a score of government operatives had combed that part of the town without securing a trace of anything tangible. On the average of once a night the phone at headquarters would ring and some one at the other end would send in a hurry call for help up in the Bronx or in Harlem or some other distant part of the city where he thought he had turned up a clue. The men on duty would leap into the machine that always waited at the curb and fracture every speed law ever made—only to find, when they arrived, that it was a false alarm.

Finally, after several weeks of that sort of thing, conditions commenced to get on Dick's nerves.

"I'm going to tackle this thing on my own," he announced. "Luck is going to play as much of a part in landing von Ewald as anything else—and luck never hunted with more than one man. Good-by! See you fellows later."

But it was a good many weeks—August, to be precise—before the men in the Federal Building had the opportunity of talking to Walters. He would report over the phone, of course, and drop down there every few days—but he'd only stay long enough to find out if there was any real news or any orders from Washington. Then he'd disappear uptown.

"Dick's sure got a grouch these days," was the comment that went around after Walters had paid one of his flying visits.

"Yeh," grunted Barry, who was on duty that night, "either the von Ewald case's got on his nerves or he's found a girl that can't see him."

Neither supposition missed the mark very far.

Walters was getting sick and tired of the apparently[47] fruitless chase after an elusive German. He had never been known to flinch in the face of danger—often went out of his way to find it, in fact—but this constant search for a man whom nobody knew, a man of whom there wasn't the slightest description, was nerve-racking, to say the least.

Then, too, he had met Mary McNilless.

He'd wandered into the Public Library one evening just before closing time, and, like many another man, had fallen victim to Mary's red hair and Mary's Irish eyes. But a brick wall was a soft proposition compared to Mary McNilless. Snubbing good-looking young men who thought that the tailors were missing an excellent model was part of the day's work with the little library girl—though she secretly admitted to herself that this one was a bit above the average.

Dick didn't get a rise that night, though, or for some days after. Every evening at seven found him at the desk over which Miss McNilless presided, framing some almost intelligent question about books in order to prolong the conversation. Mary would answer politely and—that was all.

But, almost imperceptibly, a bond of friendship sprang up between them. Maybe it was the fact that Dick's mother had been Irish, too, or possibly it was because he admitted to himself that this girl was different from the rest, and, admitting it, laid the foundation for a deep-souled respect that couldn't help but show in his manner.

Within the month Dick was taking her home, and in six weeks they were good pals, bumming around to queer, out-of-the-way restaurants and planning outings which Dick, in his heart, knew could never materialize—not until von Ewald had been run to cover, at any rate.

Several times Mary tried to find out her companion's[48] profession—diplomatically, of course, but nevertheless she was curious. Naturally, Dick couldn't tell her. Said he had "just finished a job on the Coast and was taking a vacation in New York." But Mary had sense enough to know that he wasn't at leisure. Also that he was working on something that kept his mind constantly active—for several times he had excused himself in a hurry and then returned, anywhere from half an hour to an hour later, with a rather crestfallen expression.

After they had reached the "Dick and Mary" stage she came right out one night and asked him.

"Hon," he told her, "that's one thing that I've got to keep from you for a while. It's nothing that you would be ashamed of, though, but something that will make you mighty proud. At least," he added, "it'll make you proud if I don't fall down on the job almighty hard. Meanwhile, all I can do is to ask you to trust me. Will you?"

The tips of her fingers rested on the back of his hand for just a moment before she said, "You know I will, Dick"—and neither of them mentioned the subject from that time on.

On the night of the Black Tom explosion, early in August, Dick didn't show up at the Library at the usual hour, and, while this didn't worry Mary, because it had happened several times before, she began to be annoyed when three nights passed the same way. Of course, she had no way of knowing that the Service had received a tip from a stool pigeon on the pay roll of the New York police force that "a bunch of Germans were planning a big explosion of some kind" just a few hours before the earth rocked with the force of the blow-up in Jersey. Every government operative in the city had been informed of the rumor, but few of them had taken it seriously and not one[49] had any reason to expect that the plot would culminate so close to New York. But the echo of the first blast had hardly died away before there were a dozen agents on the spot, weaving a network around the entire district. All they got for their pains, however, was a few suspects who very evidently didn't know a thing.

So it was a very tired and disgusted Dick who entered the Library four nights later and almost shambled up to Mary's desk.

"I'll be off duty in half an hour," she told him. "From the way you look, you need a little comforting."

"I do that," he admitted. "Don't make me wait any longer than you have to," and he amused himself by glancing over the late seekers after knowledge.

When they had finally seated themselves in a cozy corner of a little restaurant in the upper Forties, Dick threw caution to the winds and told Mary all about his troubles.

"I haven't the least business to do it," he confessed, "and if the chief found it out I'd be bounced so fast that it would make my head swim. But, in the first place, I want you to marry me, and I know you wouldn't think of doing that unless you knew something more about me."

There was just the flicker of a smile around Mary's mouth as she said, almost perfunctorily, "No, of course not!" But her intuition told her that this wasn't the time to joke, and, before Walters could go on, she added, "I know you well enough, Dick, not to worry about that end of it."

So Walters told her everything from the beginning—and it didn't take more than five minutes at that. Outside of the fact that his people lived in Des Moines, that he had been in the Secret Service for eight years, and that he[50] hadn't been able to do a thing toward the apprehension of a certain German spy that the government was extremely anxious to locate, there was pitifully little to tell.

"The whole thing," he concluded, "came to a head the other night—the night I didn't show up. We knew that something was going to break, somewhere, but we couldn't discover where until it was too late to prevent the explosion across the river. Now that they've gotten away with that, they'll probably lay their lines for something even bigger."

"Well, now that I've told you, what d'you think?"

"You mean you'd like to marry me?" Mary asked with a smile.

"I don't know how to put it any plainer," Dick admitted—and what followed caused the waiter to wheel around and suddenly commence dusting off a table that already was bright enough to see your face in.

"There wasn't the slightest clue left after the Black Tom affair?" Mary asked, as she straightened her hat.

"Not one. We did find two of the bombs that hadn't exploded—devilishly clever arrangements, with a new combination of chemicals. Something was evidently wrong with the mixture, though, for they wouldn't go off, even when our experts started to play with them. The man who made them evidently wasn't quite sure of his ground. But there wasn't a thing about the bombs themselves that would provide any indication of where they came from."

"The man who made them must have had a pretty thorough knowledge of chemistry," Mary mused.

"Mighty near perfect," admitted Walters. "At least six exploded on time, and, from what I understand, they were loaded to the muzzle with a mixture that no one but an expert would dare handle."[51]

"And," continued Mary, with just a hint of excitement in her voice, "the bomb-maker would continue to investigate the subject. He would want to get the latest information, the most recent books, the—"

"What are you driving at?" Walters interrupted.

"Just this," and Mary leaned across the table so that there was no possibility of being overheard. "We girls have a good deal of time on our hands, so we get into the habit of making conjectures and forming theories about the 'regulars'—the people who come into the Library often enough for us to know them by sight.

"Up to a month ago there was a man who dropped into the reference room nearly every day to consult books from Shelf Forty-five. Naturally he came up to my desk, and, as he usually arrived during the slack periods, I had plenty of time to study him. Maybe it was because I had been reading Lombroso, or possibly it's because I am just naturally observant, but I noticed that, in addition to each of his ears being practically lobeless, one of them was quite pointed at the top—almost like a fox's.

"For a week he didn't show up, and then one day another man came in and asked for a book from Shelf Forty-five. Just as he turned away I had a shock. Apparently he wasn't in the least like the other man in anything save height—but neither of his ears had any lobes to speak of and the top of them was pointed! When he returned the book I looked him over pretty thoroughly and came to the conclusion that, in spite of the fact that his general appearance differed entirely from the other man's, they were really one and the same!"

"But what," grumbled Walters, "has that to do with the Black Tom explosion?"

"The last time this man came to the Library," said Mary, "was two days before the night you failed to[52] arrive—two days before the explosion. And—Do you know what books are kept on Shelf Forty-five?"

"No. What?"

"The latest works on the chemistry of explosives!"

Walters sat up with a jerk that threatened to overthrow the table.

"Mary," he said, in a whisper, "I've a hunch that you've succeeded where all the rest of us fell down! The disguises and the constant reference to books on explosives are certainly worth looking into. What name did this man give?"

"Names," she corrected. "I don't recall what they were or the addresses, either. But it would be easy to find them on the cards. We don't have very many calls for books from Shelf Forty-five."

"It doesn't matter, though," and Walters slipped back into his disconsolate mood. "He wouldn't leave a lead as open as that, of course."

"No, certainly not," agreed Mary. "But the last time he was there he asked for Professor Stevens's new book. It hadn't come in then, but I told him we expected it shortly. So, unless you men have scared him off, he'll be back in a day or two—possibly in a new disguise. Why don't you see the librarian, get a place as attendant in the reference room, and I'll tip you off the instant I spot that pointed ear. That's one thing he can't hide!"

The next morning there was a new employee in the reference room. No one knew where he came from and no one—save the librarian and Mary McNilless—knew what he was there for, because his principal occupation appeared to be lounging around inconspicuously in the neighborhood of the information desk. There he stayed for three days, wondering whether this clue, like all the rest, would dissolve into thin air.[53]

About five o'clock on the afternoon of the third day a man strolled up to Mary's desk and asked if Professor Stevens's book had come in yet. It was reposing at that moment on Shelf Forty-five, as Mary well knew, but she said she'd see, and left the room, carefully arranging her hair at the back of her neck with her left hand—a signal which she and Dick had agreed upon the preceding evening.

Before she returned the new attendant had vanished, but Dick Walters, in his usual garb, was loitering around the only entrance to the reference room, watching the suspect out of the corner of his eye.

"I'm sorry," Mary reported, "but the Stevens book won't be in until to-morrow," and she was barely able to keep the anxiety out of her voice as she spoke.

Had Dick gotten her signal? Would he be able to trail his man? Could he capture him without being injured? These and a score of other questions rushed through her mind as she saw the German leave the room. Once outside—well, she'd have to wait for Dick to tell her what happened then.

The man who was interested in the chemistry of explosives apparently wasn't in the least afraid of being followed, for he took a bus uptown, alighted at Eighty-third Street, and vanished into one of the innumerable small apartment houses in that section of the city. Walters kept close behind him, and he entered the lobby of the apartment house in time to hear his quarry ascending to the fourth floor. Then he signaled to the four men who had followed him up the Avenue in a government-owned machine—men who had been stationed outside the Library in the event of just such an occurrence—and instructed two of them to guard the rear of the house, while the other two remained in front.[54]

"I'm going to make this haul myself," Walters stated, "but I want you boys to cover up in case anything happens to me. No matter what occurs, don't let him get away. Shoot first and ask questions afterward!" and he had re-entered the house almost before he finished speaking.

On the landing at the third floor he paused long enough to give the men at the rear a chance to get located. Then—a quick ring at the bell on the fourth floor and he waited for action.

Nothing happened. Another ring—and still no response.

As he pressed the button for the third time the door swung slowly inward, affording only a glimpse of a dark, uninviting hall. But, once he was inside, the door closed silently and he heard a bolt slipped into place. Simultaneously a spot light, arranged over the doorway, flashed on and Dick was almost dazzled by the glare. Out of the darkness came the guttural inquiry:

"What do you want?"

"Not a thing in the world," replied Walters, "except to know if a man named Simpson liveshere."

"No," came the voice, "he does not. Get out!"

"Sure I will if you'll pull back that bolt. What's the idea, anyhow? You're as mysterious as if you were running a bomb factory or something—"

As he spoke he ducked, for if the words had the effect he hoped, the other would realize that he was cornered and attempt to escape.

A guttural German oath, followed by a rapid movement of the man's hand toward his hip pocket was the reply. In a flash Dick slipped forward, bending low to avoid the expected attack, and seized the German in a half nelson that defied movement. Backing out of the circle of light, he held the helpless man in front of him—as a shelter in[55] case of an attack from other occupants of the apartment—and called for assistance. The crash of glass at the rear told him that reinforcements had made their way up the fire escape and had broken in through the window. A moment later came the sound of feet on the stairs and the other two operatives were at the door, revolvers drawn and ready for action.

But there wasn't any further struggle. Von Ewald—or whatever his real name was, for that was never decided—was alone and evidently realized that the odds were overwhelming. Meekly, almost placidly, he allowed the handcuffs to be slipped over his wrists and stood by as the Secret Service men searched the apartment. Not a line or record was found to implicate anyone else—but what they did discover was a box filled with bombs precisely like those picked up on the scene of the Black Tom explosion, proof sufficient to send the German to the penitentiary for ten years—for our laws, unfortunately, do not permit of the death penalty for spies unless caught red-handed by the military authorities.

That he was the man for whom they were searching—the mysterious "No. 859"—was apparent from the fact that papers concealed in his desk contained full details as to the arrangement of the Nemours plant at Wilmington, Delaware, with a dozen red dots indicative of the best places to plant bombs. Of his associates and the manner in which he managed his organization there wasn't the slightest trace. But the Black Tom explosion, if you recall, was the last big catastrophe of its kind in America—and the capture of von Ewald was the reason that more of the German plots didn't succeed.

The Treasury Department realized this fact when Mary McNilless, on the morning of the day she was to be married to Dick Walters, U. S. S. S., received a very handsome[56] chest of silver, including a platter engraved, "To Miss Mary McNilless, whose cleverness and keen perception saved property valued at millions of dollars."

No one ever found out who sent it, but it's a safe bet that the order came from Washington by way of Wilmington, where the Nemours plant still stands—thanks to the quickness of Mary's Irish eyes.

[57]

V
PHYLLIS DODGE, SMUGGLER EXTRAORDINARY

Bill Quinn tossed aside his evening paper and, cocking his feet upon a convenient chair, remarked that, now that peace was finally signed, sealed, and delivered, there ought to be a big boom in the favorite pastime of the idle rich.

"Meaning what?" I inquired.

"Smuggling, of course," said Quinn, who only retired from Secret Service when an injury received in action forced him to do so.

"Did you ever travel on a liner when four out of every five people on board didn't admit that they were trying to beat the customs officials one way or another—and the only reason the other one didn't follow suit was because he knew enough to keep his mouth shut. That's how Uncle Sam's detectives pick up a lot of clues. The amateur crook never realizes that silence is golden and that oftentimes speech leads to a heavy fine.

"Now that the freedom of the seas is an accomplished fact the whole crew of would-be smugglers will doubtless get to work again, only to be nabbed in port. Inasmuch as ocean travel has gone up with the rest of the cost of living, it'll probably be a sport confined to the comparatively rich, for a couple of years anyhow.

"It was different in the old days. Every steamer that came in was loaded to the eyes and you never knew when[58] you were going to spot a hidden necklace or a packet of diamonds that wasn't destined to pay duty. There were thrills to the game, too, believe me.

"Why, just take the case of Phyllis Dodge...."

Mrs. Dodge [Quinn continued, after he had packed his pipe to a condition where it was reasonably sure to remain lighted for some time] was, theoretically at least, a widow. Her full name, as it appeared on many passenger lists during the early part of 1913, was Mrs. Mortimer C. Dodge, of Cleveland, Ohio. When the customs officials came to look into the matter they weren't able to find anyone in Cleveland who knew her, but then it's no penal offense to give the purser a wrong address, or even a wrong name, for that matter.

While there may have been doubts about Mrs. Dodge's widowhood—or whether she had ever been married, for that matter—there could be none about her beauty. In the language of the classics, she was there. Black hair, brown eyes, a peaches-and-cream complexion that came and went while you watched it, and a figure that would have made her fortune in the Follies. Joe Gregory said afterward that trailing her was one of the easiest things he had ever done.

To get the whole story of Phyllis and her extraordinary cleverness—extraordinary because it was so perfectly obvious—we'll have to cut back a few months before she came on the scene.

For some time the Treasury Department had been well aware that a number of precious stones, principally pearl necklaces, were being smuggled into the country. Agents abroad—the department maintains a regular force in Paris, London, Rotterdam, and other European points, you know—had reported the sale of the jewels and they had turned up a few weeks later in New York[59] or Chicago. But the Customs Service never considers it wise to trace stones back from their owners on this side. There are too many ramifications to any well-planned smuggling scheme, and it is too easy for some one to claim that he had found them in a long-forgotten chest in the attic or some such story as that. The burden of proof rests upon the government in a case of this kind and, except in the last extremity, it always tries to follow the chase from the other end—to nab the smuggler in the act and thus build up a jury-proof case.

Reports of the smuggling cases had been filtered into the department half a dozen times in as many months, and the matter finally got on the chief's nerves to such a degree that he determined to thrash it out if it took every man he had.

In practically every case the procedure was the same—though the only principals known were different each time.

Rotterdam, for example, would report: "Pearl necklace valued at $40,000, sold to-day to man named Silverburg. Have reason to believe it is destined for States"—and then would follow a technical description of the necklace. Anywhere from six weeks to three months later the necklace would turn up in the possession of a jeweler who bore a shady reputation. Sometimes the article wouldn't appear at all, which might have been due to the fact that they weren't brought into this country or that the receivers had altered them beyond recognition. However, the European advices pointed to the latter supposition—which didn't soothe the chief's nerves the least bit.

Finally, along in the middle of the spring of nineteen thirteen, there came a cable from Paris announcing the sale of the famous Yquem emerald—a gorgeous stone that[60] you couldn't help recognizing once you got the description. The purchaser was reported to be an American named Williamson. He paid cash for it, so his references and his antecedents were not investigated at the time.

Sure enough, it wasn't two months later when a report came in from Chicago that a pork-made millionaire had added to his collection a stone which tallied to the description of the Yquem emerald.

"Shall we go after it from this end, Chief?" inquired one of the men on the job in Washington. "We can make the man who bought it tell us where he got it and then sweat the rest of the game out of the go-betweens."

"Yes," snorted the chief, "and be laughed out of court on some trumped-up story framed by a well-paid lawyer. Not a chance! I'm going to land those birds and land 'em with the goods. We can't afford to take any chances with this crowd. They've evidently got money and brains, a combination that you've got to stay awake nights to beat. No—we'll nail 'em in New York just as they're bringing the stones in.

"Send a wire to Gregory to get on the job at once and tell New York to turn loose every man they've got—though they've been working on the case long enough, Heaven knows!"

The next morning when Gregory and his society manner strolled into the customhouse in New York he found the place buzzing. Evidently the instructions from Washington had been such as to make the entire force fear for their jobs unless the smuggling combination was broken up quickly. It didn't take Joe very long to get the details. They weren't many and he immediately discarded the idea of possible collusion between the buyers of the stones abroad. It looked to be a certainty on the face of it, but, once you had discovered that, what good[61] did it do you? It wasn't possible to jail a man just because he bought some jewels in Europe—and, besides, the orders from Washington were very clear that the case was to be handled strictly from this side—at least, the final arrest was to be made on American soil, to avoid extradition complications and the like.

So when Joe got all the facts they simply were that some valuable jewels had been purchased in Europe and had turned up in America, without going through the formality of visiting the customhouse, anywhere from six weeks to three months later.

"Not much to work on," grumbled Gregory, "and I suppose, as usual, that the chief will be as peevish as Hades if we don't nab the guilty party within the week."

"It's more than possible," admitted one of the men who had handled the case.

Gregory studied the dates on which the jewels had been purchased and those on which they had been located in this country for a few moments in silence. Then:

"Get me copies of the passenger lists of every steamer that has docked here in the past year," he directed. "Of course it's possible that these things might have been landed at Boston or Philadelphia, but New York's the most likely port."

When the lists had been secured Gregory stuffed them into his suit case and started for the door.

"Where you going?" inquired McMahon, the man in charge of the New York office.

"Up to the Adirondacks for a few days," Gregory replied.

"What's the idea? Think the stuff is being brought over by airplane and landed inland? Liners don't dock upstate, you know."

"No," said Gregory, "but that's where I'm going to[62] dock until I can digest this stuff," and he tapped his suit case. "Somewhere in this bunch of booklets there's a clue to this case and it's up to me to spot it. Good-by."

Five days later when he sauntered back into the New York office the suit case was surprisingly light. Apparently every one of the passenger lists had vanished. As a matter of fact, they had been boiled down to three names which were carefully inscribed in Joe's notebook.

"Did you pick up any jewels in the Catskills?" was the question that greeted him when he entered.

28

"Wasn't in the Catskills," he growled. "Went up to a camp in the Adirondacks—colder'n blazes. Any more stuff turn up?"

"No, but a wire came from Washington just after you left to watch out for a hundred-thousand-dollar string of pearls sold at a private auction in London last week to an American named—"

"I don't care what *his* name was," Gregory cut in. "What was the date they were sold?"

"The sixteenth."

Gregory glanced at the calendar.

"And to-day is the twenty-second," he mused. "What boats are due in the next three days?"

"The *Cretic* docks this afternoon and the *Tasmania* ought to get in to-morrow. That'll be all until the end of the week."

"Right!" snapped Gregory. "Don't let a soul off the *Cretic* until I've had a look at her passenger list. It's too late to go down the harbor now, but not a person's to get off that ship until I've had a chance to look 'em over. Also cable for a copy of the *Tasmania's* passenger list. Hurry it up!"

Less than ten minutes after he had slipped on board the *Cretic*, however, Gregory gave the signal which permitted[63] the gangplank to be lowered and the passengers to proceed as usual—except for the fact that the luggage of everyone and the persons of not a few were searched with more than the average carefulness. But not a trace of the pearls was found, as Joe had anticipated. A careful inspection of the passenger list and a few moments with the purser had convinced him that none of his three suspects were on board.

Shortly after he returned to the office, the list of the *Tasmania's* passengers began to come over the cables. Less than half a page had been received when Gregory uttered a sudden exclamation, reached for his notebook, compared a name in it with one which appeared on the cabled report, and indulged in the luxury of a deep-throated chuckle.

"Greg's got a nibble somewhere," commented one of the bystanders.

"Yes," admitted his companion, "but landin' the fish is a different matter. Whoever's on the other end of that line is a mighty cagy individual."

But, though he undoubtedly overheard the remark, Gregory didn't seem to be the least bit worried. In fact, his hat was at a more rakish angle than usual and his cane fairly whistled through the air as he wandered up the Avenue half an hour later.

The next the customs force heard of him was when he boarded the quarantine boat the next morning, clambering on the liner a little later with all the skill of a pilot.

"You have a passenger on board by the name of Dodge," he informed the purser, after he had shown his badge. "Mrs. Mortimer C. Dodge. What do you know about her?"

"Not a thing in the world," said the purser, "except that she is a most beautiful and apparently attractive woman. Crossed with us once before—"[64]

"Twice," corrected Gregory. "Came over in January and went right back."

"That's right," said the purser, "so she did. I'd forgotten that. But, beyond that fact, there isn't anything that I can add."

"Seem to be familiar with anyone on board?"

"Not particularly. Mixes with the younger married set and I've noticed her on deck with the Mortons quite frequently. Probably met them on her return trip last winter. They were along then, if I remember rightly."

"Thanks," said the customs operative. "You needn't mention anything about my inquiries, of course," and he mixed with the throng of newspaper reporters who were picking up news in various sections of the big vessel.

When the *Tasmania* docked, Gregory was the first one off.

"Search Mrs. Mortimer C. Dodge to the skin," he directed the matron. "Take down her hair, tap the heels of her shoes, and go through all the usual stunts, but be as gentle as you can about it. Say that we've received word that some uncut diamonds—not pearls, mind you—are concealed on the *Tasmania* and that orders have been given to go over everybody thoroughly. Pass the word along the line to give out the same information, so she won't be suspicious. I don't think you'll find anything, but you never can tell."

At that, Joe was right. The matron didn't locate a blessed thing out of the way. Mrs. Dodge had brought in a few dutiable trinkets, but they were all down on her declaration, and within the hour she was headed uptown in a taxi, accompanied by a maid who had met her as she stepped out of the customs office.

Not far behind them trailed another taxi, top up and Gregory's eyes glued to the window behind the chauffeur.[65]

The first machine finally drew up at the Astor, and Mrs. Dodge and the maid went in, followed by a pile of luggage which had been searched until it was a moral certainty that not a needle would have been concealed in it.

Gregory waited until they were out of sight and then followed.

In answer to his inquiries at the desk he learned that Mrs. Dodge had stopped at the hotel several times before and the house detective assured him that there was nothing suspicious about her conduct.

"How about the maid?" inquired Gregory.

"Don't know a thing about her, either, except that she is the same one she had before. Pretty little thing, too—though not as good-looking as her mistress."

For the next three days Joe hung around the hotel or followed the lady from the *Tasmania* wherever she went. Something in the back of his head—call it intuition or a hunch or whatever you please, but it's the feeling that a good operative gets when he's on the right trail—told him that he was "warm," as the kids say. Appearances seemed to deny that fact. Mrs. Dodge went only to the most natural places—a few visits to the stores, a couple to fashionable modistes and milliners, and some drives through the Park, always accompanied by her maid and always in the most sedate and open manner.

But on the evening of the third day the house detective tipped Joe off that his prey was leaving in the morning.

"Guess she's going back to Europe," reported the house man. "Gave orders to have a taxi ready at nine and her trunks taken down to the docks before them. Better get busy if you want to land her."

"I'm not ready for that just yet," Gregory admitted with a scowl.[66]

When Mrs. Dodge's taxi drove off the following morning Joe wasn't far away, and, acting on orders which he had delivered over the phone, no less than half a dozen operatives watched the lady and the maid very closely when they reached the dock.

Not a thing came of it, however. Both of them went to the stateroom which had been reserved and the maid remained to help with the unpacking until the "All-ashore-that-'re-going-ashore" was bellowed through the boat. Then she left and stood on the pier until the ship had cleared the dock.

"It beats me," muttered Gregory. "But I'm willing to gamble my job that I'm right." And that night he wired to Washington to keep a close lookout for the London pearls, adding that he felt certain they would turn up before long.

"In that case," muttered the chief at the other end of the wire, "why in Heaven's name didn't he get them when they came in?"

Sure enough, not a fortnight had passed before St. Louis reported that a string of pearls, perfectly matched, answering to the description of the missing jewels, had been offered for sale there through private channels.

The first reaction was a telegram to Gregory that fairly burned the wires, short but to the point. "Either the man who smuggled that necklace or your job in ten days," it read.

And Gregory replied, "Give me three weeks and you'll have one or the other."

Meanwhile he had been far from inactive. Still playing his hunch that Phyllis Dodge had something to do with the smuggling game, he had put in time cultivating the only person on this side that appeared to know her—the maid.[67]

It was far from a thankless task, for Alyce—she spelled it with a "y"—was pretty and knew it. Furthermore, she appeared to be entirely out of her element in a cheap room on Twenty-fourth Street. Most of the time she spent in wandering up the Avenue, and it was there that Gregory made her acquaintance—through the expedient of bumping her bag out of her hands and restoring it with one of his courtly bows. The next minute he was strolling alongside, remarking on the beauty of the weather.

But, although he soon got to know Alyce well enough to take her to the theater and to the cabarets, it didn't seem to get him anywhere. She was perfectly frank about her position. Said she was a hair dresser by trade and that she acted as lady's maid to a Mrs. Dodge, who spent the better part of her time abroad.

"In fact," she said, "Mrs. Dodge is only here three or four days every two months or so."

"And she pays you for your time in between?"

"Oh yes," Alyce replied; "she's more than generous."

"I should say she was," Gregory thought to himself—but he considered it best to change the subject.

During the days that followed, Joe exerted every ounce of his personality in order to make the best possible impression. Posing as a man who had made money in the West, he took Alyce everywhere and treated her royally. Finally, when he considered the time ripe, he injected a little love into the equation and hinted that he thought it was about time to settle down and that he appeared to have found the proper person to settle with.

But there, for the first time, Alyce balked. She didn't refuse him, but she stated in so many words that she had a place that suited her for the time being, and that, until the fall, at least, she preferred to keep on with it.[68]

"That suits me all right," declared Gregory. "Take your time about it. Meanwhile we'll continue to be good friends and trail around together, eh?"

"Certainly," said Alyce, "er—that is—until Tuesday."

"Tuesday?" inquired Joe. "What's coming off Tuesday?"

"Mrs. Dodge will arrive on the *Atlantic*," was the reply, "and I'll have to be with her for three days at least."

"Three days—" commenced Gregory, and halted himself. It wasn't wise to show too much interest. But that night he called the chief on long distance and inquired if there had been any recent reports of suspicious jewel sales abroad. "Yes," came the voice from Washington, "pearls again. Loose ones, this time. And your three weeks' grace is up at noon Saturday." The click that followed as the receiver hung up was finality itself.

The same procedure, altered in a few minor details, was followed when Mrs. Dodge landed. Again she was searched to the skin; again her luggage was gone over with microscopic care, and again nothing was found.

This time she stayed at the Knickerbocker, but Alyce was with her as usual.

Deprived of his usual company and left to his own devices, Gregory took a long walk up the Drive and tried to thrash out the problem.

"Comes over on a different boat almost every trip," he thought, "so that eliminates collusion with any of the crew. Doesn't stay at the same hotel two times running, so there's nothing there. Has the same maid and always returns—"

Then it was that motorists on Riverside Drive were treated to the sight of a young and extremely prepossessing man, dressed in the height of fashion, throwing[69] his hat in the air and uttering a yell that could be heard for blocks. After which he disappeared hurriedly in the direction of the nearest drug store.

A hasty search through the phone book gave him the number he wanted—the offices of the Black Star line.

"Is Mr. MacPherson, the purser of the *Atlantic*, there?" he inquired. Then: "Hello! Mr. MacPherson? This is Gregory, Customs Division. You remember me, don't you? Worked on the Maitland diamond case with you two years ago.... Wonder if you could tell me something I want to know—is Mrs. Mortimer C. Dodge booked to go back with you to-morrow?... She is? What's the number of her stateroom? And—er—what was the number of the room she had coming over?... I thank you."

If the motorists whom Gregory had startled on the Drive had seen him emerge from the phone booth they would have marveled at the look of keen satisfaction and relief that was spread over his face. The cat that swallowed the canary was tired of life, compared with Joe at that moment.

Next morning the Customs operatives were rather surprised to see Gregory stroll down to the *Atlantic* dock about ten o'clock.

"Thought you were somewhere uptown on the chief's pet case," said one of them.

"So I was," answered Joe. "But that's practically cleaned up."

With that he went aboard, and no one saw him until just before the "All-ashore" call. Then he took up his place beside the gangplank, with three other men placed near by in case of accident.

"Follow my lead," he directed. "I'll speak to the girl. Two of you stick here to make certain that she[70] doesn't get away, and you, Bill, beat it on board then and tell the captain that the boat's not to clear until we give the word. We won't delay him more than ten minutes at the outside."

When Alyce came down the gangplank a few minutes later, in the midst of people who had been saying good-by to friends and relatives, she spotted Joe waiting for her, and started to move hurriedly away. Gregory caught up with her before she had gone a dozen feet.

"Good morning, Alyce," he said. "Thought I'd come down to meet you. What've you got in the bag there?" indicating her maid's handbag.

"Not—not a thing," said the girl, flushing. Just then the matron joined the party, as previously arranged, and Joe's tone took on its official hardness.

"Hurry up and search her! We don't want to keep the boat any longer than we have to."

Less than a minute later the matron thrust her head out of the door long enough to report: "We found 'em—the pearls. She had 'em in the front of her dress."

Gregory was up the gangplank in a single bound. A moment later he was knocking at the door of Mrs. Dodge's stateroom. The instant the knob turned he was inside, informing Phyllis that she was under arrest on a charge of bringing jewels into the United States without the formality of paying duty. Of course, the lady protested—but the *Atlantic* sailed, less than ten minutes behind schedule time, without her.

Promptly at twelve the phone on the desk of the chief of the Customs Division in Washington buzzed noisily.

"Gregory speaking," came through the receiver. "My time's up—and I've got the party you want. Claims to be from Cleveland and sails under the name of Mrs.[71] Mortimer C. Dodge—first name Phyllis. She's confessed and promises to turn state's evidence if we'll go light with her."

"That," added Quinn, "was the finish of Mrs. Dodge, so far as the government was concerned. In order to land the whole crew—the people who were handling the stuff on this side as well as the ones who were mixed up in the scheme abroad—they let her go scot-free, with the proviso that she's to be rushed to Atlanta if she ever pokes her nose into the United States again. The last I heard of her she was in Monaco, tangled up in a blackmail case there.

"Gregory told me all about it sometime later. Said that the first hunch had come to him when he studied the passengers' lists in the wilds of the Adirondacks. Went there to be alone and concentrate. He found that of all the people listed, only three—two men and a Mrs. Dodge—had made the trip frequently in the past six months. The frequency of Mrs. Dodge's travel evidently made it impracticable for her to use different aliases. Some one would be sure to spot her.

"But it wasn't until that night on Riverside Drive that the significance of the data struck him. Each time she took the same boat on which she had come over! Did she have the same stateroom? The phone call to MacPherson established the fact that she did—this time at least. The rest was almost as obvious as the original plan. The jewels were brought aboard, passed on to Phyllis, and she tucked them away somewhere in her stateroom. Her bags and her person could, of course, be searched with perfect safety. Then, what was more natural than that her maid should accompany her on board when she was leaving? Nobody ever pays any[72] attention to people who board the boat at *this* end, so Alyce was able to walk off with the stuff under the very eyes of the customs authorities—and they found later that she had the nerve to place it in the hands of the government for the next twenty-four hours. She sent it by registered mail to Pittsburgh and it was passed along through an underground "fence" channel until a prospective purchaser appeared.

"Perfectly obvious and perfectly simple—that's why the plan succeeded until Gregory began to make love to Alyce and got the idea that Mrs. Dodge was going right back to Europe hammered into his head. It had occurred to him before, but he hadn't placed much value on it...."

"O-o-o-o!" yawned Quinn. "I'm getting dry. Trot out some grape juice and put on that Kreisler record—'Drigo's Serenade.' I love to hear it. Makes me think of the time when they landed that scoundrel Weimar."

[73]

VI
A MATTER OF RECORD

"What was that you mentioned last week—something about the record of Kreisler's 'Drigo's Serenade' reminding you of the capture of some one?" I asked Bill Quinn one summer evening as he painfully hoisted his game leg upon the porch railing.

"Sure it does," replied Quinn. "Never fails. Put it on again so I can get the necessary atmosphere, as you writers call it, and possibly I'll spill the yarn—provided you guarantee to keep the ginger ale flowing freely. That and olive oil are about the only throat lubricants left us."

So I slipped on the record, rustled a couple of bottles from the ice box, and settled back comfortably, for when Quinn once started on one of his reminiscences of government detective work he didn't like to be interrupted.

"That's the piece, all right," Bill remarked, as the strains of the violin drifted off into the night. "Funny how a few notes of music like that could nail a criminal while at the same time it was saving the lives of nobody knows how many other people—"

Remember Paul Weimar [continued Quinn, picking up the thread of his story]. He was the most dangerous of the entire gang that helped von Bernstorff, von Papen, and the rest of that crew plot against the United States at a time when we were supposed to be entirely neutral.[74]

An Austrian by birth, Weimar was as thoroughly a Hun at heart as anyone who ever served the Hohenzollerns and, in spite of his size, he was as slippery as they make 'em. Back in the past somewhere he had been a detective in the service of the Atlas Line, but for some years before the war was superintendent of the police attached to the Hamburg-American boats. That, of course, gave him the inside track in every bit of deviltry he wanted to be mixed up in, for he had made it his business to cultivate the acquaintance of wharf rats, dive keepers, and all the rest of the scum of the Seven Seas that haunts the docks.

Standing well over six feet, Weimar had a pair of fists that came in mighty handy in a scuffle, and a tongue that could curl itself around all the blasphemies of a dozen languages. There wasn't a water front where they didn't hate him—neither was there a water front where they didn't fear him.

Of course, when the war broke in August, 1914, the Hamburg-American line didn't have any further official use for Weimar. Their ships were tied up in neutral or home ports and Herr Paul was out of a job—for at least ten minutes. But he was entirely too valuable a man for the German organization to overlook for longer than that, and von Papen, in Washington, immediately added him to his organization—with blanket instructions to go the limit on any dirty work he cared to undertake. Later, he worked for von Bernstorff; Doctor Dumba, the Austrian ambassador; and Doctor von Nuber, the Austrian consul in New York—but von Papen had first claim upon his services and did not hesitate to press them, as proven by certain entries in the checkbook of the military attaché during the spring and summer of 1915.

Of course, it didn't take the Secret Service and the men[75] from the Department of Justice very long to get on to the fact that Weimar was altogether too close to the German embassy for the safety and comfort of the United States government. But what were they to do about it? We weren't at war then and you couldn't arrest a man merely because he happened to know von Papen and the rest of his precious companions. You had to have something on him—something that would stand up in court—and Paul Weimar was too almighty clever to let that happen.

When you remember that it took precisely one year to land this Austrian—one year of constant watching and unceasing espionage—you will see how well he conducted himself.

And the government's sleuths weren't the only ones who were after him, either.

Captain Kenney, of the New York Police Force, lent mighty efficient aid and actually invented a new system of trailing in order to find out just what he was up to.

In the old days, you told a man to go out and follow a suspect and that was all there was to it. The "shadow" would trail along half a block or so in the rear, keeping his man always in view, and bring home a full account of what he had done all day. But you couldn't do that with Weimar—he was too foxy. From what some of the boys have told me, I think he took a positive delight in throwing them off the scent, whether he had anything up his sleeve or not.

One day, for example, you could have seen his big bulk swinging nonchalantly up Broadway, as if he didn't have a care in the world. A hundred feet or more behind him was Bob Dugan, one of Kenney's men. When Weimar disappeared into the Subway station at Times Square, Dugan was right behind him, and when the Austrian boarded the local for Grand Central Station, Dugan was[76] on the same train—on the same car, in fact. But when they reached the station, things began to happen. Weimar left the local and commenced to stroll up and down the platform, waiting until a local train and an express arrived at the same time. That was his opportunity. He made a step or two forward, as if to board the express, and Dugan—not wishing to make himself too conspicuous—slipped on board just as the doors were closing, only to see Weimar push back and jam his way on the local!

Variations of that stunt occurred time after time. Even the detailing of two men to follow him failed in its purpose, for the Austrian would enter a big office building, leap into an express elevator just as it was about to ascend, slip the operator a dollar to stop at one of the lower floors, and be lost for the day or until some one picked him up by accident.

So Cap Kenney called in four of his best men and told them that it was essential that Weimar be watched.

"Two of you," he directed, "stick with him all the time. Suppose you locate him the first thing in the morning at his house on Twenty-fourth Street, for example. You, Cottrell, station yourself two blocks up the street. Gary, you go the same distance down. Then, no matter which way he starts he'll have one of you in front of him and one behind. The man in front will have to use his wits to guess which way he intends to go and to beat him to it. If he boards a car, the man in front can pick him up with the certainty that the other will cover the trail in the rear. In that way you ought to be able to find out where he is going and, possibly, what he is doing there."

The scheme, thanks to the quick thinking of the men assigned to the job, worked splendidly for months—at least it worked in so far as keeping a watch on Weimar was[77] concerned. But that was all. In the summer of 1915 the government knew precisely where Weimar had been for the past six months, with whom he had talked, and so on—but the kernel of the nut was missing. There wasn't the least clue to what he had talked about and what deviltry he had planned!

Without that information, all the dope the government had was about as useful as a movie to a blind man.

Washington was so certain that Weimar had the key to a number of very important developments—among them the first attempt to blow up the Welland Canal—that the chief of the Secret Service made a special trip to New York to talk to Kenney.

"Isn't it possible," he suggested, "to plant your men close enough to Weimar to find out, for example, what he talks about over the phone?"

Kenney smiled, grimly.

"Chief," he said, "that's been done. We've tapped every phone that Weimar's likely to use in the neighborhood of his house and every time he talks from a public station one of our men cuts in from near-by—by an arrangement with Central—and gets every word. But that bird is too wary to be caught with chaff of that kind. He's evidently worked out a verbal code of some kind that changes every day. He tells the man at the other end, for example, to be at the drug store on the corner of Seventy-third and Broadway at three o'clock to-morrow afternoon and wait for a phone call in the name of Williams. Our man is always at the place at the appointed hour, but no call ever arrives. 'Seventy-third and Broadway' very evidently means some other address, but it's useless to try and guess which one. You'd have to have a man at every pay station in town to follow that lead."[78]

"How about overhearing his directions to the men he meets in the open?"

"Not a chance in the world. His rendezvous are always public places—the Pennsylvania or Grand Central Station, a movie theater, a hotel lobby, or the like. There he can put his back against the wall and make sure that no one is listening in. He's on to all the tricks of the trade and it will take a mighty clever man—or a bunch of them—to nail him."

"H-m-m!" mused the chief. "Well, at that, I believe I've got the man."

"Anyone I know?"

"Yes, I think you do—Morton Maxwell. Remember him? Worked on the Castleman diamond case here a couple of years ago for the customs people and was also responsible for uncovering the men behind the sugar-tax fraud. He isn't in the Service, but he's working for the Department of Justice, and I'm certain they'll turn him loose on this if I ask them to. Maxwell can get to the bottom of Weimar's business, if anyone can. Let me talk to Washington—"

And within an hour after the chief had hung up the receiver Morton Maxwell, better known as "Mort," was headed toward New York with instructions to report at Secret Service headquarters in that city.

Once there, the chief and Kenney went over the whole affair with him. Cottrell and Gary and the other men who had been engaged in shadowing the elusive Weimar were called in to tell their part of the story, and every card was laid upon the table.

When the conference concluded, sometime after midnight, the chief turned to Maxwell and inquired:

"Well, what's your idea about it?"

For a full minute Mort smoked on in silence and gazed[79] off into space. Men who had just met him were apt to think this a pose, a play to the grand stand—but those who knew him best realized that Maxwell's alert mind was working fastest in such moments and that he much preferred not to make any decision until he had turned things over in his head.

"There's just one point which doesn't appear to have been covered," he replied. Then, as Kenney started to cut in, "No, Chief, I said *appeared* not to have been covered. Very possibly you have all the information on it and forgot to hand it out. Who does this Weimar live with?"

"He lives by himself in a house on Twenty-fourth Street, near Seventh Avenue—boards there, but has the entire second floor. So far as we've been able to find out he has never been married. No trace of any wife on this side, anyhow. Never travels with women—probably afraid they'd talk too much."

"Has he any relatives?"

"None that I know of—"

"Wait a minute," Cottrell interrupted. "I dug back into Weimar's record before the war ended his official connection with the steamship company, and one of the points I picked up was that he had a cousin—a man named George Buch—formerly employed on one of the boats.

"Where is Buch now?" asked Maxwell.

"We haven't been able to locate him," admitted the police detective. "Not that we've tried very hard, because the trail didn't lead in his direction. I don't even know that he is in this country, but it's likely that he is because he was on one of the boats that was interned here when the war broke."

Again it was a full minute before Maxwell spoke.[80]

"Buch," he said, finally, "appears to be the only link between Weimar and the outer world. It's barely possible that he knows something, and, as we can't afford to overlook any clue, suppose we start work along that line. I'll dig into it myself the first thing in the morning, and I certainly would appreciate any assistance that your men could give me, Chief. Tell them to make discreet inquiries about Buch, his appearance, habits, etc., and to try and find out whether he is on this side. Now I'm going to turn in, for something seems to tell me that the busy season has arrived."

At that Maxwell wasn't far wrong. The weeks that followed were well filled with work, but it was entirely unproductive of results. Weimar was shadowed day and night, his telephones tapped and his mail examined. But, save for the fact that his connection with the German embassy became increasingly apparent, no further evidence was forthcoming.

The search for Buch was evidently futile, for that personage appeared to have disappeared from the face of the earth. All that Maxwell and the other men who worked on the matter could discover was that Buch—a young Austrian whose description they secured—had formerly been an intimate of Weimar. The latter had obtained his appointment to a minor office in the Hamburg-American line and Buch was commonly supposed to be a stool pigeon for the master plotter.

But right there the trail stopped.

No one appeared to know whether the Austrian was in New York, or the United States, for that matter, though one informant did admit that it was quite probable.

"Buch and the big fellow had a row the last time over," was the information Maxwell secured at the cost of a few drinks. "Something about some money that Weimar[81] is supposed to have owed him—fifteen dollars or some such amount. I didn't hear about it until afterward, but it appears to have been a pretty lively scrap while it lasted. Of course, Buch didn't have a chance against the big fellow—he could handle a bull. But the young Austrian threatened to tip his hand—said he knew a lot of stuff that would be worth a good deal more money than was coming to him, and all that sort of thing. But the ship docked the next day and I haven't seen or heard of him since."

The idea of foul play at once leaped into Maxwell's mind, but investigation of police records failed to disclose the discovery of anybody answering to the description of George Buch and, as Captain Kenney pointed out, it is a decidedly difficult matter to dispose of a corpse in such a way as not to arouse at least the suspicions of the police.

As a last resort, about the middle of September, Maxwell had a reward posted on the bulletin board of every police station in New York and the surrounding country for the "apprehension of George Buch, Austrian, age about twenty-four. Height, five feet eight inches. Hair, blond. Complexion, fair. Eyes, blue. Sandy mustache."

As Captain Kenney pointed out, though, the description would apply to several thousand men of German parentage in the city, and to a good many more who didn't have a drop of Teutonic blood in their veins.

"True enough," Maxwell was forced to admit, "but we can't afford to overlook a bet—even if it is a thousand-to-one shot."

As luck would have it, the thousand-to-one shot won!

On September 25, 1917, Detective Gary returned to headquarters, distinctly crestfallen. Weimar had given him the slip.

In company with another man, whom the detective did[82] not know, the Austrian had been walking up Sixth Avenue that afternoon when a machine swung in from Thirty-sixth Street and the Austrian had leaped aboard without waiting for it to come to a full stop.

"Of course, there wasn't a taxi in sight," said Gary, ruefully, "and before I could convince the nearest chauffeur that my badge wasn't phony they'd gone!"

"That's the first time in months," Gary replied. "He knows that he's followed, all right, and he's cagy enough to keep in the open and pretend to be aboveboard."

"Right," commented the Department of Justice operative, "and this move would appear to indicate that something was doing. Better phone all your stations to watch out for him, Cap."

But nothing more was seen or heard of Herr Weimar for five days.

Meanwhile events moved rapidly for Maxwell.

On September 26th, the day after the Austrian disappeared, one of the policemen whose beat lay along Fourteenth Street, near Third Avenue, asked to see the government detective.

"My name's Riley," announced the copper, with a brogue as broad as the toes of his shoes. "Does this Austrian, this here Buch feller ye're lookin' for, like music? Is he nuts about it?"

"Music?" echoed Maxwell. "I'm sure I don't know.... But wait a minute! Yes, that's what that chap who used to know him on the boat told me. Saying he was forever playing a fiddle when he was off duty and that Weimar threw it overboard one day in a fit of rage. Why? What's the connection?"

"Nothin' in particular, save that a little girl I'm rather sweet on wurruks in a music store on Fourteenth Street an' she an' I was talkin' things over last night an' I happened[83] to mintion th' reward offered for this Buch feller. 'Why!' says she, 'that sounds just like the Dutchy that used to come into th' shop a whole lot a year or so ago. He was crazy about music an' kep' himself pretty nigh broke a-buyin' those expensive new records. Got me to save him every violin one that came out.'"

"Um, yes," muttered Maxwell, "but has the young lady seen anything of this chap lately?"

"That she has not," Riley replied, "an' right there's th' big idear. Once a week, regular, another Dutchman comes in an' buys a record, an' he told Katy—that's me gurrul's name—last winter that th' selections were for a man that used to be a stiddy customer of hers but who was now laid up in bed."

"In bed for over a year!" exclaimed Maxwell, his face lighting up. "Held prisoner somewhere in the neighborhood of that shop on Fourteenth Street, because the big Austrian hasn't the nerve to make away with him and yet fears that he knows too much! Look here, Riley—suppose you and Miss Katy take a few nights off—I'll substitute for her and make it all right with the man who owns the store. Then I can get a line on this buyer of records for sick men."

"Wouldn't it be better, sir, if we hung around outside th' store an' let Katy give us the high sign when he come in? Then we could both trail him back to where he lives."

"You're right, Riley, it would! Where'll I meet you to-night?"

"At the corner of Fourteenth Street and Thoid Av'nue, at eight o'clock. Katy says th' man never gets there before nine."

"I'll be there," said Maxwell—and he was.

But nothing out of the ordinary rewarded their vigil the[84] first night, nor the second. On the third night, however, just after the clock in the Metropolitan Tower had boomed nine times, a rather nondescript individual sauntered into the music store, and Riley's quick eyes saw the girl behind the counter put her left hand to her chest. Then she coughed.

"That's th' signal, sir," warned the policeman in a whisper. "An' that's the guy we're after."

Had the man turned around as he made his way toward a dark and forbidding house on Thirteenth Street, not far from Fourth Avenue, he might have caught sight of two shadows skulking along not fifty feet behind him. But, at that, he would have to have been pretty quick—for Maxwell was taking no chances on losing his prey and he had cautioned the policeman not to make a sound.

When their quarry ascended the steps of No. 247 Riley started to move after him, but the Department of Justice operative halted him.

"There's no hurry," stated Maxwell. "He doesn't suspect we're here, and, besides, it doesn't make any difference if he does lock the door—I've got a skeleton key handy that's guaranteed to open anything."

Riley grunted, but stayed where he was until Maxwell gave the signal to advance.

Once inside the door, which responded to a single turn to the key, the policeman and the government agent halted in the pitch-black darkness and listened. Then from an upper floor came the sound for which Maxwell had been waiting—the first golden notes of a violin played by a master hand. The distance and the closed doorway which intervened killed all the harsh mechanical tone of the phonograph and only the wonderful melody of "Drigo's Serenade" came down to them.

On tiptoe, though they knew their movements would[85] be masked by the sounds of the music, Riley and Maxwell crept up to the third floor and halted outside the door from which the sounds came.

"Wait until the record is over," directed Maxwell, "and then break down that door. Have your gun handy and don't hesitate to shoot anyone who tries to injure Buch. I'm certain he's held prisoner here and it may be that the men who are guarding him have instructions not to let him escape at any cost. Ready? Let's go!"

The final note of the Kreisler record had not died away before Riley's shoulder hit the flimsy door and the two detectives were in the room.

Maxwell barely had time to catch a glimpse of a pale, wan figure on the bed and to sense the fact that there were two other men in the room, when there was a shout from Riley and a spurt of flame from his revolver. With a cry, the man nearest the bed dropped his arm and a pistol clattered to the floor—the barrel still singing from the impact of the policeman's bullet. The second man, realizing that time was precious, leaped straight toward Maxwell, his fingers reaching for the agent's throat. With a half laugh Mort clubbed his automatic and brought the butt down with sickening force on his assailant's head. Then he swung around and covered the man whom Riley had disarmed.

"Don't worry about him, sir," said the policeman. "His arm'll be numb half an hour from now. What do you want to do with th' lad in th' bed?"

"Get him out of here as quickly as we can. We won't bother with these swine. They have the law on their side, anyway, because we broke in here without a warrant. I only want Buch."

When he had propped the young Austrian up in a comfortable chair in the Federal Building and had given him[86] a glass of brandy to strengthen his nerves—the Lord only knows that they'll have to do in the future—Maxwell got the whole story and more than he had dared hoped for. Buch, following his quarrel with Weimar, had been held prisoner in the house on Thirteenth Street for over a year because, as Maxwell had figured, the Austrian didn't have the nerve to kill him and didn't dare let him loose. Barely enough food was allowed to keep him alive, and the only weakness that his cousin had shown was in permitting the purchase of one phonograph record a week in order to cheer him up a little.

"Naturally," said Buch, "I chose the Kreisler records, because he's an Austrian and a marvelous violinist."

"Did Weimar ever come to see you?" inquired Maxwell.

"He came in every now and then to taunt me and to say that he was going to have me thrown in the river some day soon. That didn't frighten me, but there were other things that did. He came in last week, for example, and boasted that he was going to blow up a big canal and I was afraid he might be caught or killed. That would have meant no more money for the men who were guarding me and I was too weak to walk even to the window to call for help...."

"A big canal!" Maxwell repeated. "He couldn't mean the Panama! No, that's impossible. I have it! The Welland Canal!" And in an instant he was calling the Niagara police on the long-distance phone, giving a detailed description of Weimar and his companions.

"As it turned out," concluded Quinn, reaching for his empty glass, "Weimar had already been looking over the ground. He was arrested, however, before the dynamite could be planted, and, thanks to Buch's evidence, indicted for violation of Section Thirteen of the Penal Code.[87]

"Thus did a phonograph record and thirty pieces of silver—the thirty half-dollars that Weimar owed Buch—lead directly to the arrest of one of the most dangerous spies in the German service. Let's have Mr. Drigo's Serenade once more and pledge Mort Maxwell's health in ginger ale—unless you have a still concealed around the house. And if you have I will be in duty bound to tell Jimmy Reynolds about it—he's the lad that holds the record for persistency and cleverness in discovering moonshiners."

[88]

VII
THE SECRET STILL

"July 1, 1919," said Bill Quinn, as he appropriately reached for a bottle containing a very soft drink, "by no means marked the beginning of the government's troubles in connection with the illicit manufacture of liquor.

"Of course, there's been a whole lot in the papers since the Thirst of July about people having private stills in their cellars, making drinks with a kick out of grape juice and a piece of yeast, and all that sort of thing. One concern in Pittsburgh, I understand, has also noted a tremendous and absolutely abnormal increase in the demand for its hot-water heating plants—the copper coils of which make an ideal substitute for a still—but I doubt very much if there's going to be a real movement in the direction of the private manufacture of alcoholic beverages. The Internal Revenue Department is too infernally watchful and its agents too efficient for much of that to get by.

"When you get right down to it, there's no section in the country where the art of making 'licker' flourishes to such an extent as it does in eastern Tennessee and western North Carolina. Moonshine there is not only a recognized article of trade, but its manufacture is looked upon as an inalienable right. It's tough sledding for any revenue officer who isn't mighty quick on the trigger, and[89] even then—as Jimmy Reynolds discovered a few years back—they're likely to get him unless he mixes brains with his shooting ability."

Reynolds [continued Quinn, easing his injured leg into a more comfortable position] was as valuable a man as any whose name ever appeared in the Government Blue Book. He's left the bureau now and settled down to a life of comparative ease as assistant district attorney of some middle Western city. I've forgotten which one, but there was a good reason for his not caring to remain in the East. The climate west of the Mississippi is far more healthy for Jimmy these days.

At the time of the Stiles case Jim was about twenty-nine, straight as an arrow, and with a bulldog tenacity that just wouldn't permit of his letting go of a problem until the solution was filed in the official pigeonholes which answer to the names of archives. It was this trait which led Chambers, then Commissioner of Internal Revenue, to send for him, after receipt of a message that two of his best men—Douglas and Wood, I think their names were—had been brought back to Maymead, Tennessee, with bullet holes neatly drilled through their hearts.

"Jim," said the Commissioner, "this case has gone just far enough. It's one thing for the mountaineers of Tennessee to make moonshine whisky and defy the laws of the United States. But when they deliberately murder two of my best men and pin a rudely scribbled note to 'Bewair of this country' on the front of their shirts, that's going entirely too far. I'm going to clean out that nest of illicit stills if it takes the rest of my natural life and every man in the bureau!

"More than that, I'll demand help from the War Department, if necessary! By Gad! I'll teach 'em!" and[90] the inkwell on the Commissioner's desk leaped into the air as Chambers's fist registered determination.

Reynolds reached for a fresh cigar from the supply that always reposed in the upper drawer of the Commissioner's desk and waited until it was well lighted before he replied.

"All well and good, Chief," he commented, "but how would the army help you any? You could turn fifty thousand men in uniform loose in those mountains, and the odds are they wouldn't locate the bunch you're after. Fire isn't the weapon to fight those mountaineers with. They're too wise. What you need is brains."

"Possibly you can supply that deficiency," retorted the Commissioner, a little nettled.

"Oh, I didn't mean that you, personally, needed the brains," laughed Reynolds. "The pronoun was used figuratively and collectively. At that, I would like to have a whirl at the case if you've nothing better for me to do—"

"There isn't anything better for anyone to do at the present time," Chambers interrupted. "That's why I sent for you. We know that whisky is being privately distilled in large quantities somewhere in the mountains not far from Maymead. Right there our information ends. Our men have tried all sorts of dodges to land the crowd behind the stills, but the only thing they've been able to learn is that a man named Stiles is one of the ruling spirits. His cabin is well up in the mountains and it was while they were prospecting round that part of the country that Douglas and Wood were shot. Now what's your idea of handling the case?"

"The first thing that I want, Chief, is to be allowed to work on this absolutely alone, and that not a soul, in bureau or out of it is to know what I'm doing."[91]

"Easy enough to arrange that," assented the Commissioner, "but—"

"There isn't any 'but,'" Reynolds cut in. "You've tried putting a number of men to work on this and they've failed. Now try letting one handle it. For the past two years I've had a plan in the back of my head that I've been waiting the right opportunity to use. So far as I can see it's foolproof and I'm willing to take all the responsibility in connection with it."

"Care to outline it?" inquired Chambers.

"Not right at the moment," was Reynolds's reply, "because it would seem too wild and scatterbrained. I don't mind telling you, though, that for the next six weeks my address will be in care of the warden of the penitentiary of Morgantown, West Virginia, if you wish to reach me."

"Morgantown?" echoed the Commissioner. "What in Heaven's name are you going to do there?"

"Lay the stage setting for the first act," smiled Jimmy. "Likewise collect what authors refer to as local color—material that's essential to what I trust will be the happy ending of this drama—happy, at least, from the government's point of view. But, while you know that I'm at Morgantown, I don't want anyone else to know it and I'd much prefer that you didn't communicate with me there unless it's absolutely necessary."

"All right, I won't. You're handling the case from now on."

"Alone?"

"Entirely—if you wish it."

"Yes, Chief, I do wish it. I can promise you one of two things within the next three months: either you'll have all the evidence you want about the secret still and the men behind it or—well, you know where to ship my remains!"[92]

With that and a quick handshake he was gone.

During the weeks that followed, people repeatedly asked the Commissioner:

"What's become of Jimmy Reynolds? Haven't seen him round here for a month of Sundays."

But the Commissioner would assume an air of blank ignorance, mutter something about, "He's out of town somewhere," and rapidly change the subject.

About six weeks or so later a buzzard which was flapping its lazy way across the mountains which divide Tennessee from North Carolina saw, far below, a strange sight. A man, haggard and forlorn, his face covered with a half-inch of stubble, his cheeks sunken, his clothing torn by brambles and bleached by the sun and rain until it was almost impossible to tell its original texture, stumbled along with his eyes fixed always on the crest of a hill some distance off. It was as if he were making a last desperate effort to reach his goal before the sun went down.

Had the buzzard been so minded, his keen eyes might have noted the fact that the man's clothes were marked by horizontal stripes, while his head was covered with hair the same length all over, as if he had been shaved recently and the unkempt thatch had sprouted during the last ten days.

Painfully but persistently the man in convict's clothes pressed forward. When the sun was a little more than halfway across the heavens he glimpsed a cabin tucked away on the side of a mountain spur not far away. At the sight he pressed forward with renewed vigor, but distances are deceptive in that part of the country and it was not until nearly dark that he managed to reach his destination.

In fact, the Stiles family was just sitting down to what passes for supper in that part of the world—fat bacon[93] and corn bread, mostly—when there was the sound of a man's footstep some fifty feet away.

Instantly the houn' dog rose from his accustomed place under the table and crouched, ready to repel invaders. Old Man Stiles—his wife called him Joe, but to the entire countryside he was just "Old Man Stiles"—reached for his rifle with a muttered imprecation about "Rev'nue officers who never let a body be."

But the mountaineer had hardly risen from his seat when there was a sound as of a heavy body falling against the door—and then silence.

Stiles looked inquiringly at his wife and then at Ruth, their adopted daughter. None of them spoke for an appreciable time, but the hound continued to whine and finally backed off into a corner.

"Guess I'll have to see what et is," drawled the master of the cabin, holding his rifle ready for action.

Slowly he moved toward the door and cautiously, very cautiously, he lifted the bolt that secured it. Even if it were a revenue officer, he argued to himself, his conscience was clear and his premises could stand the formality of a search because, save for a certain spot known to himself alone, there was nothing that could be considered incriminating.

As the door swung back the body of a man fell into the room—a man whose clothing was tattered and whose features were concealed under a week's growth of stubbly beard. Right into the cabin he fell, for the door had supported his body, and, once that support was removed, he lay as one dead.

In fact, it wasn't until at least five minutes had elapsed that Stiles came to the conclusion that the intruder was really alive, after all. During that time he had worked over him in the rough mountain fashion, punching and[94] pulling and manhandling him in an effort to secure some sign of life. Finally the newcomer's eyes opened and he made an effort to sit up.

"Wait a minute, stranger," directed Stiles, motioning his wife toward a closet in the corner of the room. Mrs. Stiles—or 'Ma,' as she was known in that part of the country—understood the movement. Without a word she opened the cupboard and took down a flask filled with a clear golden-yellow liquid. Some of this she poured into a cracked cup on the table and handed it to her husband.

"Here," directed the mountaineer, "throw yo' haid back an' drink this. Et's good fur what ails yer."

The moment after he had followed instructions the stranger gulped, gurgled, and gasped as the moonshine whisky burnt its way down his throat. The man-sized drink, taken on a totally empty stomach, almost nauseated him. Then it put new life in his veins and he tried to struggle to his feet.

Ruth Stiles was beside him in an instant and, with her father's help, assisted him to a chair at the table.

"Stranger," said Stiles, stepping aside and eying the intruder critically, "I don't know who or what you are, but I do know that yo' look plumb tuckered out. Nobody's goin' hungry in my house, so fall to an' we'll discuss other matters later."

Whereupon he laid his rifle in its accustomed place, motioned to his wife and daughter to resume their places at the table, and dragged up another chair for himself.

Beyond a word or two of encouragement to eat all he wanted of the very plain fare, none of the trio addressed the newcomer during the remainder of the meal. All three of them had noted the almost-obliterated stripes that encircled his clothing and their significance was unmistakable. But Stiles himself was far from being convinced. He had heard too much of the tricks of government agents to be misled by what might prove, after all, only a clever disguise.

Therefore, when the womenfolk had cleared away the supper things and the two men had the room to themselves, the mountaineer offered his guest a pipeful of tobacco and saw to it that he took a seat before the fire where the light would play directly upon his features. Then he opened fire.

"Stranger," he inquired, "what might yo' name be?"

"Patterson," said the other. "Jim Patterson."

"Whar you come from?"

"Charlestown first an' Morgantown second. Up for twelve years for manslaughter—railroaded at that," was Patterson's laconic reply.

"How'd you get away?"

At that the convict laughed, but there was more of a snarl than humor in his tone as he answered: "Climbed th' wall when th' guards weren't lookin'. They took a coupla pot shots at me, but none of them came within a mile. Then I beat it south, travelin' by night an' hidin' by day. Stole what I could to eat, but this country ain't overly well filled with farms. Hadn't had a bite for two days, 'cept some berries, when I saw your cabin an' came up here."

Stiles puffed away in silence for a moment. Then he rose, as if to fetch something from the other side of the room. Once behind Patterson, however, he reached forward and, seizing the stubble that covered his face, yanked it as hard as he could.

"What th'——?" yelled the convict, springing to his feet and involuntarily raising his clenched hand.

"Ca'm yo'self, stranger, ca'm yo'self," directed the mountaineer, with a half smile. "Jes' wanted to see for myself ef that beard was real, that's all. Thought you might be a rev'nue agent in disguise."

"A rev'nue agent?" queried Patterson, and then as if the thought had just struck him that he was in the heart of the moonshining district, he added: "That's rich! Me, just out of th' pen an' you think I'm a bull. That's great. Here"—reaching into the recesses of his frayed shirt—"here's something that may convince you."

And he handed over a tattered newspaper, more than a week old, and pointed to an article on the first page.

"There, read that!"

"Ruth does all th' reading for this fam'ly," was Stiles's muttered rejoinder. "Ruth! Oh, Ruth! Come here a minute an' read somethin' to yo' pappy!"

Patterson had not failed to note, during supper, that Ruth Stiles came close to being a perfect specimen of a mountain flower, rough and undeveloped, but with more than a trace of real beauty, both in her face and figure. Standing in front of the fire, with its flickering light casting a sort of halo around her, she was almost beautiful—despite her homespun dress and shapeless shoes.

Without a word the convict handed her the paper and indicated the article he had pointed out a moment before.

"Reward offered for convict's arrest," she read. "James Patterson, doing time for murder, breaks out of Morgantown. Five hundred dollars for capture. Prisoner scaled wall and escaped in face of guards' fire." Then followed an account of the escape, the first of its kind in several years.

"Even if you can't read," said Patterson, "there's my picture under the headline—the picture they took for the rogues' gallery," and he pointed to a fairly distinct photograph which adorned the page.[97]

Stiles took the paper closer to the fire to secure a better look, glanced keenly at the convict, and extended his hand.

"Guess that's right, stranger," he admitted. "You're no rev'nue agent."

Later in the evening, as she lay awake, thinking about the man who had shattered the monotony of their mountain life, Ruth Stiles wondered if Patterson had not given vent to what sounded suspiciously like a sigh of relief at that moment. But she was too sleepy to give much thought to it, and, besides, what if he had?...

In the other half of the cabin, divided from the women's room only by a curtain of discolored calico, slept Patterson and Stiles—the former utterly exhausted by his travels, the latter resting with keen hair trigger consciousness of danger always only a short distance away. Nothing happened, however, to disturb the peace of the Stiles domicile. Even the hound slept quietly until the rosy tint of the eastern sky announced another day.

After breakfast, at which the fat-back and corn bread were augmented by a brownish liquid which passed for coffee, Stiles informed his guest that he "reckoned he'd better stick close to th' house fer a few days," as there was no telling whether somebody might not be on his trail.

Patterson agreed that this was the proper course and put in his time helping with the various chores, incidentally becoming a little better acquainted with Ruth Stiles. That night he lay awake for several hours, but nothing broke the stillness save a few indications of animal life outside the cabin and the labored breathing of the mountaineer in the bunk below him.

For three nights nothing occurred. But on the fourth night, Saturday, supper was served a little earlier than usual and Patterson noted just a suspicion of something[98] almost electrical in the air. He gave no indication of what he had observed, however, and retired to his bunk in the usual manner. After an hour or more had elapsed he heard Stiles slip quietly off his mattress and a moment later there was the guarded scratch of a match as a lantern was lighted.

Suspecting what would follow, Patterson closed his eyes and continued his deep, regular breathing. But he could sense the fact that the lantern had been swung up to a level with his bunk and he could almost feel the mountaineer's eyes as Stiles made certain that he was asleep. Stifling an impulse to snore or do something to convince his host that he wasn't awake, Patterson lay perfectly still until he heard the door close. Then he raised himself guardedly on one elbow and attempted to look through the window beside the bunk. But a freshly applied coat of whitewash prevented that, so he had to content himself with listening.

Late in the night—so late that it was almost morning—he heard the sounds of men conversing in whispers outside the cabin, but he could catch nothing beyond his own name. Soon Stiles re-entered the room, slipped into bed, and was asleep instantly.

So things went for nearly three weeks. The man who had escaped from prison made himself very useful around the cabin, and, almost against his will, found that he was falling a victim to the beauty and charm of the mountain girl.

"I mustn't do it," he told himself over and over again. "I can't let myself! It's bad enough to come here and accept the old man's hospitality, but the girl's a different proposition."

It was Ruth herself who solved the riddle some three weeks after Patterson's arrival. They were wandering[99] through the woods together, looking for sassafras roots, when she happened to mention that Stiles was not her own father.

"He's only my pappy," she said, "my adopted father. My real father was killed when I was a little girl. Shot through the head because he had threatened to tell where a still was hidden. He never did believe in moonshining. Said it was as bad as stealin' from the government. So somebody shot him and Ma Stiles took me in, 'cause she said she was sorry for me even if my pa was crazy."

"Do you believe that moonshining is right?" asked her companion.

"Anything my pa believed was the truth," replied the girl, her eyes flashing. "Everybody round these parts knows that Pappy Stiles helps run the big still the rev'nue officers been lookin' for the past three years. Two of 'em were shot not long ago, too—but that don't make it right. 'Specially when my pa said it was wrong. What you smilin' at?"

Patterson resisted an inclination to tell her that the smile was one of relief and replied that he was just watching the antics of a chipmunk a little way off. But that night he felt a thrill of joy as he lay, listening as always, in his bunk.

Things had been breaking rather fast of late. The midnight gatherings had become more frequent and, convinced that he had nothing to fear from his guest, Stiles was not as cautious as formerly. He seldom took the trouble to see that the escaped prisoner was asleep and he had even been known to leave the door unlatched as he went out into the night.

That night, for example, was one of the nights that he was careless—and, as usually happens, he paid dearly for it.[100]

Waiting until Stiles was well out of the house, Patterson slipped silently out of his bunk in his stocking feet and, inch by inch, reopened the door. Outside, the moon was shining rather brightly, but, save for the retreating figure of the mountaineer—outlined by the lantern he carried—there was nothing else to be seen.

Very carefully Patterson followed, treading softly so as to avoid even the chance cracking of a twig. Up the mountainside went Stiles and, some fifty feet behind him, crouched the convict, his faded garments blending perfectly with the underbrush. After half a mile or so of following a rude path, Stiles suddenly disappeared from view—not as if he had turned a corner, but suddenly, as if the earth had swallowed him.

After a moment Patterson determined to investigate. When he reached the spot where he had last seen Stiles he looked around and almost stumbled against the key to the entire mystery. There in the side of the mountain was an opening, the entrance to a natural cave, and propped against it was a large wooden door, completely covered with vines.

"Not a chance of finding it in the daytime unless you knew where it was," thought the convict as he slipped silently into the cave. Less than thirty feet farther was an abrupt turn, and, glancing round this, Patterson saw what he had been hoping for—a crowd of at least a dozen mountaineers gathered about a collection of small but extremely efficient stills. Ranged in rows along the sides of the cave were scores of kegs, the contents of which were obvious from the surroundings.

Pausing only long enough to make certain of his bearings, the convict returned to the cabin and, long before Stiles came back, was sound asleep.

It was precisely four weeks from the day when the[101] buzzard noted the man on the side of the mountain, when a sheriff's posse from another county, accompanied by half a dozen revenue officers, rode clattering through Maymead and on in the direction of the Stiles cabin. Before the mountaineers had time to gather, the posse had surrounded the hill, rifles ready for action.

Stiles himself met them in front of his rude home and, in response to his challenge as to what they wanted, the sheriff replied that he had come for a prisoner who had escaped from Morgantown a month or so before. Stiles was on the verge of declaring that he had never heard of the man when, to his amazement, Patterson appeared from the woods and surrendered.

The instant the convict had gained the shelter of the government guns, however, a startling change took place. He held a moment's whispered conversation with one of the revenue officials and the latter slipped him a spare revolver from his holster. Then— "Hands up!" ordered the sheriff, and Stiles's hands shot above his head.

Leaving three men to guard the cabin and keep watch over Old Man Stiles, whose language was searing the shrubbery, the remainder of the posse pushed up the mountain, directed by the pseudoconvict. It took them some time to locate the door to the cave, but, once inside, they found all the evidence they wanted—evidence not only directly indicative of moonshining, but the two badges which had belonged to Douglas and Wood and which the mountaineers had kept as souvenirs of the shooting, thus unwittingly providing a firm foundation for the government's case in court.

The next morning, when Commissioner Chambers reached his office, he found upon his desk a wire which read:[102]

Stiles gang rounded up without the firing of a single shot. Direct evidence of complicity in Woods-Douglas murders. Secret still is a secret no longer.

The signature to the telegram was "James Reynolds, alias Jim Patterson."

"Jim Patterson," mused the commissioner. "Where have I heard that name.... Of course. He's the prisoner that broke out of Morgantown a couple of months ago! Jimmy sure did lay the local color on thick!"

"But," I inquired, as Quinn paused, "don't you consider that rather a dirty trick on Reynolds's part—worming himself into the confidence of the mountaineers and then betraying them? Besides, what about the girl?"

"Dirty trick!" snorted the former Secret Service agent. "Would you think about ethics if some one had murdered two of the men you work next to in the office? It was the same thing in this case. Jimmy knew that if he didn't turn up that gang they'd probably account for a dozen of his pals—to say nothing of violating the law every day they lived! What else was there for him to do?

"The girl? Oh, Reynolds married her. They sometimes do that, even in real life, you know. As I said, they're living out in the Middle West, for Ruth declared she never wanted to see a mountain again, and both of them admitted that it wouldn't be healthy to stick around within walking distance of Tennessee. That mountain crowd is a bad bunch to get r'iled, and it must be 'most time for Stiles and his friends to get out of jail.

"It's a funny thing the way these government cases work out. Here was one that took nearly three months to solve, and the answer was the direct result of hard work and careful planning—while the Trenton taxicab tangle, for example, was just the opposite!"

[103]

VIII
THE TAXICAB TANGLE

We'd been sitting on the front porch—Bill Quinn and I—discussing things in general for about half an hour when the subject of transportation cropped up and, as a collateral idea, my mind jumped to taxicabs, for the reason that the former Secret Service operative had promised to give me the details of a case which he referred to as "The Trenton Taxicab Tangle."

"Yes," he replied, reminiscently, when I reminded him of the alliterative title and inquired to what it might refer, "that was one of the branch cases which grew out of the von Ewald chase—you remember Mary McNilless and the clue of Shelf Forty-five? Well, Dick Walters, the man who landed von Ewald, wasn't the only government detective working on that case in New York—not by some forty-five or fifty—and Mary wasn't the only pretty woman mixed up in it, either. There was that girl at the Rennoc switchboard....

"That's another story, though. What you want is the taxicab clue."

If you remember the incidents which led up to the von Ewald affair [continued Quinn, as he settled comfortably back in his chair] you will recall that the German was the slipperiest of slippery customers. When Walters stumbled on his trail, through the quick wit of Mary McNilless, there wasn't the slightest indication that there[104] was such a man. He was a myth, a bugaboo—elusive as the buzz of a mosquito around your ear.

During the months they scoured New York in search for him, a number of other cases developed. Some of these led to very interesting conclusions, but the majority, as usual, flivvered into thin air.

The men at headquarters, the very cream of the government services, gathered from all parts of the country, were naturally unable to separate the wheat from the chaff in advance. Night after night they went out on wild-goose chases and sometimes they spent weeks in following a promising lead—to find only blue sky and peaceful scenery at the end of it.

Alan Whitney, who had put in two or three years rounding up counterfeiters for the Service, and who had been transferred to the Postal Inspection Service at the time of those registered mail robberies in the Middle West—only to be detailed to Secret Service work in connection with the von Ewald case—was one of the bitterest opponents of this forced inaction.

"I don't mind trouble," Whitney would growl, "but I do hate this eternal strain of racing around every time the bell goes off and then finding that some bonehead pulled the alarm for the sheer joy of seeing the engines come down the street. There ought to be a law against irresponsible people sending in groundless 'tips'—just as there's a law against scandal or libel or any other information that's not founded on fact."

But, just the same, Al would dig into every new clue with as much interest and energy as the rest of the boys—for there's always the thrill of thinking that the tip you're working on may be the right one after all.

Whitney was in the office one morning when the phone rang and the chief answered it.[105]

"Yes," he heard the chief say, "this is the right place—but if your information is really important I would suggest that you come down and give it in person. Telephones are not the most reliable instruments in the world."

A pause followed and the chief's voice again:

"Well, of course we are always very glad to receive information that tends to throw any light on those matters, but I must confess that yours sounds a little vague and far-fetched. Maybe the people in the taxi merely wanted to find a quiet place to talk.... They got out and were away for nearly two hours? Hum! Thanks very much. I'll send one of our men over to talk to you about it, if you don't mind. What's the address?"

A moment or two later, after the chief had replaced the receiver, he called out to Whitney and with a smile that he could barely conceal told him to catch the next train to Trenton, where, at a certain address, he would find a Miss Vera Norton, who possessed—or thought she possessed—information which would be of value to the government in running down the people responsible for recent bomb outrages and munition-plant explosions.

"What's the idea, Chief?" inquired Al.

"This young lady—at least her voice sounded young over the phone—says that she got home late from a party last night. She couldn't sleep because she was all jazzed up from dancing or something, so she sat near her window, which looks out upon a vacant lot on the corner. Along about two o'clock a taxicab came putt-putting up the street, stopped at the corner, and two men carrying black bags hopped out. The taxicab remained there until nearly four o'clock—three-forty-eight, Miss Norton's watch said—and then the two men came back, without the bags, jumped in, and rolled off. That's all she knows, or, at least, all she told.[106]

"When she picked up the paper round eleven o'clock this mornin' the first thing that caught her eye was the attempt to blow up the powder plant 'bout two miles from the Norton home. One paragraph of the story stated that fragments of a black bag had been picked up near the scene of the explosion, which only wrecked one of the outhouses, and the young lady leaped to the conclusion that her two night-owls were mixed up in the affair. So she called up to tip us off and get her name in history. Better run over and talk to her. There might be something to the information, after all."

"Yes, there *might*," muttered Whitney, "but it's getting so nowadays that if you walk down the street with a purple tie on, when some one thinks you ought to be wearing a green one, they want you arrested as a spy. Confound these amateurs, anyhow! I'm a married man, Chief. Why don't you send Giles or one of the bachelors on this?"

"For just that reason," was the reply. "Giles or one of the others would probably be impressed by the Norton's girl's blond hair—it must be blond from the way she talked—and spend entirely too much time running the whole thing to earth. Go on over and get back as soon as you can. We can't afford to overlook anything these days—neither can we afford to waste too much time on harvesting crops of goat feathers. Beat it!"

And Whitney, still protesting, made his way to the tube and was lucky enough to catch a Trenton train just about to pull out of the station.

Miss Vera Norton, he found, was a blond—and an extremely pretty one, at that. Moreover, she appeared to have more sense than the chief had given her credit for. After Whitney had talked to her for a few minutes he admitted to himself that it was just as well that Giles[107] hadn't tackled the case—he might never have come back to New York, and Trenton isn't a big enough place for a Secret Service man to hide in safety, even when lured by a pair of extremely attractive gray-blue eyes.

Apart from her physical charms, however, Whitney was forced to the conclusion that what she had seen was too sketchy to form anything that could be termed a real clue.

"No," she stated, in reply to a question as to whether she could identify the men in the taxi, "it was too dark and too far off for me to do that. The arc light on the corner, however, gave me the impression that they were of medium height and rather thick set. Both of them were dressed in dark suits of some kind and each carried a black leather bag. That's what made me think that maybe they were mixed up in that explosion last night."

"What kind of bags were they?"

"Gladstones, I believe you call them. Those bags that are flat on the bottom and then slant upward and lock at the top."

"How long was the taxi there?"

"I don't know just when it did arrive, for I didn't look at my watch then, but it left at twelve minutes to four. I was getting mighty sleepy, but I determined to see how long it would stay in one place, for it costs money to hire a car by the hour—even one of those Green-and-White taxis."

"Oh, it was a Green-and-White, eh?"

"Yes, and I got the number, too," Miss Norton's voice fairly thrilled with the enthusiasm of her detective ability. "After the men had gotten out of the car I remembered that my opera glasses were on the bureau and I used them to get a look at the machine. I couldn't see anything of the chauffeur beyond the fact that he was hunched down[108] on the front seat, apparently asleep, and the men came back in such a hurry that I didn't have time to get a good look at them through the glasses."

"But the number," Whitney reminded her.

"I've got it right here," was the reply, as the young lady dug down into her handbag and drew out a card. "N. Y. four, three, three, five, six, eight," she read. "I got that when the taxi turned around and headed back—to New York, I suppose. But what on earth would two men want to take a taxi from New York all the way to Trenton for? Why didn't they come on the train?"

"That, Miss Norton," explained Whitney, "is the point of your story that makes the whole thing look rather suspicious. I will confess that when the chief told me what you had said over the phone I didn't place much faith in it. There might have been a thousand good reasons for men allowing a local taxi to wait at the corner, but the very fact of its bearing a New York number makes it a distinctly interesting incident."

"Then you think that it may be a clue, after all?"

"It's a clue, all right," replied the operative, "but what it's a clue to I can't say until we dig farther into the matter. It is probable that these two men had a date for a poker party or some kind of celebration, missed the train in New York, and took a taxi over rather than be left out of the party. But at the same time it's distinctly within the realms of possibility that the men you saw were implicated in last night's explosion. It'll take some time to get at the truth of the matter and, meanwhile, might I ask you to keep this information to yourself?"

"Indeed I shall!" was the reply. "I won't tell a soul, honestly."[109]

After that promise, Al left the Norton house and made his way across town to where the munitions factory reared its hastily constructed head against the sky. Row after row of flimsy buildings, roofed with tar paper and giving no outward evidence of their sinister mission in life—save for the high barbed-wire fence that inclosed them—formed the entire plant, for there shells were not made, but loaded, and the majority of the operations were by hand.

When halted at the gate, Whitney found that even his badge was of no use in securing entrance. Evidently made cautious by the events of the preceding night, the guard refused to admit anyone, and even hesitated about taking Al's card to the superintendent. The initials "U. S. S. S." finally secured him admittance and such information as was available.

This, however, consisted only of the fact that some one had cut the barbed wire at an unguarded point and had placed a charge of explosive close to one of the large buildings. The one selected was used principally as a storehouse. Otherwise, as the superintendent indicated by an expressive wave of his hand, "it would have been good night to the whole place."

"Evidently they didn't use a very heavy charge," he continued, "relying upon the subsequent explosions from the shells inside to do the damage. If they'd hit upon any other building there'd be nothing but a hole in the ground now. As it is, the damage won't run over a few thousand dollars."

"Were the papers right in reporting that you picked some fragments of a black bag not far from the scene of the explosion?" Whitney asked.

"Yes, here they are," and the superintendent produced three pieces of leather from a drawer in his desk. "Two pieces of the top and what is evidently a piece of the side."[110]

Whitney laid them on the desk and examined them carefully for a few moments. Then:

"Notice anything funny about these?" he inquired.

"No. What's the matter?"

"Not a thing in the world, except that the bag must have had a very peculiar lock."

"What's that?"

"Here—I'll show you," and Whitney tried to put the two pieces of metal which formed the lock together. But, inasmuch as both of them were slotted, they wouldn't join.

"Damnation!" exclaimed the superintendent. "What do you make of that."

"That there were two bags instead of one," stated Whitney, calmly. "Coupled with a little information which I ran into before I came over here, it begins to look as if we might land the men responsible for this job before they're many hours older."

Ten minutes later he was on his way back to New York, not to report at headquarters, but to conduct a few investigations at the headquarters of the Green-and-White Taxicab Company.

"Can you tell me," he inquired of the manager in charge, "just where your taxi bearing the license number four, three, three, five, six, eight was last night?"

"I can't," said the manager, "but we'll get the chauffeur up here and find out in short order.

"Hello!" he called over an office phone. "Who has charge of our cab bearing license number four, three, three, five, six, eight?... Murphy? Is he in?... Send him up—I'd like to talk to him."

A few moments later a beetle-jawed and none too cleanly specimen of the genus taxi driver swaggered in and didn't even bother to remove his cap before sitting down.[111]

"Murphy," said the Green-and-White manager, "where was your cab last night?"

"Well, let's see," commenced the chauffeur. "I took a couple to the Amsterdam Theayter in time for th' show an' then picked up a fare on Broadway an' took him in the Hunnerd-an'-forties some place. Then I cruised around till the after-theater crowd began to come up an'—an' I got one more fare for Yonkers. Another long trip later on made it a pretty good night."

"Murphy," cut in Whitney, edging forward into the conversation, "where and at just what hour of the night did those two Germans offer you a hundred dollars for the use of your car all evening?"

"They didn't offer me no hunnerd dollars," growled the chauffeur, "they gave me...." Then he checked himself suddenly and added, in an undertone, "I don't know nothin' 'bout no Goimans."

"The hell you don't!" snarled Whitney, edging toward the door. "Back up against that desk and keep your hands on top of it, or I'll pump holes clean through you!"

His right hand was in his coat pocket, the fingers closed around what was very palpably the butt of an automatic. Murphy could see the outline of the weapon and obeyed instructions, while Whitney slammed the door with his left hand.

"Now look here," he snapped, taking a step nearer to the taxi driver, "I want the truth and I want it quick! Also, it's none of your business why I want it! But you better come clean if you know what's good for you. Out with it! Where did you meet 'em and where did you drive 'em?"

Realizing that escape was cut off and thoroughly cowed by the display of force, Murphy told the whole story—or as much of it as he knew.[112]

"I was drivin' down Broadway round Twenty-eig't Street last night, 'bout ten o'clock," he confessed. "I'd taken that couple to the the-ayter, just as I told you, an' that man up to Harlem. Then one of these t'ree guys hailed me...."

"Three?" interrupted Whitney.

"That's what I said—t'ree! They said they wanted to borrow my machine until six o'clock in th' mornin' an' would give me two hunnerd dollars for it. I told 'em there was nothin' doin' an' they offered me two-fifty, swearin' that they'd have it back at th' same corner at six o'clock sharp. Two hunnerd an' fifty bones being a whole lot more than I could make in a night, I gambled with 'em an' let 'em have th' machine, makin' sure that I got the coin foist. They drove off, two of 'em inside, an' I put in th' rest of th' night shootin' pool. When I got to th' corner of Twenty-eig't at six o'clock this mornin', there wasn't any sign of 'em—but th' car was there, still hot from the hard ride they give her. That's all I know—'shelp me Gawd!"

"Did the men have any bags with them?"

"Bags? No, not one."

"What did they look like?"

"The one that talked with me was 'bout my heig't an' dressed in a dark suit. He an' th' others had their hats pulled down over their eyes, so's I couldn't see their faces."

"Did he talk with a German accent?"

"He sure did. I couldn't hardly make out what he was sayin'. But his money talked plain enough."

"Yes, and it's very likely to talk loud enough to send you to the pen if you're not careful!" was Whitney's reply. "If you don't want to land there, keep your mouth shut about this. D'you get me?"

"I do, boss, I do."[113]

"And you've told me all the truth—every bit of it?"

"Every little bit."

"All right. Clear out!"

When Murphy left the room, Whitney turned to the manager and, with a wry smile, remarked: "Well, we've discovered where the car came from and how they got it. But that's all. We're really as much in the dark as before."

"No," replied the manager, musingly. "Not quite as much. Possibly you don't know it, but we have a device on every car that leaves this garage to take care of just such cases as this—to prevent drivers from running their machines all over town without pulling down the lever and then holding out the fares on us. Just a minute and I'll show you.

"Joe," he called, "bring me the record tape of Murphy's machine for last night and hold his car till you hear from me."

"This tape," he explained, a few minutes later, "is operated something along the lines of a seismograph or any other instrument for detecting change in direction. An inked needle marks these straight lines and curves all the time the machine is moving, and when it is standing still it oscillates slightly. By glancing at these tapes we can tell when any chauffeur is holding out on us, for it forms a clear record—not only of the distance the machine has traveled, but of the route it followed."

"Doesn't the speedometer give you the distance?" asked Whitney.

"Theoretically, yes. But it's a very simple matter to disconnect a speedometer, while this record is kept in a locked box and not one driver in ten even knows it's there. Now, let's see what Murphy's record tape tells us....[114]

"Yes, here's the trip to the theater around eight-thirty. See the sharp turn from Fifth Avenue into Forty-second Street, the momentary stop in front of the Amsterdam, and the complete sweep as he turned around to get back to Broadway. Then there's the journey up to the Bronx or Harlem or wherever he went, another complete turn and an uninterrupted trip back down on Broadway."

"Then this," cut in Whitney, unable to keep the excitement out of his voice, "is where he stopped to speak to the Germans?"

"Precisely," agreed the other, "and, as you'll note, that stop was evidently longer than either of the other two. They paid their fares, while Murphy's friends had to be relieved of two hundred and fifty dollars."

"From there on is what I'm interested in," announced Whitney. "What does the tape say?"

"It doesn't *say* anything," admitted the manager, with a smile. "But it *indicates* a whole lot. In fact, it blazes a blood-red trail that you ought to be able to follow with very little difficulty. See, when the machine started it kept on down Broadway—in fact, there's no sign of a turn for several blocks."

"How many?"

"That we can't tell—now. But we can figure it up very accurately later. The machine then turned to the right and went west for a short distance only—stopped for a few moments—and then went on, evidently toward the ferry, for here's a delay to get on board, here's a wavy line evidently made by the motion of the boat when the hand ought to have been practically at rest, and here's where they picked up the trip to Trenton. Evidently they didn't have to stop until they got there, because we have yards of tape before we reach a stop point, and then the paper is worn completely through by the action of[115] the needle in oscillating, indicative of a long period of inaction. The return trip is just as plain."

"But," Whitney objected, "the whole thing hinges on where they went before going to Trenton. Murphy said they didn't have any bags, so they must have gone home or to some rendezvous to collect them. How are we going to find the corner where the machine turned?"

"By taking Murphy's car and driving it very carefully south on Broadway until the tape indicates precisely the distance marked on this one—the place where the turn was made. Then, driving down that street, the second distance shown on the tape will give you approximately the house you're looking for!"

"Good Lord," exclaimed Whitney, "that's applying science to it! Sherlock Holmes wasn't so smart, after all!"

Al and the manager agreed that there was too much traffic on Broadway in the daytime or early evening to attempt the experiment, but shortly after midnight, belated pedestrians might have wondered why a Green-and-White taxicab containing two men proceeded down Broadway at a snail's pace, while every now and then it stopped and one of the men got out to examine something inside.

"I think this is the corner," whispered the garage manager to Whitney, when they reached Eighth Street, "but to be sure, we'll go back and try it over again, driving at a normal pace. It's lucky that this is a new instrument and therefore very accurate."

The second trial produced the same result as the first—the place they sought lay a few blocks west of Broadway, on Eighth.

Before they tried to find out the precise location of the house, Whitney phoned to headquarters and requested loan of a score of men to assist him in the contemplated raid.

"Tell 'em to have their guns handy," he ordered, "because[116] we may have to surround the block and search every house."

But the taxi tape rendered that unnecessary. It indicated any one of three adjoining houses on the north side of the street, because, as the manager pointed out, the machine had not turned round again until it struck a north-and-south thoroughfare, hence the houses must be on the north side.

By this time the reserves were on hand and, upon instructions from Whitney, spread out in a fan-shaped formation, completely surrounding the houses, front and rear. At a blast from a police whistle they mounted the steps and, not waiting for the doors to be opened, went through them shoulders first.

It was Whitney, who had elected to assist in the search of the center house, who captured his prey in a third-floor bedroom.

Before the Germans knew what was happening Al was in the room, his flashlight playing over the floor and table in a hasty search for incriminating evidence. It didn't take long to find it, either. In one corner, only partly concealed by a newspaper whose flaring headlines referred to the explosion of the night before, was a collection of bombs which, according to later expert testimony was sufficient to blow a good-sized hole in the city of New York.

That was all they discovered at the time, but a judicious use of the third degree—coupled with promises of leniency—induced one of the prisoners to loosen up the next day and he told the whole story—precisely as the taxi tape and Vera Norton had told it. The only missing ingredient was the power behind the plot—the mysterious "No. 859"—whom Dick Walters later captured because of the clue on Shelf forty-five.

[117]

"So you see," commented Quinn as he finished, "the younger Pitt wasn't so far wrong when he cynically remarked that 'there is a Providence that watches over children, imbeciles, and the United States.' In this case the principal clues were a book from the Public Library, the chance observations of a girl who couldn't sleep and a piece of white paper with some red markings on it.

"At that, though, it's not the first time that German agents have gotten into trouble over a scrap of paper."

"What happened to Vera Norton?" I inquired.

"Beyond a little personal glory, not a thing in the world," replied Quinn. "Didn't I tell you that Al was married? You're always looking for romance, even in everyday life. Besides, if he had been a bachelor, Whitney was too busy trying to round up the other loose ends of the Ewald case. 'Number eight fifty-nine' hadn't been captured then, you remember.

"Give me a match—my pipe's gone out. No, I can't smoke it here; it's too late. But speaking of small clues that lead to big things, some day soon I'll tell you the story of how a match—one just like this, for all I know—led to the uncovering of one of the most difficult smuggling cases that the Customs Service ever tried to solve."

IX
A MATCH FOR THE GOVERNMENT

"I wonder how long it will take," mused Bill Quinn, as he tossed aside a copy of his favorite fictional monthly, "to remove the ethical restrictions which the war placed upon novels and short stories? Did you ever notice the changing style in villains, for example? A decade or so ago it was all the rage to have a Japanese do the dirty work—for then we were taking the 'yellow peril' rather seriously and it was reflected in our reading matter. The tall, well-dressed Russian, with a sinister glitter in his black eyes, next stepped upon the scene, to be followed by the villain whose swarthy complexion gave a hint of his Latin ancestry.

"For the past few years, of course, every real villain has had to have at least a touch of Teutonic blood to account for the various treacheries which he tackles. I don't recall a single novel—or a short story, either—that has had an English or French villain who is foiled in the last few pages. I suppose you'd call it the *entente cordiale* of the novelists, a sort of concerted attempt by the writing clan to do their bit against the Hun. And mighty good propaganda it was, too....

"But, unfortunately, the detective of real life can't always tell by determining a man's nationality whether he's going to turn out to be a crook or a hero. When you come right down to it, every country has about the same proportion of each and it's only by the closest observation that one can arrive at a definite and fact-supported conclusion.

"Details—trifles unnoticed in themselves—play a far larger part in the final dénouement than any preconceived ideas or fanciful theories. There was the case of Ezra Marks and the Dillingham diamonds, for example...."

Ezra [continued the former Secret Service operative, when he had eased his game leg into a position where it no longer gave him active trouble] was all that the name implied. Born in Vermont, of a highly puritanical family, he had been named for his paternal grandfather and probably also for some character from the Old Testament. I'm not awfully strong on that Biblical stuff myself.

It wasn't long after he grew up, however, that life on the farm began to pall. He found a copy of the life of Alan Pinkerton somewhere and read it through until he knew it from cover to cover. As was only natural in a boy of his age, he determined to become a great detective, and drifted down to Boston with that object in view. But, once in the city, he found that "detecting" was a little more difficult than he had imagined, and finally agreed to compromise by accepting a very minor position in the Police Department. Luckily, his beat lay along the water front and he got tangled up in two or three smuggling cases which he managed to unravel in fine shape, and, in this way, attracted the attention of the Customs Branch of the Treasury Department, which is always on the lookout for new timber. It's a hard life, you know, and one which doesn't constitute a good risk for an insurance company. So there are always gaps to be filled—and Ezra plugged up one of them very nicely.

As might have been expected, the New Englander was hardly ever addressed by his full name. "E. Z." was the title they coined for him, and "E. Z." he was from that time on—at least to everyone in the Service. The people on the other side of the fence, however, the men and women who look upon the United States government as a joke and its laws as hurdles over which they can jump whenever they wish—found that this Mark was far from an easy one. He it was who handled the Wang Foo opium case in San

Diego in nineteen eleven. He nailed the gun runners at El Paso when half a dozen other men had fallen down on the assignment, and there were at least three Canadian cases which bore the imprint of his latent genius on the finished reports.

His particular kind of genius was distinctly out of the ordinary, too. He wasn't flashy and he was far from a hard worker. He just stuck around and watched everything worth watching until he located the tip he wanted. Then he went to it—and the case was finished!

The chap who stated that "genius is the capacity for infinite attention to details" had Ezra sized up to a T. And it was one of these details—probably the most trifling one of all—that led to his most startling success.

Back in the spring of nineteen twelve the European agents of the Treasury Department reported to Washington that a collection of uncut diamonds, most of them rather large, had been sold to the German representative of a firm in Rotterdam. From certain tips which they picked up, however, the men abroad were of the opinion that the stones were destined for the United States and advised that all German boats be carefully watched, because the Dillingham diamonds—as the collection was known—had been last heard of en route to Hamburg and it was to be expected that they would clear from there.[121]

The cablegram didn't cause any wild excitement in the Treasury Department. European agents have a habit of trying to stir up trouble in order to make it appear that they are earning their money and then they claim that the people over here are not always alert enough to follow their tips. It's the old game of passing the buck. You have to expect it in any business.

But, as events turned out, the men on the other side were dead right.

Almost before Washington had time officially to digest the cable and to mail out the stereotyped warnings based upon it, a report filtered in from Wheeling, West Virginia, that one of the newly made coal millionaires in that section had invested in some uncut diamonds as large as the end of your thumb. The report came in merely as a routine statement, but it set the customs authorities to thinking.

Uncut stones, you know, are hard to locate, either when they are being brought in or after they actually arrive. Their color is dull and slatelike and there is little to distinguish them from other and far less valuable pebbles. Of course, there might not be the slightest connection in the world between the Wheeling diamonds and those of the Dillingham collection—but then, on the other hand, there might....

Hence, it behooved the customs people to put on a little more speed and to watch the incoming steamers just as carefully as they knew how.

Some weeks passed and the department had sunk back into a state of comfortable ease—broken only occasionally by a minor case or two—when a wire arrived one morning stating that two uncut diamonds had appeared in New York under conditions which appeared distinctly suspicious. The owner had offered them at a[122] price 'way under the market figure, and then, rather than reply to one or two questions relative to the history of the stones, had disappeared. There was no record of the theft of any diamonds answering to the description of those seen in Maiden Lane, and the police force inquired if Washington thought they could have been smuggled.

"Of course they could," snorted the chief. "But there's nothing to prove it. Until we get our hands upon them and a detailed description of the Dillingham stones, it's impossible to tell."

So he cabled abroad for an accurate list of the diamonds which had been sold a couple of months earlier, with special instructions to include any identifying marks, as it was essential to spot the stones before a case could be built up in court.

The following Tuesday a long dispatch from Rotterdam reached the department, stating, among other things, that one of the Dillingham diamonds could be distinguished by a heart-shaped flaw located just below the surface. That same afternoon came another wire from New York to the effect that two rough stones, answering to the description of the ones alluded to in a previous message, had turned up in the jewelry district after passing through half a dozen underground channels.

"Has one of the diamonds a heart-shaped flaw in it?" the chief inquired by wire.

"It has," came back the response. "How did you know it?"

"I didn't," muttered the head of the Customs Service, "but I took a chance. The odds were twenty to one against me, but I've seen these long shots win before. Now," ringing for Mahoney, his assistant, "we'll see what can be done to keep the rest of that collection from drifting in—if it hasn't already arrived."[123]

"Where's Marks located now?" the chief inquired when Mahoney entered.

"Somewhere in the vicinity of Buffalo, I believe. He's working on that Chesbro case, the one in connection with—"

"I know," cut in the chief. "But that's pin money compared with this matter of the Dillingham diamonds. Thousands of dollars are at stake here, against hundreds there. Besides, if this thing ever leaks out to the papers we'll never hear the last of it. The New York office isn't in any too strong as it is. Wire Marks to drop the trail of those silk hounds and beat it to New York as fast as he can. He'll find real work awaiting him there—something that ought to prove a test of the reputation he's built up on the other three borders. Hurry it up!"

"E. Z." found the message awaiting him when he returned to his hotel that night, and without the slightest symptom of a grouch grabbed the next train for New York. As he told me later, he didn't mind in the least dropping the silk matter, because he had put in the better part of a month on it and didn't seem any closer than when he started.

It took Ezra less than five minutes to get all the dope the New York office had on the case—and it took him nearly six months to solve it.

"The two diamonds in Wheeling and the two that turned up here are the only ones we know about," said the man in charge of the New York office. "The original Dillingham collection contained twenty-one rough stones—but whether the other seventeen have already been brought in or whether the people who are handling them have shipped them elsewhere is wholly problematical. The chief learned about the heart-shaped flaw from our man at Rotterdam, so that identifies one of the stones.[124] But at the same time it doesn't help us in the least—for we can't handle the case from this end."

"Same rules as on the Coast, eh?" inquired Marks.

"Precisely. You've got to tackle the other end of the game. No rummaging around here, trying to pick up the trail that ends with the stone in Maiden Lane. As you know, this bunch is pretty well organized, wheels within wheels and fences on fences. You get something on one of them and the rest of the crowd will perjure themselves black in the face to get him off, with the result that your case will be laughed out of court and the man you're really after—the chap who's running the stones under your nose—is a thousand miles away with a grin on his face. You've got to land him first and the others later, if the chief wants them. The chances are, though, that he'll be well satisfied to have the goods on the crook that's doing the main part of the work."

"Well," drawled Marks, "I trust he gets his satisfaction. Got any ideas on the matter?"

"Nary an idea. The stones were sold abroad and presumably they were headed for Hamburg—which would appear to point to a German boat. Four of them, supposedly—one of them, certainly—turned up here without passing through the office or paying the customary duty. Now go to it!"

When Marks got back to his hotel and started to think the problem over, he had to admit that there wasn't very much to "go to." It was the thinnest case he had ever tackled—a perfect circle of a problem, without the slightest sign of a beginning, save the one which was barred.

Anxious as he was to make good, he had to concede that the department's policy of working from the other end of the case was the right course to follow. He had heard of too many arrests that fell flat, too many weary[125] weeks of work that went for nothing—because the evidence was insufficient—not to realize the justice of the regulations that appeared to hamper him.

"No," he thought, as he half dreamed over a pipe-load of tobacco, "the case seems to be impregnable. But there must be some way to jimmy into it if you try long enough."

His first move was the fairly obvious one of searching the newspaper files to discover just what ships had docked during the ten days previous to the appearance of the stones in Wheeling. But this led nowhere, because that week had been a very busy one in maritime circles. The *Celtic*, the *Mauretania*, the *Kaiser Wilhelm der Grosse*, the *Kronprinzessin Cecelie*, the *Deutschland* and a host of other smaller vessels had landed within that time.

Just as a check upon his observations, he examined the records for the week preceding the first appearance of the diamonds in New York. Here again he ran into a snag, but one which enabled him to eliminate at least half of the vessels he had considered before. However, there still remained a sufficient number to make it impossible to watch all of them or even to fix upon two or three which appeared more suspicious than the others.

The information from abroad pointed to the fact that a German boat was carrying the diamonds, but, Marks figured, there was nothing in the world to prevent the stones from being taken into England or France or Italy and reshipped from there. They had turned up in the United States, so why couldn't they have been slipped through the customs of other countries just as easily?

The one point about the whole matter that appeared significant to him was that two stones had been reported in each case—a pair in Wheeling and another pair in New York. This evidence would be translated either to mean[126] that the smugglers preferred to offer the diamonds in small lots, so as not to center suspicion too sharply in their movements, or that the space which they used to conceal the stones was extremely limited.

Marks inclined to the latter theory, because two stones, rather than one, had been offered in each instance. If the whole lot had been run in, he argued, the men responsible would market them singly, rather than in pairs. This would not detract in the slightest from the value of the stones, as it isn't easy to match rough diamonds and thus increase their market value.

Having settled this matter to his own satisfaction and being convinced that, as not more than two stones were being run in at one time, it would take at least eight more trips to import the entire shipment, "E. Z." settled down to a part of the government detective's work which is the hardest and the most necessary in his life—that which can best be characterized by the phrase "watchful waiting."

For weeks at a time he haunted the docks and wharves along the New York water front. His tall, angular figure became a familiar sight at every landing place and his eyes roamed restlessly over the crowds that came down the gangplank. In a number of instances he personally directed the searching of bags and baggage which appeared to be suspicious. Save for locating a few bolts of valuable lace and an oil painting concealed in the handle of a walking stick which was patently hollow, he failed to turn up a thing.

The only ray of hope that he could glimpse was the fact that, since he had been assigned to the case, four more stones had been reported—again in pairs. This proved that his former reasoning had been correct and also that the smugglers evidently intended to bring in all of the[127] twenty-one stones, two at a time. But when he came to catalog the hiding places which might be used to conceal two articles of the size of the stones already spotted, he was stumped. The list included a walking stick, the heels of a pair of women's shoes, two dummy pieces of candy concealed in a box of real confections, a box of talcum, a bag of marbles, the handle of an umbrella, or any one of a number of other trinkets which travelers carry as a matter of course or bring home as curios or gifts.

Finally, after two solid months of unproductive work, he boarded the midnight train for Washington and strolled into the chief's office the following morning, to lay his cards on the table.

"Frankly," he admitted, "I haven't accomplished a thing. I'm as far from breaking into the circle as I was at the beginning, and, so far as I can see, there isn't any hope of doing it for some time to come."

"Well," inquired the chief, "do you want to be relieved of the case or do you want me to drop the matter entirely—to confess that the Customs Service has been licked by a single clever smuggler?"

"Not at all!" and Marks's tone indicated that such a thought had never entered his head. "I want the Service to stick with the case and I want to continue to handle it. But I do want a definite assurance of time."

"How much time?"

"That I can't say. The only lead I've located—and that isn't sufficient to be dignified by the term 'clue'—will take weeks and probably months to run to earth. I don't see another earthly trail to follow, but I would like to have time to see whether this one leads anywhere."

"All right," agreed the chief, fully realizing what "E. Z." was up against and not being hurried by any pressure from the outside—for the case had been carefully[128] kept out of the newspapers—"this is September. Suppose we say the first of the year? How does that suit you?"

"Fair enough, if that's the best you can do."

"I'm afraid it is," was the comment from across the desk, "because that's all the case is worth to us. Your time is valuable and we can't afford to spend a year on any case—unless it's something as big as the sugar frauds. Stick with it until New Year's, and if nothing new develops before then we'll have to admit we're licked and turn you loose on something else."

"Thanks, Chief," said Marks, getting up from his chair. "You can depend upon my doing everything possible in the next three months to locate the leak and I surely appreciate your kindness in not delivering an ultimatum that you want the smuggler or my job. But then I guess you know that I couldn't work any harder than I'm going to, anyhow."

"Possibly," agreed the head of the Service, "and then, again, it may be because I have confidence that you'll turn the trick within the year. Want any help from this end?"

"No, thanks. This looks like a one-man game and it ought not to take more than one man to finish it. A whole bunch of people always clutter up the place and get you tangled in their pet theories and personal ideas. What I would like, though, is to be kept in close touch with any further developments concerning stones that appear later on—where they are located—their exact weight and diameter, and any other facts that might indicate a possible hiding place."

"You'll get that, all right," promised the chief. "And I trust that you'll develop a red-hot trail of your own before January first."[129]

With that Marks shook hands and started back to New York, fairly well pleased with the results of his trip, but totally disgusted with the lack of progress which he had made since leaving Buffalo.

Early in October a message from Washington informed him that a couple of uncut diamonds had turned up in Cincinnati, stones which answered to the description of a pair in the Dillingham collection.

Around the 10th of November another pair was heard from in Boston, and anyone who was familiar with Marks and his methods would have noted a tightening of the muscles around his mouth and a narrowing of his eyes which always indicated that he was nearing the solution of a difficulty.

After receiving the November message he stopped haunting the wharves and commenced to frequent the steamship offices of the Hamburg-American, North German Lloyd and Llanarch lines. The latter, as you probably know, is operated by Welsh and British capital and runs a few small boats carrying passengers who would ordinarily travel second class, together with a considerable amount of freight.

When the first day of December dawned, Marks drew a deep-red circle around the name of the month on his calendar and emitted a prayerful oath, to the effect he'd "be good and eternally damned if that month didn't contain an unexpected Christmas present for a certain person." He made no pretense of knowing who the person was—but he did feel that he was considerably closer to his prey than he had been five months before.

Fate, as some one has already remarked, only deals a man a certain number of poor hands before his luck changes. Sometimes it gets worse, but, on the average, it improves. In Ezra Marks's case Fate took the form of a[130] storm at sea, one of those winter hurricanes that sweep across the Atlantic and play havoc with shipping.

Ezra was patiently waiting for one of three boats. Which one, he didn't know—but by the process of elimination he had figured to a mathematical certainty that one of them ought to carry two uncut diamonds which were destined never to visit the customs office. Little by little, through the months that had passed, he had weeded out the ships which failed to make port at the time the diamonds arrived—calculating the time by the dates on which the stones appeared elsewhere—and there were only three ships left. One of them was a North German Lloyder, the second belonged to the Hamburg-American fleet, and the third possessed an unpronounceable Welsh name and flew the pennant of the Llanarch line.

As it happened, the two German ships ran into the teeth of the gale and were delayed three days in their trip, while the Welsh boat missed the storm entirely and docked on time.

Two days later came a message from Washington to the effect that two diamonds, uncut, had been offered for sale in Philadelphia.

"Have to have one more month," replied Marks. "Imperative! Can practically guarantee success by fifteenth of January"—for that was the date on which the Welsh ship was due to return.

"Extension granted," came the word from Washington. "Rely on you to make good. Can't follow case any longer than a month under any circumstances."

Marks grinned when he got that message. The trap was set, and, unless something unforeseen occurred, "E. Z." felt that the man and the method would both be in the open before long.

When the Welsh ship was reported off quarantine in [131] January, Marks bundled himself into a big fur coat and went down the bay in one of the government boats, leaving instructions that, the moment the ship docked, she was to be searched from stem to stern.

"Don't overlook as much as a pill box or a rat hole," he warned his assistants, and more than a score of men saw to it that his instructions were carried out to the letter.

Beyond exhibiting his credentials, Marks made no effort to explain why the ship was under suspicion. He watched the deck closely to prevent the crew from throwing packages overboard, and as soon as they reached dock he requested all officers to join him in one of the big rooms belonging to the Customs Service. There he explained his reasons for believing that some one on board was guilty of defrauding the government out of duty on a number of uncut diamonds.

"What's more," he concluded, at the end of an address which was purposely lengthy in order to give his men time to search the ship, "I am willing to stake my position against the fact that two more diamonds are on board the ship at this moment!"

Luckily, no one took him up—for he was wrong.

The captain, pompous and self-assertive, preferred to rise and rant against the "infernal injustice of this high-handed method."

Marks settled back to listen in silence and his fingers strayed to the side pocket of his coat where his pet pipe reposed. His mind strayed to the thought of how his men were getting along on the ship, and he absent-mindedly packed the pipe and struck a match to light it.

It was then that his eye fell upon the man seated beside him—Halley, the British first mate of the steamer. He had seen him sitting there before, but had paid little [132] attention to him. Now he became aware of the fact that the mate was smoking a huge, deep-bowled meerschaum pipe. At least, it had been in his mouth ever since he entered, ready to be smoked, but unlighted.

Almost without thinking about it, Marks leaned forward and presented the lighted match, holding it above the mate's pipe.

"Light?" he inquired, in a matter-of-fact tone.

To his amazement, the other started back as if he had been struck, and then, recovering himself, muttered: "No, thanks. I'm not smoking."

"Not smoking?" was the thought that flashed through Marks's head, "then why—"

But the solution of the matter flashed upon him almost instantly. Before the mate had time to move, Marks's hand snapped forward and seized the pipe. With the same movement he turned it upside down and rapped the bowl upon the table. Out fell a fair amount of tobacco, followed by two slate-colored pebbles which rolled across the table under the very eyes of the captain!

"I guess that's all the evidence we need!" Marks declared, with a laugh of relief. "You needn't worry about informing your consul and entering a protest, Captain Williams. I'll take charge of your mate and these stones and you can clear when you wish."

[133]

X

THE GIRL AT THE SWITCHBOARD

"When you come right down to it," mused Bill Quinn, "women came as near to winning the late but unlamented war as did any other single factor.

"The Food Administration placarded their statement that 'Food Will Win the War' broadcast throughout the country, and that was followed by a whole flock of other claimants, particularly after the armistice was signed. But there were really only two elements that played a leading role in the final victory—men and guns. And women backed these to the limit of their powerful ability—saving food, buying bonds, doing extra work, wearing a smile when their hearts were torn, and going 'way out of their usual sphere in hundreds of cases—and making good in practically every one of them.

"So far as we know, the Allied side presented no analogy to Mollie Pitcher or the other heroines of past conflicts, for war has made such forward steps that personal heroism on the part of women is almost impossible. Of course, we had Botchkareva and her 'Regiment of Death,' not to mention Edith Cavell, but the list is not a long one.

"When it is finally completed, however, there are a few names which the public hasn't yet heard which will stand well toward the front. For example, there was Virginia Lang—"[134]

"Was she the girl at the switchboard that you mentioned in connection with the von Ewald case?" I interrupted.

"That's the one," said Quinn, "and, what's more, she played a leading role in that melodrama, a play in which they didn't use property guns or cartridges."

Miss Lang [continued Quinn] was one of the few women I ever heard of that practically solved a Secret Service case "on her own." Of course, in the past, the different governmental detective services have found it to their advantage to go outside the male sex for assistance.

There have been instances where women in the employ of the Treasury Department rendered valuable service in trailing smugglers—the matter of the Deauville diamonds is a case in point—and even the Secret Service hasn't been above using women to assist in running counterfeiters to earth, while the archives of the State Department would reveal more than one interesting record of feminine co-operation in connection with underground diplomacy.

But in all these cases the women were employed to handle the work and they were only doing what they were paid for, while Virginia Lang—

Well, in the first place, she was one of the girls in charge of the switchboard at the Rennoc in New York. You know the place—that big apartment hotel on Riverside Drive where the lobby is only a shade less imposing than the bell-boys and it costs you a month's salary to speak to the superintendent. They never have janitors in a place like that.

Virginia herself—I came to know her fairly well in the winter of nineteen seventeen, after Dave Carroll had gone to the front—was well qualified by nature to be the[135] heroine of any story. Rather above the average in size, she had luckily taken advantage of her physique to round out her strength with a gymnasium course. But in spite of being a big woman, she had the charm and personality which are more often found in those less tall. When you couple this with a head of wonderful hair, a practically perfect figure, eyes into which a man could look and, looking, lose himself, lips which would have caused a lip stick to blush and—Oh, what's the use? Words only caricature a beautiful woman, and, besides, if you haven't gotten the effect already, there's nothing that I could tell you that would help any.

In the spring of nineteen sixteen, when the von Ewald chase was at its height, Miss Lang was employed at the Rennoc switchboard and it speaks well for her character when I can tell you that not one of the bachelor tenants ever tried a second time to put anything over. Virginia's eyes could snap when they wanted to and Virginia's lips could frame a cutting retort as readily as a pleasant phrase.

In a place like the Rennoc, run as an apartment hotel, the guests change quite frequently, and it was some task to keep track of all of them, particularly when there were three girls working in the daytime, though only one was on at night. They took it by turns—each one working one week in four at night and the other three holding down the job from eight to six. So, as it happened, Virginia did not see Dave Carroll until he had been there nearly a month. He blew in from Washington early one evening and straightway absented himself from the hotel until sometime around seven the following morning, following the schedule right through, every night.

Did you ever know Carroll? He and I worked together on the Farron case out in St. Louis, the one where a bookmaker[136] at the races tipped us off to the biggest counterfeiting scheme ever attempted in this country, and after that he took part in a number of other affairs, including the one which prevented the Haitian revolution in nineteen thirteen.

Dave wasn't what you would call good-looking, though he did have a way with women. The first night that he came downstairs—after a good day's sleep—and spotted Virginia Lang on the switchboard, he could have been pardoned for wandering over and trying to engage her in a conversation. But the only rise he got was from her eyebrows. They went up in that "I-am-sure-I-have-never-met-you" manner which is guaranteed to be cold water to the most ardent male, and the only reply she vouchsafed was "What number did you wish?"

"You appear to have mine," Dave laughed, and then asked for Rector 2800, the private branch which connected with the Service headquarters.

When he came out of the booth he was careful to confine himself to "Thank you" and the payment of his toll. But there was something about him that made Virginia Lang feel he was "different"—a word which, with women, may mean anything—or nothing. Then she returned to the reading of her detective story, a type of literature to which she was much addicted.

Carroll, as you have probably surmised, was one of the more than twoscore Government operatives sent to New York to work on the von Ewald case. His was a night shift, with roving orders to wander round the section in the neighborhood of Columbus Circle and stand ready to get anywhere in the upper section of the city in a hurry in case anything broke. But, beyond reporting to headquarters regularly every hour, the assignment was not exactly eventful.[137]

The only thing that was known about von Ewald at that time was that a person using such a name—or alias—was in charge of the German intrigues against American neutrality. Already nearly a score of bomb outrages, attempts to destroy shipping, plots against munition plants, and the like had been laid at his door, but the elusive Hun had yet to be spotted. Indeed, there were many men in the Service who doubted the existence of such a person, and of these Carroll was one.

But he shrugged his shoulders and stoically determined to bear the monotony of strolling along Broadway and up, past the Plaza, to Fifth Avenue and back again every night—a program which was varied only by an occasional séance at Reisenweber's or Pabst's, for that was in the days before the one-half of one per cent represented the apotheosis of liquid refreshment.

It was while he was walking silently along Fifty-ninth Street, on the north side, close to the Park, a few nights after his brush with Virginia Lang, that Carroll caught the first definite information about the case that anyone had obtained.

He hadn't noted the men until he was almost upon them, for the night was dark and the operative's rubber heels made no sound upon the pavement. Possibly he wouldn't have noticed them then if it hadn't been for a phrase or two of whispered German that floated out through the shrubbery.

"He will stay at Conner's" was what reached Carroll's ears. "That will be our chance—a rare opportunity to strike two blows at once, one at our enemy and the other at this smug, self-satisfied nation which is content to make money out of the slaughter of Germany's sons. Once he is in the hotel, the rest will be easy."[138]

"How?" inquired a second voice.

"A bomb, so arranged to explode with the slightest additional pressure, in a—"

"Careful," growled a third man. "Eight fifty-nine would hardly care to have his plans spread all over New York. This cursed shrubbery is so dense that there is no telling who may be near. Come!"

And Carroll, crouched on the outside of the fence which separates the street from the Park, knew that seconds were precious if he was to get any further information. A quick glance down the street showed him that the nearest gate was too far away to permit of entrance in that manner. So, slipping his automatic into the side pocket of his coat he leaped upward and grasped the top of the iron fence. On the other side he could hear the quick scuffle of feet as the Germans, alarmed, began to retreat rapidly.

A quick upward heave, a purchase with his feet, and he was over, his revolver in his hand the instant he lighted on the other side.

"Halt!" he called, more from force of habit than from anything else, for he had no idea that any of the trio would stop.

But evidently one of them did, for from behind the shelter of a near-by bush came the quick spat of a revolver and a tongue of flame shot toward him. The bullet, however, sung harmlessly past and he replied with a fusillade of shots that ripped through the bush and brought a shower of German curses from the other side. Then another of the conspirators opened fire from a point at right angles to the first, and the ruse was successful, for it diverted Carroll's attention long enough to permit the escape of the first man, and the operative was still flat on the ground, edging his way cautiously forward when[139] the Park police arrived, the vanguard of a curious crowd attracted by the shots.

"What's the trouble?" demanded the "sparrow cop."

"None at all," replied Dave, as he slipped the still warm revolver into his pocket and brushed some dirt from his sleeve. "Guy tried to hold me up, that's all, and I took a pot shot at him. Cut it! Secret Service!" and he cautiously flashed his badge in the light of the electric torch which the park policeman held.

"Huh!" grunted the guard, as he made his way to the bush from behind which Carroll had been attacked. "You evidently winged him. There's blood on the grass here, but no sign of the bird himself. Want any report to headquarters?" he added, in an undertone.

"Not a word," said Carroll. "I'm working this end of the game and I want to finish it without assistance. It's the only thing that's happened in a month to break the monotony and there's no use declaring anyone else in on it. By the way, do you know of any place in town known as Conner's?"

"Conner's? Never heard of it. Sounds as though it might be a dive in the Bowery. Plenty of queer places down there."

"No, it's hardly likely to be in that section of the city," Dave stated. "Farther uptown, I think. But it's a new one on me."

"On me, too," agreed the guard, "and I thought I knew the town like a book."

When he reported to headquarters a few moments later, Carroll told the chief over the wire of his brush with the trio of Germans, as well as what he had heard. There was more than a quiver of excitement in the voice from the other end of the wire, for this was the first actual proof of the existence of the mysterious "No. 859."[140]

"Still believe von Ewald is a myth?" inquired the Chief.

"Well, I wouldn't go so far as to say that," was the answer, "because the bullet that just missed me was pretty material. Evidently some one is planning these bomb outrages and it's up to us to nab him—if only for the sake of the Service."

"Did you catch the name of the man to whom your friends were alluding?" asked the chief.

"No, they just referred to him as 'he.'"

"That might mean any one of a number of people," mused the chief. "Sir Cecil Spring-Rice is in town, you know. Stopping at the Waldorf. Then there's the head of the French Mission at the Vanderbilt with a bunch of people, and Lord Wimbledon, who's spent five million dollars for horses in the West, stopping at the same place you are. You might keep an eye on him and I'll send Kramer and Fleming up to trail the other two."

"Did you ever hear of the place they called Conner's, Chief?"

"No, but that doesn't mean anything. It may be a code word—a prearranged name to camouflage the hotel in the event anyone were listening in."

"Possibly," replied Carroll, just before he hung up, "but somehow I have a hunch that it wasn't. I'll get back on the job and let you know if anything further develops."

His adventure for the night appeared to have ended, for he climbed into bed the following morning without having been disturbed, but lay awake for an hour or more—obsessed with the idea that he really held the clue to the whole affair, but unable to figure out just what it was.

Where was it that they intended to place the bomb? Why would they arrange it so as to explode upon pressure,[141] rather than concussion or by a time fuse? Where was Conner's? Who was the man they were plotting against?

These were some of the questions which raced through his brain, and he awoke in the late afternoon still haunted by the thought that he really ought to know more than he did.

That night at dinner he noted, almost subconsciously, that he was served by a new waiter, a fact that rather annoyed him because he had been particularly pleased at the service rendered by the other man.

"Where's Felix?" he inquired, as the new attendant brought his soup.

"He isn't on to-night, sir," was the reply. "He had an accident and won't be here for a couple of days."

"An accident?"

"Yes, sir," was the laconic answer.

"Anything serious?"

"No, sir. He—he hurt his hand," and the waiter disappeared without another word. Carroll thought nothing more of it at the time, but later, over his coffee and a good cigar, a sudden idea struck him. Could it be that Felix was one of the men whom he had surprised the night before, the one he had fired at and hit? No, that was too much of a coincidence. But then Felix was manifestly of foreign origin, and, while he claimed to be Swiss, there was a distinct Teutonic rasp to his words upon occasion.

Signaling to his waiter, Dave inquired whether he knew where Felix lived. "I'd like to know if there is anything that I can do for him," he gave as his reason for asking.

"I haven't the slightest idea," came the answer, and Carroll was aware that the man was lying, for his demeanor[142] was sullen rather than subservient and the customary "sir" was noticeable by its absence.

Once in the lobby, Dave noticed that the pretty telephone operator was again at the switchboard, and the idea occurred to him that he might find out Felix's address from the hotel manager or head waiter.

"I understand that my waiter has been hurt in an accident," the operative explained to the goddess of the wires, "and I'd like to find out where he lives. Who would be likely to know?"

"The head waiter ought to be able to tell you," was the reply, accompanied by the flash of what Carroll swore to be the whitest teeth he had ever seen. "Just a moment and I will get him on the wire for you." Then, after a pause, "Booth Number Five, please."

But Carroll got no satisfaction from that source, either. The head waiter maintained that he knew nothing of Felix's whereabouts and hung up the receiver in a manner which was distinctly final, not to say impolite. The very air of mystery that surrounded the missing man was sufficient to incline him to the belief that, after all, there might be something to the idea that Felix was the man he had shot at the night before. In that event, it was practically certain that Lord Wimbledon was the object of the Germans' attention—but that didn't solve the question of where the bomb was to be placed, nor the location of "Conner's."

"Just the same," he muttered, half aloud, "I'm going to stick around here to-night."

"Why that momentous decision?" came a voice almost at his elbow, a voice which startled and charmed him with its inflection.

Looking up, he caught the eyes of the pretty telephone girl, laughing at him.[143]

"Talking to yourself is a bad habit," she warned him with a smile which seemed to hold an apology for her brusqueness of the night before, "particularly in your business."

"My business?" echoed Dave. "What do you know about that?"

"Not a thing in the world—except," and here her voice dropped to a whisper—"except that you are a government detective and that you've discovered something about Lord Wimbledon, probably some plot against His Lordship."

"Where—how—what in the world made you think that?" stammered Carroll, almost gasping for breath.

"Very simple," replied the girl. "Quite elementary, as Sherlock Holmes used to say. You called the headquarters number every night when you came down—the other girls tipped me off to that, for they know that I'm fond of detective stories. Then everybody around here knows that Felix, the waiter that you inquired about, is really German, though he pretends to be Swiss, and that he, the head waiter, and the pastry cook are thick as thieves."

"You'd hardly expect me to say 'Yes,' would you? Particularly as I am supposed to be a government operative."

"Now I know you are," smiled the girl. "Very few people use the word 'operative.' They'd say 'detective' or 'agent.' But don't worry, I won't give you away."

"Please don't," laughed Carroll, half banteringly, half in earnest, for it would never do to have it leak out that a girl had not only discovered his identity, but his mission. Then, as an after-thought, "Do you happen to know of any hotel or place here in town known as 'Conner's'?" he asked.[144]

"Why, of course," was the reply, amazing in its directness. "The manager's name—" But then she halted abruptly, picked up a plug, and said, "What number, please?" into the receiver.

Carroll sensed that there was a reason for her stopping in the middle of her sentence and, looking around, found the pussy-footed head waiter beside him, apparently waiting for a call. Silently damning the custom that made it obligatory for waiters to move without making a sound, Carroll wandered off across the lobby, determined to take a stroll around the block before settling down to his night's vigil. A stop at the information desk, however, rewarded him with the news that Lord Wimbledon was giving a dinner in his apartments the following evening to the British ambassador—that being all the hotel knew officially about his Grace's movements.

"I'll take care to have half a dozen extra men on the job," Carroll assured himself, "for that's undoubtedly the time they would pick if they could get away with it. A single bomb then would do a pretty bit of damage."

The evening brought no further developments, but shortly after midnight he determined to call the Rennoc, in the hope that the pretty telephone girl was still on duty and that she might finish telling him what she knew of Conner's.

"Hotel Rennoc," came a voice which he recognized instantly.

"This is Dave Carroll speaking," said the operative. "Can you tell me now what it was you started to say about Conner's?"

"Not now," came the whispered reply. Then, in a louder voice, "Just a moment, please, and I'll see if he's registered." During the pause which followed Dave[145] realized that the girl must be aware that she was watched by some one. Was it the silent-moving head waiter?

"No, he hasn't arrived yet," was the next phrase that came over the wires, clearly and distinctly, followed by instructions, couched in a much lower tone, "Meet me, Drive entrance, one-five sure," and then a click as the plug was withdrawn.

It was precisely five minutes past one when Carroll paused in front of the Riverside Drive doorway to the Rennoc, considering it the part of discretion to keep on the opposite side of the driveway. A moment later a woman, alone, left the hotel, glanced around quickly, and then crossed to where he was standing.

"Follow me up the street," she directed in an undertone as she passed. "Michel has been watching like a hawk."

Dave knew that Michel was the head waiter, and out of the corner of his eye he saw a shadow slip out of another of the hotel doorways, farther down the Drive, and start toward them. But when he looked around a couple of blocks farther up the drive, there was no one behind them.

"Why all the mystery?" he inquired, as he stepped alongside the girl.

"Something's afoot in the Rennoc," she replied, "and they think I suspect what it is and have told you about it. Michel hasn't taken his eyes off me all evening. I heard him boast one night that he could read lips, so I didn't dare tell you anything when you called up, even though he was across the lobby. Conner's, the place you asked about, is the Rennoc. Spell it backward. Conner is the manager—hence the name of the hotel."

"Then," said Carroll, "that means that they've got a plan under way to bomb Lord Wimbledon and probably[146] the British ambassador at that dinner to-morrow evening. I overheard one of them say last night that a bomb, arranged to explode at the slightest pressure, would be placed in the—" and then he stopped.

"In the cake!" gasped the girl, as if by intuition. But her next words showed that her deduction had a more solid foundation. "This is to be a birthday dinner, in honor of Lord

Percy Somebody who's in Lord Wimbledon's party, as well as in honor of Lord Cecil. The pastry cook, who's almost certainly mixed up in the plot, has plenty of opportunity to put the bomb there, where it would never be suspected. The instant they cut the cake—"

But her voice trailed off in midair as something solid came down on her head with a crash. At the same moment Dave was sent reeling by a blow from a blackjack, a blow which sent him spinning across the curb and into the street. He was dimly aware that two men were leaping toward him and that a third was attacking the telephone girl.

Panting, gasping, fighting for time in which to clear his head of the effects of the first blow, Carroll fought cautiously, but desperately, realizing that his opponents desired to avoid gun-play for fear of attracting the police. A straight left to the jaw caught one of the men coming in and knocked him sprawling, but the second, whom Carroll recognized as Michel, was more wary. He dodged and feinted with the skill of a professional boxer, and then launched an uppercut which went home on the point of Dave's jaw.

It was at that moment that the operative became aware of another participant in the fray—a figure in white with what appeared to be a halo of gold around her head. The thought flashed through his mind that he must be[147] dreaming, but he had sense enough left to leap aside when a feminine voice called "Look out!" and the arc light glinted off the blade of a knife as it passed perilously close to his ribs. Then the figure in white brought something down on Michel's head and, wheeling, seized the wrist of the third man in a grip of iron.

Ten seconds later the entire trio was helpless and Carroll was blowing a police whistle for assistance.

"There was really nothing to it at all," protested the telephone girl, during the ride in the patrol. "They made the mistake of trying to let Felix, with his wounded hand, take care of me. I didn't have two years of gym work and a complete course in jiu jitsu for nothing, and that blackjack came in mighty handy a moment or two later. All Felix succeeded in doing was to knock my hat off, and I shed my coat the instant I had attended to him."

"That's why I thought you were a goddess in white," murmured Dave.

"No goddess at all, just a girl from the switchboard who was glad to have a chance at the brutes. Anyhow, that few minutes beats any book I ever read for action!"

Dave's hand stole out in the darkness as they jolted forward, and when it found what it was seeking, "Girl," he said, "do you realize that I don't even know your name?"

"Lang," said a voice in the dark. "My friends call me Virginia."

"After what you just did for me, I think we ought to be at least good friends," laughed Carroll, and the thrill of the fight which has just passed was as nothing when she answered:

"At least that ... Dave!"

[148]

Quinn paused for a moment to repack his pipe and I took advantage of the interruption to ask what happened at the Wimbledon dinner the following night.

"Not a thing in the world," replied Quinn. "Everything went off like clockwork—everything but the bomb. As the Podunk *Gazette* would say, 'A very pleasant time was had by all.' But you may be sure that they were careful to examine the cake and the other dishes before they were sampled by the guests. Michel, Felix, and the cook were treated to a good dose of the third degree at headquarters, but without results. They wouldn't even admit that they knew any such person as 'Number Eight-fifty-nine' or von Ewald. Two of them got off with light sentences for assault and battery. The pastry cook, however, went to the pen when they found a quantity of high explosives in his room."

"And Miss Lang?"

"If you care to look up the marriage licenses for October, nineteen sixteen, you'll find that one was issued in the names of David Carroll and Virginia Lang. She's the wife of a captain now, for Dave left the Service the following year and went to France to finish his fight with the Hun. I saw him not long ago and the only thing that's worrying him is where he is going to find his quota of excitement, for he says that there is nothing left in the Service but chasing counterfeiters and guarding the resident, and he can't stand the idea of staying in the army and drawing his pay for wearing a uniform."

[149]

XI
"LOST—$100,000!"

"I stopped on my way here to-night and laid in a supply of something that I don't often use—chewing gum," said Bill Quinn, formerly of the Secret Service, as he settled back comfortably to enjoy an evening's chat. "There are some professional reformers who maintain that the great American habit of silently working the jaws over a wad of chewing gum is harmful in the extreme, but if you'll look into the matter you'll find that agitators of that type want you to cut out all habits except those which they are addicted to.

"Personally, I'm not a habitual worshiper at the shrine of the great god Goom, but there's no use denying the fact that it does soothe one's nerves occasionally. Incidentally, it has other uses—as Elmer Allison discovered not very long ago."

"Yes?" I inquired, sensing the fact that Quinn had a story up his sleeve and was only awaiting the opportunity to spring it. "Didn't you mention a post-office case in which a wad of gum played a prominent role?"

"That's the one," said the former government operative, easing his wounded leg into a less cramped position. "Here, have a couple of sticks just to get the proper atmosphere and I'll see if I can recall the details."

For some reason that's hard to define [Quinn went on, after he had peeled two of the dun-colored sticks and commenced[150] work on them] crooks in general and amateur crooks in particular seem to regard the United States mails as particularly easy prey. Possibly they figure that, as millions of dollars are handled by the Post-office Department every year, a little here and there won't be missed. But if they knew the high percentage of mail robberies that are solved they wouldn't be so keen to tackle the game.

Lifting valuables, once they have passed into the hands of Uncle Sam's postman, is a comparatively easy crime to commit. There are dozens of ways of doing it—methods which range all the way from fishing letters out of a post-box with a piece of string and a hairpin, to holding up the mail car in a deserted portion of a railroad track. But getting away with it is, as our Yiddish friends say, something else again.

The annals of the Postal Inspection Service are filled with incidents which indicate that the High Cost of Living is down around zero compared to the High Cost of Crime, when said crime is aimed at the mails. There are scores of men in Atlanta, Leavenworth, and other Federal prisons whose advice would be to try murder, forgery, or arson rather than attempt to earn a dishonest living by stealing valuable letters.

The majority of persons realize that it pays to register their money and insure their packages because, once this precaution has been attended to, the government exercises special care in the handling of these and makes it extremely difficult for crooks to get anywhere near them. If a registered letter disappears there is a clean-cut trail of signed receipts to follow and somebody has to bear the burden of the loss. But even with these precautions, the Registered Section is looted every now and then.

One of the biggest cases of this kind on record was that[151] which occurred in Columbus when letters with an aggregate value of one hundred thousand dollars just vanished into thin air. Of course, they didn't all disappear at one time, but that made it all the more mysterious—because the thefts were spread out over a period of some five or six weeks and they went on, just as regularly as clockwork, in spite of the precautions to the contrary.

The first of the losses, as I recall it, was a shipment of ten thousand dollars in large bills sent by a Chicago bank to a financial concern in Columbus. When working on that single case, of course, the officials of the department were more or less in the dark as to the precise place that the disappearance had taken place, in spite of the fact that there were the usual signed slips indicating that the package had been received at the Columbus Post Office. But clerks who are in a hurry sometimes sign receipts without being any too careful to check up the letters or packages to which they refer—a highly reprehensible practice, but one which is the outgrowth of the shortage of help. It was quite within the bounds of possibility, for example, for the package to have been abstracted from the Chicago office without the loss being discovered until Columbus checked up on the mail which was due there.

But a week or ten days later came the second of the mysterious disappearances—another envelope containing bills of large denomination, this time en route from Pittsburgh to Columbus. When a third loss occurred the following fortnight, the headquarters of the Postal Inspection Service in Washington became distinctly excited and every man who could be spared was turned loose in an effort to solve the problem. Orders were given to shadow all the employees who had access to the registered mail with a view to discovering whether they had made any[152] change in their personal habits, whether they had displayed an unusual amount of money within the past month, or whether their family had shown signs of exceptional prosperity.

It was while the chief was waiting for these reports that Elmer Allison blew into Washington unexpectedly and strolled into the room in the big gray-stone tower of what was then the Post-office Department Building, with the news that he had solved the "poison-pen case" in Kansas City and was ready to tackle something else.

The chief, to put it mildly, was surprised and inquired why in the name of the seven hinges of Hades Allison hadn't made his report directly to the office by mail.

"That was a pretty important case, Chief," Elmer replied, "and I didn't want to take any chances of the findings being lost in the registered mail." Then, grinning, he continued, "Understand you've been having a bit of trouble out in Columbus?"

"Who told you about that?" growled the chief.

"Oh, you can't keep things like that under your hat even if you do succeed in keeping them out of the papers," retorted Allison. "A little bird tipped me off to it three weeks ago and—"

"And you determined to leap back here as soon as you could so that you would be assigned to the case, eh?"

"You guessed it, Chief. I wanted a try at the Columbus affair and I was afraid I wouldn't get it unless I put the matter personally up to you. How 'bout it?"

"As it happens, you lost about two days of valuable time in coming here, instead of wiring for further instructions from Kansas City," the chief told him. "I had intended taking you off that anonymous letter case by noon to-morrow, whether you'd finished it or not, for this is a far more important detail. Somebody's gotten[153] away with fifty thousand dollars so far, and there's no—"

"Pardon me, sir, but here's a wire which has just arrived from Rogers, in Columbus. Thought you'd like to see it at once," and the chief's secretary laid a yellow slip face upward on his desk. Allison, who was watching closely, saw a demonstration of the reason why official Washington maintained that the chief of the Postal Inspection Service had the best "poker face" in the capital. Not a muscle in his countenance changed as he read the telegram and then glanced up at Allison, continuing his sentence precisely where he had been interrupted:

"Reason to suppose that the thief is going to stop there. This wire from Rogers, the postmaster at Columbus, announces the loss of a fourth package of bills. Fifty thousand this time. That's the biggest yet and it brings the total deficit up to one hundred thousand dollars. Rogers says that the banks are demanding instant action and threatening to take the case to headquarters, which means that it'll spread all over the papers. Congress will start an investigation, some of us will lose our official heads, and, in the mix-up, the man who's responsible for the losses will probably make a clean getaway."

Then, with a glance at the clock which faced his desk, "There's a train for Columbus in twenty minutes, Allison. Can you make it?"

"It's less than ten minutes to the station," replied the operative. "That gives me plenty of leeway."

"Well, move and move fast," snapped the chief. "I'll wire Columbus that you've been given complete charge of the case; but try to keep it away from the papers as long as you can. The department has come in for enough criticism lately without complicating the issue from the[154]outside. Good luck." And Allison was out of the door almost before he had finished speaking.

Allison reached Columbus that night, but purposely delayed reporting for work until the following morning. In the first place there was no telling how long the case would run and he felt that it was the part of wisdom to get all the rest he could in order to start fresh. The "poison-pen" puzzle hadn't been exactly easy to solve, and his visit to Washington, though brief, had been sufficiently long for him to absorb some of the nervous excitement which permeated the department. Then, too, he figured that Postmaster Rogers would be worn out by another day of worry and that both of them would be the better for a night's undisturbed sleep.

Nine o'clock the next morning, however, saw him seated in one of the comfortable chairs which adorned the postmaster's private office. Rogers, who did not put in an appearance until ten, showed plainly the results of the strain under which he was laboring, for he was a political appointee who had been in office only a comparatively short time, a man whose temperament resented the attacks launched by the opposition and who felt that publication of the facts connected with the lost one hundred thousand dollars would spell ruin, both to his own hopes and those of the local organization.

Allison found that the chief had wired an announcement of his coming the day before and that Rogers was almost pitifully relieved to know that the case was in the hands of the man who had solved nearly a score of the problems which had arisen in the Service during the past few years.

"How much do you know about the case?" inquired the postmaster.

"Only what I learned indirectly and from what the chief told me," was Allison's reply. "I understand that[155] approximately one hundred thousand dollars is missing from this post office" (here Rogers instinctively winced as he thought of the criticism which this announcement would cause if it were made outside the office), "but I haven't any of the details."

"Neither have we, unfortunately," was the answer. "If we had had a few more we might have been able to prevent the last theft. You know about that, of course."

"The fifty thousand dollars? Yes. The chief told me that you had wired."

"Well, that incident is typical of the other three. Banks in various parts of the country have been sending rather large sums of money through the mails to their correspondents here. There's nothing unusual in that at this time of the year. But within the past five or six weeks there have been four packages—or, rather, large envelopes—of money which have failed to be accounted for. They ranged all the way from ten thousand dollars, the first loss, to the fifty thousand dollars which disappeared within the past few days. I purposely delayed wiring Washington until we could make a thorough search of the whole place, going over the registry room with a fine-tooth comb—"

"Thus warning every man in it that he was under suspicion," muttered Allison.

"What was that?" Rogers inquired.

"Nothing—nothing at all. Just talking to myself. Far from a good habit, but don't mind it. I've got some queer ones. You didn't find anything, of course?"

"In the building? No, not a thing. But I thought it best to make a thorough clean-up here before I bothered Washington with a report."

"What about the men who've been working on the case up to this time?"[156]

"Not one of them has been able to turn up anything that could be dignified by the term clue, as I believe you detectives call it."

"Yes, that's the right word," agreed the operative. "At least all members of the Detective-Story-Writers' Union employ it frequently enough to make it fit the case. What lines have Boyd and the other men here been following?"

"At my suggestion they made a careful examination into the private lives of all employees of the post-office, including myself," Rogers answered, a bit pompously. "I did not intend to evade the slightest responsibility in the matter, so I turned over my bankbook, the key to my safe-deposit vault and even allowed them to search my house from cellar to garret."

"Was this procedure followed with respect to all the other employees in the building?"

"No, only one or two of the highest—personal friends of mine whom I could trust to keep silent. I didn't care to swear out search warrants for the residences of all the people who work here, and that's what it would have meant if they had raised any objection. In their cases the investigation was confined to inquiries concerning their expenditures in the neighborhood, unexpected prosperity, and the like."

"With what result?"

"None at all. From all appearances there isn't a soul in this building who has had ten cents more during the past six weeks than he possessed in any like period for two years back."

"Did Boyd or any of the other department operatives ask to see the plans of the post office?" inquired Allison, taking another tack.

"The what?"[157]

"The plans of the post-office—the blue print prepared at the time that the building was erected."

"No. Why should they?"

72

"I thought they might have been interested in it, that's all," was Allison's answer, but anyone who knew him would have noted that his tone was just a trifle too nonchalant to be entirely truthful.

"By the way," added the operative, "might I see it?"

"The blue print?"

"Yes. You will probably find it in the safe. If you'll have some one look it up, I'll be back in half an hour to examine it," said Allison. "Meanwhile, I'll talk to Boyd and the other men already on the ground and see if I can dig anything out of what they've discovered."

But Boyd and his associates were just as relieved as Rogers had been to find that the case had been placed in Allison's hands. Four weeks and more of steady work had left them precisely where they had commenced—"several miles back of that point," as one of them admitted, "for three more stunts have been pulled off right under our eyes." The personal as well as the official record of every man and woman in the Columbus post office had been gone over with a microscope, without the slightest result. If the germ of dishonesty was present, it was certainly well hidden.

"We'll try another and more powerful lens," Allison stated, as he turned back to the postmaster's private office. "By the way, Boyd, have you or any of your men been in the Service more than four years?"

"No, I don't think any of us has. What has that got to do with it?"

"Not a thing in the world, as far as your ability is concerned, but there is one point that every one of you overlooked—because you never heard of it. I'm going[158] to try it out myself now and I'll let you know what develops."

With that Allison turned and sauntered back into Rogers's office.

There, spread upon the desk, was the missing blue print, creased and dusty from disuse.

"First time you ever saw this, eh?" Allison inquired of the postmaster.

"The first time I even knew it was there," admitted that official. "How'd you know where to find it?"

"I didn't—but there's an ironclad rule of the department that plans of this nature are to be kept under lock and key for just such emergencies as this. But I guess your predecessor was too busy to worry you with details."

Rogers grunted. It was an open secret that the postmaster who had preceded him had not been any too friendly to his successor.

Allison did not pursue the subject but spread the plan upon an unoccupied table so that he could examine it with care.

"If you'll be good enough to lock that door, Postmaster," he directed, "I'll show you something else about your building that you didn't know. But I don't want anybody else coming in while we're discussing it."

Puzzled, but feeling that the government detective ought to be allowed to handle things in his own way, Rogers turned the key in the lock and came over to the table where Allison stood.

"Do you see that little square marked with a white star and the letter 'L'?" asked Elmer.

"Yes, what is it?"

"What is this large room next to it?" countered the operative.

"That's the—why, that's the registry room!"[159]

"Precisely. And concealed in the wall in a spot known only to persons familiar with this blue print, is a tiny closet, or 'lookout.' That's what the 'L' means and that's the reason that there's a strict rule about guarding plans of this nature very carefully."

"You mean to say that a place has been provided for supervision of the registry division—a room from which the clerks can be watched without their knowledge?"

"Exactly—and such a precaution has been taken in practically every post office of any size in the country. Only the older men in the Service know about it, which is the reason that neither Boyd nor any of his men asked to see this set of plans. The next step is to find the key to the lookout and start in on a very monotonous spell of watchful waiting. You have the bunch of master keys, of course?"

"Yes, they're in the safe where the plans were kept. Just a moment and I'll get them."

When Rogers produced the collection of keys, Allison ran hurriedly over them and selected one which bore, on the handle, a small six-pointed star corresponding to the mark on the blue print.

"Want to go up with me and investigate the secret chamber?" he inquired.

"I certainly do," agreed Rogers. "But there's one point where this room won't help us in the slightest. How did the thief get the mail containing the money out of the building? You know the system that maintains in the registry room? It's practically impossible for a sheet of paper to be taken out of there, particularly when we are on guard, as we are now."

"That's true," Allison admitted, "but it's been my experience that problems which appear the most puzzling are, after all, the simplest of explanation. You remember[160] the Philadelphia mint robbery—the one that Drummond solved in less than six hours? This may prove to be just as easy."

There Allison was wrong, dead wrong—as he had to admit some ten days later, when, worn with the strain of sitting for hours at a time with his eyes glued to the ventilator which masked the opening to the lookout, he finally came to the conclusion that something would have to be done to speed things up. It was true that no new robberies had occurred in the meantime, but neither had any of the old ones been punished. The lost one hundred thousand dollars was still lost; though the department, with the aid of the Treasury officials, had seen that the banks were reimbursed.

"The decoy letter," thought Allison, "is probably the oldest dodge in the world. But, who knows, it may work again in this case—provided we stage-manage it sufficiently carefully."

With the assistance of the cashier of one of the local banks Elmer arranged to have a dummy package of money forwarded by mail from New York. It was supposed to contain thirty-five thousand dollars in cash, and all the formalities were complied with precisely as if thirty-five thousand-dollar bills were really inside the envelope, instead of as many sheets of blank paper carefully arranged.

On the morning of the day the envelope was due to reach Columbus, Allison took up his position close to the grille in the lookout, his eyes strained to catch the slightest suspicious movement below. Hour after hour passed uneventfully until, almost immediately below him, he saw a man drop something on the floor. Two envelopes had slipped from his hands and he stooped to pick them up—that was all.[161]

But what carried a thrill to the operative in the lookout was the fact that one of the envelopes was the dummy sent from New York and that, when the man straightened up, he had only *one* of the two in his hands. The dummy had disappeared!

Allison rubbed his eyes and looked again. No, he was right. The postal clerk had, in some manner, disposed of the envelope supposed to contain thirty-five thousand dollars and he was going about his work in precisely the same way as before.

"Wait a minute," Allison argued to himself. "There's something missing besides the envelope! What is it?"

A moment later he had the clue to the whole affair—the jaws of the clerk, which Allison had previously and subconsciously noted were always hard at work on a wad of gum, now were at rest for the first time since the operative had entered the lookout! The chewing gum and the dummy packet had disappeared at the same time!

It didn't take Elmer more than thirty seconds to reach Rogers's office, and he entered with the startling announcement that "an envelope containing thirty-five thousand dollars had just disappeared from the registry room."

"What?" demanded the postmaster. "How do you know? I haven't received any report of it."

"No, and you probably wouldn't for some time," Elmer retorted. "But it happens that I saw it disappear."

"Then you know where it is?"

"I can lay my hands on it—and probably the rest of the missing money—inside of one minute. Let's pay a visit to the registry room."

Before entering the section, however, Allison took the precaution of posting men at both of the doors.

"After I'm inside," he directed, "don't allow anyone[162] to leave on any pretext whatever. And stand ready for trouble in case it develops. Come on, Mr. Rogers."

Once in the room devoted to the handling of registered mail, Allison made directly for the desk under the lookout. The occupant regarded their approach with interest but, apparently, without a trace of anxiety.

"I'd like to have that letter supposed to contain thirty-five thousand dollars which you dropped on the floor a few moments ago," Elmer remarked in a quiet, almost conversational tone.

Except for a sudden start, the clerk appeared the picture of innocence.

"What letter?" he parried.

"You know what one!" snapped Allison, dropping his suave manner and moving his hand significantly toward his coat pocket. "Will you produce it—or shall I?"

"I—I don't know what you are talking about," stammered the clerk.

"No? Well, I'll show you!" and the operative's hands flashed forward and there was a slight click as a pair of handcuffs snapped into place. "Now, Mr. Rogers, you'll be good enough to watch me carefully, as your evidence will probably be needed in court. I'll show you as simple and clever a scheme as I've ever run across."

With that Allison dropped to the floor, wormed his way under the table-desk, tugged at something for a moment and then rose, holding five large envelopes in his hands!

"There's your lost one hundred thousand dollars," he explained, "and a dummy packet of thirty-five thousand dollars to boot. Thought you could get away with it indefinitely, eh?" he inquired of the handcuffed clerk. "If you'd stopped with the one hundred thousand dollars, as you'd probably intended to do, you might have. But that extra letter turned the trick. Too bad it contained[163] only blank paper"—and he ripped the envelope open to prove his assertion.

"But—but—I don't understand," faltered Rogers. "How did this man work it right under our eyes?"

"He didn't," declared Allison. "He tried to work it right under mine, but he couldn't get away with it. The plan was simplicity itself. He'd slip an envelope which he knew contained a large sum of money out of the pile as it passed him—he hadn't signed for them, so he wasn't taking any special risk—drop it on the floor, stoop over, and, if he wasn't being watched, attach it to the *bottom* of his desk with a wad of chewing gum. You boasted that you went over the room with a fine-tooth comb, but who would think of looking on the under side of this table. The idea, of course, was that he'd wait for the storm to blow over—because the letters could remain in their hiding places for months, if necessary—and then start on a lifelong vacation with his spoils as capital. But he made the error of overcapitalization and I very much fear that he'll put in at least ten years at Leavenworth or Morgantown. But I'd like to bet he never chews another piece of gum!"

"That," continued Quinn, as he tossed another pink wrapper into the wastebasket, "I consider the simplest and cleverest scheme to beat the government that I ever heard of—better even than Cochrane's plan in connection with the robbery of the Philadelphia mint, because it didn't necessitate any outside preparation at all. The right job, a piece of gum, and there you are. But you may be sure that whenever an important letter disappears nowadays, one of the first places searched by the Postal Inspection operatives is the lower side of the desks and tables. You can't get away with a trick twice in the same place."

[164]

XII
"THE DOUBLE CODE"

It was one night in early fall that Bill Quinn and I were browsing around the library in the house that he had called "home" ever since a counterfeiter's bullet incapacitated him from further active work in the Secret Service. Prior to that time he had lived, as he put it, "wherever he hung his hat," but now there was a comfortable little house with a den where Quinn kept the more unusual, and often gruesome, relics which brought back memories of the past.

There, hanging on the wall with a dark-brown stain still adorning the razorlike edge, was a Chinese hatchet which had doubtless figured in some tong war on the Coast. Below was an ordinary twenty-five-cent piece, attached to the wall paper with chewing gum—"just as it once aided in robbing the Treasury of nearly a million dollars," Quinn assured me. In another part of the room was a frame containing what appeared to be a bit torn from the wrapping of a package, with the canceled stamp and a half-obliterated postmark as the only clues to the murder of the man who had received it, and, beside the bookcases, which contained a wide range of detective literature, hung a larger frame in which were the finger prints of more than a score of criminals, men bearing names practically unknown to the public, but whose exploits were bywords in the various governmental detective services.[165]

It was while glancing over the contents of the bookcase that I noted one volume which appeared strangely out of place in this collection of the fictional romances of crime.

"What's this doing here?" I inquired, taking down a volume of *The Giant Raft*, by Jules Verne. "Verne didn't write detective stories, did he?"

"No," replied Quinn, "and it's really out of place in the bookcase. If possible, I'd like to have it framed and put on the wall with the rest of the relics—for it's really more important than any of them, from the standpoint of value to the nation. That quarter on the wall over there—the one which figured in the Sugar Fraud case—cost the government in the neighborhood of a million dollars, but this book probably saved a score of millions and hundreds of lives as well. If it hadn't been for the fact that Thurber of the Navy Department knew his Jules Vernes even better than he did his Bible, it's quite possible that—

"Well, there's no use telling the end of the story before the beginning. Make yourself comfortable and I'll see if I can recall the details of the case."

Remember Dr. Heinrich Albert? [Quinn inquired, after we had both stretched out in front of the open fire]. Theoretically, the Herr Doktor was attached to the German embassy in Washington merely in an advisory and financial capacity. He and Haniel von Heimhausen—the same counselor that the present German government wanted to send over here as ambassador after the signing of the peace treaty—were charged with the solution of many of the legal difficulties which arose in connection with the business of the big red brick dwelling on Massachusetts Avenue. But while von Heimhausen was occupied with the legal end of the game, Doctor Albert attended[166] to many of the underground details which went unsuspected for many years.

It was he, for example, who managed the bidding for the wireless station in the Philippines—the plan which permitted the German government to dictate the location of the station and to see to it that the towers were so placed where they would be most useful to Berlin. He undoubtedly worked with von Papen and Boy-Ed during the early years of the war—years in which this precious trio, either with or without the knowledge of Count von Bernstorff, sought by every means to cripple American shipping, violate American neutrality, and make a laughingstock of American diplomatic methods. What's more, they got away with it for months, not because the Secret Service and the Department of Justice weren't hot on their trail, but because the Germans were too cagy to be caught and you can't arrest a diplomat just on suspicion.

During the months which followed the first of August, nineteen fourteen, practically every one of the government's detective services was called upon in some way to pry into the affairs of the embassy staff. But the brunt of the work naturally devolved upon the two organizations directly concerned with preventing flagrant breaches of neutrality—the Secret Service and the Department of Justice.

Every time that Doctor Albert, or any other official of the German government, left Washington he was trailed by anywhere from one to five men. Every move he made was noted and reported to headquarters, with the result that the State Department had a very good idea of the names of the men who were being used to forward Germany's ends, even though it knew comparatively little about what was actually planned. The attachés were entirely too clever to carry on compromising conversations[167] in the open, and their appointments were made in such a manner as effectually to prevent the planting of a dictaphone or any other device by which they might be overheard.

The directions to the men who were responsible for the working of the two Services were:

Every attaché of the German embassy is to be guarded with extreme care, day and night. Reports are to be made through the usual channels and, in the event that something unusual is observed, Divisional Headquarters is to be notified instantly, the information being transmitted to Washington before any final action is taken.

This last clause, of course, was inserted to prevent some hot-headed operative from going off half-cocked and thus spoiling the State Department's plans. As long as Albert and his associates were merely "guarded" they couldn't enter any formal complaint. But, given half a chance, they would have gotten on their official dignity and demanded that the espionage cease.

From the State Department's point of view it was an excellent rule, but Gene Barlow and the other Service men assigned to follow Albert couldn't see it in that light.

"What's the idea, anyhow?" Gene growled one night as his pet taxicab dashed down Massachusetts Avenue in the wake of the big touring car that was carrying the German attaché to the Union Station. "Here we have to be on the job at all hours, just to watch this Dutchman and see what he does. And," with a note of contempt, "he never does anything worth reporting. Sees half a dozen people, lunches at the German-American Club, drops in at two or three offices downtown, and then back here again. If they'd only let us waylay him and get hold of that black bag that he always carts around there'd[168] be nothing to it. Some day I'm going to do that little thing, just to see what happens."

But Barlow took it out in threats. Secret Service men find pleasure in stating what they are going to do "some day"—but the quality of implicit obedience has been drilled into them too thoroughly for them to forget it, which is possibly the reason why they take such a sheer and genuine delight in going ahead when the restrictions are finally lifted.

It was in New York, more than two years after the war had commenced, that Barlow got his first opportunity to "see what would happen." In the meantime, he had been assigned to half a dozen other cases, but always returned to the shadowing of Doctor Albert because he was the one man who had been eminently successful in that work. The German had an almost uncanny habit of throwing his pursuers off the trail whenever he wanted to and in spite of the efforts of the cleverest men in the Service had disappeared from time to time. The resumption of unrestricted submarine warfare and the delicacy of the diplomatic situation which ensued made it imperative that the "man with the saber scar," as Doctor Albert was known, be kept constantly under surveillance.

"Stick to him, Gene, and don't bother about reporting until you are certain that he will stay put long enough for you to phone," were the instructions that Barlow received. "The doctor must be watched every moment that he's away from the Embassy and it's up to you to do it."

"Anything else beside watching him?" inquired the operative, hopefully.

"No," smiled the chief, "there isn't to be any rough stuff. We're on the verge of an explosion as it is, and anyone who pulls the hair trigger will not only find himself[169] out of a job, but will have the doubtful satisfaction of knowing that he's responsible for wrecking some very carefully laid plans. Where Albert goes, who he talks with and, if possible, a few details of what they discuss, is all that's wanted."

"Wouldn't like to have a piece of the Kaiser's mustache or anything of that kind, would you, Chief?" Barlow retorted. "I could get that for you a whole lot easier than I could find out what the man with the saber scar talks about. He's the original George B. Careful. Never was known to take a chance. Wouldn't bet a nickel against a hundred dollars that the sun would come up to-morrow and always sees to it that his conferences are held behind bolted doors. They even pull down the shades so that no lip reader with a pair of field glasses can get a tip as to what they're talking about."

"That's the reason you were picked for this case," was the chief's reply. "Any strong-arm man could whale Albert over the head and throw him in the river. That wouldn't help any. What we need is information concerning what his plans are, and it takes a clever man to get that."

"All bull and a yard wide!" laughed Gene, but the compliment pleased him, nevertheless. "I'll watch him, but let me know when the lid comes off and I can use other methods."

The chief promised that he would—and it was not more than three weeks later that he had an opportunity to make good.

"Barlow," he directed, speaking over the long-distance phone to the operative in New York, "the Department of Justice has just reported that Doctor Albert is in receipt of a document of some kind—probably a letter of instruction from Berlin—which it is vital that we have at once.[170] Our information is that the message is written on a slip of oiled paper carried inside a dummy lead pencil. It's possible that the doctor has destroyed it, but it isn't probable. Can you get it?"

"How far am I allowed to go?" inquired Gene, hoping for permission to stage a kidnaping of the German attaché, but fully expecting these instructions which followed—orders that he was to do nothing that would cause an open breach, nothing for which Doctor Albert could demand reparation or even an apology.

"In other words," Barlow said to himself, as he hung up the phone, "I'm to accomplish the impossible, blindfolded and with my hands tied. Wonder whether Paula would have a hunch—"

Paula was Barlow's sweetheart, a pretty little brunette who earned a very good salary as private secretary to one of the leading lights of Wall Street—which accounted for the fact that the operative had learned to rely upon her quick flashes of intuitive judgment for help in a number of situations which had required tact as well as action. They were to be married whenever Gene's professional activities subsided sufficiently to allow him to remain home at least one night a month, but, meanwhile, Paula maintained that she would as soon be the wife of an African explorer—"Because at least I would know that he wouldn't be back for six months, while I haven't any idea whether you'll be out of town two days or two years."

After they had talked the Albert matter over from all angles, Paula inquired, "Where would your friend with the saber scar be likely to carry the paper?"

"Either in his pocket or in the black bag that he invariably has with him."

"Hum!" she mused, "if it's in his pocket I don't see that there is anything you can do, short of knocking him down[171] and taking it away from him, and that's barred by the rules of the game. But if it is in the mysterious black bag.... Is the doctor in town now?"

"Yes, he's at the Astor, probably for two or three days. I left Dwyer and French on guard there while I, presumably, snatched a little sleep. But I'd rather have your advice than any amount of rest."

"Thanks," was the girl's only comment, for her mind was busy with the problem. "There's apparently no time to lose, so I'll inform the office the first thing in the morning that I won't be down, meet you in front of the Astor, and we'll see what happens. Just let me stick with you, inconspicuously, and I think that I can guarantee at least an opportunity to lift the bag without giving the German a chance to raise a row."

Thus it was that, early the next day, Gene Barlow was joined by a distinctly personable young woman who, after a moment's conversation, strolled up and down Broadway in front of the hotel.

Some twenty minutes later a man whose face had been disfigured by a saber slash received at Heidelberg came down the steps and asked for a taxi. But Barlow, acting under directions from Paula, had seen that there were no taxis to be had. A flash of his badge and some coin of the realm had fixed that. So Dr. Heinrich Albert, of the German embassy, was forced to take a plebeian surface car—as Paula had intended that he should. The Secret Service operative and his pretty companion boarded the same car a block farther down, two other government agents having held it sufficiently long at Forty-fourth Street to permit of this move.

Worming their way through the crowd when their prey changed to the Sixth Avenue Elevated, Gene and Paula soon reached points of vantage on either side of the[172] German, who carried his black bag tightly grasped in his right hand, and the trio kept this formation until they reached Fiftieth Street, when the girl apparently started to make her way toward the door. Something caused her to stumble, however, and she pitched forward right into the arms of the German, who by that time had secured a seat and had placed his bag beside him, still guarding it with a protecting arm.

Before the foreigner had time to gather his wits, he found himself with a pretty girl literally in his lap—a girl who was manifestly a lady and who blushed to the tips of her ears as she apologized for her awkwardness. Even if the German had been a woman-hater there would have been nothing for him to do but to assist her to her feet, and that, necessarily, required the use of both hands. As it happened, Doctor Albert was distinctly susceptible to feminine charms, and there was something about this girl's smile which was friendly, though embarrassed.

So he spent longer than was strictly essential in helping her to the door—she appeared to have turned her ankle—and then returned to his seat only to find that his portfolio was missing!

Recriminations and threats were useless. A score of people had left the car and, as the guard heartlessly refused to stop the train before the next station, there was naturally not a trace of the girl or the man who had accompanied her. By that time, in fact, Barlow and Paula had slipped into the shelter of a neighboring hotel lobby and were busy inspecting the contents of Doctor Albert's precious brief case.

"Even if there's nothing in it," laughed the girl, "we've had the satisfaction of scaring him to death."

Gene said nothing, but pawed through the papers in frantic haste.[173]

"A slip of oiled paper," he muttered. "By the Lord Harry! here it is!" and he produced a pencil which his trained fingers told him was lighter than it should be. With a wrench he broke off the metal tip that held the eraser, and from within the wooden spindle removed a tightly wrapped roll of very thin, almost transparent paper, covered with unintelligible lettering.

"What's on it?" demanded Paula.

"I'll never tell you," was Barlow's reply. "It would take a better man than I am to decipher this," and he read off:

"I i i t f b b t t x o...."

"Code?" interrupted the girl.

"Sure it is—and apparently a peach." The next moment he had slipped the paper carefully into an inside pocket, crammed the rest of the papers back into the brief case, and was disappearing into a phone booth.

"Better get down to work, dear," he called over his shoulder. "I'm going to report to the office here and then take this stuff down to Washington!" And that was the last that Paula saw of him for a week.

Six hours later Barlow entered the chief's office in the Treasury Department and reported that he had secured the code message.

"So New York phoned," was the only comment from the man who directed the destinies of the Secret Service. "Take it right up to the Navy Department and turn it over to Thurber, the librarian. He'll be able to read it, if anybody can."

Thurber, Gene knew, was the man who was recognizedly the leading authority on military codes and ciphers in the United States, the man who had made a hobby as[174] well as a business of decoding mysterious messages and who had finally deciphered the famous "square letter" code, though it took him months to do it.

"He'll have to work faster than that this time," thought Barlow, as he made his way toward the librarian's office on the fourth floor of the big gray-stone building. "Time's at a premium and Germany moves too fast to waste any of it."

But Thurber was fully cognizant of the necessity for quick action. He had been warned that Barlow was bringing the dispatch and the entire office was cleared for work.

Spreading the oiled paper on a table top made of clear glass, the Librarian turned on a battery of strong electric lights underneath so that any watermark or secret writing would have been at once apparent. But there was nothing on the sheet except line after line of meaningless letters.

"It's possible, of course, that there may be some writing in invisible ink on the sheet," admitted the cipher expert. "But the fact that oiled paper is used would seem to preclude that. The code itself may be any one of several varieties and it's a matter of trying 'em all until you hit upon the right one."

"I thought that Poe's story of 'The Gold Bug' claimed that any cipher could be read if you selected the letter that appeared most frequently and substituted for it the letter 'e,' which is used most often in English, and so on down the list," stated Barlow.

"So it did. But there are lots of things that Poe didn't know about codes." Thurber retorted, his eyes riveted to the sheet before him. "Besides, that was fiction and the author knew just how the code was constructed, while this is fact and we have to depend upon hard work and blind luck.[175]

"There are any number of arbitrary systems which might have been used in writing this message," he continued. "The army clock code is one of them—the one in which a number is added to every letter figure, dependent upon the hour at which the message is written. But I don't think that applies in this case. The cipher doesn't look like it—though I'll have to admit that it doesn't look like any that I've come across before. Let's put it on the blackboard and study it from across the room. That often helps in concentrating."

"You're not going to write the whole thing on the board?" queried the operative.

"No, only the first fifteen letters or so," and Thurber put down this line:
I i i t f b b t t x o r q w s b b

"Translated into what we call 'letter figures,'" he went on, "that would be 9 9 9 20 6 2 2 20 20 24 15 18 17 23 19 2 2—the system where 'a' is denoted by 1, 'b' by 2, and so on. No, that's still meaningless. That repetition of the letter 'i' at the beginning of the message is what makes it particularly puzzling.

"If you don't mind, I'll lock the door and get to work on this in earnest. Where can I reach you by phone?"

Barlow smiled at this polite dismissal and, stating that he would be at headquarters for the rest of the evening and that they would know where to reach him after that, left the office—decidedly doubtful as to Thurber's ability to read the message.

Long after midnight Gene answered a ring from the phone beside his bed and through a haze of sleep heard the voice of the navy librarian inquiring if he still had the other papers which had been in Doctor Albert's bag.[176]

"No," replied the operative, "but I can get them. They are on top of the chief's desk. Nothing in them, though. Went over them with a microscope."

"Just the same," directed Thurber, "I'd like to have them right away. I think I'm on the trail, but the message is impossible to decipher unless we get the code word. It may be in some of the other papers."

Barlow found the librarian red-eyed from his lack of sleep and the strain of the concentration over the code letter. But when they had gone over the papers found in the black bag, even Thurber had to admit that he was checkmated.

"Somewhere," he maintained, "is the one word which will solve the whole thing. I know the type of cipher. It's one that is very seldom used; in fact, the only reference to it that I know of is in Jules Verne's novel *The Giant Raft*. It's a question of taking a key word, using the letter figures which denote this, and adding these to the letter figures of the original letter. That will give you a series of numbers which it is impossible to decipher unless you know the key word. I feel certain that this is a variation of that system, for the fact that two letters appear together so frequently would seem to indicate that the numbers which they represent are higher than twenty-six, the number of the letters in the alphabet."

"One word!" muttered Barlow. Then, seizing what was apparently a memorandum sheet from the pile of Albert's papers, he exclaimed: "Here's a list that neither the chief nor I could make anything of. See? It has twelve numbers, which might be the months of the year, with a name or word behind each one!"

"Yes," replied Thurber, disconsolately, "I saw that the first thing. But this is October and the word corresponding[177] to the number ten is 'Wilhelmstrasse'—and that doesn't help at all. I tried it."

"Then try 'Hohenzollern,' the September word!" snapped Barlow. "This message was presumably written in Berlin and therefore took some time to get over here."

"By George! that's so! A variation of the 'clock code' as well as Verne's idea. Here, read off the letters and I'll put them on the board with the figures representing Hohenzollern underneath. Take the first fifteen as before."

When they had finished, the blackboard bore the following, the first line being the original code letters, the second the letter figures of these, and the third the figures of the word "Hohenzollern" with the first "h" repeated for the fifteenth letter:

I i i t f b b t t x o r q w s b b

i		b		t						b

5	0	8	6	4	5	8	7	3	9	8

5		4	6	5	2	2		8		4

"Why thirty-five for that double 'i' and twenty-eight for the double 'b's'?" asked Barlow.

"Add twenty-six—the total number of letters in the alphabet—to the letter figure for the letter itself," said Thurber. "That's the one beauty of this code, one of the things which helps to throw you off the scent. Now subtracting the two lines we have:

"1 20 12 1 14 20 9 3 6 12 5 5 20"

"We've got it!" he cried an instant later, as he stepped back to look at the figures and read off:

"A t l a n t i c   f l e e t"

[178]

"It was a double code, after all," Thurber stated when he had deciphered the entire message by the same procedure and had reported his discovery to the Secretary of the

Navy over the phone. "Practically infallible, too, save for the fact that I, as well as Doctor Albert, happened to be familiar with Jules Verne. That, plus the doctor's inability to rely on his memory and therefore leaving his key words in his brief case, rendered the whole thing pretty easy."

"Yes," thought Gene, "plus my suggestion of the September word, rather than the October one, and plus Paula's quick wit—that's really all there was to it!" But he kept his thoughts to himself, preferring to allow Thurber to reap all the rewards that were coming to him for the solution of the "double code."

"Do you know what the whole message was?" I inquired, as Quinn stopped his narrative.

"You'll find it pasted on the back of that copy of *The Giant Raft*," replied the former operative. "That's why I claim that the book ought to be preserved as a souvenir of an incident that saved millions of dollars and hundreds of lives."

Turning to the back of the Verne book I saw pasted there the following significant lines:

Atlantic Fleet sails (from) Hampton Roads (at) six (o'clock) morning of seventeenth. Eight U-boats will be waiting. Advise necessary parties and be ready (to) seek safety. Success (of) attack inevitable.

"That means that if Thurber hadn't been able to decipher that code the greater part of our fleet would have been sunk by an unexpected submarine attack, launched[179] by a nation with whom we weren't even at war?" I demanded, when I had finished the message.

"Precisely," agreed Quinn. "But if you'll look up the records you'll find that the fleet did not sail on schedule, while Dr. Heinrich Albert and the entire staff from the house on Massachusetts Avenue were deported before many more weeks had passed. There was no sense in raising a fuss about the incident at the time, for von Bernstorff would have denied any knowledge of the message and probably would have charged that the whole thing was a plant, designed to embroil the United States in the war. So it was allowed to rest for the time being and merely jotted down as another score to be wiped off the slate later on.

"But you have to admit that a knowledge of Jules Verne came in very handy—quite as much so, in fact, as did a knowledge of the habits and disposition of white mice in another case."

"Which one was that?"

Quinn merely pointed to the top of his bookcase, where there reposed a stuffed white mouse, apparently asleep.

"That's a memento of the case," replied the former operative. "I'll tell you of it the next time you drop in."

[180]

XIII
THE TRAIL OF THE WHITE MICE

"The United States Secret Service," announced Bill Quinn, "is by long odds the best known branch of the governmental detective bureaus. The terror which the continental crook feels at the sound of the name 'Scotland Yard' finds its echo on this side of the Atlantic whenever a criminal knows that he has run afoul of the U. S. S. S. For Uncle Sam never forgives an injury or forgets a wrong. Sooner or later he's going to get his man—no matter how long it takes nor how much money it costs.

"But the Secret Service, strictly speaking, is only one branch of the organization. There are others which work just as quietly and just as effectively. The Department of Justice, which had charge of the violation of neutrality laws, banking, and the like; the Treasury Department, which, through the Customs Service and the Bureau of Internal Revenue, wages constant war on the men and women who think they can evade the import regulations and the laws against illicit manufacture of alcohol; the Pension Bureau of the Interior Department, which is called upon to handle hundreds of frauds every year; and the Post Office Department, which guards the millions of dollars intrusted to the mails.

"Each of these has its own province. Each works along its own line in conjunction with the others, and[181] each of them is, in reality, a secret organization which performs a vastly important service to the nation as a whole. When you speak of the Secret Service, the Treasury Department's organization comes immediately to mind—coupled with a panorama of counterfeiters, anarchists, revolutionaries, and the like. But the field of the Secret Service is really limited when compared to the scope of the other organizations.

"Look around this room"—and he made a gesture which included the four walls of the library den in which we were seated, a room in which the usual decorations had been replaced by a strange collection of unusual and, in a number of instances, gruesome relics. "Every one of those objects is a memento of some exploit of the men engaged in Secret Service," Quinn went on. "That Chinese hatchet up there came very close to being buried in the skull of a man in San Diego, but its principal mission in life was the solution of the mystery surrounding the smuggling of thousands of pounds of opium. That water-stained cap was fished out of the Missouri after its owner had apparently committed suicide—but the Pension Bureau located him seven years later, with the aid of a fortune teller in Seattle. At the side of the bookcase there you will find several of the original poison-pen letters which created so much consternation in Kansas City a few years ago, letters which Allison of the Postal Inspection Service finally traced to their source after the local authorities had given up the case as impossible of solution.

"The woman whose picture appears on the other wall was known as Mrs. Armitage—and that was about all that they did know about her, save that she was connected with one of the foreign organizations and that in some mysterious way she knew everything that was going[182]on in the State Department almost as soon as it was started. And there, under that piece of silk which figured in one of the boldest smuggling cases that the Treasury Department ever tackled, is the blurred postmark which eventually led to the discovery of the man who murdered Montgomery Marshall—a case in which our old friend Sherlock Holmes would have reveled. But it's doubtful if he could have solved it any more skillfully than did one of the Post Office operatives."

"What's the significance of that white mouse on the mantelpiece?" I inquired, sensing the fact that Quinn was in one of his story-telling moods.

"It hasn't any significance," replied the former government agent, "but it has a story—one which illustrates my point that all the nation's detective work isn't handled by the Secret Service, by a long shot. Did you ever hear of H. Gordon Fowler, alias W. C. Evans?"

"No," I replied, "I don't think I ever did."

"Well, a lot of people have—to their sorrow," laughed Quinn, reaching for his pipe.

No one appears to know what Fowler's real name is [continued the former operative]. He traveled under a whole flock of aliases which ran the gamut of the alphabet from Andrews to Zachary, but, to save mixing things up, suppose that we assume that his right name was Fowler. He used it for six months at one time, out in Minneapolis, and got away with twenty thousand dollars' worth of stuff.

For some time previous to Fowler's entrance upon the scene various wholesale houses throughout the country had been made the victims of what appeared to be a ring of bankruptcy experts—men who would secure credit for goods, open a store, and then "fail." Meanwhile the[183] merchandise would have mysteriously vanished and the proprietor would be away on a "vacation" from which, of course, he would never return.

On the face of it this was a matter to be settled solely by the Wholesalers' Credit Association, but the Postal Inspection Service got into it through the fact that the mails were palpably being used with intent to defraud and therefore Uncle Sam came to the aid of the business men.

On the day that the matter was reported to Washington the chief of the Postal Inspection Service pushed the button which operated a buzzer in the outer office and summoned Hal Preston, the chap who later on was responsible for the solution of the Marshall murder mystery.

"Hal," said the chief, with a smile, "here's a case I know you'll like. It's right in the line of routine and it ought to mean a lot of traveling around the country—quick jumps at night and all that sort of stuff."

Preston grunted, but said nothing. You couldn't expect to draw the big cases every time, and, besides, there was no telling when something might break even in the most prosaic of assignments.

"Grant, Wilcox & Company, in Boston, report that they've been stung twice in the same place by a gang of bankruptcy sharks," the chief went on. "And they're not the only ones who have suffered. Here's a list of the concerns and the men that they've sold to. You'll see that it covers the country from Hoquiam, Washington, to Montclair, New Jersey—so they appear to have their organization pretty well in hand. Ordinarily we wouldn't figure in this thing at all—but the gang made the mistake of placing their orders through the mail and now it's up to us to land 'em. Here's the dope. Hop to it!"

That night, while en route to Mount Clemens, Michigan, where the latest of the frauds had been perpetrated,[184] Preston examined the envelope full of evidence and came to a number of interesting conclusions. In the first place the failures had been staged in a number of different localities—Erie, Pennsylvania, had had one of them under the name of "Cole & Hill"; there had been another in Sioux City, where Immerling Brothers had failed; Metcalf and Newman, Illinois, had likewise contributed their share, as had Minneapolis, Newark, Columbus, White Plains, and Newburg, New York; San Diego, California; Hoquiam, Washington, and several other points.

But the point that brought Hal up with a jerk was the dates attached to each of these affairs. No two of them had occurred within six months of the other and several were separated by as much as a year.

"Who said this was a gang?" he muttered. "Looks a lot more like the work of a single man with plenty of nerve and, from the amount of stuff he got away with, he ought to be pretty nearly in the millionaire class by now. There's over two hundred thousand dollars' worth of goods covered by this report alone and there's no certainty that it is complete. Well, here's hoping—it's always easier to trail one man than a whole bunch of 'em."

In Mount Clemens Preston found further evidence which tended to prove that the bankruptcy game was being worked by a single nervy individual, posing under the name of "Henry Gerard."

Gerard, it appeared, had entered the local field about a year before, apparently with plenty of capital, and had opened two prosperous stores on the principal street. In August, about two months before Preston's arrival, the proprietor of the Gerard stores had left on what was apparently scheduled for a two weeks' vacation. That was the last that had been heard of him, in spite of the fact that a number of urgent creditors had camped upon[185] his trail very solicitously. The stores had been looted, only enough merchandise being left to keep up the fiction of a complete stock, and Gerard had vanished with the proceeds.

After making a few guarded inquiries in the neighborhood of the store, Preston sought out the house where Gerard had boarded during his stay in Mount Clemens. There he found that the missing merchant, in order to allay suspicion, had paid the rental of his apartment for three months in advance, and that the place had not been touched since, save by the local authorities who had been working on the case.

"You won't find a thing there," the chief of police informed Hal, in response to a request for information. "Gerard's skipped and that's all there is to it. We've been over the place with a fine-tooth comb and there ain't a scrap of evidence. We did find some telegrams torn up in his waste basket, but if you can make anything out of 'em it's more than I can," and he handed over an envelope filled with scraps of finely torn yellow paper.

"Not the slightest indication of where Gerard went?" inquired Preston as he tucked the envelope in an inside pocket.

"Not a bit," echoed the chief. "He may be in China now, so far as we know."

"Was he married?"

"Nobody here knows nothin' about him," the chief persisted. "They do say as how he was right sweet on a girl named Anna Something-or-other who lived in the same block. But she left town before he did, and she 'ain't come back, neither."

"What did you say her name was?"

"Anna Vaughan, I b'lieve she called herself. You might ask Mrs. Morris about her. She had a room at[186] her place, only a few doors away from where Gerard stayed."

The apartment of the man who had vanished, Preston found, was furnished in the manner typical of a thousand other places. Every stick of furniture appeared to have seen better days and no two pieces could be said to match. Evidently Gerard had been practicing economy in his domestic arrangements in order to save all the money possible for a quick getaway. What was more, he had carefully removed everything of a personal nature, save a row of books which decorated the mantel piece in one of the rooms.

It was toward these that Preston finally turned in desperation. All but one of them were the cheaper grade of fiction, none of which bore any distinguishing marks, but the exception was a new copy of the latest Railroad Guide. Just as Preston pounced upon this he heard a chuckle from behind him and, whirling, saw the chief of police just entering the door.

"Needn't worry with that, young man," he urged. "I've been all through it and there ain't nothin' in it. Just thought I'd drop up to see if you'd found anything," he added, in explanation of his sudden appearance. "Have you?"

"No," admitted the postal operative. "Can't say that I have. This is the first piece of personal property that I've been able to locate and you say there is nothing in this?"

"Nary a clue," persisted the chief, but Preston, as if loath to drop the only tangible reminder of Gerard, idly flipped the pages of the Guide, and then stood it on edge on the table, the covers slightly opened. Then, as the chief watched him curiously, he closed the book, opened it again and repeated the operation.[187]

"What's the idea? Tryin' to make it do tricks?" the chief asked as Hal stood the book on edge for the third time.

"Hardly that. Just working on a little theory of my own," was the response, as the post-office man made a careful note of the page at which the Guide had fallen open—the same one which had presented itself to view on the two other occasions. "Here, would you like to try it?" and he handed the volume to the chief. But that functionary only shrugged his shoulders and replaced the Guide upon the mantelpiece.

"Some more of your highfalutin' detective work, eh?" he muttered. "Soon you'll be claimin' that books can talk."

"Possibly not out loud," smiled Hal. "But they can be made to tell very interesting stories now and then, if you know how to handle 'em. There doesn't seem to be much here, Chief, so I think I'll go back to the hotel. Let me know if anything comes up, will you?" And with that he left.

But before returning to the hotel he stopped at the house where Anna Vaughan had resided and found out from the rather garrulous landlady that Gerard had appeared to be rather smitten with the beautiful stranger.

"She certainly was dressed to kill," said the woman who ran the establishment. "A big woman and strong as all outdoors. Mr. Gerard came here three or four nights a week while she was with us and he didn't seem to mind the mice at all."

"Mind the what?" snapped Preston.

"The mice—the white mice that she used to keep as pets," explained the landlady. "Had half a dozen or more of them running over her shoulders, but I told her that I couldn't stand for that. She could keep 'em in her[188] room if she wanted to, but I had to draw the line somewhere. Guess it was on their account that she didn't have any other visitors. S'far as I know Mr. Gerard was the only one who called on her."

"When did Miss Vaughan leave?" Hal inquired.

"Mrs. Vaughan," corrected the woman. "She was a widow—though she was young and pretty enough to have been married any time she wanted to be. Guess the men wouldn't stand for them mice, though. She didn't stay very long—just about six weeks. Left somewheres about the middle of July."

"About two weeks before Gerard did?"

"About that—though I don't just remember the date."

A few more inquiries elicited the fact that Mrs. Vaughan's room had been rented since her departure, so Preston gave up the idea of looking through it for possible connecting links with the expert in bankruptcy.

Returning to the hotel, the operative settled down to an examination of the scraps of torn telegrams which the chief had handed him. Evidently they had been significant, he argued, for Gerard had been careful to tear them into small bits, and it was long past midnight before he had succeeded in piecing the messages together, pasting the scraps on glass in case there had been any notations on the reverse of the blank.

But when he had finished he found that he had only added one more puzzling aspect to the case.

There were three telegrams, filed within a week and all dated just before Gerard had left town.

"Geraldine, Anna, May, and Florence are in Chicago," read the message from Evanston, Illinois.

"George, William, Katherine, Ray, and Stephen still in St. Louis," was the wire filed from Detroit.

The third message, from Minneapolis, detailed the fact[189] that "Frank, Vera, Marguerite, Joe, and Walter are ready to leave St. Paul."

None of the telegrams was signed, but, merely as a precaution, Preston wired Evanston, Detroit, and Minneapolis to find out if there was any record of who had sent them.

"Agent here recalls message," came the answer from Detroit the next day. "Filed by woman who refused to give her name. Agent says sender was quite large, good-looking, and very well dressed."

"Anna Vaughan!" muttered Preston, as he tucked the telegram in his pocket and asked to be shown a copy of the latest Railway Guide.

Referring to a note which he had made on the previous evening, Hal turned to pages 251-2, the part of the book which had fallen open three times in succession when he had examined it in Gerard's rooms, and noted that it was the Atchinson, Topeka & Santa Fé time-table, westbound. Evidently the missing merchant had invested in a copy of the Guide rather than run the risk of leaving telltale time-tables around his apartment, but he had overstepped himself by referring to only one portion of the book.

"Not the first time that a crook has been just a little too clever," mused Preston, with a smile. "If it had been an old copy, there wouldn't have been any evidence—but a new book, opened several times at the same place, can be made to tell tales—his honor, the chief of police, to the contrary."

It was clear, therefore, that Preston had three leads to work on: Anna Vaughan, a large, beautiful woman, well-dressed and with an affection for white mice; the clue that Gerard was somewhere in the Southwest and at least the first names of fourteen men and women connected with the gang.[190]

But right there he paused. Was there any gang? The dates of the various disappearances tended to prove that there wasn't, but the messages received by Gerard certainly appeared to point to the fact that others were connected with the conspiracy to defraud.

Possibly one of the clerks who had been connected with the Gerard stores would be able to throw a little light upon the situation....

It wasn't until Hal interviewed the woman who had acted as cashier and manager for the second store that he found the lead he was after. In response to his inquiry as to whether she had ever heard the missing proprietor speak of any of the persons mentioned in the wires, the cashier at first stated definitely that she hadn't, but added, a moment later:

"Come to think of it, he did. Not as people, but as trunks."

"What's that?" exclaimed the operative. "Trunks?"

"Yes. I remember sometime last spring, when we were figuring on how much summer goods we ought to carry, I mentioned the matter to Mr. Gerard, and almost automatically he replied, 'I'll wire for Edna and Grace.' Thinking he meant saleswomen, I reminded him that we had plenty, particularly for the slack season. He colored up a bit, caught his breath, and turned the subject by stating that he always referred to trunks of goods in terms of people's first names—girls for the feminine stuff and men's for the masculine. But Edna and Grace weren't on your list, were they?"

"No," replied Preston. "But that doesn't matter. Besides, didn't the two trunks of goods arrive?"

"Yes, they came in a couple of weeks later."

"Before Mrs. Vaughan came to town?"

"Oh yes, some time before she arrived."[191]

"I thought so," was Preston's reply, and, thanking the girl, he wandered back to the hotel—convinced that he had solved at least one of the mysteries, the question of what Gerard did with his surplus "bankrupt stock." It was evidently packed in trunks and shipped to distant points, to be forwarded by the Vaughan woman upon instructions from Gerard himself. The wires he had torn up were merely confirmatory messages, sent so that he would have the necessary information before making a getaway.

"Clever scheme, all right," was Hal's mental comment. "Now the next point is to find some town in the Southwest where a new store has been opened within the past two months."

That night the telegraph office at Mount Clemens did more business than it had had for the past year. Wires, under the government frank, went out to every town on the Atchison, Topeka & Santa Fé and to a number of adjacent cities. In each case the message was the same:

Wire name of any new clothing store opened within past two months. Also description of proprietor. Urgent.

PRESTON,
U. S. P. I. S.

Fourteen chiefs of police replied within the next forty-eight hours, but of these only two—Leavenworth and Fort Worth—contained descriptions which tallied with that of Henry Gerard.

So, to facilitate matters, Preston sent another wire:

Has proprietor mentioned in yesterday's wire a wife or woman friend who keeps white mice as pets?

Fort Worth replied facetiously that the owner of the new store there was married, but that his wife had a cat—which[192] might account for the absence of the mice. Leavenworth, however, came back with:

Yes, Mrs. Noble, wife of owner of Outlet Store, has white mice for pets. Why?

Never mind reason [Preston replied]. Watch Noble and wife until I arrive. Leaving to-day.

Ten minutes after reaching Leavenworth Preston was ensconced in the office of the chief of police, outlining the reason for his visit.

"I'm certain that Noble is the man you want," said the chief, when Hal had finished. "He came here some six weeks or more ago and at once leased a store, which he opened a few days later. The description fits him to a T, except for the fact that he's evidently dispensed with the mustache. The Vaughan woman is posing as his wife and they've rented a house on the outskirts of town. What do you want me to do? Nab 'em right away?"

"No," directed the operative. "I'd rather attend to that myself, if you don't object. After trailing them this far, I'd like to go through with it. You might have some men handy, though, in case there's any fuss."

Just as Mr. and Mrs. C. K. Noble were sitting down to dinner there was a ring at their front-door bell and Noble went to see who it was.

"I'd like to speak to Mr. H. Gordon Fowler," said Preston, his hand resting carelessly in the side pocket of his coat.

"No Mr. Fowler lives here," was the growling reply from the inside.

"Then Mr. W. C. Evans or Mr. Henry Gerard will do!" snapped the operative, throwing his shoulder against the partly opened door. Noble—or Fowler, as he was afterward[193] known—stepped aside as Hal plunged through, and then slammed the door behind him.

89

"Get him, Anna!" he called, throwing the safety bolt into position.

The next thing that Preston knew, a pair of arms, bare and feminine but strong as iron, had seized him around the waist and he was in imminent danger of being bested by a woman. With a heave and a wriggling twist he broke the hold and turned, just in time to see Fowler snatch a revolver from a desk on the opposite side of the room and raise it into position. Without an instant's hesitation he leaped to one side, dropped his hand into his coat pocket, and fired. Evidently the bullet took effect, for the man across the room dropped his gun, spun clean around and then sank to the floor. As he did so, however, the woman hurled a heavy vase directly at Preston's head and the operative sank unconscious.

"Well, go on!" I snapped, when Quinn paused. "You sound like a serial story—to be continued in our next. What happened then?"

"Nothing—beyond the fact that three policemen broke in some ten seconds after Hal fired, grabbed Mrs. Vaughan or whatever her name was, and kept her from beating Hal to death, as she certainly would have done in another minute. Fowler wasn't badly hurt. In fact, both of them stood trial the next spring—Fowler drawing six years and Anna Vaughan one. Incidentally, they sent 'em back to Leavenworth to do time and, as a great concession, allowed the woman to take two of her white mice with her. I managed to get one of the other four, and, when it died, had it stuffed as a memento of a puzzling case well solved.

"It's a hobby of mine—keeping these relics. That[194] hatchet, for example.... Remind me to tell you about it some time. The mice were responsible for finding one man in fifty million—which is something of a job in itself—but the hatchet figured in an even more exciting affair...."

[195]

XIV
WAH LEE AND THE FLOWER OF HEAVEN

"Yes, there's quite a story attached to that," remarked Bill Quinn one evening as the conversation first lagged and then drifted away into silence. We were seated in his den at the time—the "library" which he had ornamented with relics of a score or more of cases in which the various governmental detective services had distinguished themselves—and I came to with a start.

"What?" I exclaimed. "Story in what?"

"In that hatchet—the one on the wall there that you were speculating about. It didn't take a psychological sleuth to follow your eyes and read the look of speculation in them. That's a trick that a 'sparrow cop' could pull!"

"Well, then, suppose you pay the penalty for your wisdom—and spin the yarn," I retorted, none the less glad of the opportunity to hear the facts behind the sinister red stain which appeared on the blade of the Chinese weapon, for I knew that Quinn could give them to me if he wished.

"Frankly, I don't know the full history of the hatchet," came the answer from the other side of the fireplace. "Possibly it goes back to the Ming dynasty—whenever that was—or possibly it was purchased from a mail-order house in Chicago. Chop suey isn't the only Chinese article made in this country, you know. But my interest in it commenced with the night when Ezra Marks[196]—

"However, let's start at the beginning."

Marks [continued the former operative] was, as you probably recall, one of the best men ever connected with the Customs Service. It was he who solved the biggest diamond-smuggling case on record, and he was also responsible for the discovery of the manner in which thirty thousand yards of very valuable silk was being run into the country every year without visiting the custom office. That's a piece of the silk up there, over the picture of Mrs. Armitage....

It wasn't many months before the affair of the Dillingham diamonds that official Washington in general and the offices of the Customs Service in particular grew quite excited over the fact that a lot of opium was finding its way into California. Of course, there's always a fair amount of "hop" on the market, provided you know where to look for it, and the government has about as much chance of keeping it out altogether as it has of breaking up the trade in moonshine whisky. The mountaineer is going to have his "licker" and the Chink is going to have his dope—no matter what you do. But it's up to the Internal Revenue Bureau and the Customs Service to see that neither one arrives in wholesale quantities. And that was just what was happening on the Coast.

In fact, it was coming in so fast that the price was dropping every day and the California authorities fairly burned up the wires 'cross continent with their howls for help.

At that time Marks—Ezra by name and "E. Z." by nickname—was comparatively a new member of the force. He had rendered valuable service in Boston, however, and the chief sent for him and put the whole thing in his hands.[197]

"Get out to San Diego as quickly as you know how," snapped the chief, tossing over a sheaf of yellow telegraph slips. "There's all the information we have, and apparently you won't get much more out there—unless you dig it up for yourself. All they seem to know is that the stuff is coming in by the carload and is being peddled in all the hop joints at a lower price than ever before. It's up to you to get the details. Any help you need will be supplied from the San Francisco office, but my advice is to play a lone hand—you're likely to get further than if you have a gang with you all the time."

"That's my idear, Chief," drawled Ezra, who hailed from Vermont and had all the New Englander's affection for single-handed effort, not because he had the least objection to sharing the glory, but simply because he considered it the most efficient way to work. "I'll get right out there and see how the land lays."

"Needn't bother to report until you discover something worth while," added the chief. "I'll know that you're on the job and the farther you keep away from headquarters the less suspicion you're likely to arouse."

This was the reason that, beyond the fact they knew that an operative named Marks had been sent from Washington to look into the opium matter, the government agents on the Coast were completely in the dark as to the way in which the affair was being handled. In fact, the chief himself was pretty well worried when two months slipped by without a word from Ezra....

But the big, raw-boned Yankee was having troubles of his own. Likewise, he took his instructions very seriously and didn't see the least reason for informing Washington of the very patent fact that he had gotten nowhere and found out nothing.

"They know where they can reach me," he argued to[198] himself one night, about the time that the chief began to wonder if his man were floating around the bay with a piece of Chinese rope about his neck. "Unless I get a wire they won't hear anything until I have at least a line on this gang."

Then, on going over the evidence which he had collected during the weeks that he had been in San Diego, he found that there was extremely little of it. Discreet questioning had developed the fact, which he already knew, that opium was plentiful all along the

Coast, and that, presumably, it was supplied from a point in the south of the state. But all his efforts to locate the source of the drug brought him up against a blank wall.

In order to conduct his investigations with a minimum of suspicion, Marks had elected to enter San Diego in the guise of a derelict—a character which he had played to such perfection that two weeks after he arrived he found himself in court on the charge of vagrancy. Only the fact that the presiding magistrate did not believe in sentencing first offenders saved him from ten days in the workhouse, an opportunity which he was rather sorry to miss because he figured that he might pick up some valuable leads from the opium addicts among his fellow prisoners.

The only new point which he had developed during his stay in the underworld was that some one named Sprague, presumably an American, was the brains of the opium ring and had perfected the entire plan. But who Sprague was or where he might be found were matters which were kept in very watchful secrecy.

"I give it up," muttered the operative, shrugging his arms into a threadbare coat and shambling out of the disreputable rooming house which passed for home. "Work doesn't seem to get me anywhere. Guess I'll have[199] to trust to luck," and he wandered out for his nightly stroll through the Chinese quarter, hoping against hope that something would happen.

It did—in bunches!

Possibly it was luck, possibly it was fate—which, after all, is only another name for luck—that brought him into an especially unsavory portion of the city shortly after midnight.

He had wandered along for three hours or more, with no objective in view save occasional visits to dives where he was known, when he heard something which caused him to whirl and automatically reach for his hip pocket. It was the cry of a woman, shrill and clear—the cry of a woman in mortal danger!

It had only sounded once, but there was a peculiar muffled quality at the end of the note, suggestive of a hand or a gag having been placed over the woman's mouth. Then—silence, so still as to be almost oppressive.

Puzzled, Marks stood stock still and waited. So far as he could remember that was the first time that he had heard anything of the kind in Chinatown. He knew that there were women there, but they were kept well in the background and, apparently, were content with their lot. The woman who had screamed, however, was in danger of her life. Behind one of those flimsy walls some drama was being enacted in defiance of the law—something was being done which meant danger of the most deadly kind to him who dared to interfere.

For a full minute Marks weighed the importance of his official mission against his sense of humanity. Should he take a chance on losing his prey merely to try to save a woman's life? Should he attempt to find the house from which the scream had come and force the door? Should he....[200]

But the question was solved for him in a manner even more startling than the cry in the night.

While he was still debating the door of a house directly in front of him opened wide and a blinding glare of light spread fanwise into the street. Across this there shot the figure of what Marks at first took to be a man—a figure attired in a long, heavily embroidered jacket and silken trousers. As it neared him, however, the operative sensed that it was a woman, and an instant later he knew that it was the woman whose stifled scream had halted him only a moment before.

Straight toward Marks she came and, close behind her—their faces set in a look of deadly implacable rage—raced two large Chinamen.

Probably realizing that she stood no chance of escape in the open street, the woman darted behind Marks and prepared to dodge her pursuers. As she did so the operative caught her panting appeal: "Save me! For the sake of the God, save me!"

That was all that was necessary. Ezra sensed in an instant the fact that he had become embroiled in what bade fair to be a tragedy and braced himself for action. He knew that he had no chance for holding off both men, particularly as he did not care to precipitate gun play, but there was the hope that he might divert them until the girl escaped.

As the first of the two men leaped toward him, Marks swung straight for his jaw, but his assailant ducked with what was almost professional rapidity and the blow was only a glancing one. Before the operative had time to get set the other man was upon him and, in utter silence save for their labored breathing and dull thuds as blows went home, they fought their way back to the far side of the street. As he retreated, Marks became conscious that[201]instead of making her escape, the girl was still behind him. The reason for this became apparent when the larger of the Chinamen suddenly raised his arm and the light from the open doorway glinted on the blade of a murderous short-handled axe—the favorite weapon of Tong warfare. Straight for his head the blade descended, but the girl's arm, thrust out of the darkness behind him, diverted the blow and the hatchet fairly whistled as it passed within an inch of his body.

Realizing that his only hope of safety lay in reaching the opposite side of the sidewalk, where he would be able to fight with his back against the wall, Marks resumed his retreat, his arms moving like flails, his fists crashing home blows that lost much of their power by reason of the heavily padded jackets of his opponents. Finally, after seconds that seemed like hours, one of his blows found the jaw of the man nearest him, and Marks wheeled to set himself for the onrush of the other—the man with the hatchet.

But just at that moment his foot struck the uneven curbing and threw him off his balance. He was conscious of an arc of light as the blade sang through the air; he heard a high, half-muffled cry from the girl beside him; and he remembered trying to throw himself out of the way of the hatchet. Then there was a stinging, smarting pain in the side of his head and in his left shoulder—followed by the blackness of oblivion.

From somewhere, apparently a long distance off, there came a voice which brought back at least a part of the operative's fast failing consciousness, a voice which called a name vaguely familiar to him:

"Sprague! Sprague!"

"Sprague?" muttered Marks, trying to collect himself. "Who—is—Sprague?"[202]

Then, as he put it later, he "went off."

How much time elapsed before he came to he was unable to say, but subsequent developments indicated that it was at least a day and a night. He hadn't the slightest idea what had occurred meanwhile—he only knew that he seemed to drift back to consciousness and a realization that his head was splitting as if it would burst. Mechanically he stretched his legs and tried to rise, only to find that what appeared to be a wooden wall closed him in on all sides, leaving an opening only directly above him.

For an appreciable time he lay still, trying to collect his thoughts. He recalled the fight in the open street, the intervention of the girl, the fall over the curb and then—there was something that he couldn't remember, something vital that had occurred just after he had tried to dodge the hatchet blade.

"Yes," he murmured, as memory returned, "it was some one calling for 'Sprague—Sprague!'"

"Hush!" came a whispered command out of the darkness which surrounded him, and a hand, soft and very evidently feminine, covered his mouth. "You must not mention that name here. It means the death, instant and terrible! They are discussing your fate in there now, but if they had thought that you knew Wah Lee your life would not be worth a yen."

"Wah Lee? Who is he?" Marks replied, his voice pitched in an undertone. "I don't remember any Wah Lee. And who are you?"

"Who I am does not matter," came out of the darkness, "but Wah Lee—he is the master of life and death—the high priest of the Flower of Heaven. Had it not been for him you would have been dead before this."

"But I thought—"[203]

"That he desired your life? So he did—and does. But they have to plan the way in which it is to be taken and the disposition which is to be made of your body. That was what gave me my opportunity for binding up your wound and watching for you to wake."

In spite of himself Marks could not repress a slight shudder. So they were saving him for the sacrifice, eh? They were going to keep him here until their arrangements were complete and then make away with him, were they?

Moving cautiously, so as to avoid attracting attention, the operative slipped his right hand toward his hip pocket, only to find that his automatic was missing. As he settled back with a half moan, he felt something cold slipped into the box beside him, and the girl's voice whispered:

"Your revolver. I secured it when they brought you in here. I thought you might need it later. But be very careful. They must not suspect that you have wakened."

"I will," promised Marks, "but who are you? Why should you take such an interest in me?"

"You tried to save me from something that is worse than death," replied the girl. "You failed, but it was not your fault. Could I do less than to help you?"

"But what was it you feared?"

"Marriage! Marriage to the man I loathe above all others—the man who is responsible for the opium that is drugging my people—the man who is known as Wah Lee, but who is really an American." Here she hesitated for a moment and then hissed:

"Sprague!"

"Sprague?" Marks echoed, sitting bolt upright. But the girl had gone, swallowed up somewhere in the impenetrable darkness which filled the room.

His brain cleared by the realization that he had blundered[204] into the heart of the opium-runners' den, it took Ezra only a few seconds to formulate a plan of action. The first thing, of course, was to get away. But how could that be accomplished when he did not even know where he was or anything about the house? The girl had said something about the fact that "they were considering his fate." Who were "they" and where were they?

Obviously, the only way to find this out was to do a little scouting on his own account, so, slowly and carefully, he raised himself clear of the boxlike arrangement in which he had been placed and tried to figure out his surroundings. His hand, groping over the side, came into almost instant contact with the floor and he found it a simple matter to step out into what appeared to be a cleared space in the center of a comparatively large room. Then, curious as to the place where he had been concealed, he felt the box from one end to the other. The sides were about two feet high and slightly sloping, with an angle near the head. In fact, both ends of the affair were narrower than the portion which had been occupied by his shoulders. Piled up at either end of this box were others, of the same shape and size. What could their purpose be? Why the odd shape?

Suddenly the solution of the mystery flashed across the operative's mind—coffins! Coffins which appeared to be piled up on all sides of the storeroom. Was this the warehouse for a Chinese undertaker or was it—

One coffin over which he nearly tripped gave him the answer. It was partly filled with cans, unlabeled and quite heavy—containers which Marks felt certain were packed full of opium and smuggled in some manner inside the coffins.

Just as he arrived at this conclusion Marks' eye was[205] caught by a tiny streak of light filtering through the wall on the opposite side of the room. Making his way carefully toward this, he found that the crack presented a fairly complete view of an adjoining apartment in which three Chinese, evidently of high degree, were sorting money and entering accounts in large books.

As he looked, a fourth figure entered the room—a man who caused him to catch his breath and flatten himself against the wall, for he recognized the larger of the two Chinamen who had attacked him the night before—or whenever it was. This was the man to whom the girl had alluded as "Wah Lee, High Priest of the Flower of Heaven"—which was merely another way of saying that he had charge of the opium shipments.

As he entered the others rose and remained standing until he had seated himself. Then one of them commenced to speak in rapid, undistinguishable Chinese. Before he had had time to pronounce more than a few words, however, Wah Lee interrupted him with a command couched in English to: "Cut that out! You know I don't understand that gibberish well enough to follow you."

"Beg pardon," replied the other. "I always forget. You are so like one of us that, even in private, I find it hard to remember."

Wah Lee said nothing, but, slipping off his silken jacket, settled back at his ease. A moment later Marks was amazed to see him remove his mandarin's cap, and with it came a wig of coal-black hair!

For the first time the government agent realized what the girl had meant when she intimated that Wah Lee and Sprague were one and the same—an American who was masquerading as Chinese in order to further his smuggling plans!

"Word has just arrived," continued the man who had[206] first spoken, "that the boat will be off Point Banda to-night. That will allow us to pick up the coffins before daybreak and bury them until such time as the American hounds are off their guard."

"Yes," grunted Sprague, "and let's hope that that's soon. We must have fifty thousand dollars' worth of the stuff cached on the other side of the border and orders are coming in faster than we can fill them. I think it would be best to run this cargo right in. We can stage a funeral, if necessary, and avoid suspicion in that way. Wait a minute! I've got a hunch! What about the bum we carried in here last night—the one that tried to help Anita in her getaway?"

"Anita?"

"Yes, my girl. I can't remember that rigmarole you people call her. Anita's her name from now on."

"He is in the next room, unconscious. Two of the men dumped him in one of the empty coffins and let him stay there."

"Good," chuckled Sprague. "We'll just let him remain—run him across the border, and bring his body back in a big hearse. The coffin and the body will be real, but there'll be enough cans of dope packed in and around him and in the carriages of the 'mourners' to make us all rich. It's the chance of a lifetime for a big play, because no one will ever suspect us or even inquire into his identity."

Behind the thin wall which separated him from the next room Marks stiffened and his fingers wound themselves even more tightly around the butt of his automatic. It is not given to many men to hear their death sentence pronounced in a manner as dramatic and cold-blooded as were the words which came from the outer apartment. By listening intently, Ezra learned that the coup would[207] be sprung sometime within the next few hours, the conspirators feeling that it would not be safe to delay, as the opium shipment was due before dawn.

Moving silently and aided somewhat by the fact that his eyes had become a little accustomed to the inky blackness, Marks made his way back to the place where he had awakened. He knew that that was where they would expect to find him and he also knew that this was the one place to avoid. So he located the door and, finding it bolted from the outside, placed himself where he would be at least partly sheltered when the party entered.

After what seemed to be an interminable time he finally heard a sound from the hallway—the soft slip-slip of felt shoes approaching. Then the bolt was withdrawn and the door opened, admitting the four men whom he had seen in the other room, and behind them, carrying a lantern, came the girl.

Nerving himself for a supreme leap, Marks waited until all five visitors were inside the room, and then started to slip through the open doorway. But his movement attracted the attention of the man called Sprague and, with a cry of warning, he wheeled and fired before the operative could gain the safety of the hall. Knowing that his body, outlined against the light from outside, would make an ideal target, Ezra dropped to the floor and swung his automatic into action. As he did so the girl extinguished the lantern with a single swift blow, leaving the room in total blackness, save for the path made by the light in the hallway.

For probably twenty seconds there wasn't a sound. Then Marks caught a glimpse of a moving figure and fired, leaping to one side as he did so in order to avoid the fusillade directed at the flash of his revolver. By a cry from the other side of the room he knew that his shot[208] had gone home, and a moment later he had an opportunity to wing another of his assailants, again drawing a volley of shots. The last shot in his clip was fired with a prayer—but it evidently went home, for only silence, punctuated by moans from the opposite side of the room, ensued.

"That night," concluded Quinn, "a big sailing vessel was met off Point Banda and they found a full month's supply of opium aboard of her. A search of Lower California, near the border, also disclosed a burying ground with many of the graves packed with cans of the drug. The raid, of course, was a violation of Mexican neutrality—but they got away with it."

"The girl?" I cut in. "What became of her?"

"When the police reached the house a few moments after Marks had fired the last shot, they found that Sprague was dead with one of Ezra's bullets through his brain. The three Chinamen were wounded, but not fatally. The girl, however, was huddled in a corner, dead. No one ever discovered whether she stopped one of the bullets from Marks's revolver or whether she was killed by Sprague's men as a penalty for putting out the lantern. Undoubtedly, that saved Ezra's life—which was the reason that he saw that she was given a decent funeral and an adequate memorial erected over her grave.

"He also kept her jacket as a memento of the affair, turning the hatchet over to me for my collection. Under it you will find a copy of the wire he sent the chief."

Curious, I went over and read the yellow slip framed beneath the weapon:

Opium smuggled in coffins. American, at head of ring, dead. Gang broken up. Opium seized. What next?

MARKS.

[209]

"Didn't wait long for another assignment, did he?" I inquired.

"No," was the response. "When you're working for Uncle Sam you come to find that excitement is about the only thing that keeps your nerves quiet. Sometimes, as in Marks's case, it's the thrill of the actual combat. But more often it's the search for a tangible clue—the groping in the dark for something you know exists but which you can't lay your hands on. That was the trouble with the Cheney case...."

[210]

XV
THE MAN WITH THREE WIVES

One of the first things to strike the eye of the visitor who enters the library-den of William J. Quinn—known to his friends and former associates in the United States Secret Service as "Bill"—is a frame which stands upon the mantel and contains the photographs of three exceptionally pretty women.

Anyone who doesn't know that this room is consecrated to relics of the exploits of the various governmental detective services might be pardoned for supposing that the three pictures in the single frame are photographs of relatives. Only closer inspection will reveal the fact that beneath them appears a transcript from several pages of a certain book of records—the original of which is kept at the New York City Hall.

These pages state that....

But suppose we let Quinn tell the story, just as he told it one cold November night while the wind was whistling outside and the cheery warmth of the fire made things extremely snug within.

Secret Service men [said Quinn] divide all of their cases into two classes—those which call for quick action and plenty of it and those which demand a great deal of thought and only an hour or so of actual physical work. Your typical operative—Allison, who was responsible for solving the poison-pen puzzle, for example, or Hal Preston,[211] who penetrated the mystery surrounding the murder of Montgomery Marshall—is essentially a man of action. He likes to tackle a job and get it over with. It doesn't make any difference if he has to round up a half dozen counterfeiters at the point of a single revolver—as Tommy Callahan once did—or break up a gang of train robbers who have sworn never to be taken alive. As long as he has plenty of thrills and excitement, as long as he is able to get some joy out of life, he doesn't give a hang for the risk. That's his business and he loves it.

But it's the long-drawn-out cases which he has to ponder over and consider from a score of angles that, in the vernacular of vaudeville, capture his Angora. Give him an assignment where he can trail his man for a day or two, get the lay of the land, and then drop on the bunch like a ton o' brick and everything's fine. Give him one of the other kind and—well, he's just about as happy as Guy Randall was when they turned him loose with instructions to get something on Carl Cheney.

Remember during the early days of the war when the papers were full of stories from New York, Philadelphia, Boston, Milwaukee and points west about gatherings of pro-German sympathizers who were determined to aid the Fatherland? Theoretically, we were neutral at that time and these people had all the scope they wanted. They did not confine themselves to talk, however, but laid several plans which were destined to annoy the government and to keep several hundred operatives busy defeating them—for they were aimed directly at our policy of neutrality.

As a campaign fund to assure the success of these operations, the German sympathizers raised not less than sixteen million dollars—a sum which naturally excited the cupidity not only of certain individuals within their[212] own ranks, but also of persons on the outside—men who were accustomed to live by their wits and who saw in this gigantic collection the opportunity of a lifetime.

When you consider that you can hire a New York gangster to commit murder for a couple of hundred dollars—and the "union scale" has been known to be even lower—it's no wonder that the mere mention of sixteen million dollars caused many a crook of international reputation to figure how he could divert at least a part of this to his own bank account. That's the way, as it afterward turned out, that Carl Cheney looked at it.

Cheney had rubbed elbows with the police on several occasions prior to nineteen fourteen. It was suspected that he had been mixed up in a number of exceptionally clever smuggling schemes and that he had had a finger in one or two operations which came perilously close to blackmail. But no one had ever been able to get anything on him. He was the original Finnigin—"In agin, gone agin." By the time the plan came to a successful conclusion all that remained of "Count Carl's" connection with it was a vague and distinctly nebulous shadow—and you simply can't arrest shadows, no matter how hard you try.

The New York police were the first to tip Washington off to the fact that Cheney, who had dropped his aristocratic alias for the time being, was back in this country and had been seen in the company of a number of prominent members of a certain German-American club which wasn't in any too good repute with the Department of Justice by reason of the efforts of some of its members to destroy the neutral stand of the nation.

Have no indications of what Cheney is doing [the report admitted], but it will be well to trail him. Apparently he has[213] some connection, officially or unofficially, with Berlin. Advise what action you wish us to take.

Whereupon the chief wired back:

Operative assigned to Cheney case leaves to-night. Meanwhile please watch.

It wasn't until after the wire had been sent that Guy Randall was summoned to the inner sanctum of the Secret Service and informed that he had been elected to trail the elusive suspect and find out what he was up to.

"So far as our records show," stated the chief, "no one has ever been able to catch this Cheney person in the act of departing from the straight and narrow path. However, that's a matter of the past. What we've got to find out is what he is planning now—why he is in New York and why he has attached himself to the pro-German element which has all kinds of wild schemes up its sleeve."

"And I'm the one who's got to handle it?" inquired Guy, with a grimace.

"Precisely," grinned the chief. "Oh, I know it doesn't look like much of a job and I grant you that the thrill element will probably be lacking. But you can't draw a snap every time. All that's asked is that you get something on Cheney—something which will withstand the assaults of the lawyers he will undoubtedly hire the minute we lay hands on him. Therefore you've got to be mighty careful to have the right dope. If you're satisfied that he's doing nothing out of the way, don't hesitate to say so. But I don't expect that your report will clear him, for, from what we already know of the gentleman, he's more likely to be implicated in some plan aimed directly at a violation of neutrality, and it's essential[214] that we find out what that is before we take any radical step."

"What do you know about Cheney?" was Randall's next question, followed by an explanation from the chief that the "count" had been suspected in a number of cases and had barely been able to escape in time.

"But," added the head of the Secret Service, "he did escape. And that's what we have to prevent this time. He's a fast worker and a clever one—which means that you've got to keep continually after him. Call in all the help you need, but if you take my advice you'll handle the case alone. You're apt to get a lot further that way."

Agreeing that this was the best method to pursue, Randall caught the midnight train for New York and went at once to police headquarters, where he requested a full description of Cheney's previous activities.

"You're asking for something what ain't," he was informed, ungrammatically, but truthfully. "We've never been able to get a thing on the count, though we're dead certain that he had a finger in several crooked plays. The Latimer letters were never directly traced to him, but it's a cinch that he had something to do with their preparation, just as he had with the blackmailing of old man Branchfield and the smuggling of the van Husen emeralds. You remember that case, don't you? The one where the stones were concealed in a life preserver and they staged a 'man overboard' stunt just as the ship came into the harbor. Nobody ever got the stones or proved that they were actually smuggled—but the count happened to be on the ship at the time, just as he 'happened' to be in Paris when they were sold. We didn't even dare arrest him, which accounts for the fact that his photograph doesn't ornament the Rogues' Gallery."

"Well, what's the idea of trailing him, then?"[215]

"Just to find out what he is doing. What d'ye call those birds that fly around at sea just before a gale breaks—stormy petrels? That's the count! He's a stormy petrel of crookedness. Something goes wrong every time he hits a town—or, rather, just after he leaves, for he's too clever to stick around too long. The question now is, What's this particular storm and when is it goin' to break?"

"Fine job to turn me loose on," grumbled Randall.

"It is that," laughed the captain who was dispensing information. "But you can never tell what you'll run into, me boy. Why I remember once—"

Randall, however, was out of the office before the official had gotten well started on his reminiscences. He figured that he had already had too much of a grouch to listen patiently to some long-winded story dug out of the musty archives of police history and he made his way at once to the hotel where Carl Cheney was registered, flaunting his own name in front of the police whom he must have known were watching him.

Neither the house detective nor the plain-clothes man who had been delegated to trail Cheney could add anything of interest to the little that Randall already knew. The "count," they said, had conducted himself in a most circumspect manner and had not been actually seen in conference with any of the Germans with whom he was supposed to be in league.

"He's too slick for that," added the man from the Central Office. "Whenever he's got a conference on he goes up to the Club and you can't get in there with anything less than a battering ram and raiding squad. There's no chance to plant a dictaphone, and how else are you going to get the information?"

"What does he do at other times?" countered Guy,[216] preferring not to reply to the former question until he had gotten a better line on the case.

"Behaves himself," was the laconic answer. "Takes a drive in the Park in the afternoon, dines here or at one of the other hotels, goes to the theater and usually finishes up with a little supper somewhere among the white lights."

"Any women in sight?"

"Yes—two. A blond from the girl-show that's playin' at the Knickerbocker and a red-head. Don't know who she is—but they're both good lookers. No scandal, though. Everything appears to be on the level—even the women."

"Well," mused the government operative after a moment's silence, "I guess I better get on the job. Probably means a long stretch of dull work, but the sooner I get at it the sooner I'll get over it. Where is Cheney now?"

"Up in his room. Hasn't come down to breakfast yet. Yes. There he is now. Just getting out of the elevator—headed toward the dinin' room," and the plain-clothes man indicated the tall figure of a man about forty, a man dressed in the height of fashion, with spats, a cane, and a morning coat of the most correct cut. "Want me for anything?"

"Not a thing," said Randall, absently. "I'll pick him up now. You might tell the chief to watch out for a hurry call from me—though I'm afraid he won't get it."

As events proved, Randall was dead right. The Central Office heard nothing from him for several months, and even Washington received only stereotyped reports indicative of what Cheney was doing—which wasn't much.

Shortly after the first of the year, Guy sent a wire to the chief, asking to be relieved for a day or two in order that he might be free to come to Washington. Sensing the[217] fact that the operative had some plan which he wished to discuss personally, the chief put another man on Cheney's trail and instructed Randall to report at the Treasury Department on the following morning.

"What's the matter?" inquired the man at the head of the Service as Guy, a little thinner than formerly and showing by the wrinkles about his eyes the strain under which he was working, strolled into the office.

"Nothing's the matter, Chief—and that's where the trouble lies. You know I've never kicked about work, no matter how much of it I've had. But this thing's beginning to get on my nerves. Cheney is planning some coup. I'm dead certain of that. What it's all about, though, I haven't the least idea. The plans are being laid in the German-American Club and there's no chance of getting in there."

"How about bribing one of the employees to leave?"

"Can't be done. I've tried it—half a dozen times. They're all Germans and, as such, in the organization. However, I have a plan. Strictly speaking, it's outside the law, but that's why I wanted to talk things over with you...."

When Randall had finished outlining his plan the chief sat for a moment in thought. Then, "Are you sure you can put it over?" he inquired.

"Of course I can. It's done every other day, anyhow, by the cops themselves. Why shouldn't we take a leaf out of their book?"

"I know. But there's always the possibility of a diplomatic protest."

"Not in this case, Chief. The man's only a waiter and, besides, before the embassy has a chance to hear about it I'll have found out what I want to know. Then, if they want to raise a row, let 'em."[218]

The upshot of the matter was that, about a week later, Franz Heilman, a waiter employed at the German-American Club in New York, was arrested one night and haled into Night Court on a charge of carrying concealed weapons—a serious offense under the Sullivan Act. In vain he protested that he had never carried a pistol in his life. Patrolman

Flaherty, who had made the arrest, produced the weapon which he claimed to have found in Heilman's possession and the prisoner was held for trial.

Bright and early the next morning Randall, disguised by a mustache which he had trained for just such an occasion and bearing a carefully falsified letter from a German brewer in Milwaukee, presented himself at the employee's entrance of the German-American Club and asked for the steward. To that individual he told his story—how he had tried to get back to the Fatherland and had failed, how he had been out of work for nearly a month, and how he would like to secure employment of some kind at the Club where he would at least be among friends.

After a thorough examination of the credentials of the supposed German—who had explained his accent by the statement that he had been brought to the United States when very young and had been raised in Wisconsin—the steward informed him that there was a temporary vacancy in the Club staff which he could fill until Heilman returned.

"The duties," the steward added, "are very light and the pay, while not large, will enable you to lay by a little something toward your return trip to Germany."

Knowing that his time was limited, Randall determined to let nothing stand in the way of his hearing all that went on in the room where Cheney and his associates held their conferences. It was the work of only a few moments to bore holes in the door which connected this room with an[219] unused coat closet—plugging up the holes with corks stained to simulate the wood itself—and the instant the conference was on the new waiter disappeared.

An hour later he slipped out of the side entrance to the Club and the steward is probably wondering to this day what became of him. Had he been able to listen in on the private wire which connected the New York office of the Secret Service with headquarters at Washington, he would have had the key to the mystery.

"Chief," reported Randall, "I've got the whole thing. There's a plot on foot to raise one hundred and fifty thousand German reservists—men already in this country—mobilizing them in four divisions, with six sections. The first two divisions are to assemble at Silvercreek, Michigan—the first one seizing the Welland Canal and the second capturing Wind Mill Point, Ontario. The third is to meet at Wilson, N. Y., and will march on Port Hope. The fourth will go from Watertown, N. Y., to Kingston, Ontario, while the fifth will assemble somewhere near Detroit and proceed toward Windsor. The sixth will stage an attack on Ottawa, operating from Cornwall.

"They've got their plans all laid for the coup, and Cheney reported to-day that he intends to purchase some eighty-five boats to carry the invading force into the Dominion. The only thing that's delaying the game is the question of provisions for the army. Cheney's holding out for another advance—from what I gathered he's already received a lot—and claims that he will be powerless unless he gets it. I didn't stay to listen to the argument, for I figured that I'd better leave while the leaving was good."

The reply that came back from Washington was rather startling to the operative, who expected only commendation and the statement that his task was completed.[220]

"What evidence have you that this invasion is planned?"

"None besides what I heard through holes which I bored in one of the doors of the German-American Club this morning."

"That won't stand in court! We don't dare to arrest this man Cheney on that. You've got to get something on him."

"Plant it?"

"No! Get it straight. And we can't wait for this expedition to start, either. That would be taking too much of a chance. It's up to you to do a little speedy work in the research line. Dig back into the count's past and find something on which we can hold him, for he's very evidently the brains of the organization, in spite of the fact that he probably is working only for what he can get of that fund that the Germans have raised. I understand that it's sixteen million dollars and that's enough to tempt better men than Cheney. Now go to it, and remember—you've got to work fast!"

Disappointed, chagrined by the air of finality with which the receiver at the Washington end of the line was hung up, Randall wandered out of the New York office with a scowl on his face and deep lines of thought between his eyes. If he hadn't been raised in the school which holds that a man's only irretrievable mistake is to quit under fire, he'd have thrown up his job right there and let some one else tackle the work of landing the count. But he had to admit that the chief was right and, besides, there was every reason to suppose that grave issues hung in the balance. The invasion of Canada meant the overthrow of American neutrality, the failure of the plans which the President and the State Department had so carefully laid.

Cheney was the crux of the whole situation. Once[221] held on a charge that could be proved in court, the plot would fall through for want of a capable leader—for the operative had learned enough during his hour in the cloak-room to know that "the count" was the mainspring of the whole movement, despite the fact that he undoubtedly expected to reap a rich financial harvest for himself.

Selecting a seat on the top of a Fifth Avenue bus, Randall resigned himself to a consideration of the problem.

"The whole thing," he figured, "simmers down to Cheney himself. In its ramifications, of course, it's a question of peace or war—but in reality it's a matter of landing a crook by legitimate means. I can't plant a gun on him, like they did on Heilman, and there's mighty little chance of connecting him with the Branchfield case or the van Husen emeralds at this late date. His conduct around town has certainly been blameless enough. Not even any women to speak of. Wait a minute, though! There were two. The blond from the Knickerbocker and that red-haired dame. He's still chasing around with the blond—but what's become of Miss Red-head?"

This train of thought had possibilities. If the girl had been cast aside, it was probable that she would have no objection to telling what she knew—particularly as the color of her hair hinted at the possession of what the owner would call "temperament," while the rest of the world forgets to add the last syllable.

It didn't take long to locate the owner of the fiery tresses. A quick round-up of the head waiters at the cafés which Cheney frequented, a taxi trip to Washington Square and another to the section above Columbus Circle, and Randall found that the red-haired beauty was known as Olga Brainerd, an artist's model, whose face had appeared upon the cover of practically every popular publication[222] in the country. She had been out of town for the past two months, he learned, but had just returned and had taken an apartment in a section of the city which indicated the possession of considerable capital.

"Miss Brainerd," said Randall, when he was face to face with the Titian beauty in the drawing-room of her suite, "I came with a message from your friend, Carl Cheney."

Here he paused and watched her expression very closely. As he had hoped, the girl was unable to master her feelings. Rage and hate wrote themselves large across her face and her voice fairly snapped as she started to reply. Randall, however, interrupted her with a smile and the statement:

"That's enough! I'm going to lay my cards face up on the table. I am a Secret Service operative seeking information about Cheney. Here is my badge, merely to prove that I'm telling the truth. We have reason to believe that 'the Count,' as he is called, is mixed up with a pro-German plot which, if successful, would imperil the peace of the country. Can you tell us anything about him?"

"Can I?" echoed the girl. "The beast! He promised to marry me, more than two months ago, and then got infatuated with some blond chit of a chorus girl. Just because I lost my head and showed him a letter I had received—a letter warning me against him—he flew into a rage and threatened.... Well, never mind what he did say. The upshot of the affair was that he sent me out of town and gave me enough money to last me some time. But he'll pay for his insults!"

"Have you the letter you received?" asked Randall, casually—as if it meant little to him whether the girl produced it or not.

"Yes. I kept it. Wait a moment and I'll get it for[223] you." A few seconds later she was back with a note, written in a feminine hand—a note which read:

If you are wise you will ask the man who calls himself Carl Cheney what he knows of Paul Weiss, of George Winters, and Oscar Stanley. You might also inquire what has become of Florence and Rose.

(Signed) AMELIA.

Randall looked up with a puzzled expression. "What's all this about?" he inquired. "Sounds like Greek to me."

"To me, too," agreed the girl. "But it was enough to make Carl purple with rage and, what's more, to separate him from several thousand dollars."

"Weiss, Winters, and Stanley," mused Guy. "Those might easily be Cheney's former aliases. Florence, Rose, and Amelia? I wonder.... Come on, girl, we're going to take a ride down to City Hall! I've got a hunch!"

Late that afternoon when Carl Cheney arrived at his hotel he was surprised to find a young man awaiting him in his apartment—a man who appeared to be perfectly at ease and who slipped over and locked the door once the count was safely within the room.

"What does this mean?" demanded Cheney. "By what right—"

"It means," snapped Randall, "that the game's up!" Then, raising his voice, he called, "Mrs. Weiss!" and a tall woman parted the curtains at the other end of the room; "Mrs. Winters!" and another woman entered; "Mrs. Stanley!" and a third came in. With his fingers still caressing the butt of the automatic which nestled in his coat pocket, Randall continued:

"Cheney—or whatever your real name is—there won't be any invasion of Canada. We know all about your plans—in fact, the arsenal on West Houston Street is in[224] possession of the police at this moment. It was a good idea and undoubtedly you would have cleaned up on it—were it not for the fact that I am under the far from painful necessity of arresting you on a charge of bigamy—or would you call it 'trigamy'? The records at City Hall gave you away, after one of these ladies had been kind enough to provide us with a clue to the three aliases under which you conducted your matrimonial operations.

"Come on, Count. The Germans may need you worse than we do—but we happen to have you!"

[225]

XVI
AFTER SEVEN YEARS

Bill Quinn was disgusted. Some one, evidently afflicted with an ingrowing sense of humor, had sent him the prospectus of a "school" which professed to be able to teach budding aspirants the art of becoming a successful detective for the sum of twenty-five dollars, and Quinn couldn't appreciate the humor.

"*How to Become a Detective—in Ten Lessons*," he snorted. "It only takes one for the man who's got the right stuff in him, and the man that hasn't better stay out of the game altogether."

"Well," I retorted, anxious to stir up any kind of an argument that might lead to one of Quinn's tales about the exploits of Uncle Sam's sleuths, "just what does it take to make a detective?"

It was a moment or two before Quinn replied. Then: "There are only three qualities necessary," he replied. "Common sense, the power of observation, and perseverance. Given these three, with possibly a dash of luck thrown in for good measure, and you'll have a crime expert who could stand the heroes of fiction on their heads.

"Take Larry Simmons, for example. No one would ever have accused him of having the qualifications of a detective—any more than they would have suspected him of being one. But Larry drew a good-sized salary from[226] the Bureau of Pensions because he possessed the three qualities I mentioned. He had the common sense of a physician, the observation of a trained newspaper reporter, and the perseverance of a bulldog. Once he sunk his teeth in a problem he never let loose—which was the reason that very few people ever put anything over on the Pension Bureau as long as Larry was on the job.

"That cap up there," and Quinn pointed to a stained and dilapidated bit of headgear which hung upon the wall of his den, "is a memento of one of Simmons's cases. The man who bought it would tell you that I'm dead right when I say that Larry was persevering. That's putting it mildly."

Quite a while back [continued Quinn, picking up the thread of his story] there was a man out in Saint Joseph, Missouri, named Dave Holden. No one appeared to know where he came from and, as he conducted himself quietly and didn't mix in with his neighbors' affairs, no one cared very much.

Holden hadn't been in town more than a couple of weeks when one of the older inhabitants happened to inquire if he were any kin to "Old Dave Holden," who had died only a year or two before.

"No," said Holden, "I don't believe I am. My folks all came from Ohio and I understand that this Holden was a Missourian."

"That's right," agreed the other, "and a queer character, too. Guess he was pretty nigh the only man that fought on the Union side in the Civil War that didn't stick th' government for a pension. Had it comin' to him, too, 'cause he was a captain when th' war ended. But he always said he didn't consider that Uncle Sam owed[227] him anything for doin' his duty. Spite of th' protests of his friends, Dave wouldn't ever sign a pension blank, either."

A few more questions, carefully directed, gave Holden the history of his namesake, and that night he lay awake trying to figure out whether the plan which had popped into his head was safe. It promised some easy money, but there was the element of risk to be considered.

"After all," he concluded, "I won't be doing anything that isn't strictly within the law. My name is David Holden—just as the old man's was. The worst that they can do is to turn down the application. I won't be committing forgery or anything of the kind. And maybe it'll slip through—which would mean a pile of money, because they'll kick in with all that accumulated during the past fifty years."

So it was that, in the course of time, an application was filed at the Bureau of Pensions in Washington for a pension due "David Holden" of Saint Joseph, Missouri, who had fought in the Civil War with the rank of captain. But, when the application had been sent over to the War Department so that it might be compared with the records on file there, it came back with the red-inked notation that "Capt. David Holden had died two years before"—giving the precise date of his demise as evidence.

The moment that the document reached the desk of the Supervisor of Pensions he pressed one of the little pearl buttons in front of him and asked that Larry Simmons be sent in. When Larry arrived the chief handed him the application without a word.

"Right! I'll look into this," said Larry, folding the paper and slipping it into the pocket of his coat.

"Look into it?" echoed the supervisor. "You'll do more than that! You'll locate this man Holden—or[228] whatever his right name is—and see that he gets all that's coming to him. There've been too many of these cases lately. Apparently people think that all they have to do is to file an application for a pension and then go off and spend the money. Catch the first train for Saint Joe and wire me when you've landed your man. The district attorney will attend to the rest of the matter."

The location of David Holden, as Simmons found, was not the simplest of jobs. The pension applicant, being comparatively a newcomer, was not well known in town, and Simmons finally had to fall back upon the expedient of watching the post-office box which Holden had given as his address, framing a dummy letter so that the suspect might not think that he was being watched.

Holden, however, had rented the box for the sole purpose of receiving mail from the Pension Bureau. He had given the number to no one else and the fact that the box contained what appeared to be an advertisement from a clothing store made him stop and wonder. By that time, however, Simmons had him well in sight and followed him to the boarding-house on the outskirts of the town where he was staying.

That evening, while he was still wondering at the enterprise of a store that could obtain a post-office box number from a government bureau at Washington, the solution of the mystery came to him in a decidedly unexpected manner. The house in which Holden was staying was old-fashioned, one of the kind that are heated, theoretically at least, by "registers," open gratings in the wall. Holden's room was directly over the parlor on the first floor and the shaft which carried the hot air made an excellent sound-transmitter.

It so happened that Simmons, after having made a number of inquiries around town about the original Dave[229] Holden, called at the boarding house that night to discover what the landlady knew about the other man of the same name, who was seated in the room above.

Suddenly, like a voice from nowhere, came the statement in a high-pitched feminine voice: "I really don't know anything about him at all. Mr. Holden came here about six weeks ago and asked me to take him in to board. He seemed to be a very nice, quiet gentleman, who was willing to pay his rent in advance. So I let him have one of the best rooms in the house."

At the mention of his name Holden listened intently. Who was inquiring about him, and why?

There was only a confused mumble—apparently a man's reply, pitched in a low tone—and then the voice of the landlady again came clearly through the register:

"Oh, I'm sure he wouldn't do anything like that. Mr. Holden is...."

But that was all that the pension applicant waited for. Moving with the rapidity of a frightened animal, he secured one or two articles of value from his dresser, crammed a hat into his pocket, slipped on a raincoat, and vaulted out of the window, alighting on the sloping roof of a shed just below. Before he had quitted the room, however, he had caught the words "arrest on a charge of attempting to obtain money under false pretenses."

Some two minutes later there was a knock on his door and a voice demanded admittance. There was no reply. Again the demand, followed by a rattling of the doorknob and a tentative shake of the door. In all, it was probably less than five minutes after Larry Simmons had entered the parlor before he had burst in the door of Holden's room. But the bird had flown and the open window pointed to the direction of his flight.

Unfortunately for the operative the night was dark[230] and the fugitive was decidedly more familiar with the surrounding country than Larry was. By the time he had secured the assistance of the police half an hour had elapsed, and there weren't even any telltale footprints to show in which direction the missing man had gone.

"See that men are placed so as to guard the railroad station," Simmons directed, "and pass the word up and down the line that a medium-sized man, about thirty-five years of age, with black hair and a rather ruddy complexion—a man wanted by the government on a charge of false pretenses—is trying to make his escape. If anyone reports him, let me know at once."

That, under the circumstances, was really all that Larry could do. It ought to be an easy matter to locate the fugitive, he figured, and it would only be a question of a few days before he was safely in jail.

Bright and early the next morning the operative was awakened by a bell-boy who informed him that the chief of police would like to see him.

"Show him in," said Larry, fully expecting to see the chief enter with a handcuffed prisoner. But the head of the police force came in alone, carrying a bundle, which he gravely presented to Simmons.

"What's this?" inquired the pension agent.

"All that's left of your friend Holden," was the reply. "One of my men reported late last night that he had heard a splash in the river as though some one had jumped off the wharf, but he couldn't find out anything more. To tell the truth, he didn't look very hard—because we had our hands full with a robbery of Green's clothing store. Some one broke in there and—"

"Yes—but what about Holden?" Simmons interrupted.

"Guess you'll have to drag the river for him," answered the chief. "We found his coat and vest and raincoat on[231] the dock this mornin', and on top of them was this note, addressed to you."

The note, as Larry found an instant later, read:

I'd rather die in the river than go to jail. Tell your boss that he can pay two pensions now—one for each of the Dave Holdens.

The signature, almost illegible, was that of "David Holden (Number two)."

"No doubt that your man heard the splash when Holden went overboard last night?" inquired the operative.

"Not the least in the world. He told me about it, but I didn't connect it with the man you were after, and, besides, I was too busy right then to give it much thought."

"Any chance of recovering the body?"

"Mighty little at this time of the year. The current's good and strong an' the chances are that he won't turn up this side of the Mississippi, if then. It was only by accident that we found his cap. It had lodged under the dock and we fished it out less 'n half an hour ago—" and the chief pointed to a water-soaked piece of cloth which Simmons recognized as the one which Holden had been wearing the evening before.

"Well, I don't suppose there's anything more that we can do," admitted Larry. "I'd like to have the river dragged as much as possible, though I agree with you that the chances for recovering the body are very slim. Will you look after that?"

"Sure I will, and anything else you want done." The chief was nothing if not obliging—a fact which Simmons incorporated in his official report, which he filed a few days later, a report which stated that "David Holden, wanted on a charge of attempting to obtain money under[232]false pretenses, had committed suicide by drowning rather than submit to arrest."

The body has not been recovered [the report admitted], but this is not to be considered unusual at this time of the year when the current is very strong. The note left by the fugitive is attached.

Back from Washington came the wire:

Better luck next time. Anyhow, Holden won't bother us again.

If this were a moving picture [Quinn continued, after a pause], there would be a subtitle here announcing the fact that seven years are supposed to elapse. There also probably would be a highly decorated explanatory title informing the audience that "Uncle Sam Never Forgets Nor Forgives"—a fact that is so perfectly true that it's a marvel that people persist in trying to beat the government. Then the scene of the film would shift to Seattle, Washington.

They would have to cut back a little to make it clear that Larry Simmons had, in the meantime, left the Pension Bureau and entered the employment of the Post-office Department, being desirous of a little more excitement and a few more thrills than his former job afforded. But he was still working for Uncle Sam, and his memory—like that of his employer—was long and tenacious.

One of the minor cases which had been bothering the department for some time past was that of a ring of fortune-tellers who, securing information in devious ways, would pretend that it had come to them from the spirit world and use it for purposes which closely approximated[233]blackmail. Simmons, being in San Francisco at the time, was ordered to proceed to Seattle and look into the matter.

Posing as a gentleman of leisure with plenty of money and but little care as to the way in which he spent it, it wasn't long before he was steered into what appeared to be the very center of the ring—the residence of a Madame Ahara, who professed to be able to read the stars, commune with spirits, and otherwise obtain information of an occult type. There Larry went through all the usual stages—palmistry, spiritualism, and clairvoyance—and chuckled when he found, after his third visit, that his pocket had been picked of a letter purporting to contain the facts about an escapade in which he had been mixed up a few years ago. The letter, of course, was a plant placed there for the sole purpose of providing a lead for madame and her associates to follow. And they weren't long in taking the tip.

The very next afternoon the government agent received a telephone call notifying him that madame had some news of great importance which she desired to impart—information which had come to her from the other world and in which she felt certain he would be interested.

Larry asked if he might bring a friend with him, but the request—as he had expected—was promptly refused. The would-be blackmailers were too clever to allow first-hand evidence to be produced against them. They wished to deal only with principals or, as madame informed him over the phone, "the message was of such a nature that only he should hear it."

"Very well," replied Simmons, "I'll be there at eleven this evening."

It was not his purpose to force the issue at this time. In fact, he planned to submit to the first demand for money[234] and trust to the confidence which this would inspire to render the blackmailers less cautious in the future. But something occurred which upset the entire scheme and, for a time at least, threatened disaster to the Post-office schemes.

Thinking that it might be well to look the ground over before dark, Larry strolled out to Madame Ahara's about five o'clock in the afternoon and took up his position on the opposite side of the street, studying the house from every angle. While he was standing there a man came out—a man who was dressed in the height of fashion, but whose face was somehow vaguely familiar. The tightly waxed mustache and the iron-gray goatee seemed out of place, for Simmons felt that the last time he had seen the man he had been clean shaven.

"Where was it?" he thought, as he kept the man in sight, though on the opposite side of the street. "New York? No. Washington? Hardly. Saint Louis? No, it was somewhere where he was wearing a cap—a cap that was water-stained and ... I've got it! In Saint Joseph! The man who committed suicide the night I went to arrest him for attempting to defraud the Pension Bureau! It's he, sure as shooting!"

But just as Simmons started to cross the street the traffic cop raised his arm, and when the apparently interminable stream of machines had passed, the man with the mustache was nowhere to be seen. He had probably slipped into one of the near-by office buildings. But which? That was a question which worried Larry for a moment or two. Then he came to the conclusion that there was no sense in trying to find his man at this moment. The very fact that he was in Seattle was enough. The police could find him with little difficulty.

But what had Holden been doing at the clairvoyant's?[235] Had he fallen into the power of the ring or was it possible that he was one of the blackmailers himself?

The more Larry thought about the matter, the more he came to the conclusion that here was an opportunity to kill two birds with a single stone—to drive home at least the entering wedge of the campaign against the clairvoyants and at the same time to land the man who had eluded him seven years before.

The plan which he finally evolved was daring, but he realized that the element of time was essential. Holden must not be given another opportunity to slip through the net.

That night when Larry kept his appointment at madame's he saw to it that a cordon of police was thrown around the entire block, with instructions to allow no one to leave until after a prearranged signal.

"Don't prevent anyone from coming into the house," Simmons directed, "but see that not a soul gets away from it. Also, you might be on the lookout for trouble. The crowd's apt to get nasty and we can't afford to take chances with them."

A tall dark-skinned man, attired in an Arabian burnoose and wearing a turban, answered the ring at the door, precisely as Larry anticipated—for the stage was always well set to impress visitors. Madame herself never appeared in the richly decorated room where the crystal-gazing séances were held, preferring to remain in the background and to allow a girl, who went by the name of Yvette, to handle visitors, the explanation being that "Madame receives the spirit messages and transmits them to Yvette, her assistant."

Simmons therefore knew that, instead of dealing with an older and presumably more experienced woman, he would only have to handle a girl, and it was upon this that he placed his principal reliance.[236]

Everything went along strictly according to schedule. Yvette, seated on the opposite side of a large crystal ball in which she read strange messages from the other world—visions transmitted from the cellar by means of a cleverly constructed series of mirrors—told the operative everything that had been outlined in the letter taken from his pocket on the preceding night, adding additional touches founded on facts which Larry had been "careless" enough to let slip during his previous visits. Then she concluded with a very thinly veiled threat of blackmail if the visitor did not care to kick in with a certain sum of money.

Larry listened to the whole palaver in silence, but his eyes were busy trying to pierce the dim light in which the room was shrouded. So far as he could see, the door through which he had entered formed the only means of getting into the room—but there were a number of rugs and draperies upon the walls, any one of which might easily mask a doorway.

When the girl had finished, the operative leaned forward and hitched his chair around so that he could speak in a whisper.

"If you know what's good for you," he cautioned, "don't move! I've got you covered, in the first place, and, secondly, there's a solid cordon of police around this house! Careful—not a sound! I'm not after you. I want the people who're behind you. Madame and her associates. This blackmailing game has gone about far enough, but I'll see that you get off with a suspended sentence if you do as I tell you. If not—" and the very abruptness with which he stopped made the threat all the more convincing.

"What—what do you want me to do?" stammered the girl, her voice barely audible.[237]

"Turn state's evidence and tip me off to everyone who's in on this thing," was Larry's reply, couched in the lowest of tones. "There's not a chance of escape for any of you, so you might as well do it and get it over with. Besides that, I want to know where I can find a man with a waxed mustache and iron-gray goatee who left this house at ten minutes past five this afternoon."

"Madame!" exclaimed the girl. "Davidson!"

"Yes—Madame and Davidson, if that's the name he goes by now. It was Holden the last time I saw him."

"He"—and the girl's voice was a mere breath—"he is madame!"

"What?"

"Yes, there is no Madame Ahara. Davidson runs the whole thing. He is—"

But at that moment one of the rugs on the wall which Larry was facing swung outward and a man sprang into the room, a man whose face was purple with rage and who leaped sidewise as he saw Larry's hand snap an automatic into view above the pedestal on which the crystal ball reposed. In a flash Simmons recognized two things—his danger and the fact that the man who had just entered was Holden, alias Davidson, blackmailer and potential thief.

Before the government agent had time to aim the head of the clairvoyant ring fired. But his bullet, instead of striking Larry, shattered the crystal ball into fragments and the room was plunged into total darkness. In spite of the fact that he knew the shot would bring speedy relief from outside the house, Simmons determined to capture his man single-handed and alive. Half-leaping, half-falling from the chair in which he had been seated, the operative sprang forward in an attempt to nail his man while the latter was still dazed by the darkness. But[238] his foot, catching in one of the thick rugs which carpeted the floor, tripped him and he fell—a bullet from the other's revolver plowing through the fleshy part of his arm.

The flash, however, showed him the position of his adversary, and it was the work of only a moment to slip forward and seize the blackmailer around the waist, his right hand gripping the man's wrist and forcing it upward so that he was powerless to use his revolver. For a full minute they wrestled in the inky darkness, oblivious to the fact that the sound of blows on the outer door indicated the arrival of reinforcements.

Then suddenly Larry let go of the blackmailer's arm and, whirling him rapidly around, secured a half nelson that threatened to dislocate his neck.

"Drop it!" he snarled. "Drop that gun before I wring your head off!" and the muffled thud as the revolver struck the floor was the signal that Holden had surrendered. A moment later the light in the center of the room was snapped on and the police sergeant inquired if Larry needed any assistance.

"No," replied Simmons, grimly, "but you might lend me a pair of bracelets. This bird got away from me once, some seven years ago, and I'm not taking any more chances!"

[239]
XVII
THE POISON-PEN PUZZLE

Beside the bookcase in the room which Bill Quinn likes to dignify by the name of "library"—though it's only a den, ornamented with relics of scores of cases in which members of the different government detective services have figured—hangs a frame containing four letters, each in a different handwriting.

Beyond the fact that these letters obviously refer to some secret in the lives of the persons to whom they are addressed, there is little about them that is out of the ordinary. A close observer, however, would note that in none of the four is the secret openly stated. It is only hinted at, suggested, but by that very fact it becomes more mysterious and alarming.

It was upon this that I commented one evening as I sat, discussing things in general, with Quinn.

"Yes," he agreed, "the writer of those letters was certainly a genius. As an author or as an advertising writer or in almost any other profession where a mastery of words and the ability to leave much to the imagination is a distinct asset, they would have made a big success."

"They?" I inquired. "Did more than one person write the letters?"

"Don't look like the writing of the same person, do they?" countered Quinn. "Besides, that was one of the[240] many phases of the matter which puzzled Elmer Allison, and raised the case above the dead level of ordinary blackmailing schemes."

Allison [Quinn went on, settling comfortably back in his big armchair] was, as you probably remember, one of the star men of the Postal Inspection Service, the chap who solved the mystery of the lost one hundred thousand dollars in Columbus. In fact, he had barely cleared up the tangle connected with the letters when assigned to look into the affair of the missing money, with what results you already know.

The poison-pen puzzle, as it came to be known in the department, first bobbed up some six months before Allison tackled it. At least, that was when it came to the attention of the Postal Inspection Service. It's more than likely that the letters had been arriving for some time previous to that, because one of the beauties of any blackmailing scheme—such as this one appeared to be—is that 90 per cent of the victims fear to bring the matter to the attention of the law. They much prefer to suffer in silence, kicking in with the amounts demanded, than to risk the exposure of their family skeletons by appealing to the proper authorities.

A man by the name of Tyson, who lived in Madison, Wisconsin, was the first to complain. He informed the postmaster in his city that his wife had received two letters, apparently in a feminine handwriting, which he considered to be very thinly veiled attempts at blackmailing.

Neither of the letters was long. Just a sentence or two. But their ingenuity lay in what they suggested rather than in their actual threats.

The first one read:[241]

Does your husband know the details of that trip to Fond du Lac? He might be interested in what Hastings has to tell him.

The second, which arrived some ten days later, announced:

The photograph of the register of a certain hotel in Fond du Lac for June 8 might be of interest to your husband—who can tell?

That was all there was to them, but it doesn't take an expert in plot building to think of a dozen stories that could lie back of that supposedly clandestine trip on the eighth of June.

Tyson didn't go into particulars at the time. He contented himself with turning the letters over to the department, with the request that the matter be looked into at once. Said that his wife had handed them to him and that he knew nothing more about the matter.

All that the postal authorities could do at the time was to instruct him to bring in any subsequent communications. But, as the letters stopped suddenly and Tyson absolutely refused to state whether he knew of anyone who might be interested in causing trouble between his wife and himself, there was nothing further to be done. Tracing a single letter, or even two of them, is like looking for a certain star on a clear night—you've got to know where to look before you have a chance of finding it—and the postmark on the letters wasn't of the least assistance.

Some three or four weeks later a similar case cropped up. This time it was a woman who brought in the letters—a woman who was red-eyed from lack of sleep and worry. Again the communications referred to a definite escapade, but still they made no open demand for money.

By the time the third case cropped up the postal[242] authorities in Madison were appealing to Washington for assistance. Before Bolton and Clarke, the two inspectors originally assigned to the case, could reach the Wisconsin capital another set of the mysterious communications had been received and called to the attention of the department.

During the three months which followed no less than six complaints were filed, all of them alleging the receipt of veiled threats, and neither the local authorities nor the men from Washington could find a single nail on which to hang a theory. Finally affairs reached such a stage that the chief sent for Allison, who had already made something of a name for himself, and told him to get on the job.

"Better make the first train for Madison," were the directions which Elmer received. "So far as we can tell, this appears to be the scheme of some crazy woman, intent upon causing domestic disturbances, rather than a well-laid blackmailing plot. There's no report of any actual demand for money. Just threats or suggestions of revelations which would cause family dissension. I don't have to tell you that it's wise to keep the whole business away from the papers as long as you can. They'll get next to it some time, of course, but if we can keep it quiet until we've landed the author of the notes it'll be a whole lot better for the reputation of the department.

"Bolton and Clarke are in Madison now, but their reports are far from satisfactory, so you better do a little investigating of your own. You'll have full authority to handle the case any way that you see fit. All we ask is action—before somebody stirs up a real row about the inefficiency of the Service and all that rot."

Elmer smiled grimly, knowing the difficulties under which the department worked, difficulties which make it hard for any bureau to obtain the full facts in a case[243] without being pestered by politicians and harried by local interests which are far from friendly. For this reason you seldom know that Uncle Sam is conducting an investigation until the whole thing is over and done with and the results are ready to be presented to the grand jury. Premature publicity has ruined many cases and prevented many a detective from landing the men he's after, which was the reason that Allison slipped into town on rubber heels, and his appearance at the office of the postmaster was the first indication that official had of his arrival.

"Mr. Gordon," said Allison, after they had completed the usual preliminaries connected with credentials and so forth, "I want to tackle this case just as if I were the first man who had been called in. I understand that comparatively little progress has been made—"

"'Comparatively little' is good," chuckled the postmaster.

"And I don't wish to be hindered by any erroneous theories which may have been built up. So if you don't mind we'll run over the whole thing from the beginning."

"Well," replied the postmaster, "you know about the Tyson letters and—"

"I don't know about a thing," Elmer cut in. "Or at least we'll work on the assumption that I don't. Then I'll be sure not to miss any points and at the same time I'll get a fresh outline of the entire situation."

Some two hours later Postmaster Gordon finished his résumé of the various cases which were puzzling the police and the postal officials, for a number of the best men on the police force had been quietly at work trying to trace the poison-pen letters.

"Are these all the letters that have been received?" Allison inquired, indicating some thirty communications which lay before him on the desk.[244]

"All that have been called to the attention of this office. Of course, there's no telling how many more have been written, about which no complaint has been made. Knowing human nature, I should say that at least three times that number have been received and possibly paid for. But the recipients didn't report the matter—for reasons best known to themselves. As a matter of fact—But you're not interested in gossip."

"I most certainly am!" declared Allison. "When you're handling a matter of this kind, where back-stairs intrigue and servants-hall talk is likely to play a large part, gossip forms a most important factor. What does Dame Rumor say in this case?"

"So far as these letters are concerned, nothing at all. Certain influences, which it's hardly necessary to explain in detail, have kept this affair out of the papers—but gossip has it that at least three divorces within as many months have been caused by the receipt of anonymous letters, and that there are a number of other homes which are on the verge of being broken up for a similar reason."

"That would appear to bear out your contention that other people have received letters like these, but preferred to take private action upon them. Also that, if blackmail were attempted, it sometimes failed—otherwise the matter wouldn't have gotten as far as the divorce court."

Then, after a careful study of several of the sample letters on the desk, Allison continued, "I suppose you have noted the fact that no two of these appear to have been written by the same person?"

"Yes, but that is a point upon which handwriting experts fail to agree. Some of them claim that each was written by a different person. Others maintain that one woman was responsible for all of them, and a third school[245] holds that either two or three people wrote them. What're you going to do when experts disagree?"

"Don't worry about any of 'em," retorted Allison. "If we're successful at all we won't have much trouble in proving our case without the assistance of a bunch of so-called experts who only gum up the testimony with long words that a jury can't understand. Where are the envelopes in which these letters were mailed?"

"Most of the people who brought them in failed to keep the envelopes. But we did manage to dig up a few. Here they are," and the postmaster tossed over a packet of about half a dozen, of various shapes and sizes.

"Hum!" mused the postal operative, "all comparatively inexpensive stationery. Might have been bought at nearly any corner drug store. Any clue in the postmarks?"

"Not the slightest. As you will note, they were mailed either at the central post office or at the railroad station—places so public that it's impossible to keep a strict watch for the person who mailed 'em. In one case—that of the Osgoods—we cautioned the wife to say nothing whatever about the matter, and then ordered every clerk in the post office to look out for letters in that handwriting which might be slipped through the slot. In fact, we closed all the slots save one and placed a man on guard inside night and day."

"Well, what happened?" inquired Allison, a trifle impatiently, as the postmaster paused.

"The joke was on us. Some two days later a letter which looked suspiciously like these was mailed. Our man caught it in time to dart outside and nail the person who posted it. Fortunately we discovered that she was Mrs. Osgood's sister-in-law and that the letter was a perfectly innocent one."[246]

"No chance of her being mixed up in the affair?"

"No. Her husband is a prominent lawyer here, and, besides, we've watched every move she's made since that time. She's one of the few people in town that we're certain of."

"Yet, you say her handwriting was similar to that which appears on these letters?"

"Yes, that's one of the many puzzling phases of the whole matter. Every single letter is written in a hand which closely resembles that of a relative of the person to whom it is addressed! So much so, in fact, that at least four of the complainants have insisted upon the arrest of these relatives, and have been distinctly displeased at our refusal to place them in jail merely because their handwriting is similar to that of a blackmailer."

"Why do you say blackmailer? Do you know of any demand for money which has been made?"

"Not directly—but what other purpose could a person have than to extract money? They'd hardly run the risk of going to the pen in order to gratify a whim for causing trouble."

"How about the Tysons and the Osgoods and the other people who brought these letters in—didn't they receive subsequent demands for money?"

"They received nothing—not another single letter of any kind."

"You mean that the simple fact of making a report to your office appeared to stop the receipt of the threats."

"Precisely. Now that you put it that way, it does look odd. But that's what happened."

Allison whistled. This was the first ray of light that had penetrated a very dark and mysterious case, and, with its aid, he felt that he might, after all, be successful.

Contenting himself with a few more questions, including[247] the names of the couples whom gossip stated had been separated through the receipt of anonymous communications, Allison bundled the letters together and slipped them into his pocket.

"It's quite possible," he stated, as he opened the door leading out of the postmaster's private office, "that you won't hear anything more from me for some time. I hardly think it would be wise to report here too often, or that if you happen to run into me on the street that you would register recognition. I won't be using the name of Allison, anyhow, but that of Gregg—Alvin Gregg—who has made a fortune in the operation of chain stores and is looking over the field with a view to establishing connections here. Gregg, by the way, is stopping at the Majestic Hotel, if you care to reach him," and with that he was gone.

Allison's first move after establishing his identity at the hotel, was to send a wire to a certain Alice Norcross in Chicago—a wire which informed her that "My sister, Mrs. Mabel Kennedy, requests your presence in Madison, Wisconsin. Urgent and immediate." The signature was "Alvin Gregg, E. A.," and to an inquisitive telegraph operator who inquired the meaning of the initials, Allison replied: "Electrical Assistant, of course," and walked away before the matter could be further discussed.

The next evening Mrs. Mabel Kennedy registered at the Majestic Hotel, and went up to the room which Mr. Gregg had reserved for her—the one next to his.

"It's all right, Alice," he informed her a few moments later, after a careful survey had satisfied him that the hall was clear of prying ears. "I told them all about you—that you were my sister 'n' everything. So it's quite respectable."

"Mrs. Kennedy," or Alice Norcross, as she was known[248] to the members of the Postal Service whom she had assisted on more than one occasion when the services of a woman with brains were demanded, merely smiled and continued to fix her hair before the mirror.

"I'm not worrying about that," she replied. "You boys can always be trusted to arrange the details—but traveling always did play the dickens with my hair! What's the idea, anyhow? Why am I Mrs. Mabel Kennedy, and what's she supposed to do?"

In a few words Allison outlined what he was up against—evidently the operation of a very skillful gang of blackmailers who were not only perfectly sure of their facts, but who didn't run any risks until their victims were too thoroughly cowed to offer any resistance.

"The only weak spot in the whole plan," concluded the operative, "is that the letters invariably cease when the prospective victims lay their case before the postmaster."

"You mean that you think he's implicated?"

"No—but some one in his office is!" snapped Allison. "Else how would they know when to lay off? That's the only lead we have, and I don't want to work from it, but up to it. Do you know anyone who's socially prominent in Madison?"

"Not a soul, but it's no trick to get letters of introduction—even for Mrs. Mabel Kennedy."

"Fine! Go to it! The minute you get 'em start a social campaign here. Stage several luncheons, bridge parties, and the like. Be sure to create the impression of a woman of means—and if you can drop a few hints about your none too spotless past, so much the better."

"You want to draw their fire, eh?"

"Precisely. It's unfortunate that we can't rig up a husband for you—that would make things easier, but when it's known that I, Alvin Gregg, am your brother,[249] I think it's more than likely that they'll risk a couple of shots."

It was about a month later that Mrs. Kennedy called up her brother at the Hotel Majestic and asked him to come over to her apartment at once.

"Something stirring?" inquired Allison as he entered the drawing-room of the suite which his assistant had rented in order to bolster up her social campaign.

"The first nibble," replied the girl, holding out a sheet of violet-tinted paper, on which appeared the words:

Of course your brother and your friends know all about the night you spent alone with a certain man in a cabin in the Sierras?

"Great Scott!" ejaculated Allison. "Do you mean to say it worked?"

"Like clockwork," was the girl's reply. "Acting on your instructions, I made a special play for Snaith, the postmaster's confidential secretary and general assistant. I invited him to several of my parties and paid particular attention to what I said when he was around. The first night I got off some clever little remark about conventions—laughing at the fact that it was all right for a woman to spend a day with a man, but hardly respectable for her to spend the evening. The next time he was there—and he was the only one in the party who had been present on the previous occasion—I turned the conversation to snowstorms and admitted that I had once been trapped in a storm in the Sierra Nevadas and had been forced to spend the night in a cabin. But I didn't say anything then about any companion. The third evening—when an entirely different crowd, with the exception of Snaith, was present—some one brought up the subject of what constitutes a gentleman, and my contribution was[250] a speech to the effect that 'one never knows what a man is until he is placed in a position where his brute instincts would naturally come to the front.'

"Not a single one of those remarks was incriminating or even suspicious—but it didn't take a master mind to add them together and make this note! Snaith was the only man who could add them, because he was the only one who was present when they were all made!"

"Fine work!" applauded Allison. "But there's one point you've overlooked. This letter, unlike the rest of its kind, is postmarked Kansas City, while Snaith was here day before yesterday when this was mailed. I know, because Clarke's been camping on his trail for the past three weeks."

"Then that means—"

"That Snaith is only one of the gang—the stool-pigeon—or, in this case, the lounge-lizard—who collects the information and passes it on to his chief? Exactly. Now, having Mr. Snaith where I want him and knowing pretty well how to deal with his breed, I think the rest will be easy. I knew that somebody in the postmaster's office must be mixed up in the affair and your very astute friend was the most likely prospect. Congratulations on landing him so neatly!"

"Thanks," said the girl, "but what next?"

"For you, not a thing. You've handled your part to perfection. The rest is likely to entail a considerable amount of strong-arm work, and I'd rather not have you around. Might cramp my style."

That night—or, rather, about three o'clock on the following morning—Sylvester Snaith, confidential secretary to the postmaster of Madison, was awakened by the sound of some one moving stealthily about the bedroom of his bachelor apartment. Before he could utter a sound[251] the beam of light from an electric torch blazed in his eyes and a curt voice from the darkness ordered him to put up his hands. Then:

"What do you know about the anonymous letters which have been sent to a number of persons in this city?" demanded the voice.

"Not—not a thing," stammered the clerk, trying to collect his badly scattered senses.

"That's a lie! We know that you supplied the information upon which those letters were based! Now come through with the whole dope or, by hell I'll—" the blue-steel muzzle of an automatic which was visible just outside the path of light from the torch completed the threat. Snaith, thoroughly cowed, "came through"—told more than even Allison had hoped for when he had planned the night raid on a man whom he had sized up as a physical coward.

Less than an hour after the secretary had finished, Elmer was on his way to Kansas City, armed with information which he proceeded to lay before the chief of police.

"'Spencerian Peter,' eh?" grunted the chief. "Sure, I know where to lay my hands on him—been watching him more or less ever since he got out of Leavenworth a couple of years back. But I never connected him with this case."

"What do you mean—this case?" demanded Allison. "Did you know anything about the poison-pen letters in Madison?"

"Madison? No—but I know about the ones that have set certain people here by the ears for the past month. I thought that was what you wanted him for. Evidently the game isn't new."

"Far from it," Elmer replied. "I don't know how much he cleaned up in Wisconsin, but I'll bet he got away[252] with a nice pile. Had a social pet there, who happened to be the postmaster's right-hand man, collect the scandal for him and then he'd fix up the letters—faking some relative's handwriting with that infernal skill of his. Then his Man Friday would tip him off when they made a holler to headquarters and he'd look for other suckers rather than run the risk of getting the department on his trail by playing the same fish too long. That's what finally gave him away—that and the fact that his assistant was bluffed by an electric torch and an empty gun."

"Well, I'll be hanged," muttered the chief. "You might have been explaining the situation here—except that we don't know who his society informant is. I think we better drop in for a call on 'Spencerian' this evening."

"The call was made on scheduled time," Quinn concluded, "but it was hardly of a social nature. You wouldn't expect a post-office operative, a chief of police, and half a dozen cops to stage a pink tea. Their methods are inclined to be a trifle more abrupt—though Pete, as it happened, didn't attempt to pull any rough stuff. He dropped his gun the moment he saw how many guests were present, and it wasn't very long before they presented him with a formal invitation to resume his none too comfortable but extremely exclusive apartment in Leavenworth. Snaith, being only an accomplice, got off with two years. The man who wrote the letters and who was the principal beneficiary of the money which they produced, drew ten."

"And who got the credit for solving the puzzle?" I inquired. "Allison or the Norcross girl?"

"Allison," replied Quinn. "Alice Norcross only worked on condition that her connection with the Service be kept[253] quite as much of a secret as the fact that her real name was Mrs. Elmer Allison."

"What? She was Allison's wife?" I demanded.

"Quite so," said the former operative. "If you don't believe me, there's a piece of her wedding dress draped over that picture up there," and he pointed to a strip of white silk that hung over one of the framed photographs on the wall.

"But I thought you said—"

"That that was part of the famous thirty thousand yards which was nailed just after it had been smuggled across the Canadian border? I did. But Allison got hold of a piece of it and had it made up into a dress for Alice. So that bit up there has a double story. You know one of them. Remind me to tell you the other sometime."

[254]

XVIII
THIRTY THOUSAND YARDS OF SILK

"I'd sure like to lead the life of one of those fictional detective heroes," muttered Bill Quinn, formerly of the United States Secret Service, as he tossed aside the latest volume of crime stories that had come to his attention. "Nothing to do but trail murderers and find the person who lifted the diamond necklace and stuff of that kind. They never have a case that isn't interesting or, for that matter, one in which they aren't successful. Must be a great life!"

"But aren't the detective stories of real life interesting and oftentimes exciting?" I inquired, adding that those which Quinn had already told me indicated that the career of a government operative was far from being deadly monotonous.

"Some of them are," he admitted, "but many of them drag along for months or even years, sometimes petering out for pure lack of evidence. Those, of course, are the cases you never hear of—the ones where Uncle Sam's men fall down on the job. Oh yes, they're fallible, all right. They can't solve every case—any more than a doctor can save the life of every patient he attends. But their percentage, though high, doesn't approach the success of your Sherlock Holmeses and your Thinking Machines, your Gryces and Sweetwaters and Lecoqs."

"How is it, then, that every story you've told dealt[255] with the success of a government agent—never with his failure?"

Quinn smiled reminiscently for a moment.

Then, "What do doctors do with their mistakes?" he asked. "They bury 'em. And that's what any real detective will do—try to forget, except for hoping that some day he'll run up against the man who tricked him. Again, most of the yarns I've told you revolved around some of the relics of this room"—waving his hand to indicate the walls of his library—"and these are all mementoes of successful cases. There's no use in keeping the other kind. Failures are too common and brains too scarce. That bit of silk up there—"

"Oh yes," I interrupted, "the one that formed part of Alice Norcross's wedding dress."

"And figured in one of the most sensational plots to defraud the government that was ever uncovered," added Quinn. "If Ezra Marks hadn't located that shipment I wouldn't have had that piece of silk and there wouldn't be any story to tell. So you see, it's really a circle, after all."

Marks [Quinn went on] was one of the few men connected with any branch of the government organizations who really lived up to the press-agent notices of the detectives you read about. In the first place, he looked like he might have stepped out of a book—big and long-legged and lanky. A typical Yankee, with all of the New-Englander's shrewdness and common sense. If you turned Ezra loose on a case you could be sure that he wouldn't sit down and try to work it out by deduction. Neither would he plunge in and attempt by sheer bravado and gun play to put the thing over. He'd mix the two methods and, more often than not, come back with the answer.[256]

Then, too, Marks had the very happy faculty of drawing assignments that turned out to be interesting. Maybe it was luck, but more than likely it was because he followed plans that made 'em so—preferring to wait until he had all the strings to a case and then stage a big round-up of the people implicated. You remember the case of the Englishman who smuggled uncut diamonds in the bowl of his pipe and the one you wrote under the title of "Wah Lee and the Flower of Heaven"? Well, those were typical of Ezra's methods—the first was almost entirely analytical, the second mainly gun play plus a painstaking survey of the field he had to cover.

But when Marks was notified that it was up to him to find out who was running big shipments of valuable silks across the Canadian border, without the formality of visiting the customhouse and making the customary payments, he found it advisable to combine the two courses.

It was through a wholesale dealer in silks in Seattle, Washington, that the Customs Service first learned of the arrival of a considerable quantity of this valuable merchandise, offered through certain underground channels at a price which clearly labeled it as smuggled. Possibly the dealer was peeved because he didn't learn of the shipment in time to secure any of it. But his reasons for calling the affair to the attention of the Treasury Department don't really matter. The main idea was that the silk was there, that it hadn't paid duty, and that some one ought to find out how it happened.

When a second and then a third shipment was reported, Marks was notified by wire to get to Seattle as fast as he could, and there to confer with the Collector of the Port.

It wasn't until after he had arrived that Ezra knew what the trouble was, for the story of the smuggled silk[257] hadn't penetrated as far south as San Francisco, where he had been engaged in trying to find a cargo of smuggled coolies.

"Here's a sample of the silk," announced the Collector of the Port at Seattle, producing a piece of very heavy material, evidently of foreign manufacture. "Beyond the fact that we've spotted three of the shipments and know where to lay our hands on them if wanted, I've got to admit that we don't know a thing about the case. The department, of course, doesn't want us to trace the silk from this end. The minute you do that you lay yourself open to all sorts of legal tangles and delays—to say nothing of giving the other side plenty of time to frame up a case that would sound mighty good in court. Besides, I haven't enough men to handle the job in the short space of time necessary. So you'll have to dig into it and find out who got the stuff in and how. Then we'll attend to the fences who've been handling it here."

"The old game of passing the buck," thought Ezra, as he fingered the sample of silk meditatively. "I'll do the work and they'll get the glory. Oh, well—"

"Any idea of where the shipments came from?" he inquired.

"There's no doubt but that it's of Japanese manufacture, which, of course, would appear to point to a shipping conspiracy of some nature. But I hardly think that's true here. Already eighteen bolts of silk have been reported in Seattle, and, as you know, that's a pretty good sized consignment. You couldn't stuff 'em into a pill box or carry 'em inside a walking stick, like you could diamonds. Whoever's handling this job is doing it across the border, rather than via the shipping route."

"No chance of a slip-up in your information, is there, Chief?" Ezra inquired, anxiously. "I'd hate to start[258] combing the border and then find that the stuff was being slipped in through the port."

"No," and the Collector of Customs was positive in his reply. "I'm not taking a chance on that tip. I know what I'm talking about. My men have been watching the shipping like hawks. Ever since that consignment of antique ivory got through last year we've gone over every vessel with a microscope, probing the mattresses and even pawing around in the coal bins. I'm positive that there isn't a place big enough to conceal a yard of silk that the boys haven't looked into—to say nothing of eighteen bolts.

"Besides," added the Collector, "the arrival of the silk hasn't coincided with the arrival of any of the ships from Japan—not by any stretch of the imagination."

"All right, I'll take up the trail northward then," replied Marks. "Don't be surprised if you fail to hear from me for a couple of months or more. If Washington inquires, tell them that I'm up on the border somewhere and let it go at that."

"Going to take anybody with you?"

"Not a soul, except maybe a guide that I'll pick up when I need him. If there is a concerted movement to ship silk across the line—and it appears that there is—the more men you have working with you the less chance there is for success. Border runners are like moonshiners, they're not afraid of one man, but if they see a posse they run for cover and keep out of sight until the storm blows over. And there isn't one chance in a thousand of finding 'em meanwhile. You've got to play them, just like you would a fish, so the next time you hear from me you will know that I've either landed my sharks or that they've slipped off the hook!"

It was about a month later that the little town of Northport,[259] up in the extreme northeastern corner of Washington, awoke to find a stranger in its midst. Strangers were something of a novelty in Northport, and this one—a man named Marks, who stated that he was "prospectin' for some good lumber"—caused quite a bit of talk for a day or two. Then the town gossips discovered that he was not working in the interest of a large company, as had been rumored, but solely on his own hook, so they left him severely alone. Besides, it was the height of the logging season and there was too much work to be done along the Columbia River to worry about strangers.

Marks hadn't taken this into consideration when he neared the eastern part of the state, but he was just as well pleased. If logs and logging served to center the attention of the natives elsewhere, so much the better. It would give him greater opportunity for observation and possibly the chance to pick up some information. Up to this time his trip along the border had been singularly uneventful and lacking in results. In fact, it was practically a toss-up with him whether he would continue on into Idaho and Montana, on the hope that he would find something there, or go back to Seattle and start fresh.

However, he figured that it wouldn't do any harm to spend a week or two in the neighborhood of the Columbia—and, as events turned out, it was a very wise move.

Partly out of curiosity and partly because it was in keeping with his self-assumed character of lumber prospector, Marks made a point of joining the gangs of men who worked all day and sometimes long into the night keeping the river clear of log jams and otherwise assisting in the movement of timber downstream. Like everyone who views these operations for the first time, he marveled at the dexterity of the loggers who perched upon the treacherous slippery trunks with as little thought[260] for danger as if they had been crossing a country road. But their years of familiarity with the current and the logs themselves had given them a sense of balance which appeared to inure them to peril.

Nor was this ability to ride logs confined wholly to the men. Some of the girls from the near-by country often worked in with the men, handling the lighter jobs and attending to details which did not call for the possession of a great amount of strength.

One of these, Marks noted, was particularly proficient in her work. Apparently there wasn't a man in Northport who could give her points in log riding, and the very fact that she was small and wiry provided her with a distinct advantage over men who were twice her weight. Apart from her grace and beauty, there was something extremely appealing about the girl, and Ezra found himself watching her time after time as she almost danced across the swirling, bark-covered trunks—hardly seeming to touch them as she moved.

The girl was by no means oblivious of the stranger's interest in her ability to handle at least a part of the men's work. She caught his eye the very first day he came down to the river, and after that, whenever she noted that he was present she seemed to take a new delight in skipping lightly from log to log, lingering on each just long enough to cause it to spin dangerously and then leaping to the next.

But one afternoon she tried the trick once too often. Either she miscalculated her distance or a sudden swirl of the current carried the log for which she was aiming out of her path, for her foot just touched it, slipped and, before she could recover her balance, she was in the water—surrounded by logs that threatened to crush the life out of her at any moment.[261]

Startled by her cry for help, three of the lumbermen started toward her—but the river, like a thing alive, appeared to thwart their efforts by opening up a rift in the jam on either side, leaving a gap too wide to be leaped, and a current too strong to be risked by men who were hampered by their heavy hobnailed shoes.

Marks, who had been watching the girl, had his coat off almost as soon as she hit the water. An instant later he had discarded his shoes and had plunged in, breasting the river with long overhand strokes that carried him forward at an almost unbelievable speed. Before the men on the logs knew what was happening, the operative was beside the girl, using one hand to keep her head above water, and the other to fend off the logs which were closing in from every side.

"Quick!" he called. "A rope! A—" but the trunk of a tree, striking his head a glancing blow, cut short his cry and forced him to devote every atom of his strength to remaining afloat until assistance arrived. After an interval which appeared to be measured in hours, rather than seconds, a rope splashed within reach and the pair were hauled to safety.

The girl, apparently unhurt by her drenching, shook herself like a wet spaniel and then turned to where Marks was seated, trying to recover his breath.

"Thanks," she said, extending her hand. "I don't know who you are, stranger, but you're a man!"

"It wasn't anything to make a fuss about," returned Ezra, rising and turning suspiciously red around the ears, for it was the first time that a girl had spoken to him in that way for more years than he cared to remember. Then, with the Vermont drawl that always came to the surface when he was excited or embarrassed, he added: "It was worth gettin' wet to have you speak like that."[262]

This time it was the girl who flushed, and, with a palpable effort to cover her confusion, she turned away, stopping to call back over her shoulder, "If you'll come up to dad's place to-night I'll see that you're properly thanked."

"Dad's place?" repeated Ezra to one of the men near by. "Where's that?"

"She means her stepfather's house up the river," replied the lumberman. "You can't miss it. Just this side the border. Ask anybody where Old Man Petersen lives."

Though the directions were rather vague, Marks started "up the river" shortly before sunset, and found but little difficulty in locating the big house—half bungalow and half cabin—where Petersen and his stepdaughter resided, in company with half a dozen foremen of lumber gangs, and an Indian woman who had acted as nurse and chaperon and cook and general servant ever since the death of the girl's mother a number of years before.

While he was still stumbling along, trying to pierce the gloom which settled almost instantly after sunset, Marks was startled to see a white figure rise suddenly before him and to hear a feminine voice remark, "I wondered if you'd come."

"Didn't you know I would?" replied Ezra. "Your spill in the river had me scared stiff for a moment, but it was a mighty lucky accident for me."

At the girl's suggestion they seated themselves outside, being joined before long by Petersen himself, who, with more than a trace of his Slavic ancestry apparent in his voice, thanked Marks for rescuing his daughter. It was when the older man left them and the girl's figure was outlined with startling distinctness by the light from the open door, that Ezra received a shock which brought him to earth with a crash.[263]

In the semidarkness he had been merely aware that the girl was wearing a dress which he would have characterized as "something white." But once he saw her standing in the center of the path of light which streamed from the interior of the house there could be no mistake.

The dress was of white silk!

More than that, it was made from material which Marks would have sworn had been cut from the same bolt as the sample which the Collector had shown him in Seattle!

"What's the matter, Mr. Marks?" inquired the girl, evidently noting the surprise which Ezra was unable completely to suppress. "Seen a ghost or something?"

"I thought for a moment I had," was the operative's reply, as he played for time. "It must be your dress. My—my sister had one just like it once."

"It is rather pretty, isn't it? In spite of the fact that I made it myself—out of some silk that dad—that dad brought home."

Ezra thought it best to change the subject, and as soon as he could find the opportunity said good night, with a promise to be on hand the next day to see that the plunge in the river wasn't repeated.

But the next morning he kept as far away from the girl—Fay Petersen—as he could, without appearing to make a point of the matter. He had thought the whole thing over from every angle and his conclusion was always the same. The Petersens were either hand in glove with the gang that was running the silk across the border or they were doing the smuggling themselves. The lonely cabin, the proximity to the border, the air of restraint which he had noted the previous evening (based principally upon the fact that he had not been invited indoors), the silk dress—all were signs which pointed at least to a knowledge of the plot to beat the customs.[264]

More than that, when Marks commenced to make some guarded inquiries about the family of the girl whom he had saved from drowning, he met with a decidedly cool reception.

"Old Man Petersen has some big loggin' interests in these parts," declared the most loquacious of his informants, "an' they say he's made a pile o' money in the last few months. Some say it's timber an' others say it's—well, it ain't nobody's concern how a man makes a livin' in these parts, s'long as he behaves himself."

"Isn't Petersen behaving himself?" asked Ezra.

"Stranger," was the reply, "it ain't always healthy to pry into another man's affairs. Better be satisfied with goin' to see the girl. That's more than anybody around here's allowed to do."

"So there was an air of mystery about the Petersen house, after all!" Marks thought. It hadn't been his imagination or an idea founded solely upon the sight of the silk dress!

The next fortnight found the operative a constant and apparently a welcome visitor at the house up the river. But, hint as he might, he was never asked indoors—a fact that made him all the more determined to see what was going on. While he solaced himself with the thought that his visits were made strictly in the line of duty, that his only purpose was to discover Petersen's connection with the smuggled silk, Ezra was unable entirely to stifle another feeling—something which he hadn't known since the old days in Vermont, when the announcement of a girl's wedding to another man had caused him to leave home and seek his fortunes in Boston.

Fay Petersen was pretty. There was no denying that fact. Also she was very evidently prepossessed in favor of the man who had saved her from the river. But this[265] fact, instead of soothing Marks's conscience, only irritated it the more. Here he was on the verge of making love to a girl—really in love with her, as he admitted to himself—and at the same time planning and hoping to send her stepfather to the penitentiary. He had hoped that the fact that Petersen was not her own father might make things a little easier for him, but the girl had shown in a number of ways that she was just as fond of her foster-parent as she would have been of her own.

"He's all the daddy I ever knew," she said one night, "and if anything ever happened to him I think it would drive me crazy," which fell far short of easing Ezra's mind, though it strengthened his determination to settle the matter definitely.

The next evening that he visited the Petersens he left a little earlier than usual, and only followed the road back to Northport sufficiently far to make certain that he was not being trailed. Then retracing his steps, he approached the house from the rear, his soft moccasins moving silently across the ground, his figure crouched until he appeared little more than a shadow between the trees.

Just as he reached the clearing which separated the dwelling from the woods, he stumbled and almost fell. His foot had caught against something which felt like the trunk of a fallen tree, but which moved with an ease entirely foreign to a log of that size.

Puzzled, Marks waited until a cloud which had concealed the moon had drifted by, and then commenced his examination. Yes, it was a log—and a big one, still damp from its immersion in the river. But it was so light that he could lift it unaided and it rang to a rap from his knuckles. The end which he first examined was solid, but at the other end the log was a mere shell, not more than an inch of wood remaining inside the bark.[266]

It was not until he discovered a round plug of wood—a stopper, which fitted precisely into the open end of the log—that the solution of the whole mystery dawned upon him. The silk had been shipped across the border from Canada inside the trunks of trees, hollowed out for the purpose! Wrapping the bolts in oiled silk would keep them perfectly waterproof and the plan was so simple as to be impervious to detection, save by accident.

Emboldened by his discovery, Marks slipped silently across the cleared space to the shadow of the house, and thence around to the side, where a few cautious cuts of his bowie knife opened a peep hole in the shutter which covered the window. Through this he saw what he had hoped for, yet feared to find—Petersen and three of his men packing bolts of white silk in boxes for reshipment. What was more, he caught snatches of their conversation which told him that another consignment of the smuggled goods was due from Trail, just across the border, within the week.

Retreating as noiselessly as he had come, Marks made his way back to Northport, where he wrote two letters—or, rather, a letter and a note. The first, addressed to the sheriff, directed that personage to collect a posse and report to Ezra Marks, of the Customs Service, on the second day following. This was forwarded by special messenger, but Marks pocketed the note and slipped it cautiously under the door of the Petersen house the next evening.

"It's a fifty-fifty split," he consoled his conscience. "The government gets the silk and the Petersens get their warning. I don't suppose I'll get anything but the devil for not landing them!"

The next morning when the sheriff and his posse arrived they found, only an empty house, but in the main room were piled boxes containing no less than thirty[267] thousand yards of white silk—valued at something over one hundred thousand dollars. On top of the boxes was an envelope addressed to Ezra Marks, Esq., and within it a note which read, "I don't know who you are, Mr. Customs Officer, but you're a man!"

There was no signature, but the writing was distinctly feminine.

"And was that all Marks ever heard from her?" I asked, when Quinn paused.

"So far as I know," said the former operative. "Of course, Washington never heard about that part of the case. They were too well satisfied with Ezra's haul and the incoming cargo, which they also landed, to care much about the Petersens. So the whole thing was entered on Marks's record precisely as he had figured it—a fifty-fifty split. You see, even government agents aren't always completely successful—especially when they're fighting Cupid as well as crooks!"

[268]
XIX
THE CLUE IN THE CLASSIFIED COLUMN

Quinn tossed his evening paper aside with a gesture in which disgust was mingled in equal proportion with annoyance.

"Why is it," he inquired, testily, "that some fools never learn anything?"

"Possibly that's because they're fools," I suggested. "What's the trouble now?"

"Look at that!" And the former Secret Service operative recovered the paper long enough to indicate a short news item near the bottom of the first page—an item which bore the headline, "New Fifty-Dollar Counterfeit Discovered."

"Yes," I agreed, "there always are people foolish enough to change bills without examining them any too closely. But possibly this one is very cleverly faked."

"Fools not to examine them!" echoed Quinn. "That isn't the direction in which the idiocy lies. The fools are the people who think they can counterfeit Uncle Sam's currency and get away with it. Barnum must have been right. There's a sucker born every minute—and those that don't try to beat the ponies or buck the stock market turn to counterfeiting for a living. They get it, too, in Leavenworth or Atlanta or some other place that maintains a federal penitentiary.

"They never seem to learn anything by others' experience,[269] either. You'd think, after the Thurene case, it would be perfectly apparent that no one could beat the counterfeiting game for long."

"The Thurene case? I don't seem to remember that. The name is unusual, but—"

"Yes, and that wasn't the only part of the affair that was out of the ordinary," Quinn cut in. "Spencer Graham also contributed some work that was well off the beaten path—not forgetting the assistance rendered by a certain young woman."

Probably the most remarkable portion of the case [continued Quinn] was the fact that Graham didn't get in on it until Thurene had been arrested. Nevertheless, if it hadn't been for his work in breaking through an ironclad alibi the government might have been left high and dry, with a trunkful of suspicions and mighty little else.

Somewhere around the latter part of August the New York branch of the Secret Service informed Washington that a remarkably clever counterfeit fifty-dollar bill had turned up in Albany—a bill in which the engraving was practically perfect and the only thing missing from the paper was the silk fiber. This, however, was replaced by tiny red and blue lines, drawn in indelible ink. The finished product was so exceptionally good that, if it had not been for the lynxlike eyes of a paying teller—plus the highly developed sense of touch which bank officials accumulate—the note would have been changed without a moment's hesitation.

The man who presented it, who happened to be well known to the bank officials, was informed that the bill was counterfeit and the matter was reported through the usual channels. A few days later another bill, evidently from the same batch, was picked up in Syracuse, and[270]from that time on it rained counterfeits so hard that every teller in the state threw a fit whenever a fifty-dollar bill came in, either for deposit or for change.

Hardly had the flow of upstate counterfeits lessened than the bills began to make their appearance in and around New York, sometimes in banks, but more often in the resorts patronized by bookmakers from Jamaica and the other near-by race tracks.

The significance of this fact didn't strike the Secret Service men assigned to the case until the horses had moved southward. The instant one of the bills was reported in Baltimore two operatives were ordered to haunt the *pari-mutuel* booths at Pimlico, with instructions to pay particular attention to the windows where the larger wagers were laid. An expert in counterfeits also took up his position inside the cage, to signal the men outside as soon as a phony bill was presented.

It was during the rush of the betting after the two-year-olds had gone to the post for the first race that the signal came—indicating that a man about forty-five years of age, well dressed and well groomed, had exchanged two of the counterfeits for a one hundred-dollar ticket on the favorite.

Hollister and Sheehan, the Secret Service men, took no chances with their prey. Neither did they run the risk of arresting him prematurely. Figuring that it was well within the realms of possibility that he had received the bills in exchange for other money, and that he was therefore ignorant of the fact that they were spurious, they contented themselves with keeping close to him during the race and the interval which followed.

When the favorite won, the man they were watching cashed his bet and stowed his winnings away in a trousers pocket. Then, after a prolonged examination of the[271] jockeys, the past performances and the weights of the various horses, he made his way back to the window to place another bet.

Again the signal—and this time Hollister and Sheehan closed in on their man, notifying him that he was under arrest and advising him to come along without creating any disturbance.

"Arrest for what?" he demanded.

"Passing counterfeit money," replied Hollister, flashing his badge. Then, as the man started to protest, Sheehan counseled him to reserve his arguments until later, and the trio made their way out of the inclosure in silence.

When searched, in Baltimore, two sums of money were found upon the suspect—one roll in his left-hand trousers pocket being made up of genuine currency, including that which he had received for picking the winner of the first race, and the one in the right-hand pocket being entirely of counterfeit fifty-dollar bills—forty-eight in number.

When questioned, the prisoner claimed that his name was Robert J. Thurene of New Haven, and added that there were plenty of people in the Connecticut city who would vouch for his respectability.

"Then why," inquired the chief of the Secret Service, who had come over from Washington to take charge of the case, "do you happen to have two thousand four hundred dollars in counterfeit money on you?"

At that moment Thurene dropped his bomb—or, rather, one of the many which rendered the case far from monotonous.

"If you'll search my room at the Belvedere," he suggested, "you'll find some five thousand dollars more."

"What?" demanded the chief. "Do you admit that you deliberately brought seven thousand five hundred dollars of counterfeit money here and tried to pass it?"[272]

"I admit nothing," corrected the arrested man. "You stated that the fifty-dollar bills which you found upon me when I was searched against my will were false. I'll take your word for that. But if they are counterfeit, I'm merely telling you that there are a hundred more like them in my room at the hotel."

"Of course you're willing to state where they came from?" suggested the chief, who was beginning to sense the fact that something underlay Thurene's apparent sincerity.

"Certainly. I found them."

"Old stuff," sneered one of the operatives standing near by. "Not only an old alibi, but one which you'll have a pretty hard time proving."

"Do you happen to have a copy of yesterday's *News* handy?" Thurene asked.

When the paper was produced he turned rapidly to the Lost and Found column and pointed to an advertisement which appeared there:

FOUND—An envelope containing a sum of money. Owner may recover same by notifying Robert J. Thurene, Belvedere Hotel, and proving property.

"There," he continued, after reading the advertisement aloud, "that is the notice which I inserted after finding the money which you say is counterfeit."

"Where did you find it?"

"In the Pennsylvania station, night before last. I had just come in from New York, and chanced to see the envelope lying under one of the rows of seats in the center of the waiting room. It attracted my attention, but when I examined it I was amazed to find that it contained one hundred and fifty fifty-dollar bills, all apparently brand new. Naturally, I didn't care to part with the money[273] unless I was certain that I was giving it up to the rightful owner, so I carried it with me to the hotel and advertised the loss at once.

"The next afternoon I went out to the track and found, when it was too late, that the only money I had with me was that contained in the envelope. I used a couple of the bills, won, and, being superstitious, decided to continue betting with that money. That's the reason I used it this afternoon. Come to think of it, you won't find the original five thousand dollars in my room. Part of it is the money which I received at the track and which I replaced in order to make up the sum I found. But most of the bills are there."

"You said," remarked the chief, striking another tack, "that your name is Thurene and that you live in New Haven. What business are you in?"

"Stationery. You'll find that my rating in Bradstreet's is excellent, even though my capital may not be large. What's more"—and here the man's voice became almost aggressive—"any bank in New Haven and any member of the Chamber of Commerce will vouch for me. I've a record of ten years there and some ten in Lowell, Mass., which will bear the closest possible inspection."

And he was right, at that.

In the first place, a search of his room at the hotel brought to light a large official envelope containing just the sum of money he had mentioned, counterfeit bills and real ones. Secondly, a wire to New Haven elicited the information that "Robert J. Thurene, answering to description in inquiry received, has operated a successful stationery store here for the past ten years. Financial standing excellent. Wide circle of friends, all of whom vouch for his character and integrity."

When this wire was forwarded to Washington, the chief[274] having returned to headquarters, Spencer Graham received a hurry-up call to report in the main office. There he was informed that he was to take charge of the Thurene case and see what he could find out.

"I don't have to tell you," added the chief, "that it's rather a delicate matter. Either the man is the victim of circumstances—in which case we'll have to release him with profound apologies and begin all over again—or he's a mighty clever crook. We can't afford to take any chances. The case as it finally stands will have to be presented in court, and, therefore, must be proof against the acid test of shrewd lawyers for the defense, lawyers who will rely upon the newspaper advertisement and Thurene's spotless record as indications of his innocence."

"That being the case, Chief, why take any chances right now? The case hasn't gotten into the papers, so why not release Thurene?"

"And keep him under constant surveillance? That wouldn't be a bad idea. The moment he started to leave the country we could nab him, and meanwhile we would have plenty of time to look into the matter. Of course, there's always the danger of suicide—but that's proof of guilt, and it would save the Service a lot of work in the long run. Good idea! We'll do it."

So it was that Robert J. Thurene of New Haven was released from custody with the apologies of the Secret Service—who retained the counterfeit money, but returned the real bills—while Spencer Graham went to work on the Baltimore end of the case, four operatives took up the job of trailing the stationer, and Rita Clarke found that she had important business to transact in Connecticut.

Anyone who didn't know Rita would never have suspected that, back of her brown eyes lay a fund of[275] information upon a score of subjects—including stenography, the best methods of filing, cost accounting, and many other points which rendered her invaluable around an office. Even if they found this out, there was something else which she kept strictly to herself—the fact that she was engaged to a certain operative in the United States Secret Service, sometimes known as Number Thirty-three, and sometimes as Spencer Graham.

In reply to Spencer's often-repeated requests that she set a day for their wedding, Miss Clarke would answer: "And lose the chance to figure in any more cases? Not so that you could notice it! As long as I'm single you find that you can use me every now and then, but if I were married I'd have too many domestic cares. No, Spencer, let's wait until we get one more BIG case, and then—well, we'll say one month from the day it's finished."

Which was the reason that Graham and his fiancée had a double reason for wanting to bring Thurene to earth.

The first place that Graham went to in Baltimore was the Pennsylvania station, where he made a number of extended inquiries of certain employees there. After that he went to the newspaper office, where he conferred with the clerk whose business it was to receive the lost and found advertisements, finally securing a copy of the original notice in Thurene's handwriting. Also some other information which he jotted down in a notebook reserved for that purpose.

Several days spent in Baltimore failed to turn up any additional leads and Graham returned to Washington with a request for a list of the various places where counterfeit fifty-dollar bills had been reported during the past month. The record sounded like the megaphonic call of a train leaving Grand Central Station—New York,[276] Yonkers, Poughkeepsie, Syracuse, Troy, and points north, with a few other cities thrown in for good measure. So Spencer informed the chief that he would make his headquarters in New York for the next ten days or so, wired Rita to the same effect, and left Washington on the midnight train.

In New York he discovered only what he had already known, plus one other very significant bit of evidence—something which would have warranted him in placing Thurene again under arrest had he not been waiting for word from Rita. He knew that it would take her at least a month to work up her end of the case, so Graham put in the intervening time in weaving his net a little stronger, for he had determined that the next time the New Haven stationer was taken into custody would be the last—that the government would have a case which all the lawyers on earth couldn't break.

Early in December he received a wire from Rita—a telegram which contained the single word, "Come"—but that was enough. He was in New Haven that night, and, in a quiet corner of the Taft grille the girl gave him an account of what she had found.

"Getting into Thurene's store was the easiest part of the whole job," she admitted. "It took me less than a day to spot one of the girls who wanted to get married, bribe her to leave, and then arrive bright and early the following morning, in response to the 'stenographer wanted' advertisement."

"Thurene's had a lot of practice writing ads lately," remarked Graham, with a smile.

"What do you mean?"

"Nothing. Tell you later. What'd you find in the store?"

"Not a thing—until day before yesterday. I thought[277] it best to move slowly and let matters take their own course as far as possible. So I contented myself with doing the work which had been handled by the girl whose place I took—dictation, typing, and the rest. Then I found that the correspondence files were in shocking shape. I grabbed the opportunity to do a little night work by offering to bring them up to date.

"'Certainly,' said the boss, and then took good care to be on hand when I arrived after dinner that night. The very way he hung around and watched every movement I made convinced me that the stuff was somewhere on the premises. But where? That's what I couldn't figure out.

"Having demonstrated my ability by three hours of stiff work on the files, I suggested a few days later that I had a first-hand knowledge of cost accounting and that I would be glad to help get his books in shape for the holiday business, the old man who usually attends to this being sick. Again Thurene assented and again he blew in, 'to explain any entries which might prove troublesome.' I'll say this for him, though—there isn't a single incriminating entry on the books. Every purchase is accounted for, down to the last paper of pins.

"Then, when I felt that I had wormed myself sufficiently well into his good graces, I hinted that I might be able to help out by supervising the system in the engraving department—checking up the purchases, watching the disbursements, keeping an eye on the stock and so on. Rather to my surprise, he didn't offer any objection. Said that my work had been of so much help elsewhere that he would be glad to have me watch the engravers' work.

"It was there that I got my first real lead—at least I hope it's a lead. Back of the engraving department is a[278] small room, locked and padlocked, where the boss is supposed to ride his personal hobby of amateur photography. I asked one of the men the reason for guarding a dark room so carefully, and he replied that Thurene claimed to be on the verge of making a great discovery in color photography, but that the process took a long time and he didn't want to run the risk of having it disturbed. I'm to have a look at his color process to-night."

"What?" cried Graham. "He's going to show you what is in the double-locked room?"

"That's what he's promised to do. I haven't the least hope of seeing anything incriminating—all the evidence will probably be well hidden—but this morning I expressed a casual interest in photography and remarked that I understood he was working on a new color process. I did it mainly to see how he would react. But he never batted an eyelid. 'I've been making some interesting experiments recently,' he said, 'and they ought to reach a climax to-night. If you'd care to see how they turn out, suppose you meet me here at nine o'clock and we'll examine them together.'"

"But Rita," Graham protested, "you don't mean to say that you're going to put yourself entirely in this man's power?"

The girl's first answer was a laugh, and then, "What do you mean, 'put myself in his power'?" she mocked. "You talk like the hero of a melodrama. This isn't the first time that I've been alone in the store with him after dark. Besides, he doesn't suspect a thing and it's too good a chance to miss. Meet me here the first thing in the morning—around eight-thirty—and I'll give you the details of Thurene's secret chamber, provided it contains anything interesting."

"Rita, I can't—" Graham started to argue, but the[279] girl cut in with, "You can't stop me? No, you can't. What's more, I'll have to hurry. It's ten minutes to nine now. See you in the morning."

The next thing Graham knew she had slipped away from the table and was on her way out of the grille.

When Rita reached the Thurene establishment, promptly at nine, she found the proprietor waiting for her.

"On time, as usual," he laughed. "Now you'd better keep your hat and coat on. There's no heat in the dark room and I don't want you to catch cold. The plates ought to be ready by this time. We'll go right down and take a look at them."

Guided by the light from the lantern which the stationer held high in the air, the girl started down the steps leading to the basement where the engraving department was located. She heard Thurene close the door behind him, but failed to hear him slip the bolt which, as they afterward found, had been well oiled.

In fact, it was not until they had reached the center of the large room, in one corner of which was the door to the private photographic laboratory, that she knew anything was wrong. Then it was too late.

Before she could move, Thurene leaned forward and seized her—one arm about her waist, the other over her mouth. Struggle as she might, Rita was unable to move. Slowly, relentlessly, Thurene turned her around until she faced him, and then, with a sudden movement of the arm that encircled her waist, secured a wad of cotton waste, which he had evidently prepared for just such an emergency. When he had crammed this in the girl's mouth and tied her hands securely, he moved forward to open the door to the dark room.

"Thought I was easy, didn't you?" he sneered. "Didn't think I'd see through your scheme to get a position here[280] and your infernal cleverness with the books and the accounts? Want to see something of my color process, eh? Well, you'll have an opportunity to study it at your leisure, for it'll be twelve good hours before anyone comes down here, and by that time I'll be where the rest of your crowd can't touch me."

"Come along! In with you!"

At that moment there was a crash of glass from somewhere near the ceiling and something leaped into the room—something that took only two strides to reach Thurene and back him up against the wall, with the muzzle of a very businesslike automatic pressed into the pit of his stomach.

The whole thing happened so quickly that by the time Rita recovered her balance and turned around she only saw the stationer with his hands well above his head and Spencer Graham—her Spencer—holding him up at the point of a gun.

"Take this," snapped the operative, producing a penknife, "and cut that girl's hands loose! No false moves now—or I'm likely to get nervous!"

A moment later Rita was free and Thurene had resumed his position against the wall.

"Frisk him!" ordered Graham, and then, when the girl had produced a miscellaneous collection of money, keys and jewelry from the man's pockets, Spencer allowed him to drop his arms long enough to snap a pair of handcuffs in place.

"This time," announced the Secret Service man, "you won't be released merely because of a fake ad. and the testimony of your friends. Pretty clever scheme, that. Inserting a 'found advertisement' to cover your possession of counterfeit money in case you were caught. But you overlooked a couple of points. The station in Baltimore[281] was thoroughly swept just five minutes before your train arrived from New York and every man on duty there is ready to swear that he wouldn't have overlooked anything as large as the envelope containing that phony money. Then, too, the clerk in the *News* office received your advertisement shortly after noon the next day—so you didn't advertise it 'at once,' as you said you did.

"But your biggest mistake was in playing the game too often. Here"—producing a page from the classified section of a New York newspaper—"is the duplicate of your Baltimore ad., inserted to cover your tracks in case they caught you at Jamaica. I've got the original, in your handwriting, in my pocket."

"But how'd you happen to arrive here at the right moment?" exclaimed Rita.

"I wasn't any too well convinced that you'd fooled our friend here," Graham replied. "So I trailed you, and, attracted by the light from Thurene's lantern, managed to break in that window at the time you needed me."

"There's only one thing that puzzles me," the operative continued, turning to Thurene. "What made you take up counterfeiting? Your business record was clear enough before that, and, of course, being an engraver, it wasn't hard for you to find the opportunity. What was the motive?"

For a full sixty seconds the man was silent and then, from between his clenched teeth, came two words, "Wall Street."

"I might have guessed that," replied Graham. "I'll see you safely in jail first and then have a look through your room. Want to come along, Rita?"

"No, thanks, Spencer. I've had enough for one[282] evening. Let's see. This is the sixth of December. Suppose we plan a certain event for the sixth of January?"

"And so they were married and lived happily ever after?" I added, as Quinn paused.

"And so they were married," he amended. "I can't say as to the rest of it—though I'm inclined to believe that they were happy. Anyhow, Rita knew when she had enough—and that's all you can really ask for in a wife."

[283]

XX
IN THE SHADOW OF THE CAPITOL

"It won't be long until they're all back—with their pretty clothes and their jeweled bags and their air of innocent sophistication—but until at least a dozen of them gather here Washington won't be itself again."

Bill Quinn and I had been discussing the change which had come over Washington since peace had disrupted the activities of the various war organizations, and then, after a pause, the former member of the Secret Service had referred to "them" and to "their pretty clothes."

"Who do you mean?" I inquired. "With the possible exception of some prominent politicians I don't know anyone whose presence is essential to make Washington 'itself again.' And certainly nobody ever accused politicians, with the possible exception of J. Ham Lewis, of wearing pretty clothes. Even he didn't carry a jeweled bag."

"I wasn't thinking of Congressmen or Senators or even members of the Cabinet," replied Quinn with a smile. "Like the poor, they are always with us, and also like the poor, there are times when we would willingly dispense with them. But the others—they make life worth living, particularly for members of the Secret Service, who are apt to be a bit bored with the monotony of chasing counterfeiters and guarding the President.

"The ones I refer to are the beautifully gowned women whose too perfect English often betrays their foreign[284] origin almost as certainly as would a dialect. They are sent here by various governments abroad to find out things which we would like to keep secret and their presence helps to keep Washington cosmopolitan and—interesting.

"During the war—well, if you recall the case of Jimmy Callahan and the electric sign at Norfolk—the affair which I believe you wrote under the title of 'A Flash in the Night'—you know what happened to those who were caught plotting against the government. In times of peace, however, things are different."

"Why? Isn't a spy always a spy?"

"So far as their work is concerned they are. But by a sort of international agreement, tacit but understood, those who seek to pry into the affairs of other governments during the years of peace are not treated with the same severity as when a nation is fighting for its life."

"But surely we have no secrets that a foreign government would want!" I protested. "That's one of the earmarks of a republic. Everything is aired in the open, even dirty linen."

Quinn didn't answer for a moment, and when he did reply there was a reminiscent little smile playing around the corners of his mouth.

"Do you remember the disappearance of the plans of the battleship *Pennsylvania*?" he asked.

130

"Yes, I think I do. But as I recall it the matter was never cleared up."

"Officially, it wasn't. Unofficially, it was. At least there are several persons connected with the United States Secret Service who are positive that Sylvia Sterne lifted the blue prints and afterward—well, we might as well begin the story at the first chapter."

[285]
The name she was known by on this side of the Atlantic [continued the former government agent] was not that of Sterne, though subsequent investigations proved that that was what she was called in Paris and Vienna and Rome and London. When she arrived in Washington her visiting cards bore the name of the Countess Stefani, and as there are half a dozen counts of that name to be found in the peerages of as many principalities, no one inquired too deeply into her antecedents.

Yes, she admitted that there was a count somewhere in the background, but she led those who were interested to the conclusion he had never understood her peculiar temperament and that therefore she was sojourning in Washington, seeking pleasure and nothing more. A slow, soulful glance from her violet eyes usually accompanied the statement—and caused the man to whom the statement was made (it was always a man) to wonder how anyone could fail to appreciate so charming a creature.

"Charming" is really a very good word to apply to the Countess Sylvia. Her manner was charming and her work was likewise. Charming secrets and invitations and news out of those with whom she came in contact.

Her first public appearance, so far as the Secret Service was concerned, was at one of the receptions at the British embassy. She was there on invitation, of course, but it was an invitation secured in her own original way.

Immediately upon arriving in Washington she had secured an apartment at Brickley Court, an apartment which chanced to be directly across the hall from the one occupied by a Mrs. Sheldon, a young widow with a rather large acquaintance in the diplomatic set.

Some ten days after the Countess Sylvia took up her residence on Connecticut Avenue she visited one of the department stores and made several purchases, ordering[286] them sent C. O. D. to her apartment. Only, instead of giving the number as four thirty-six, her tongue apparently slipped and she said four thirty-seven, which was Mrs. Sheldon's number. Of course, if the parcels had been paid for or charged they would have been left at the desk in the lobby, but, being collect, the boy brought them to the door of four thirty-seven.

As was only natural, Mrs. Sheldon was about to order them returned when the door across the hall opened and the countess, attired in one of her most fetching house gowns, appeared and explained the mistake.

"How stupid of me!" she exclaimed. "I must have given the girl the wrong apartment number. I'm awfully sorry for troubling you, Mrs. Sheldon."

The widow, being young, could not restrain the look of surprise when her name was mentioned by a woman who was an utter stranger, but the countess cut right in with:

"You probably don't remember me, but we met two years ago on Derby Day in London. The count and I had the pleasure of meeting you through Lord Cartwright, but it was just before the big race, and when I looked around again you had been swallowed up in the crowd."

Mrs. Sheldon had been at the Derby two years before, as the countess doubtless knew before she arrived in Washington, and also she remembered having met a number of persons during that eventful afternoon. So the rest was easy for Sylvia, particularly as the first half hour of their conversation uncovered the fact that they had many mutual friends, all of whom, however, were in Europe.

Through Mrs. Sheldon the countess met a number of the younger and lesser lights of the Diplomatic Corps and[287] the invitation to the reception at the British Embassy was hers for the suggestion.

Before the evening was over several men were asking themselves where they had met that "very charming countess" before. Some thought it must have been in Paris, others were certain that it was in Vienna, and still others maintained that her face brought back memories of their detail in Saint Petersburg (the name of the Russian capital had not then been altered). Sylvia didn't enlighten any of them. Neither did she volunteer details, save of the vaguest nature, contenting herself with knowing glances which hinted much and bits of frothy gossip which conveyed nothing. The beauty of her face and the delicate curves of her figure did the rest. Before the evening was over she had met at least the younger members of all the principal embassies and legations, not to mention three men whose names appeared upon the roster of the Senate Committee on Foreign Relations.

To one of these, Senator Lattimer, she paid particular attention, assuring him that she would be honored if he would "drop in some afternoon for tea," an invitation which the gentleman from Iowa accepted with alacrity a few days later.

As was afterward apparent, the countess had arranged her schedule with considerable care. She had arrived in Washington early in the fall, and by the time the season was well under way she had the entrée to the majority of the semiprivate functions—teas and receptions and dances to which a number of guests were invited. Here, of course, she had an opportunity to pick up a few morsels of information—crumbs which fell from the tables of diplomacy—but that wasn't what she was after. She wanted a copy of a certain confidential report referring to[288]American relations abroad, and, what's more, she'd have gotten it if she hadn't overstepped herself.

Through what might have been termed in vulgar circles "pumping" Senator Lattimer, though the countess's casual inquiries from time to time evinced only a natural interest in the affairs of the world, Sylvia found out that the report would be completed early in March and that a copy would be in the Senator's office for at least two days—or, what interested her more, two nights.

She didn't intimate that she would like to see it. That would have been too crude. In fact, she deftly turned the subject and made the Senator believe that she was interested only in his views with respect to the stabilization of currency or some such topic far removed from the point they had mentioned.

Just before he left, however, Senator Lattimer mentioned that there was going to be a big display of fireworks around the Washington Monument the following evening, and inquired if the countess would be interested in witnessing the celebration.

"Surely," said she. "Why not let's watch them from the roof here? We ought to able to get an excellent view."

"I've got a better idea than that," was the senatorial reply. "We'll go down to the State, War, and Navy Building. The windows on the south side ought to be ideal for that purpose and there won't be any trouble about getting in. I'll see to that," he added, with just a touch of pomposity.

So it happened that among the dozen or more persons who occupied choice seats in a room in the Navy Department that next night were the Hon. Arthur H. Lattimer and the Countess Stefani.

The next morning it was discovered that plans relating to certain recent naval improvements—radical changes[289] which were to be incorporated in the battleship *Pennsylvania*—were missing.

The chief learned of the loss about nine-thirty, and by ten o'clock every available man was turned loose on the case, with instructions to pry into the past records and watch the future actions of the people who had been in the room on the previous evening.

Because he particularly requested it, Owen Williams, whose connection with the Secret Service was not a matter of general information, was detailed to learn what he could of the Countess Stefani.

"I've run into her a couple of times recently," he told the chief, "and there's something not altogether on the level about the lady. I don't suppose we have time to cable abroad and trace the particular branch of the family to which she claims to belong, but I have a hunch that she is not working altogether in the interest of Europe. A certain yellow-skinned person whom we both know has been seen coming out of Brickley Court on several occasions within the past month, and—well, the countess is worth watching."

"Trail her, then!" snapped the chief. "The department has asked for quick action in this case, for there are reasons which render it inadvisable for those plans to get out of the country."

"Right!" replied Williams, settling his hat at a rather jaunty angle and picking up his gloves and stick. "I'll keep in close touch with you and report developments. If you want me within the next couple of hours I'll probably be somewhere around Brickley Court. The countess never rises until round noon."

But that morning, as Williams soon discovered, something appeared to have interfered with the routine of the fair Sylvia. She had called the office about nine o'clock,[290] made an inquiry about the New York trains, ordered a chair reserved on the eleven and a taxi for ten forty-five. All of which gave Owen just enough time to phone the chief, tell him of the sudden change in his plans, and suggest that the countess's room be searched during her absence.

"Tell New York to have some one pick up Stefani as soon as she arrives," Williams concluded. "I'm going to renew my acquaintance with her en route, find out where she's staying, and frame an excuse for being at the same hotel. But I may not be able to accompany her there, so have some one trail her from the station. I'll make any necessary reports through the New York office."

Just after the train pulled out of Baltimore the Countess Stefani saw a young and distinctly handsome man, whose face was vaguely familiar, rise from his seat at the far end of the car and come toward her. Then, as he reached her chair he halted, surprised.

"This is luck!" he exclaimed. "I never hoped to find you on the train, Countess! Going through to New York, of course?"

As he spoke the man's name came back to her, together with the fact that he had been pointed out as one of the eligible young bachelors who apparently did but little and yet had plenty of money to do it with.

"Oh, Mr. Williams! You gave me a bit of a start at first. Your face was in the shadow and I didn't recognize you. Yes, I'm just running up for a little shopping. Won't be gone for more than a day or two, for I must be back in time for the de Maury dance on Thursday evening. You are going, I suppose?"

Thankful for the opening, Williams occupied the vacant chair next to hers, and before they reached Havre de Grace they were deep in a discussion of people and affairs[291] in Washington. It was not Williams's intention, however, to allow the matter to stop there. Delicately, but certainly, he led the conversation into deeper channels, exerting every ounce of his personality to convince the countess that this was a moment for which he had longed, an opportunity to chat uninterruptedly with "the most charming woman in Washington."

"This is certainly the shortest five hours I've ever spent," he assured his companion as the porter announced their arrival at Manhattan Transfer. "Can't I see something more of you while we are in New York? I'm not certain when I'll get back to Washington and this glimpse has been far too short. Are you going to stop with friends?"

"No—at the Vanderbilt. Suppose you call up to-morrow morning and I'll see what I can do."

"Why not a theater party this evening?"

"I'm sorry, but I have an engagement."

"Right—to-morrow morning, then," and the operative said good-by with a clear conscience, having noted that one of the men from the New York office was already on the job.

Later in the evening he was informed that the countess had gone directly to her hotel, had dressed for dinner, and then, after waiting in the lobby for nearly an hour, had eaten a solitary meal and had gone back to her room, leaving word at the desk that she was to be notified immediately if anyone called. But no one had.

The next morning, instead of phoning, Williams dropped around to the Vanderbilt and had a short session with the house detective, who had already been notified that the Countess Stefani was being watched by Secret Service operatives. The house man, however, verified the report of the operative who had picked up the countess at the[292] station—she had received no callers and had seen no one save the maid.

"Any phone messages?"

"Not one."

"Any mail?"

"Just a newspaper, evidently one that a friend had mailed from Washington. The address was in a feminine hand and—"

"Tell the maid that I want the wrapper of that paper if it's in the countess's room," interrupted Williams. "I don't want the place searched for it, but if it happens to be in the wastebasket be sure I get it."

A moment later he was calling the Countess Stefani, presumably from the office of a friend of his in Wall Street.

"I'm afraid I can't see you to-day," and Sylvia's voice appeared to register infinite regret. "I wasn't able to complete a little business deal I had on last night—succumbed to temptation and went to the theater, so I'll have to pay for it to-day." (Here Williams suppressed a chuckle, both at the manner in which the lady handled the truth and at the fact that she was palpably ignorant that she had been shadowed.) "I'm returning to Washington on the Congressional, but I'll be sure to see you at the de Maurys', won't I? Please come down—for my sake!"

"I'll do it," was Owen's reply, "and I can assure you that my return to Washington will be entirely because I feel that I must see you again. Au revoir, until Thursday night."

"On the Congressional Limited, eh?" he muttered as he stepped out of the booth. "Maybe it's a stall, but I'll make the train just the same. Evidently one of the lady's plans has gone amiss."

"Here's the wrapper you wanted," said the house[293] detective, producing a large torn envelope, slit lengthwise and still showing by its rounded contour that it had been used to inclose a rolled newspaper.

"Thanks," replied Williams, as he glanced at the address. "I thought so."

"Thought what?"

"Come over here a minute," and he steered the detective to the desk, where he asked to be shown the register for the preceding day. Then, pointing to the name "Countess Sylvia Stefani" on the hotel sheet and to the same name on the wrapper, he asked, "Note everything?"

"The handwriting is the same!"

"Precisely. The countess mailed this paper herself at this hotel before she left Washington. And, if I'm not very much mistaken, she'll mail another one to herself in Washington, before she leaves New York."

"You want it intercepted?"

"I do not! If Sylvia is willing to trust the Post-office Department with her secret, I certainly am. But I intend to be on hand when that paper arrives."

Sure enough, just before leaving for the station that afternoon, Williams found out from his ally at the Vanderbilt that the countess had slipped a folded and addressed newspaper into the mail box in the lobby. She had then paid her bill and entered a taxi, giving the chauffeur instructions to drive slowly through Central Park. Sibert, the operative who was trailing her, reported that several times she appeared to be on the point of stopping, but had ordered the taxi driver to go on—evidently being suspicious that she was followed and not wishing to take any chances.

Of this, though, Williams knew nothing—for a glance into one of the cars on the Congressional Limited had been sufficient to assure him that his prey was aboard. He[294] spent the rest of the trip in the smoker, so that he might not run into her.

In Washington, however, a surprise awaited him.

Instead of returning at once to Brickley Court, the countess checked her bag at the station and hired a car by the hour, instructing the driver to take her to the Chevy Chase Club. Williams, of course, followed in another car, but had the ill fortune to lose the first taxi in the crush of machines which is always to be noted on dance nights at the club, and it was well on toward morning before he could locate the chauffeur he wanted to reach.

According to that individual, the lady had not gone into the club, at all, but, changing her mind, had driven on out into the country, returning to Washington at midnight.

"Did she meet anyone?" demanded Williams.

"Not a soul, sir. Said she just wanted to drive through the country and that she had to be at the Senate Office Building at twelve o'clock."

"The Senate Office Building?" echoed the operative. "At midnight? Did you drop her there?"

"I did, sir. She told me to wait and she was out again in five minutes, using the little door in the basement—the one that's seldom locked. I thought she was the wife of one of the Senators. Then I drove her to Union Station to get her bag, and then to Brickley Court, where she paid me and got out."

The moment the chauffeur had mentioned the Senate Office Building a mental photograph of Senator Lattimer had sprung to Williams's mind, for the affair between the countess and the Iowa statesman was public property.

Telling the chauffeur to wait in the outer room, the operative called the Lattimer home and insisted on speaking to the Senator.[295]

"Yes, it's a matter of vital importance!" he snapped. Then, a few moments later, when a gruff but sleepy voice inquired what he wanted:

"This is Williams of the Secret Service speaking, Senator. Have you any documents of importance—international importance—in your office at the present moment?"

"No, nothing of particular value. Wait a minute! A copy of a certain report to the Committee on Foreign Relations arrived late yesterday and I remember seeing it on my desk as I left. Why? What's the matter?"

"Nothing—except that I don't think that report is there now," replied Williams. "Can you get to your office in ten minutes?"

"I'll be there!"

But a thorough search by the two of them failed to reveal any trace of the document. It had gone—vanished—in spite of the fact that the door was locked as usual.

"Senator," announced the government agent, "a certain woman you know took that paper. She got in here with a false key, lifted the report and was out again in less than five minutes. The theft occurred shortly after midnight and—"

"If you know so much about it, why don't you arrest her?"

"I shall—before the hour is up. Only I thought you might like to know in advance how your friend the Countess Stefani worked. She was also responsible for the theft of the plans of the battleship *Pennsylvania*, you know."

And Williams was out of the room before the look of amazement had faded from the Senator's face.

Some thirty minutes later the Countess Sylvia was awakened by the sound of continued rapping on her door.[296] In answer to her query, "Who's there?" a man's voice replied, "Open this door, or I'll break it in!"

Williams, however, knew that his threat was an idle one, for the doors at Brickley Court were built of solid oak that defied anything short of a battering ram. Which was the reason that he had to wait a full five minutes, during which time he distinctly heard the sound of paper rattling and then the rasp of a match as it was struck.

Finally the countess, attired in a bewitching negligée, threw open the door.

"Ah!" she exclaimed. "So it is you, Mr. Williams! What do you—"

"You know what I want," growled Owen. "That paper you stole from Lattimer's office to-night. Also the plans you lifted from the Navy Department. The ones you mailed in New York yesterday afternoon and which were waiting for you here!"

"Find them!" was the woman's mocking challenge as Williams's eyes roved over the room and finally rested on a pile of crumbled ashes beside an alcohol lamp on the table. A moment's examination told him that a blue print had been burned, but it was impossible to tell what it had been, and there was no trace of any other paper in the ashes.

"Search her!" he called to a woman in the corridor. "I'm going to rifle the mail-box downstairs. She can't get away with the same trick three times!"

And there, in an innocent-looking envelope addressed to a certain personage whose name stood high on the diplomatic list, Williams discovered the report for which a woman risked her liberty and gambled six months of her life!

"But the plans?" I asked as Quinn finished.[297]

"Evidently that was what she had burned. She'd taken care to crumple the ashes so that it was an impossibility to get a shred of direct evidence, not that it would have made any difference if she hadn't. The government never prosecutes matters of this kind, except in time of war. They merely warn the culprit to leave the country and never return—which is the reason that, while you'll find a number of very interesting foreigners in Washington at the present moment, the Countess Sylvia Stefani is not among them.

Neither is the personage to whom her letter was addressed. He was 'recalled' a few weeks later."

[298]

XXI
A MILLION-DOLLAR QUARTER

"What's in the phial?" I inquired one evening, as Bill Quinn, formerly of the United States Secret Service, picked up a small brown bottle from the table in his den and slipped it into his pocket.

"Saccharine," retorted Quinn, laconically. "Had to come to it in order to offset the sugar shortage. No telling how long it will continue, and, meanwhile, we're conserving what we have on hand. So I carry my 'lump sugar' in my vest pocket, and I'll keep on doing it until conditions improve. They say the trouble lies at the importing end. Can't secure enough sugar at the place where the ships are or enough ships at the place where the sugar is.

"This isn't the first time that sugar has caused trouble, either. See that twenty-five-cent piece up there on the wall? Apparently it's an ordinary everyday quarter. But it cost the government well over a million dollars, money which should have been paid in as import duty on tons upon tons of sugar.

"Yes, back of that quarter lies a case which is absolutely unique in the annals of governmental detective work—the biggest and most far-reaching smuggling plot ever discovered and the one which took the longest time to solve.

"Nine years seems like a mighty long time to work on a single assignment, but when you consider that the[299] Treasury collected more than two million dollars as a direct result of one man's labor during that time, you'll see that it was worth while."

The whole thing really started when Dick Carr went to work as a sugar sampler [continued Quinn, his eyes fixed meditatively upon the quarter on the wall].

Some one had tipped the department off to the fact that phony sampling of some sort was being indulged in and Dick managed to get a place as assistant on one of the docks where the big sugar ships unloaded. As you probably know, there's a big difference in the duty on the different grades of raw sugar; a difference based upon the tests made by expert chemists as soon as the cargo is landed. Sugar which is only ninety-two per cent pure, for example, comes in half-a-cent a pound cheaper than that which is ninety-six per cent pure, and the sampling is accomplished by inserting a thin glass tube through the wide meshes of the bag or basket which contains the sugar.

It didn't take Carr very long to find out that the majority of the samplers were slipping their tubes into the bags at an angle, instead of shoving them straight in, and that a number of them made a practice of moistening the outside of the container before they made their tests. The idea, of course, was that the sugar which had absorbed moisture, either during the voyage or after reaching the dock—would not "assay" as pure as would the dry material in the center of the package. A few experiments, conducted under the cover of night, showed a difference of four to six per cent in the grade of the samples taken from the inside of the bag and that taken from a point close to the surface, particularly if even a small amount of water had been judiciously applied.

The difference, when translated into terms of a half-a-cent[300] a pound import duty, didn't take long to run up into hundreds of thousands of dollars, and Carr's report, made after several months' investigating, cost a number of sugar samplers their jobs and brought the wrath of the government down upon the companies which had been responsible for the practice.

After such an exposure as this, you might think that the sugar people would have been content to take their legitimate profit and to pay the duty levied by law. But Carr had the idea that they would try to put into operation some other scheme for defrauding the Treasury and during years that followed he kept in close touch with the importing situation and the personnel of the men employed on the docks.

The active part he had played in the sugar-sampling exposure naturally prevented his active participation in any attempt to uncover the fraud from the inside, but it was the direct cause of his being summoned to Washington when a discharged official of one of the sugar companies filed a charge that the government was losing five hundred thousand dollars a year by the illicit operations at a single plant.

"Frankly, I haven't the slightest idea of how it's being done," confessed the official in question. "But I am certain that some kind of a swindle is being perpetrated on a large scale. Here's the proof!"

With that he produced two documents—one the bill of lading of the steamer *Murbar*, showing the amount of sugar on board when she cleared Java, and the other the official receipt, signed by a representative of the sugar company, for her cargo when she reached New York.

"As you will note," continued the informant, "the bill of lading clearly shows that the *Murbar* carried eleven million seven hundred thirty-four thousand six hundred[301] eighty-seven pounds of raw sugar. Yet, when weighed under the supervision of the customhouse officials a few weeks later, the cargo consisted of only eleven million thirty-two thousand and sixteen pounds—a 'shrinkage' of seven hundred two thousand six hundred seventy-one pounds, about six per cent of the material shipment."

"And at the present import duty that would amount to about—"

"In the neighborhood of twelve thousand dollars loss on this ship alone," stated the former sugar official. "Allowing for the arrival of anywhere from fifty to a hundred ships a year, you can figure the annual deficit for yourself."

Carr whistled. He had rather prided himself upon uncovering the sampling frauds a few years previously, but this bade fair to be a far bigger case—one which would tax every atom of his ingenuity to uncover.

"How long has this been going on?" inquired the acting Secretary of the Treasury.

"I can't say," admitted the informant. "Neither do I care to state how I came into possession of these documents. But, as you will find when you look into the matter, they are entirely authoritative and do not refer to an isolated case. The *Murbar* is the rule, not the exception. It's now up to you people to find out how the fraud was worked."

"He's right, at that," was the comment from the acting Secretary, when the former sugar official had departed. "The information is undoubtedly the result of a personal desire to 'get even'—for our friend recently lost his place with the company in question. However, that hasn't the slightest bearing upon the truth of his charges. Carr, it's up to you to find out what there is in 'em!"

"That's a man-sized order, Mr. Secretary," smiled[302] Dick, "especially as the work I did some time ago on the sampling frauds made me about as popular as the plague with the sugar people. If I ever poked my nose on the docks at night you'd be out the price of a big bunch of white roses the next day!"

"Which means that you don't care to handle the case?"

"Not so that you could notice it!" snapped Carr. "I merely wanted you to realize the handicaps under which I'll be working, so that there won't be any demand for instant developments. This case is worth a million dollars if it's worth a cent. And, because it is so big, it will take a whole lot longer to round up the details than if we were working on a matter that concerned only a single individual. If you remember, it took Joe Gregory nearly six months to land Phyllis Dodge, and therefore—"

"Therefore it ought to take about sixty years to get to the bottom of this case, eh?"

"Hardly that long. But I would like an assurance that I can dig into this in my own way and that there won't be any 'Hurry up!' message sent from this end every week or two."

"That's fair enough," agreed the Assistant Secretary. "You know the ins and outs of the sugar game better than any man in the service. So hop to it and take your time. We'll content ourselves with sitting back and awaiting developments."

Armed with this assurance, Carr went back to New York and began carefully and methodically to lay his plans for the biggest game ever hunted by a government detective—a ring protected by millions of dollars in capital and haunted by the fear that its operations might some day be discovered.

In spite of the fact that it was necessary to work entirely in the dark, Dick succeeded in securing the manifests[303] and bills of lading of three other sugar ships which had recently been unloaded, together with copies of the receipts of their cargoes. Every one of these indicated the same mysterious shrinkage en route, amounting to about six per cent of the entire shipment, and, as Carr figured it, there were but two explanations which could cover the matter.

Either a certain percentage of the sugar had been removed from the hold and smuggled into the country before the ship reached New York, or there was a conspiracy of some kind which involved a number of the weighers on the docks.

"The first supposition," argued Carr, "is feasible but hardly within the bounds of probability. If the shortage had occurred in a shipment of gold or something else which combines high value with small volume, that's where I'd look for the leak. But when it comes to hundreds of thousands of pounds of sugar—that's something else. You can't carry that around in your pockets or even unload it without causing comment and employing so many assistants that the risk would be extremely great.

"No, the answer must lie right here on the docks—just as it did in the sampling cases."

So it was on the docks that he concentrated his efforts, working through the medium of a girl named Louise Wood, whom he planted as a file clerk and general assistant in the offices of the company which owned the *Murbar* and a number of other sugar ships.

This, of course, wasn't accomplished in a day, nor yet in a month. As a matter of fact, it was February when Carr was first assigned to the case and it was late in August when the Wood girl went to work. But, as Dick figured it, this single success was worth all the time and trouble spent in preparing for it.[304]

It would be hard, therefore, to give any adequate measure of his disappointment when the girl informed him that everything in her office appeared to be straight and aboveboard.

"You know, Dick," reported Louise, after she had been at work for a couple of months, "I'm not the kind that can have the wool pulled over my eyes. If there was anything crooked going on, I'd spot it before they'd more than laid their first plans. But I've had the opportunity of going over the files and the records and it's all on the level."

"Then how are you to account for the discrepancies between the bills of lading and the final receipts?" queried Carr, almost stunned by the girl's assurance.

"That's what I don't know," she admitted. "It certainly looks queer, but of course it is possible that the men who ship the sugar deliberately falsify the records in order to get more money and that the company pays these statements as a sort of graft. That I can't say. It doesn't come under my department, as you know. Neither is it criminal. What I do know is that the people on the dock have nothing to do with faking the figures."

"Sure you haven't slipped up anywhere and given them a suspicion as to your real work?"

"Absolutely certain. I've done my work and done it well. That's what I was employed for and that's what's given me access to the files. But, as for suspicion—there hasn't been a trace of it!"

It was in vain that Carr questioned and cross-questioned the girl. She was sure of herself and sure of her information, positive that no crooked work was being handled by the men who received the sugar when it was unloaded from the incoming ships.

Puzzled by the girl's insistence and stunned by the[305] failure of the plan upon which he had banked so much, Carr gave the matter up as a bad job—telling Louise that she could stop her work whenever she wished, but finally agreeing to her suggestion that she continue to hold her place on the bare chance of uncovering a lead.

"Of course," concluded the girl, "you may be right, after all. They may have covered their tracks so thoroughly that I haven't been able to pick up the scent. I really don't believe that they have—but it's worth the gamble to me if it is to you."

More than a month passed before the significance of this speech dawned upon Dick, and then only when he chanced to be walking along Fifth Avenue one Saturday afternoon and saw Louise coming out of Tiffany's with a small cubical package in her hand.

"Tiffany's—" he muttered. "I wonder—"

Then, entering the store, he sought out the manager and stated that he would like to find out what a lady, whom he described, had just purchased. The flash of his badge which accompanied this request turned the trick.

"Of course, it's entirely against our rules," explained the store official, "but we are always glad to do anything in our power to assist the government. Just a moment. I'll call the clerk who waited on her."

"The lady," he reported a few minutes later, "gave her name as Miss Louise Wood and her address as—"

"I know where she lives," snapped Carr. "What did she buy?"

"A diamond and platinum ring."

"The price?"

"Eight hundred and fifty dollars."

"Thanks," said the operative and was out of the office before the manager could frame any additional inquiries.[306]

When the Wood girl answered a rather imperative ring at the door of her apartment she was distinctly surprised at the identity of her caller, for she and Carr had agreed that it would not be wise for them to meet except by appointment in some out-of-the-way place.

"Dick!" she exclaimed. "What brings you here? Do you think it's safe?"

"Safe or not," replied the operative, entering and closing the door behind him. "I'm here and here I'm going to stay until I find out something. Where did you get the money to pay for that ring you bought at Tiffany's to-day?"

"Money? Ring?" echoed the girl. "What are you talking about?"

"You know well enough! Now don't stall. Come through! Where'd you get it?"

"An—an aunt died and left it to me," but the girl's pale face and halting speech belied her words.

"Try another one," sneered Carr. "Where did you get that eight hundred and fifty dollars?"

"What business is it of yours? Can't I spend my own money in my own way without being trailed and hounded all over the city?"

"You can spend your own money—the money you earn by working and the money I pay you for keeping your eyes open on the dock as you please. But—" and here Carr reached forward and grasped the girl's wrist, drawing her slowly toward him, so that her eyes looked straight into his, "when it comes to spending other money—money that you got for keeping your mouth shut and putting it over on me—that's another story."

"I didn't, Dick; I didn't!"

"Can you look me straight in the eyes and say that they haven't paid you for being blind? That they didn't[307] suspect what you came to the dock for, and declared you in on the split? No! I didn't think you could!"

With that he flung her on a couch and moved toward the door. Just as his hand touched the knob he heard a voice behind him, half sob and half plea, cry, "Dick!"

Reluctantly he turned.

"Dick, as there's a God in heaven I didn't mean to double cross you. But they were on to me from the first. They planted some stamps in my pocket during the first week I was there and then gave me my choice of bein' pulled for thieving or staying there at double pay. I didn't want to do it, but they had the goods on me and I had to. They said all I had to do was to tell you that nothing crooked was goin' on—and they'll pay me well for it."

"While you were also drawing money from me, eh?"

"Sure I was, Dick. I couldn't ask you to stop my pay. You'd have suspected. Besides, as soon as you were done with me, they were, too."

"That's where the eight hundred and fifty dollars came from?"

"Yes, and a lot more. Oh, they pay well, all right!"

For fully a minute there was silence in the little apartment, broken only by the sobs of the girl on the couch. Finally Carr broke the strain.

"There's only one way for you to square yourself," he announced. "Tell me everything you know—the truth and every word of it!"

"That's just it, Dick. I don't know anything—for sure. There's something goin' on. No doubt of that. But what it is I don't know. They keep it under cover in the scale house."

"In the scale house?"

"Yes; they don't allow anyone in there without a[308] permit. Somebody uptown tips 'em off whenever a special agent is coming down, so they can fix things. But none of the staff knows, though nearly all of them are drawin' extra money for keeping their mouths shut."

"Who are the men who appear to be implicated?"

"Mahoney, the checker for the company, and Derwent, the government weigher."

"Derwent!"

"Yes, he's in on it, too. I tell you, Dick, the thing's bigger than you ever dreamed. It's like an octopus, with tentacles that are fastened on everyone connected with the place."

"But no clue as to the location of the body of the beast?"

"Can't you guess? You know the number of their office uptown. But there's no use hoping to nab them. They're too well protected. I doubt if you can even get at the bottom of the affair on the dock."

"I don't doubt it!" Carr's chin had settled itself determinedly and his mouth was a thin red line. "I'm going to give you a chance to redeem yourself. Go back to work as usual on Monday. Don't let on, by word or gesture, that anything has changed. Just await developments. If you'll do that, I'll see that you're not implicated. More than that, I'll acknowledge you at the proper time as my agent—planted there to double cross the fraud gang. You'll have your money and your glory and your satisfaction of having done the right thing, even though you didn't intend to do it. Are you on?"

"I am, Dick. I won't say a word. I promise!"

"Good! You'll probably see me before long. But don't recognize me. You'll be just one of the girls and it'll probably be necessary to include you in the round-up. I'll fix that later. Good-by," and with that he was off.[309]

Not expecting that Carr would be able to complete his plans for at least a week, Louise was startled when the operative arrived at the dock on the following Monday morning. He had spent the previous day in Washington, arranging details, and his appearance at the company's office—while apparently casual—was part of the program mapped out in advance. What was more, Carr had come to the dock from the station, so as to prevent the "inside man" from flashing a warning of his arrival.

Straight through the office he strode, his right hand swinging at his side, his left thrust nonchalantly in the pocket of his topcoat.

Before he had crossed halfway to the door of the scale room he was interrupted by a burly individual, who demanded his business.

"I want to see Mr. Derwent or Mr. Mahoney," replied Carr.

"They're both engaged at present," was the answer. "Wait here, and I'll tell them."

"Get out of my road!" growled the operative, pulling back the lapel of his coat sufficiently to afford a glimpse of his badge. "I'll see them where they are," and before the guardian of the scale house door had recovered from his astonishment Carr was well across the portals.

The first thing that caught his eye was the figure of a man bending over the weight beam of one of the big scales, while another man was making some adjustments on the other side of the apparatus.

Derwent, who was facing the door, was the first to see Carr, but before he could warn his companion, the special agent was on top of them.

"Who are you? What business have you in here?" demanded the government weigher.

"Carr is my name," replied Dick. "Possibly you've[310] heard of me. If so, you know my business. Catching sugar crooks!"

Derwent's face went white for a moment and then flushed a deep red. Mahoney, however, failed to alter his position. He remained bending over the weight beam, his finger nails scratching at something underneath.

"Straighten up there!" ordered Carr. "You—Mahoney—I mean! Straighten up!"

"I'll see you in hell first!" snapped the other.

"You'll be there soon enough if you don't get up!" was Carr's reply, as his left hand emerged from his coat pocket, bringing to light the blue-steel barrel of a forty-five. "Get—"

Just at that moment, from a point somewhere near the door of the scale room, came a shrill, high-pitched cry—a woman's voice:

"Dick!" it called. "Lookout! Jump!"

Instantly, involuntarily, the operative leaped sidewise, and as he did so a huge bag of raw sugar crashed to the floor, striking directly on the spot where he had stood.

"Thanks, Lou," called Carr, without turning his head. "You saved me that time all right! Now, gentlemen, before any more bags drop, suppose we adjourn uptown. We're less likely to be interrupted there," and he sounded a police whistle, which brought a dozen assistants on the run.

"Search Mahoney," he directed. "I don't think Derwent has anything on him. What's that Mahoney has in his hand?"

"Nothin' but a quarter, sir, an' what looks like an old wad o' chewin' gum."

Puzzled, Carr examined the coin. Then the explanation of the whole affair flashed upon him as he investigated[311] the weight-beam and found fragments of gum adhering to the lower part, near the free end.

"So that was the trick, eh?" he inquired. "Quite a delicate bit of mechanism, this scale—in spite of the fact that it was designed to weigh tons of material. Even a quarter, gummed on to the end of the beam, would throw the whole thing out enough to make it well worth while. I think this coin and the wad of gum will make very interesting evidence—Exhibits A and B—at the trial, after we've rounded up the rest of you."

"And that," concluded Quinn, "is the story which lies behind that twenty-five-cent piece—probably the most valuable bit of money, judged from the standpoint of what it has accomplished, in the world."

"Derwent and Mahoney?" I asked. "What happened to them? And did Carr succeed in landing the men higher up?"

"Unfortunately," and Quinn smiled rather ruefully, "there is such a thing as the power of money. The government brought suit against the sugar companies implicated in the fraud and commenced criminal proceedings against the men directly responsible for the manipulation of the scales. (It developed that they had another equally lucrative method of using a piece of thin corset steel to alter the weights.) But the case was quashed upon the receipt of a check for more than two million dollars, covering back duties uncollected, so the personal indictments were allowed to lapse. It remains, however, the only investigation I ever heard of in which success was so signal and the amount involved so large.

"Todd, of the Department of Justice, handled a big affair not long afterward, but, while some of the details[312] were even more unusual and exciting, the theft was only a paltry two hundred and fifty thousand dollars."

"Which case was that?"

"The looting of the Central Trust Company," replied the former operative, rising and stretching himself. "Get along with you. It's time for me to lock up."

[313]

XXII
"THE LOOTING OF THE C. T. C."

There was a wintry quality in the night itself that made a comfortable chair and an open fire distinctly worth the payment of a luxury tax. Add to this the fact that the chairs in the library den of William J. Quinn—formerly "Bill Quinn, United States Secret Service"—were roomy and inviting, while the fire fairly crackled with good cheer, and you'll know why the conversation, after a particularly good dinner on the evening in question, was punctuated by pauses and liberally interlarded with silences.

Finally, feeling that it was really necessary that I say something, I remarked upon the fierceness of the wind and the biting, stinging sleet which accompanied a typical January storm.

"Makes one long for Florida," I added.

"Yes," agreed Quinn, "or even some point farther south. On a night like this you can hardly blame a man for heading for Honduras, even if he did carry away a quarter of a million of the bank's deposits with him."

"Huh? Who's been looting the local treasury?" I asked, thinking that I was on the point of getting some advance information.

"No one that I know of," came from the depths of Quinn's big armchair. "I was just thinking of Florida and warm weather, and that naturally led to Honduras,[314] which, in turn, recalled Rockwell to my mind. Ever hear of Rockwell?"

"Don't think I ever did. What was the connection between him and the quarter-million you mentioned?"

"Quite a bit. Rather intimate, as you might say. But not quite as much as he had planned. However, if it hadn't been for Todd—"

"Todd?"

"Yes—Ernest E. Todd, of the Department of Justice. 'Extra Ernest,' they used to call him, because he'd never give up a job until he brought it in, neatly wrapped and ready for filing. More than one man has had cause to believe that Todd's parents chose the right name for him. He may not have been much to look at—but he sure was earnest."

Take the Rockwell case, for example [Quinn went on, after a preliminary puff or two to see that his pipe was drawing well]. No one had the slightest idea that the Central Trust Company wasn't in the best of shape. Its books always balanced to a penny. There was never anything to cause the examiner to hesitate, and its officials were models of propriety. Particularly Rockwell, the cashier. Not only was he a pillar of the church, but he appeared to put his religious principles into practice on the other six days of the week as well. He wasn't married, but that only boosted his stock in the eyes of the community, many of which had daughters of an age when wedding bells sound very tuneful and orange blossoms are the sweetest flowers that grow.

When they came to look into the matter later on, nobody seemed to know much about Mr. Rockwell's antecedents. He'd landed a minor position in the bank some fifteen years before and had gradually lifted himself to the[315] cashiership. Seemed to have an absolute genius for detail and the handling of financial matters.

So it was that when Todd went back home on a vacation and happened to launch some of his ideas on criminology—ideas founded on an intensive study of Lombroso and other experts—he quickly got himself into deep water.

During the course of a dinner at one of the hotels, "E. E." commenced to expound certain theories relating to crime and the physical appearance of the criminal.

"Do you know," he inquired, "that it's the simplest thing in the world to tell whether a man—or even a boy, for that matter—has criminal tendencies? There are certain unmistakable physical details that point unerringly to what the world might call 'laxity of conscience,' but which is nothing less than a predisposition to evil, a tendency to crime. The lobes of the ears, the height and shape of the forehead, the length of the little finger, the contour of the hand—all these are of immense value in determining whether a man will go straight or crooked. Employers are using them more and more every day. The old-fashioned phrenologist, with his half-formed theories and wild guesses, has been displaced by the modern student of character, who relies upon certain rules which vary so little as to be practically immutable."

"Do you mean to say," asked one of the men at the table, "that you can tell that a man is a criminal simply by looking at him?"

"If that's the case," cut in another, "why don't you lock 'em all up?"

"But it isn't the case," was Todd's reply. "The physical characteristics to which I refer only mean that a man is likely to develop along the wrong lines. They are like the stars which, as Shakespeare remarked, 'incline, but do not compel.' If you remember, he added, 'The[316] fault, dear Brutus, lies in ourselves.' Therefore, if a detective of the modern school is working on a case and he comes across a man who bears one or more of these very certain brands of Cain, he watches that man very carefully—at least until he is convinced that he is innocent. You can't arrest a man simply because he looks like a crook, but it is amazing how often the guideposts point in the right direction."

"Anyone present that you suspect of forgery or beating his wife?" came in a bantering voice from the other end of the table.

"If you're in earnest," answered the government agent, "lay your hands on the table."

And everyone present, including Rockwell, cashier of the Central Trust Company, placed his hands, palm upward, on the cloth—though there was a distinct hesitation in several quarters.

Slowly, deliberately, Todd looked around the circle of hands before him. Then, with quite as much precision, he scanned the faces and particularly the ears of his associates. Only once did his gaze hesitate longer than usual, and then not for a sufficient length of time to make it apparent.

"No," he finally said. "I'd give every one of you a clean bill of health. Apparently you're all right. But," and he laughed, "remember, I said 'apparently.' So don't blame me if there's a murder committed before morning and one or more of you is arrested for it!"

That was all there was to the matter until Todd, accompanied by two of his older friends, left the grill and started to walk home.

"That was an interesting theory of yours," commented one of the men, "but wasn't it only a theory? Is there any real foundation of fact?"[317]

"You mean my statement that you can tell by the shape of a man's head and hands whether he has a predisposition to crime?"

"Yes."

"It's far from a theory, inasmuch as it has the support of hundreds of cases which are on record. Besides, I had a purpose in springing it when I did. In fact, it partook of the nature of an experiment."

"You mean you suspected some one present—"

"Not suspected, but merely wondered if he would submit to the test. I knew that one of the men at the table would call for it. Some one in a crowd always does—and I had already noted a startling peculiarity about the forehead, nose, and ears of a certain dinner companion. I merely wanted to find out if he had the nerve to withstand my inspection of his hands. I must say that he did, without flinching."

"But who was the man?"

"I barely caught his name," replied Todd, "and this conversation must be in strict confidence. After all, criminologists do not maintain that every man who looks like a crook is one. They simply state and prove that ninety-five per cent of the deliberate criminals, men who plan their wrong well in advance, bear these marks. And the man who sat across the table from me to-night has them, to an amazing degree."

"Across the table from you? Why that was Rockwell, cashier of the Central Trust!"

"Precisely," stated Todd, "and the only reason that I am making this admission is because I happen to know that both of you bank there."

"But," protested one of the other men, "Rockwell has been with them for years. He's worked himself up from the very bottom and had hundreds of chances to make[318] away with money if he wanted to. He's as straight as a die."

"Very possibly he is," Todd agreed. "That's the reason that I warn you that what I said was in strict confidence. Neither one of you is to say a word that would cast suspicion on Rockwell. It would be fatal to his career. On the other hand, I wanted to give you the benefit of my judgment, which, if you remember, you requested."

But it didn't take a character analyst to see that the Department of Justice man had put his foot in it, so far as his friends were concerned. They were convinced of the cashier's honesty and no theories founded on purely physical attributes could swerve them. They kept the conversation to themselves, but Todd left town feeling that he had lost the confidence of two of his former friends.

It was about a month later that he ran into Weldon, the Federal Bank Examiner for that section of the country, and managed to make a few discreet inquiries about Rockwell and the Central Trust Company without, however, obtaining even a nibble.

"Everything's flourishing," was the verdict. "Accounts straight as a string and they appear to be doing an excellent business. Fairly heavy on notes, it's true, but they're all well indorsed. Why'd you ask? Any reason to suspect anyone?"

"Not the least," lied Todd. "It's my home town, you know, and I know a lot of people who bank at the C. T. C. Just like to keep in touch with how things are going. By the way, when do you plan to make your next inspection?"

"Think I'll probably be in there next Wednesday. Want me to say 'Hello' to anybody?"

"No, I'm not popular in certain quarters," Todd[319] laughed. "They say I have too many theories—go off half cocked and all that sort of thing."

Nevertheless the Department of Justice operative arranged matters so that he reached his home city on Tuesday of the following week, discovering, by judicious inquiries, that the visit of the examiner had not been forecast. In fact, he wasn't expected for a month or more. But that's the way it is best to work. If bank officials know when to look out for an examiner, they can often fix things on their books which would not bear immediate inspection.

Weldon arrived on schedule early the following morning, and commenced his examination of the accounts of the First National, as was his habit.

As soon as Todd knew that he was in town he took up his position outside the offices of the Central Trust, selecting a vantage point which would give him a clear view of both entrances of the bank.

"Possibly," he argued to himself, "I am a damn fool. But just the same, I have a mighty well-defined hunch that Mr. Rockwell isn't on the level, and I ought to find out pretty soon."

Then events began to move even quicker than he had hoped.

The first thing he noted was that Jafferay, one of the bookkeepers of the C. T. C., slipped out of a side door of the bank and dropped a parcel into the mail box which stood beside the entrance. Then, a few minutes later, a messenger came out and made his way up the street to the State National, where—as Todd, who was on his heels—had little trouble in discovering—he cashed a cashier's check for one hundred and fifty thousand dollars, returning to the Central Trust Company with the money in his valise.[320]

"Of course," Todd reasoned, "Rockwell may be ignorant of the fact that Weldon doesn't usually get around to the State National until he has inspected all the other banks. Hence the check will have already gone to the clearing house and will appear on the books merely as an item of one hundred and fifty thousand dollars due, rather than as a check from the Central Trust. Yes, he may be ignorant of the fact—but it does look funny. Wonder what that bookkeeper mailed?"

Working along the last line of reasoning, the government operative stopped at the post office long enough to introduce himself to the postmaster, present his credentials, and inquire if the mail from the box outside the Central Trust Company had yet been collected. Learning that it had, he asked permission to inspect it.

"You can look it over if you wish," stated the postmaster, "but, of course, I have no authority to allow you to open any of it. Even the Postmaster-General himself couldn't do that."

"Certainly," agreed Todd. "I merely want to see the address on a certain parcel and I'll make affidavit, if you wish, that I have reason to suppose that the mails are being used for illegal purposes."

"That won't be necessary. We'll step down to the parcel room and soon find out what you want."

Some five minutes later Todd learned that the parcel which he recognized—a long roll covered with wrapping paper, so that it was impossible to gain even an idea of what it contained—was addressed to Jafferay, the bookkeeper, at his home address.

"Thanks! Now if you can give me some idea of when this'll be delivered I won't bother you any more. About five o'clock this afternoon? Fine!" and the man from[321] Washington was out of the post office before anyone could inquire further concerning his mission.

A telephone call disclosed the fact that Weldon was then making his examination of the Central Trust Company books and could not be disturbed, but Todd managed to get him later in the afternoon and made an appointment for dinner, on the plea of official business which he wished to discuss.

That afternoon he paid a visit to the house of a certain Mr. Jafferay and spent an hour in a vain attempt to locate the bank examiner.

Promptly at six o'clock that official walked into Todd's room at the hotel, to find the operative pacing restlessly up and down, visibly excited and clutching what appeared to be a roll of paper.

"What's the matter?" asked Weldon. "I'm on time. Didn't keep you waiting a minute?"

"No!" snapped Todd, "but where have you been for the last hour? Been trying to reach you all over town."

"Great Scott! man, even a human adding machine has a right to take a little rest now and then. If you must know, I've been getting a shave and a haircut. Anything criminal in that?"

"Can't say that there is," and Todd relaxed enough to smile at his vehemence. "But there is in this," unrolling the parcel that he still held and presenting several large sheets of ruled paper for the examiner's attention. "Recognise them?"

"They appear to be loose leaves from the ledgers at the Central Trust Company."

"Precisely. Were they there when you went over the books this morning?"

"I don't recall them, but it's possible they may have been."[322]

"No—they weren't. One of the bookkeepers mailed them to himself, at his home address, while you were still at the First National. If I hadn't visited his house this

147

afternoon, in the guise of a book agent, and taken a long chance by lifting this roll of paper, he'd have slipped them back in place in the morning and nobody'd been any the wiser."

"Then you mean that the bookkeeper is responsible for falsifying the accounts?"

"Only partially. Was the cash O. K. at the Central Trust?"

"Perfectly."

"Do you recall any record of a check for one hundred and fifty thousand dollars upon the State National drawn and cashed this morning?"

"No, there was no such check."

"Yes, there was. I was present when the messenger cashed it and he took the money back to the C. T. C. They knew you wouldn't get around to the State before morning, and by that time the check would have gone to the clearing house, giving them plenty of time to make the cash balance to a penny."

"Whom do you suspect of manipulating the funds?"

"The man who signed the check—Rockwell, the cashier! That's why I was trying to get hold of you. I haven't the authority to demand admittance to the Central Trust vaults, but you have. Then, if matters are as I figure them, I'll take charge of the case as an agent of the Department of Justice."

"Come on!" was Weldon's response. "We'll get up there right away, No use losing time over it!"

At the bank, however, they were told that the combination to the vault was known to only three persons—the president of the bank, Rockwell, and the assistant[323] cashier. The president, it developed, was out of town. Rockwell's house failed to answer the phone, and it was a good half hour before the assistant cashier put in an appearance.

When, in compliance with Weldon's orders, he swung back the heavy doors which guarded the vault where the currency was stored, he swung around, amazed.

"It's empty!" he whispered. "Not a thing there save the bags of coin. Why, I put some two hundred and fifty thousand dollars in paper money in there myself this afternoon!"

"Who was here at the time?" demanded Todd.

"Only Mr. Rockwell. I remember distinctly that he said he would have to work a little longer, but that there wouldn't be any necessity for my staying. So I put the money in there, locked the door, and went on home."

"Do you know where Rockwell is now?"

"At his house, I suppose. He lives at—"

"I know where he lives," snapped Todd. "I also know that he isn't there. I've had the place watched since five o'clock this afternoon—but Rockwell hasn't shown up. Like the money—I think we can say 'with the money'—he's gone, disappeared, vanished."

"Then," said Weldon, "it is up to you to find him. My part of the job ceased the moment the shortage was disclosed."

"I know that and if you'll attend to making a report on the matter, order the arrest of Jafferay, and spread the report of Rockwell's embezzlement through police circles, I'll get busy on my own hook. Good-by." And an instant later Todd was hailing a taxi and ordering the chauffeur to break all the speed laws in reaching the house where Rockwell boarded.

Examination of the cashier's room and an extended[324] talk with the landlady failed, however, to disclose anything which might be termed a clue. The missing official had visited the house shortly after noon, but had not come back since the bank closed.

He had not taken a valise or suit case with him, declared the mistress of the house, but he had seemed "just a leetle bit upset."

Quickly, but efficiently, Todd examined the room—even inspecting the bits of paper in the wastebasket and pawing over the books which lined the mantel. Three of the former he slipped into his pocket and then, turning, inquired:

"Was Mr. Rockwell fond of cold weather?"

"No, indeed," was the reply. "He hated winter. Said he never was comfortable from November until May. He always—"

But the "queer gentleman," as the landlady afterward referred to him, was out of the house before she could detail her pet story of the cashier's fondness for heat, no matter at what cost.

No one at the station had seen Rockwell board a train, but inquiry at the taxicab offices revealed the fact that a man, with his overcoat collar turned up until it almost met his hat brim, had taken a cab for a near-by town, where it would be easy for him to make connections either north or south.

Stopping only to wire Washington the bare outline of the case, with the suggestion that the Canadian border be watched, "though it is almost certain that Rockwell is headed south," Todd picked up the trail at the railroad ticket office, some ten miles distant, and found that a man answering to the description of his prey had bought passage as far as St. Louis. But, despite telegraphic instructions, the Saint Louis police were unable to apprehend anyone who looked like Rockwell and the government[325] operative kept right on down the river, stopping at Memphis to file a message to the authorities in New Orleans.

It was precisely a week after the looting of the Central Trust Company that Todd stood on the docks in New Orleans, watching the arrival of the passengers and baggage destined to go aboard the boat for Honduras. Singly and in groups they arrived until, when the "all ashore" signal sounded, the operative began to wonder if he were really on the right trail. Then, at the last minute, a cab drove up and a woman, apparently suffering from rheumatism, made her way toward the boat. Scenting a tip, two stewards sprang to assist her, but Todd beat them to it.

"Pardon me, madam," he said, "may I not—Drat that fly!" and with that he made a pass at something in front of his face and accidentally brushed aside the veil which hid the woman's face.

He had barely time to realize that, as he had suspected, it was Rockwell, disguised, before the "woman" had slipped out of the light wrap which she had been wearing and was giving him what he later admitted was the "scrap of his life." In fact, for several moments he not only had to fight Rockwell, but several bystanders as well—for they had only witnessed what they supposed was a totally uncalled for attack upon a woman. In the mixup that followed Rockwell managed to slip away and, before Todd had a chance to recover, was halfway across the street, headed for the entrance to a collection of shanties which provided an excellent hiding place.

Tearing himself loose, Todd whipped out his revolver and fired at the figure just visible in the gathering dusk, scoring a clean shot just above the ankle—a flesh wound, that ripped the leg muscles without breaking a bone.[326] With a groan of despair Rockwell toppled over, clawing wildly in an attempt to reach his revolver. But Todd was on top of him before the cashier could swing the gun into action, and a pair of handcuffs finished the career of the man who had planned to loot the C. T. C. of a quarter million in cold cash.

"The next time you try a trick like that," Todd advised him, on the train that night, "be careful what you leave behind in your room. The two torn letterheads of the Canadian Pacific nearly misled me, but the other one referring to the Honduran line, plus the book on Honduras and the fact that your landlady stated that you hated cold weather, gave you dead away. Of course, even without that, it was a toss-up between Canada and Central America. Those are the only two places where an embezzler is comparatively safe these days. I hope, for the sake of your comfort, they give you plenty of blankets in Joliet."

Quinn paused a moment to repack his pipe, and then, "So far as I know, he's still handling the prison finances," he added. "Yes—they found at the trial that he had had a clean record up to the moment he slipped, but the criminal tendencies were there and he wasn't able to resist temptation. He had speculated with the bank funds, covered his shortages by removing the pages from the ledger and kiting checks through the State National, and then determined to risk everything in one grand clean-up.

"He might have gotten away with it, too, if Todd hadn't spotted the peculiarities which indicated moral weakness. However, you can't always tell. No one who knew Mrs. Armitage would have dreamed that she was—what she was."

"Well," I inquired, "what was she?"[327]

"That's what puzzled Washington and the State Department for several months," replied Quinn. "It's too long a story to spin to-night. That's her picture up there, if you care to study her features."

And I went home wondering what were the crimes of which such a beautiful woman could have been guilty.

[328]

XXIII
THE CASE OF MRS. ARMITAGE

To look at him no one would have thought that Bill Quinn had a trace of sentiment in his make-up. Apparently he was just the grizzled old veteran of a hundred battles with crime, the last of which—a raid on a counterfeiter's den in Long Island—had laid him up with a game leg and a soft berth in the Treasury Department, where, for years he had been an integral part of the United States Secret Service.

But in the place of honor in Quinn's library-den there hung the photograph of a stunningly handsome woman, her sable coat thrown back just enough to afford a glimpse of a throat of which Juno might have been proud, while in her eyes there sparkled a light which seemed to hint at much but reveal little. It was very evident that she belonged to a world entirely apart from that of Quinn, yet the very fact that her photograph adorned the walls of his den proved that she had been implicated in some case which had necessitated Secret Service investigation—for the den was the shrine of relics relating to cases in which Quinn's friends had figured.

Finally, one evening I gathered courage to inquire about her.

"Armitage was her name," Quinn replied. "Lelia Armitage. At least that was the name she was known by in Washington, and even the investigations which[329] followed Melville Taylor's exposure of her foreign connections failed to reveal that she had been known by any other, save her maiden name of Lawrence."

"Where is she now?" I asked.

"You'll have to ask me something easier," and Quinn smiled, a trifle wistfully, I thought. "Possibly in London, perhaps in Paris, maybe in Rio or the Far East. But wherever she is, the center of attention is not very far away from her big violet-black eyes. Also the police of the country where she is residing probably wish that they had never been burdened with her."

"You mean—"

"That she was a crook? Not as the word is usually understood. But more than one string of valuable pearls or diamonds has disappeared when milady Armitage was in the neighborhood—though they were never able to prove that she had lifted a thing. No, her principal escapade in this country brought her into contact with the Secret Service, rather than the police officials—which is probably the reason she was nailed with the goods. You remember the incident of the 'leak' in the peace note, when certain Wall Street interests cleaned up millions of dollars?"

"Perfectly. Was she to blame for that?"

"They never settled who was to blame for it, but Mrs. Armitage was dealing through a young and decidedly attractive Washington broker at the time and her account mysteriously multiplied itself half a dozen times.

"Then there was the affair of the Carruthers Code, the one which ultimately led to her exposure at the hands of Taylor and Madelaine James."

The Carruthers Code [Quinn went on] was admittedly the cleverest and yet the simplest system of cipher communication[330] ever devised on this side of the Atlantic, with the possible exception of the one mentioned in Jules Verne's "Giant Raft"—the one that Dr. Heinrich Albert used with such success. Come to think of it, Verne wasn't an American, was he? He ought to have been, though. He invented like one.

In some ways the Carruthers system was even more efficient than the Verne cipher. You could use it with less difficulty, for one thing, and the key was susceptible of an almost infinite number of variations. Its only weakness lay in the fact that the secret had to be written down—and it was in connection with the slip of paper which contained this that Mrs. Armitage came into prominence.

For some two years Lelia Armitage had maintained a large and expensive establishment on Massachusetts Avenue, not far from Sheridan Circle. Those who claimed to know stated that there had been a Mr. Armitage, but that he had died, leaving his widow enough to make her luxuriously comfortable for the remainder of her life. In spite of the incidents of the jeweled necklaces, no one took the trouble to inquire into Mrs. Armitage's past until the leak in connection with the peace note and the subsequent investigation of Paul Connor's brokerage house led to the discovery that her name was among those who had benefited most largely by the advance information.

It was at that time that Melville Taylor was detailed to dig back into her history and see what he could discover. As was only natural, he went at once to Madelaine James, who had been of assistance to the Service in more than one Washington case which demanded feminine finesse, plus an intimate knowledge of social life in the national capital.[331]

"Madelaine," he inquired, "what do you know of a certain Mrs. Lelia Armitage?"

"Nothing particularly—except that one sees her everywhere. Apparently has plenty of money. Supposed to have gotten it from her husband, who has been dead for some time. Dresses daringly but expensively, and—while there are at least a score of men, ranging all the way from lieutenants in the army to captains of industry, who would like to marry her—she has successfully evaded scandal and almost gotten away from gossip."

"Where'd she come from?"

"London, I believe, by way of New York. Maiden name was Lawrence and the late but not very lamented Mr. Armitage was reputed to have made his money in South Africa."

"All of which," commented Taylor, "is rather vague—particularly for purposes of a detailed report."

"Report? In what connection?"

"Her name appears on the list of Connor's clients as one of the ones who cleaned up on the 'leak.' Sold short and made a barrel of money when stocks came down. The question is, Where did she get the tip?"

"Possibly from Paul Connor himself."

"Possibly—but I wish you'd cultivate her acquaintance and see if you can pick up anything that would put us on the right track."

But some six weeks later when Taylor was called upon to make a report of his investigations he had to admit that the sheet was a blank.

"Chief," he said, "either the Armitage woman is perfectly innocent or else she's infernally clever. I've pumped everyone dry about her, and a certain friend of mine, whom you know, has made a point of getting next to the lady herself. She's dined there a couple of times[332] and has talked to her at a dozen teas and receptions. But without success. Mrs. Armitage has been very frank and open about what she calls her 'good fortune' on the stock market. Says she followed her intuition and sold short when everyone else was buying. What's more, she says it with such a look of frank honesty that, according to Madelaine, you almost have to believe her."

"Has Miss James been able to discover anything of the lady's past history?"

"Nothing more than we already know—born in England—husband made a fortune in South Africa—died and left it to her. Have you tried tracing her from the other side?"

"Yes, but they merely disclaim all knowledge of her. Don't even recognize the description. That may mean anything. Well," and chief sighed rather disconsolately, for the leak puzzle had been a knotty one from the start, "I guess we'd better drop her. Too many other things going on to worry about a woman whose only offense seems to be an intuitive knowledge of the way Wall Street's going to jump."

It was at that moment that Mahoney, assistant to the chief, came in with the information that the Secretary of State desired the presence of the head of the Secret Service in his office immediately.

In answer to a snapped, "Come along—this may be something that you can take care of right away!" Taylor followed the chief to the State Department, where they were soon closeted with one of the under secretaries.

"You are familiar with the Carruthers Code?" inquired the Assistant Secretary.

"I know the principle on which it operates," the chief replied, "but I can't say that I've ever come into contact with it."[333]

"So far as we know," went on the State Department official, "it is the most efficient cipher system in the world—simple, easy to operate, almost impossible to decode without the key, and susceptible of being changed every day, or every hour if necessary, without impairing its value. However, in common with every other code, it has this weakness—once the key is located the entire system is practically valueless.

"When did you discover the disappearance of the code secret?" asked Taylor, examining his cigarette with an exaggerated display of interest.

"How did you know it was lost?" demanded the Under Secretary.

"I didn't—but the fact that your chief sent for mine and then you launch into a dissertation on the subject of the code itself is open to but one construction—some one has lifted the key to the cipher."

"Yes, some one has. At least, it was in this safe last night"—here a wave of his hand indicated a small and rather old-fashioned strong box in the corner—"and it wasn't there when I arrived this morning. I reported the matter to the Secretary and he asked me to give you the details."

"You are certain that the cipher was there last evening?" asked the chief.

"Not the cipher itself—at least not a code-book as the term is generally understood," explained the Under Secretary. "That's one of the beauties of the Carruthers system. You don't have to lug a bulky book around with you all the time. A single slip of paper—a cigarette paper would answer excellently—will contain the data covering a man's individual code. The loss or theft of one of these would be inconvenient, but not fatal. The loss of the master key, which was in that safe, is irreparable. If it[334] once gets out of the country it means that the decoding of our official messages is merely a question of time, no matter how often we switch the individual ciphers."

"What was the size of the master key, as you call it?"

"Merely a slip of government bond, about six inches long by some two inches deep."

"Was it of such a nature that it could have been easily copied?"

"Yes, but anything other than a careful tracing or a photographic copy would be valueless. The position of the letters and figures mean as much as the marks themselves. Whoever took it undoubtedly knows this and will endeavor to deliver the original—as a mark of good faith, if nothing else."

"Was this the only copy in existence?"

"There are two others—one in the possession of the Secretary, the other in the section which has charge of decoding messages. Both of these are safe, as I ascertained as soon as I discovered that my slip was missing."

A few more questions failed to bring out anything more about the mystery beyond the fact that the Assistant Secretary was certain that he had locked the safe the evening before and he knew that he had found it locked when he arrived that morning.

"All of which," as Taylor declared, "means but little. The safe is of the vintage of eighteen seventy, the old-fashioned kind where you can hear the tumblers drop clean across the room. Look!" and he pointed to the japanned front of the safe where a circular mark, some two inches in diameter, was visible close to the dial.

"Yes, but what is it?" demanded the Secretary.

"The proof that you locked the safe last night," Taylor responded. "Whoever abstracted the cipher key opened[335] the safe with the aid of some instrument that enabled them clearly to detect the fall of the tumblers. Probably a stethoscope, such as physicians use for listening to a patient's heart. Perfectly simple when you know how—particularly with an old model like this."

Finding that there was no further information available, Taylor and the chief left the department, the chief to return to headquarters, Taylor to endeavor to pick up the trail wherever he could.

"It doesn't look like an inside job," was the parting comment of the head of the Secret Service. "Anyone who had access to the safe would have made some excuse to discover the combination, rather than rely on listening to the click of the tumblers. Better get after the night watchman and see if he can give you a line on any strangers who were around the building last night."

But the night watchman when roused from his sound forenoon's sleep was certain that no one had entered the building on the previous evening save those who had business there.

"Everybody's got to use a pass now, you know," he stated. "I was on the job all night myself an' divvle a bit of anything out of the ordinary did I see. There was Mr. McNight and Mr. Lester and Mr. Greene on the job in the telegraph room, and the usual crowd of correspondents over in the press room, and a score of others who works there regular, an' Mrs. Prentice, an'—"

"Mrs. who?" interrupted Taylor.

"Mrs. Prentice, wife of th' Third Assistant Secretary. She comes down often when her husband is working late, but last night he must have gone home just before she got there, for she came back a few minutes later and said that the office was dark."

Whatever Taylor's thoughts were at the moment he[336] kept them to himself—for Prentice was the man from whose safe the cipher key had been abstracted!

So he contented himself with inquiring whether the watchman was certain that the woman who entered the building was Mrs. Prentice.

"Shure an' I'm certain," was the reply. "I've seen her and that green evening cape of hers trimmed with fur too often not to know her."

"Do you know how long it was between the time that she entered the building and the time she left?" persisted Taylor.

"That I do not, sir. Time is something that you don't worry about much when it's a matter of guarding the door to a building—particularly at night. But I'd guess somewhere about five or ten minutes?"

"Rather long for her to make her way to the office of her husband, find he wasn't there, and come right back, wasn't it?"

"Yes, sir—but you must remember I wasn't countin' the minutes, so to speak. Maybe it was only three—maybe it was ten. Anyhow, it was just nine-thirty when she left. I remember looking at the clock when she went out."

From the watchman's house, located well over in the northeastern section of the city, Taylor made his way to Madelaine James's apartment on Connecticut Avenue, discovering that young lady on the point of setting off to keep a luncheon engagement.

"I won't keep you a minute, Madelaine," promised the Secret Service operative. "Just want to ask what you know about Mrs. Mahlon Prentice?"

"Wife of the Third Assistant Secretary of State?"

Taylor nodded.

"She's a Chicago woman, I believe. Came here a[337] couple of years ago when her husband received his appointment. Rather good-looking and very popular. I happened to be at a dinner with her last evening and—"

"You what?"

"I was at a dinner at the Westovers' last night," repeated the James girl, "and Mrs. Prentice was among those present. Looked stunning, too. What's the trouble?"

"What time was the dinner?" Taylor countered.

"Eight o'clock, but of course it didn't start until nearly eight-thirty."

"And what time did Mrs. Prentice leave?"

"A few minutes after I did. She was just going up for her wraps as I came downstairs at eleven o'clock."

"You are certain that she was there all evening—that she didn't slip out for half an hour or so?"

"Of course I'm sure, Mell," the girl replied, a trace of petulance in her voice. "Why all the questions? Do you suspect the wife of the Third Assistant Secretary of State of robbing a bank?"

"Not a bank," Taylor admitted, "but it happens that the safe in her husband's office was opened last night and a highly important slip of paper abstracted. What's more, the watchman on duty in the building is ready to swear that Mrs. Prentice came in shortly before nine-thirty, and went out some five or ten minutes later, stating that her husband had evidently finished his work and left."

"That's impossible! No matter what the watchman says, there are a score of people who dined with Mrs. Prentice last evening and who know that she didn't leave the Westovers' until after eleven. Dinner wasn't over by nine-thirty, and she couldn't have gotten to the State Department and back in less than twenty minutes at the inside. It's ridiculous, that's all!"[338]

"But the watchman!" exclaimed Taylor. "He knows Mrs. Prentice and says he couldn't miss that green-and-fur coat of hers in the dark. Besides, she spoke to him as she was leaving."

Madelaine James was silent for a moment, and a tiny frown appeared between her eyes, evidence of the fact that she was doing some deep thinking.

Then: "Of course she spoke! Anyone who would go to the trouble of copying Mrs. Prentice's distinctive cloak would realize that some additional disguise was necessary. Last night, if you remember, was quite cold. Therefore it would be quite natural that the woman who impersonated Mrs. Prentice should have her collar turned up around her face and probably a drooping hat as well. The collar, in addition to concealing her features, would muffle her voice, while the watchman, not suspecting anything, would take it for granted that the green cloak was worn by the wife of the Under Secretary—particularly when she spoke to him in passing."

"You mean, then, that some one deliberately impersonated Mrs. Prentice and took a chance on getting past the watchman merely because she wore a cloak of the same color?"

"The same color—the same style—practically the same coat," argued Miss James. "What's more, any woman who would have the nerve to try that would probably watch Prentice's office from the outside, wait for the light to go out, and then stage her visit not more than five minutes later, so's to make it appear plausible. How was the safe opened?"

"Stethoscope. Placed the cup on the outside, and then listened to the tumblers as they fell. Simplest thing in the world with an antiquated box like that."

"What's missing?"[339]

By this time Taylor felt that their positions had been reversed. He, who had come to question, was now on the witness stand, while Madelaine James was doing the cross-examining. But he didn't mind. He knew the way the girl's mind worked, quickly and almost infallibly—her knowledge of women in general and Washington society in particular making her an invaluable ally in a case like this.

"A slip of paper some six inches long and two inches wide," he said, with a smile. "The key to the Carruthers Code, probably the most efficient cipher in the world, but now rendered worthless unless the original slip is located before it reaches some foreign power."

"Right!" snapped Miss James. "Get busy on your end of the matter. See what you can find out concerning this mysterious woman in the green cloak. I'll work along other and what you would probably call strictly unethical lines. I've got what a man would term a 'hunch,' but in a woman it is 'intuition'—and therefore far more likely to be right. See you later!" and with that she was off toward her car.

"But what about your luncheon engagement?" Taylor called after her.

"Bother lunch," she laughed back over her shoulder. "If my hunch is right I'll make your chief pay for my meals for the next year!"

The next that Taylor heard from his ally was a telephone call on the following evening, instructing him to dig up his evening clothes and to be present at a certain reception that evening.

"I have reason to believe," said Madelaine's voice, "that the lady of the second green cloak will be present. Anyhow, there'll be several of your friends there—including myself, Mrs. Armitage, and an ambassador who[340] doesn't stand any too well with the Administration. In fact, I have it on good authority that he's on the verge of being recalled. Naturally we don't want him to take a slip of paper, some six inches by two, with him!"

"How do you know he hasn't it already?"

"He doesn't return from New York until six o'clock this evening, and the paper is far too valuable to intrust to the mails or to an underling. Remember, I'm not certain that it is he who is supposed to get the paper eventually, but I do know who impersonated Mrs. Prentice, and I likewise know that the lady in question has not communicated with any foreign official in person. Beyond that we'll have to take a chance on the evening's developments," and the receiver was replaced before Taylor could frame any one of the score of questions he wanted to ask.

Even at the reception that night he was unable to get hold of Madelaine James long enough to find out just what she did know. In fact, it was nearly midnight before he caught the signal that caused him to enter one of the smaller and rather secluded rooms apart from the main hall.

There he found a tableau that was totally unexpected.

In one corner of the room, her back against the wall and her teeth bared in a snarl which distorted her usually attractive features into a mask of hate, stood Mrs. Armitage. Her hands were crossed in front of her in what appeared to be an unnatural attitude until Taylor caught a glimpse of polished steel and realized that the woman had been handcuffed.

"There," announced Madelaine, "in spite of your friend the watchman, stands 'Mrs. Prentice.' You'll find the green cloak in one of the closets at her home, and the stethoscope is probably concealed somewhere around the[341] house. However, that doesn't matter. The main thing is that we have discovered the missing slip of paper. You'll find it on the table over there."

Taylor followed the girl's gesture toward a table at the side of the room. But there, instead of the cipher key that he had expected, he saw only—a gold bracelet!

"What's the idea?" he demanded. "Where's the paper?"

"Snap open the bracelet," directed the girl. "What do you see?"

"It looks like—by gad! it is!—a tightly wrapped spindle of paper!" and a moment later the original of the Carruthers Code reposed safely in the Secret Service agent's vest pocket. As he tossed the empty bracelet back on the table he heard a sound behind him and turned just in time to see the woman in the corner slip to the floor in a dead faint.

"Now that we've got her," inquired Madelaine James, "what'll we do with her?"

"Take off the handcuffs, leave the room, and close the door," directed Taylor. "She'll hardly care to make any fuss when she comes to, and the fact that she is unconscious gives us an excellent opportunity for departing without a scene."

"But what I'd like to know," he asked, as they strolled back toward the main ballroom, "is how you engineered the affair?"

"I told you I had an intuition," came the reply, "and you laughed at me. Yes you did, too! It wasn't apparent on your face, but I could feel that inside yourself you were saying, 'Just another fool idea.' But Mrs. Armitage was preying on my mind. I didn't like the way she had slipped one over on us in connection with the leak on the peace note. Then, too, she seemed to have no visible means of support, but plenty of money.[342]

"I felt certain that she wasn't guilty of blackmail or any of the more sordid kinds of crime, but the fact that she was on terms of familiarity with a number of diplomats, and that she seemed to have a fondness for army and navy officials, led me to believe that she was a sort of super spy, sent over here for a specific purpose. The instant you mentioned the Carruthers Code she sprang to my mind. A bill, slipped into the fingers of her maid, brought the information about the green cloak, and the rest was easy.

"I figured that she'd have the cipher key on her to-night, for it was her first opportunity of passing it along to the man I felt certain she was working for. Sure enough, as she passed him about half an hour ago she tapped her bracelet, apparently absent-mindedly. As soon as he was out of sight I sent one of the maids with a message that some one wanted to see her in one of the smaller rooms. Thinking that it was the ambassador, she came at once. I was planted behind the door, handcuffed her before she knew what I was doing, and then signaled you!"

"Quite elementary, my dear Melville, quite elementary!"

"That," added Quinn, "was the last they heard of Mrs. Armitage. Taylor reported the matter at once, but the chief said that as they had the code they better let well enough alone. The following day the woman left Washington, and no one has heard from her since—except for a package that reached Taylor some months later. There was nothing in it except that photograph yonder, and, as Taylor was interested only in his bride, *née* Madelaine James, he turned it over to me for my collection."

[343]

XXIV
FIVE INCHES OF DEATH

"Quinn," I said one evening when the veteran of the United States Secret Service appeared to be in one of his story-spinning moods, "you've told me of cases that have to do with smuggling and spies, robberies and fingerprints and frauds, but you've never mentioned the one crime that is most common in the annals of police courts and detective bureaus."

"Murder?" inquired Quinn, his eyes shifting to the far wall of his library-den.

"Precisely. Haven't government detectives ever been instrumental in solving a murder mystery?"

"Yes, they've been mixed up in quite a few of them. There was the little matter of the Hallowell case—where the crime and the criminal were connected by a shoelace—and the incident of 'The Red Circle.' But murder, as such, does not properly belong in the province of the government detective. Only when it is accompanied by some breach of the federal laws does it come under the jurisdiction of the men from Washington. Like the Montgomery murder mystery, for example."

"Oh yes, the one connected with the postmark that's framed on your wall over there!" I exclaimed. "I'd forgotten about that. Hal Preston handled it, didn't he—the same man responsible for running down 'The Trail of the White Mice'?"[344]

"That's the one," said Quinn, and I was glad to see him settle luxuriously back in his old armchair—for that meant that he was preparing to recall the details of an adventure connected with a member of one of the government detective services.

If it hadn't been for the fact that Preston was in California at the time, working on the case of a company that was using the mails for illegal purposes, it is extremely doubtful if the mystery would ever have been solved [Quinn continued]; certainly not in time to prevent the escape of the criminal.

But Hal's investigations took him well up into the foot-hills of the Sierra Nevadas, and one morning he awoke to find the whole town in which he was stopping ablaze with a discussion of the "Montgomery mystery," as they called it.

It appeared from the details which Preston picked up in the lobby of his hotel that Marshall Montgomery had settled down in that section of the country some three years before, but that he had surrounded himself with an air of aloofness and detachment which had made him none too popular. Men who had called to see him on matters of business had left smarting under the sting of an ill-concealed snub, while it was as much as a book agent's life was worth to try to gain entrance to the house.

"It wasn't that he was stingy or close-fisted," explained one of the men who had known Montgomery. "He bought more Liberty Bonds than anyone else in town—but he bought them through his bank. Mailed the order in, just as he did with his contributions to the Red Cross and the other charitable organizations. Wouldn't see one of the people who went out to his place. In fact,[345] they couldn't get past the six or eight bulldogs that guard the house."

"And yet," said Preston, "I understand that in spite of his precautions he was killed last night?"

"Nobody knows just when he was killed," replied the native, "or how. That's the big question. When his servant, a Filipino whom he brought with him, went to wake him up this morning he found Montgomery's door locked. That in itself was nothing unusual—for every door and window in the place was securely barred before nine o'clock in the evening. But when Tino, the servant, had rapped several times without receiving any reply, he figured something must be wrong. So he got a stepladder, propped it up against the side of the house, and looked in through the window. What he saw caused him to send in a hurry call for the police."

"Well," snapped Preston, "what did he see?"

"Montgomery, stretched out on the floor near the door, stone dead—with a pool of blood that had formed from a wound in his hand!"

"In his hand?" Preston echoed. "Had he bled to death?"

"Apparently not—but that's where the queer angle to the case comes in. The door was locked from the inside—not only locked, but bolted, so there was no possibility of anyone having entered the room. The windows were tightly guarded by a patented burglar-proof device which permitted them to be open about three inches from the bottom, but prevented their being raised from the outside."

"Was there a chimney or any other possible entrance to the room?"

"None at all. Three windows and a door. Montgomery's body was sprawled out on the rug near the doorway—a revolver in his right hand, a bullet hole through[346] the palm of his left. The first supposition, of course, was that he had accidentally shot himself and had bled to death. But there wasn't enough blood for that. Just a few drops on the table and a small pool near the body. They're going to hold an autopsy later in the day and—"

It was at that moment that the Post-office operative became conscious that some one was calling his name, and, turning, he beckoned to the bell-boy who was paging him.

"Mr. Preston? Gentleman over there'd like to speak to you." Then the boy added in a whisper, "Chief o' police."

Excusing himself, Preston crossed the lobby to where a large and official-looking man was standing, well out of hearing distance of the guests who passed.

"Is this Mr. Preston of the Postal Inspection Service?" inquired the head of the local police force, adding, after the government operative had nodded. "I am the chief of police here."

"Glad to meet you, Chief," was Preston's response. "I haven't had the pleasure of making your acquaintance, though of course I know you by sight." (He neglected to add how recently this knowledge had been acquired.) "What can I do for you?"

"Have you heard about the murder of Montgomery Marshall?"

"Only the few details that I picked up in the lobby just now. But a case of that kind is entirely out of my line, you know."

"Ordinarily it would be," agreed the other, "but here's something that I think puts a different complexion on things," and he extended a bloodstained scrap of paper for Preston to examine.[347]

"That was found under the dead man's hand," the chief continued. "As you will note, it originally formed part of the wrapping of a special-delivery parcel which reached Montgomery about eight o'clock last night—just before the house was locked up, in fact. Tino, the Filipino servant, signed for it and took it in, placing it upon the table in the room in which his master was found this morning. The scrap of paper you are holding is just enough to show the postmark 'Sacramento'—but it's quite evident that the package had something to do with the murder."

"Which is the reason that you want me to look into it, eh?"

"That's the idea. I knew that you were in town, and the very fact that this box came through the mails makes it necessary for the Post-office Department to take cognizance of what otherwise would be a job for the police force alone. Am I right?"

"Perfectly," replied Preston. "Provided you have reason to believe that there was some connection between the special-delivery package and the crime itself. What was in the box?"

"Not a thing!"

"What?"

"Not a thing!" repeated the chief. "Perfectly empty—at least when we found it. The lid was lying on the table, the rest of the box on the floor. The major portion of the wrapping paper had been caught under a heavy paper weight and it appears that Montgomery, in falling, caught at the table to save himself and probably ripped away the scrap of paper I have just given you."

"But I thought his body was found near the door?"

"It was, but that isn't far from the table, which is jammed against the wall in front of one of the windows.[348] Come on up to the house with me and we'll go over the whole thing."

Glad of the excuse to look into a crime which appeared to be inexplicable, Preston accompanied the chief to the frame dwelling on the outskirts of town where Montgomery Marshall, hermit, had spent the last three years of his life.

The house was set well back from the road, with but a single gateway in a six-foot wall of solid masonry, around the top of which ran several strands of barbed wire.

"Montgomery erected the wall himself," explained the chief. "Had it put up before he ever moved into the house, and then, in addition, kept a bunch of the fiercest dogs I ever knew."

"All of which goes to prove that he feared an attack," Preston muttered. "In spite of his precautions, however, they got him! The question now is: Who are 'they' and how did they operate?"

The room in which the body had been found only added to the air of mystery which surrounded the entire problem.

In spite of what he had been told Preston had secretly expected to find some kind of an opening through which a man could have entered. But there was none. The windows, as the Postal operative took care to test for himself, were tightly locked, though open a few inches from the bottom. The bolt on the door very evidently had been shattered by the entrance of the police, and the dark-brown stain on the rug near the door showed plainly where the body had been found.

"When we broke in," explained the chief, "Montgomery was stretched out there, facing the door. The doctor said that he had been dead about twelve hours, but that it was impossible for the wound in his hand to have caused his death."[349]

"How about a poisoned bullet, fired through the opening in the window?"

"Not a chance! The only wound on the body was the one through the palm of his hand. The bullet had struck on the outside of the fleshy part near the wrist and had plowed its way through the bone, coming out near the base of the index finger at the back. And it was a bullet from his own revolver! We found it embedded in the top of the table there." And the chief pointed to a deep scar in the mahogany and to the marks made by the knives of the police when they had dug the bullet out.

"But how do you know it wasn't a bullet of the same caliber, fired from outside the window?" persisted Preston.

For answer the chief produced Montgomery's revolver, with five cartridges still in the chambers.

"If you'll note," he said, "each of these cartridges is scored or seamed. That's an old trick—makes the lead expand when it hits and tears an ugly hole, just like a 'dum-dum.' The bullet we dug out of the table was not only a forty-five, as these are, but it had been altered in precisely the same manner. So, unless you are inclined to the coincidence that the murderer used a poisoned bullet of the same size and make and character as those in Montgomery's gun, you've got to discard that theory."

"Does look like pulling the long arm of coincidence out of its socket," Preston agreed. "So I guess we'll have to forget it. Where's the box you were talking about?"

"The lid is on the table, just as we found it. The lower portion of the box is on the floor, where the dead man apparently knocked it when he fell. Except for the removal of the body, nothing in the room has been touched."

Stooping, Preston picked up the box and then proceeded to study it in connection with the lid and the torn[350] piece of wrapping paper upon the table. It was after he had examined the creases in the paper, fitting them carefully around the box itself, that he inquired: "Do you notice anything funny about the package, Chief?"

"Only that there's a hole at one end of it, just about big enough to put a lead pencil through."

"Yes, and that same hole appears in the wrapping paper," announced Preston. "Couple that with the fact that the box was empty when you found it and I think we will have—"

"What?" demanded the chief, as Preston paused.

"The solution to the whole affair," was the reply. "Or, at least, as much of it as refers to the manner in which Montgomery met his death. By the way, what do you know about the dead man?"

"Very little. He came here some three years ago, bought this place, paying cash for it; had the wall built, and then settled down. Never appeared to do any work, but was never short of money. Has a balance of well over fifty thousand dollars in the bank right now. Beyond the fact that he kept entirely to himself and refused to allow anyone but Tino, his servant, to enter the gate, he really had few eccentricities. Some folks say that he was a miser, but there are a dozen families here that wouldn't have had any Christmas dinner last year if it hadn't been for him—while his contribution to the Red Cross equaled that of anyone in town."

"Apart from his wanting to be alone, then, he was pretty close to being human?"

"That's it, exactly—and most of us have some peculiarity. If we didn't have we'd be even more unusual."

"What about Tino, the servant?" queried Preston.

"I don't think there's any lead there," the chief replied. "I hammered away at him for an hour this[351] morning. He doesn't speak English any too well, but I gathered that Montgomery picked him up in the Philippines just before he came over here. The boy was frightened half out of his senses when I told him that his master had been killed. You've got to remember, though, that if Tino had wanted to do it he had a thousand opportunities in the open. Besides, what we've got to find out first is how Montgomery met his death?"

"Does the Filipino know anything about his master's past?" asked Preston, ignoring the chief's last remark.

"He says not. Montgomery was on his way back to the States from Africa or some place—stopped off in the islands—spent a couple of months there—hired Tino and sailed for San Francisco."

"Africa—" mused the Postal operative. Then, taking another track, he inquired whether the chief had found out if Montgomery was in the habit of getting much mail, especially from foreign points.

"Saunders, the postmaster, says he didn't average a letter a month—and those he did get looked like advertisements. They remembered this special-delivery package last night because it was the first time that the man who brought it out had ever come to the house. He rang the bell at the gate, he says, turned the box over to Tino, and went along."

"Any comment about the package?"

"Only that it was very light and contained something that wabbled around. I asked him because I figured at the time that the revolver might have been in it. But the Filipino has identified that as Montgomery's own gun. Says he'd had it as long as he'd known him."

"Then all we know about this mysterious box," summarized Preston, "is that it was mailed from Sacramento, that it wasn't heavy, that it had a hole about a[352] quarter-inch wide at one end, and that it contained something that—what was the word the special-delivery man used—'wabbled'?"

"That's the word. I remember because I asked him if he didn't mean 'rattled,' and he said, 'No, wabbled, sort o' dull-like.'"

"At any rate, that clears up one angle of the case. The box was not empty when it was delivered! Granting that the Filipino was telling the truth, it was not empty when he placed it on the table in this room! That means that it was not empty when Marshall

Montgomery, after locking and bolting his door, took off the wrapping paper and lifted the lid! You've searched the room thoroughly, of course?"

"Every inch of it. We didn't leave a—"

But the chief suddenly halted, his sentence unfinished. To the ears of both men there had come a sound, faint but distinct. The sound of the rattling of paper somewhere in the room.

Involuntarily Preston whirled and scrutinized the corner from which the sound appeared to have come. The chief's hand had slipped to his hip pocket, but after a moment of silence he withdrew it and a slightly shamefaced look spread over his face.

"Sounded like a ghost, didn't it?" he asked.

"Ghosts don't rattle papers," snapped Preston. "At least self-respecting ones don't, and the other kind haven't any right to run around loose. So suppose we try to trap this one."

"Trap it? How?"

"Like you'd trap a mouse—only with a different kind of bait. Is there any milk in the house?"

"Possibly—I don't know."

"Go down to the refrigerator and find out, will you?[353] I'll stay here until you return. And bring a saucer with you."

A few moments later, when the chief returned, bearing a bottle of milk and a saucer, he found Preston still standing beside the table, his eyes fixed upon a corner of the room from which the sound of rattling paper had come.

"Now all we need is a box," said the Postal operative. "I saw one out in the hall that will suit our purposes excellently."

Securing the box, he cut three long and narrow strips from the sides, notched them and fitted them together in a rough replica of the figure 4, with the lower point of the upright stick resting on the floor beside the saucer of milk and the wooden box poised precariously at the junction of the upright and the slanting stick.

"A figure-four trap, eh?" queried the chief. "What do you expect to catch?"

"A mixture of a ghost and the figure of Justice," was Preston's enigmatic reply. "Come on—we'll lock the door and return later to see if the trap has sprung. Meanwhile, I'll send some wires to Sacramento, San Francisco, and other points throughout the state."

The telegram, of which he gave a copy to the local chief of police, "in order to save the expense of sending it," read:

Wire immediately if you know anything of recent arrival from Africa—probably American or English—who landed within past three days. Wanted in connection with Montgomery murder.

The message to San Francisco ended with the phrase "Watch outgoing boats closely," and that to Sacramento "Was in your city yesterday."

Hardly an hour later the phone rang and a voice from[354] police headquarters in Sacramento asked to speak to "Postal Inspector Preston."

"Just got your wire," said the voice, "and I think we've got your man. Picked him up on the street last night, unconscious. Hospital people say he's suffering from poisoning of some kind and don't expect him to live. Keeps raving about diamonds and some one he calls 'Marsh.' Papers on him show he came into San Francisco two days ago on the *Manu*. Won't tell his name, but has mentioned Cape Town several times."

"Right!" cried Preston. "Watch him carefully until I get there. I'll make the first train out."

That afternoon Preston, accompanied by two chiefs of police, made his way into a little room off the public ward in the hospital in Sacramento. In bed, his face drawn and haggard until the skin seemed like parchment stretched tightly over his cheekbones, lay a man at the point of death—a man who was only kept alive, according to the physicians, by some almost superhuman effort of the will.

"It's certain that he's been poisoned," said the doctor in charge of the case, "but he won't tell us how. Just lies there and glares and demands a copy of the latest newspaper. Every now and then he drifts off into delirium, but just when we think he's on the point of death he recovers."

Motioning to the others to keep in the background, Preston made his way to the bedside of the dying man. Then, bending forward, he said, very clearly and distinctly: "Marshall Montgomery is dead!"

Into the eyes of the other man there sprang a look of concentrated hatred that was almost tangible—a glare that turned, a moment later, into supreme relief.

"Thank God!" he muttered. "Now I'm ready to die!"[355]

"Tell me," said Preston, quietly—"tell me what made you do it."

"He did!" gasped the man on the bed. "He and his damned brutality. When I knew him his name was Marsh. We dug for diamonds together in South Africa—found them, too—enough to make us both rich for life. But our water was running low—barely enough for one of us. He, the skunk, hit me over the head and left me to die—taking the water and the stones with him."

He paused a moment, his breath rattling in his throat, and then continued:

"It took me five years to find him—but you say he's dead? You're not lying?"

Preston shook his head slowly and the man on the bed settled back and closed his eyes, content.

"Ask him," insisted the chief of police, "how he killed Montgomery?"

In a whisper that was barely audible came the words: "Sheep-stinger. Got me first." Then his jaws clicked and there was the unmistakable gurgle which meant that the end had come.

"Didn't he say 'sheep-stinger'?" asked the chief of police, after the doctor had stated that the patient had slipped away from the hands of the law.

"That's what it sounded like to me," replied Preston. "But suppose we go back to Montgomery's room and see what our ghost trap has caught. I told you I expected to land a figure of Justice—and if ever a man deserved to be killed it appears to have been this same Montgomery Marshall, or Marsh, as this man knew him."

The instant they entered the room it was apparent that the trap had sprung, the heavy box falling forward and completely covering the saucer of milk and whatever had disturbed the carefully balanced sticks.[356]

Warning the chief to be careful, Preston secured a poker from an adjoining room, covered the box with his automatic, and then carefully lifted the box, using the poker as a lever.

A second later he brought the head of the poker down on something that writhed and twisted and then lay still, blending in with the pattern of the carpet in such a manner as to be almost invisible.

"A snake!" cried the chief. "But such a tiny one! Do you mean to say that its bite is sufficiently poisonous to kill a man?"

"Not only one, but two," Preston declared, "as you've seen for yourself. See that black mark, like an inverted V, upon the head? That's characteristic of the cobra family, and this specimen—common to the veldts of South Africa where he is known as the 'sheep stinger'—is first cousin to the big king cobras. Montgomery's former partner evidently brought him over from Africa with this idea in mind. But when he was packing him in the box—the airhole in the end of it gave me the first inkling, by the way—he got careless and the snake bit him. Only medical attention saved his life until this afternoon, else he'd have passed along before Montgomery. I think that closes the case, Chief, and in spite of the fact that the mails were used for a distinctly illegal purpose, I believe your department ought to handle the matter—not mine."

"But the trap—the milk? How'd you happen to hit on that?"

"When you told me what the special-delivery man said about the contents of the package 'wabbling' I figured that the box must have contained a snake," explained the Postal operative. "An animal would have made some noise, while a snake, if well fed, will lie silent for hours at a time. The constant motion, however, would have[357] made it irritable—so that it struck the moment Montgomery removed the lid of the box. That explains the wound in his hand. He knew his danger and deliberately fired, hoping to cauterize the wound and drive out the poison. It was too quick for him, though, or possibly the shock stunned him so that he fell.

"Then, in spite of the fact that your men claimed to have searched the room thoroughly, that noise in the corner warned me that whatever killed Montgomery was still here. Going on the theory that the majority of snakes are fond of milk, I rigged up the trap. And there you are!"

"Yes," concluded Quinn, "the majority of the cases handled by government detectives have to do with counterfeiting or smuggling or other crimes against the federal law—offenses which ought to be exciting but which are generally dull and prosaic. Every now and then, though, they stumble across a real honest-to-goodness thrill, a story that's worth the telling.

"I've got to be away for the next couple of months or so, but drop around when I get back and I'll see if I can't recall some more of the problems that have been solved by one of the greatest, though least known, detective agencies on the face of the earth."

THE END

CPSIA information can be obtained
at www.ICGtesting.com
Printed in the USA
LVHW080002151219
640544LV00037B/1893/P